of   Mexico

Endpapers for

UNHOLY

0   50   100   150   200

Miles

ROADS ————
MOUNTAINS ⸾⸾⸾⸾⸾

Mérida

CHICHEN-ITZA
(RUINS OF
FIRST MAYAN
EMPIRE)

UXMAL
(RUINS OF
SECOND
MAYAN
EMPIRE)

Campeche   Campeche

Villahermosa

BRITISH

HONDURAS

Tuxtla Gutiérrez

GUATEMALA

HONDURAS

atepec

a   n

Unholy Crusade

Every few years Dennis Wheatley produces a new central character. This time it is 'Lucky' Adam Gordon, the son of poor Scottish fisherfolk, who, at the age of twenty-eight, has become a best-selling novelist. But was Adam really lucky? The long first chapter of this book recounts the extraordinary ups and downs of his childhood and youth, and the reason why he had made up his mind never again to fall in love.

But, of course, he did fall in love, and it is one of the strangest love stories that could be imagined.

The scene of this book is Mexico. Adam has gone there to get background colour for a novel. As a result of an accident, Adam becomes involved in a nation-wide conspiracy. His beautiful, deeply religious Chela is under the influence of an evil priest. Owing to a strange link with the past, Adam is persuaded, against his better judgement, to become the puppet head of the 'Crusaders'. On the other side are Chela's brother and Jeremy Hunterscombe of the British Secret Service, who tell him of the wholesale death, rape and torture that made previous Mexican revolutions exceptionally horrible, and they endeavour to persuade him to betray the conspirators. Caught between these two powerful influences, he tries desperately to hedge; yet cannot save himself from having to participate in revolting pagan rites. Thereafter his life is again and again in peril.

That is but half the tale. Adam's mother was fey. From her he inherited the ability to go back in time. The scenes from his past life give a fascinating picture of the magnificent but barbaric civilisation of ancient Mexico. Moreover, it propounds a logical explanation for the *white* Man-God, Quetzalcoatl, who lived in Mexico in the tenth century, who Mexican Indians still believe will return as their Saviour.

This is another Wheatley triumph. In *Unholy Crusade* he gives us again that blend of true history, modern travel, plot and counter-plot, sexual passion, desperate situations, escapes and violent death that has made his books best-sellers with both old and young, so that over twenty million copies have been sold.

THE LYMINGTON EDITION

BY DENNIS WHEATLEY

NOVELS

The Launching of Roger Brook
The Shadow of Tyburn Tree
The Rising Storm
The Man Who Killed the King
The Dark Secret of Josephine
The Rape of Venice
The Sultan's Daughter
The Wanton Princess
Evil in a Mask

The Scarlet Impostor
Faked Passports
The Black Baroness
V for Vengeance
Come Into My Parlour
Traitors' Gate
They Used Dark Forces

The Prisoner in the Mask
The Second Seal
Vendetta in Spain
Three Inquisitive People
The Forbidden Territory
The Devil Rides Out
The Golden Spaniard
Strange Conflict
Codeword—Golden Fleece
Dangerous Inheritance
Gateway to Hell

The Quest of Julian Day
The Sword of Fate
Bill for the Use of a Body

Black August
Contraband
The Island Where Time Stands Still
The White Witch of the South Seas

To the Devil—a Daughter
The Satanist

The Eunuch of Stamboul
The Secret War
The Fabulous Valley
Sixty Days to Live
Such Power is Dangerous
Uncharted Seas
The Man Who Missed the War
The Haunting of Toby Jugg
Star of Ill-Omen
They Found Atlantis
The Ka of Gifford Hillary
Curtain of Fear
Mayhem in Greece
Unholy Crusade

SHORT STORIES

Mediterranean Nights

Gunmen, Gallants and Ghosts

HISTORICAL

A Private Life of Charles II *(Illustrated by Frank C. Papé)*
Red Eagle *(The Story of the Russian Revolution)*

AUTOBIOGRAPHICAL

Stranger than Fiction *(War Papers for the Joint Planning Staff)*
Saturdays with Bricks

IN PREPARATION

The Ravishing of Lady Mary Ware *(another Roger Brook story)*
The Devil and all his Works *(Illustrated in colour)*

DENNIS WHEATLEY

Unholy Crusade

THE LYMINGTON EDITION

HUTCHINSON OF LONDON

HUTCHINSON & CO (*Publishers*) LTD
178–202 Great Portland Street, London W1

London Melbourne Sydney Auckland
Wellington Johannesburg Cape Town
and agencies throughout the world

First published 1967
The Lymington Edition May 1971

This book has been set in Times type, printed in Great Britain
on antique wove paper by Anchor Press, and
bound by Wm. Brendon, both of Tiptree, Essex

ISBN 0 09 108250 1

With love, for
'Smallest Daughter'

SHEILAKIN

With whom my wife and I
spent our happiest days
in Mexico

Contents

I

Lucky Adam Gordon

ADAM FALLSTRÖM GORDON had come to Mexico to collect material for a book.

He had recently made a big name as a writer of unusual adventure stories with authentic historical backgrounds. The adventures were the product of his mind, so it was background material for which he had come in search. But Fate plays many a strange trick and, before he was much older, he was soon to find himself, all against his will, the central figure in a series of situations more desperate than any he could have thought up.

He had arrived in Mexico City in the early hours of the previous morning and on this, his first evening, he was sampling high-life in the roof restaurant on the fourteenth floor of the Del Paseo Hotel. The big room was dimly lit; three sides of it consisted of plate-glass windows. Through them, owing to the crystal-clear air up there at seven thousand five hundred feet, could be seen the million twinkling lights that at night turned the city into a fairy-land stretching for miles.

A small band played soft, seductive music. Immaculate waiters moved softly from table to table occupied by fashionably-dressed women and prosperous-looking men. Although it was past eleven o'clock, most of them had only just started dinner—because upper-class Mexicans keep Spanish hours. Many of the women were strikingly good-looking. Here and there a table light glinted on their diamonds, emeralds or rubies. It was a scene of *grande-luxe* that could not have been surpassed anywhere in Europe.

Adam Gordon was twenty-eight. As he looked about him

while waiting for his first course of avocado pear filled with
minute eels, he felt that in fourteen years he had come a long,
long way from the poor fishing village on the east coast of
Scotland where he had been born, and that, perhaps, his
friends were right in nicknaming him 'Lucky' Gordon.

But none of them knew the whole of his story. They based
their assessment of him on his recent good fortune and, no
doubt, were a little envious of his physical attributes; for he
had a good brain, a fine body and had never known a day's
illness. He was not a giant, but he stood six foot three in his
socks, with broad shoulders, and his hands were so strong
that he could bend an iron bar. He was fair-skinned and
freckled, had pale-blue eyes a little on the small side, a straight
nose, good teeth, and thick, red-gold hair which waved despite his efforts to brush it flat. His firm chin was also covered
with short, crisp, red-gold hair; for he had grown a beard
while doing his National Service in the Royal Navy and had
decided to keep it. In his Navy days his mates had nicknamed him 'the Viking', and that had been truly apt, as he
had inherited strong strains of Norse blood from both his
mother and father.

From his late teens onward, wherever he went his striking
appearance attracted the interest of girls and women. Several
of them at nearby tables had been casting covert glances at
him ever since he had entered the restaurant, but for some
time past he had deliberately ignored such overtures. For him
women, in the persons of both Polly and Mildred, had meant
only brief periods of enjoyment followed by bitter disenchant-
ment. Finding that absorption in his work enabled him to do
without romantic attachments, he had made up his mind not
to let himself become seriously involved again.

Unlucky as he had been in love, he had certainly been
lucky in other ways—extraordinarily lucky—because Fate
had played him a number of really scurvy tricks that had
looked like destroying for good any prospect of his advancement. Yet, after each had come an entirely unexpected break,
lifting him from the rut in which it seemed he had foundered.

He had arrived in Mexico City only very late the previous
night and had no introductions; so he was dining alone. While

he drank his daiquiri cocktail he amused himself by recalling the strange seesaw of events which, interspersed with spells of desperate poverty, had now brought him to affluence.

.   .   .   .   .

Adam's father, Jamie Gordon, had come from Findhorn in Morayshire and had started life as a fisherman. Tall, strong and level-headed, he had made a useful hand on a trawler; but he had had only a rudimentary education, so had expected to spend the whole of his working life at sea. But one day in Inverness he had met Gurda Fallström. She was there to see a lawyer, as her father had recently died and, having lost her mother when she was still in her teens, she had come into his estate.

Gurda was as fine and stalwart a woman as Jamie was a man and from that very first evening, when they had supped together off kippers and tea in the house of a mutual friend, they had known that they were made for each other. But Gurda was most averse to taking a husband who would frequently be away from her for considerable periods and, through being a fisherman, might at any time be drowned in a storm.

The estate she had inherited consisted only of an old house further north in Sutherland, not far from the estuary of the Helmsdale river, and a few hundred pounds. But a cousin of hers owned the fish-net factory in the nearby village of Port-gower and it was arranged that Jamie should be given a job there.

The house was centuries old and perched on the very edge of a high cliff. It was much larger than Jamie had expected, for the Fallströms had once been comfortably off; so it contained numerous pieces of good, if worn, furniture and a collection of several hundred old books.

Jamie would have been happy to make his home with Gurda in a butte-and-ben; but to live with her in such surroundings was, to him, like being in the seventh heaven, and he worked at his new job with such a will that, within three years, he was made foreman at the net factory.

To add to their contentment the couple were blessed with five handsome and healthy children: two girls and three boys, of which Adam was the youngest and, in due course, the cleverest. His childhood in the house on the cliff could not have been happier and he was his mother's favourite.

For this there was a special reason. Gurda was a very un-usual person. Like many Scots she was that strange mixture of down-to-earth good sense and visionary subject to pyschic influences. But in her case this had developed into a definitely dual personality. Normally she was a practical, hardworking housewife, but at times she neglected everything and would sit dreaming for hours. During these periods it was evident that she was living in another world. She even talked to her-self and recited long poems in a strange language which she told her family was ancient Norse.

The only explanation for these semi-trances seemed to be that in an earlier incarnation she had been the wife of a Viking chieftain and, in that role, had known such exceptional hap-piness that, from time to time, her spirit was drawn back to re-experience episodes in it. She was herself convinced of that and, although when she returned to normal she could recall these 'dreams' only hazily, she could describe what life had been like in the time of the Scandinavian Vikings.

Her husband and elder children—all rather unimaginative people—regarded 'Mother's day-dreams' with mild amuse-ment and never questioned her about her 'other life'. But Adam, from the time he could think coherently, had been fascinated and never tired of sitting at her feet asking her about the Norsemen and the long ships in which they sailed each summer to plunder the coast towns of England, Ireland and France.

She told him of the long winters when there were only a few hours of daylight, the great storms that howled round the house and the softly-falling snow that made it impossible to travel for more than a short distance. But, snug in their houses, they saw the winter through: the men amusing them-selves making fine wood-carvings of snake-heads for the prows of their ships, or hewing oars and tools to cultivate the land, while the women worked at their weaving or sewed the skins of trapped animals into fur hoods and jackets.

Then there were the evenings of celebration: Feast days sacred to the gods, weddings and the bloodings of a *jarl*'s new sword. The long tables weighed down with roast flesh and great flagons of heady mead; the recitation by the bards of past deeds of valour, sometimes drunken quarrels with drinking horns hurled, then bloody duels with the long swords to settle matters on the spot; but laughter and the joy of living; libations poured to the red-headed Thor—the god of victories and the Jupiter of the North—with the conviction that if his votaries died in battle they would go straight to his heaven of Valhalla and there drink mead out of the skulls of their enemies.

After a time, delighted with the boy's interest, his mother had supplemented what she could tell him from her dreams by reading to him some of the old books she had inherited, which dealt with that period of history. Then, soon after his ninth birthday Adam too began to have 'dreams'. Not, to begin with, day-dreams like his mother, but vivid dreams at night. Whether he had inherited her ability to go back in time, or his dreams were a normal result of his absorption in the subject, it was impossible to say. But the former seemed probable because, during his dreams, he spoke and could understand the Norse language. On learning this, his mother began to teach him Norse, so that he could recite many of the old Icelandic runes. By then, too, he found that, occasionally, when sitting alone on the cliff or the river bank, he could see the many-oared ships of the raiders, send his mind back and seem to become Ord, the golden-haired Viking commanding the approaching fleet.

He was already aware that, when the long winter ended and spring came again, a fever of restlessness seized the menfolk. All true-bred Norsemen were fighters born and bred. They cared nothing for agriculture and left the women and slaves to cultivate the few fields about their homes that would produce enough wheat for a supply of the small, hard loaves with a hole in the centre, that resembled doughnuts in shape.

For them there were the shimmering green seas, sometimes riding mountain-high; but then all the greater challenge to courage and endurance. Beyond them lay the lands of weak peoples, living in softer climes and, therefore, easily to be overcome. From them many things could be had for the taking: strange garments made of soft, shiny material, iron helmets, strings of blue beads and ornaments of gold.

Generally their forays were made against the nearer lands: Scotland, Ireland, England, the north coast of Germany; but many of Adam's forbears and relatives had gone much further afield—to Spain, as he now realised, and by the Baltic rivers even down to Kiev in the Ukraine, to the shores of the Black Sea, and there made contact with the fabled peoples of the East who worshipped a prophet named Mohammet.

In the Norselands they had long worshipped Thor, Odin and Freyja, and, when a great chieftain died, buried him, his ship and many articles of value in the sacred bogs which, after some months, sucked them under and made them part of the earth. But by this time—about A.D. 950—certain fearless men, humble and austere, had occasionally come out of the South preaching a new religion.

It was of a Man-God who had allowed himself to be crucified so that others should be absolved of their sins. The story was difficult to believe; for it did not make sense that a god should submit himself to pain but, as a concession to the possible malice he might indulge in if ignored, they had begun to couple his name, when in danger, with that of Thor.

Then there came another strange development in Adam. Alternating with his night dreams of storm-tossed galleys at sea, burning villages in which he led his bearded henchmen to kill, rape and plunder, and the bleak, cold Norselands under winter snow, he found himself in utterly different surroundings. He was living in a country of mountains, volcanoes and vast forests where, down on the coast, there were palm trees, many exotic fruits and it was intensely hot. There were cities with great pyramids and splendid palaces. The people were brown-skinned, had hooked noses, black hair and high, sloping foreheads. They wore many-coloured cloaks with geometrical designs and, on days of celebration, the principal men among them put on gorgeous feather headdresses.

Where this other country could be he had no idea, and his mother was equally mystified; but he knew that he had been immensely happy there and infinitely preferred it to the harsh, primitive life led by the Vikings in the inhospitable North.

By the time Adam was fourteen, his older brothers and sisters were all working in the fishing-net factory; so the income of the family was, for people of their class and simple tastes, more than adequate. They all loved the roomy old house, had no desire to leave it for a city, and were leading a thoroughly contented life.

Only one worry nagged at Jamie from time to time. The base of the cliff on which the house stood was being eroded by the sea. During the greater part of each year he rarely thought about it, but on nights when the winter storms raged and great waves thundered on the beach below, causing the old house to shudder, he became troubled and felt they really ought to leave it for a safer home. Yet, owing to its precarious position, it would be next to impossible to find a purchaser, and with only a few hundred pounds put by they could not buy another. As they had always lived rent-free, even to rent a house would entail so considerable a charge on their income that they would have to give up many small luxuries to which they had long been accustomed. Still worse, instead of this roomy old home with its pleasant garden, the only sort of house they could afford would be a small one in the village.

Then, when the storm subsided, Jamie would dismiss his fears on the ground that the erosion had been going on for many years and was very slow; the house was at least two hundred years old and its foundations showed no sign of weakening. Since it had stood there for so long, there could be no real urgency about moving and resigning themselves to a greatly reduced scale of living. As spring came again each year the matter passed from his mind.

Yet at last there came the fatal night. In the roar of the storm even their nearest neighbours did not hear the cliff collapse. But in the morning the old house was gone. Jamie, Gurda, four of their children and all their possessions had disappeared into the ocean, leaving no trace that they had ever existed. Only Adam, by a fluke of Fate, survived. For the first time his world was shattered. At the age of fourteen he found himself alone, an orphan and nearly penniless.

.   .   .   .   .

Adam's escape was due to the fact that he occasionally spent a night with his mother's sister, Aunt Flora Inglis. It being two days before Christmas, she had asked him over to receive his Christmas present and carry back those she had for his brothers and sisters.

Aunt Flora was a widow, and housekeeper to Lord Ruffan at the Castle, six miles up the river. There, to the envy of her relatives, she dwelt in ease and plenty. His Lordship was an Englishman and the estate had been acquired by his grandfather in the 1890s. He came to Scotland only for the shooting and fishing; so, for the greater part of the year, Aunt Flora was mistress of all she surveyed. Even when His Lordship was in residence, as he was an elderly bachelor there was no mistress to irritate her by requiring that she should alter any of her set ways. But she was a dour, efficient woman and gave short shrift to any housemaid or kitchen hand who was pert or lazy; so Lord Ruffan considered her a treasure.

When the terrible blow fell, Adam was for some days inconsolable; but, with the resilience of youth to changed circumstances, he soon began to take stock of his situation. Aunt Flora had written at once to Lord Ruffan, giving an account of the tragedy and asking permission to keep her nephew with her. His Lordship had replied after a few days giving his consent; so at least Adam had a home. But in other respects his prospects were bleak.

Not a single possession of his or his family had survived, except the clothes he stood up in, and his parents' small nest-egg was seriously eaten into by payment of their debts and equipping him with a new outfit. Then, after some days, Mr. McPherson, who owned the fishing-net factory, had sent for him and Aunt Flora. As kindly as he could the old gentleman explained that, during the past ten years his business had suffered a serious decline, owing to competition from other factories which had more modern machinery. So, much as he would have liked to recognise Jamie Gordon's long service by making adequate provision for his orphan, he could not afford to do more than allow the boy two pounds a week until he was seventeen when, should the business continue to survive, he would take him into it.

Adam did his best to appear grateful, but such a future had little appeal for him. He had not yet made up his mind what he wanted to do except, if possible, travel. He had heard enough about the hardships of his father's early life to set him against making the sea his career, but he did feel that if he continued to do well at school he ought to be able to get a job that would enable him to see something of the world. With this in mind, he worked at his lessons harder than ever.

The life he led favoured his efforts, as it was, for a boy of his age, an exceptionally lonely one. Aunt Flora had no friends whose youngsters might have become playmates for Adam. In consequence he was never tempted to abandon his homework in order to play games with other boys and his main pleasure was to browse among the books in the fine library of the Castle. History was his favourite reading and he spent many a long, dark evening curled up in front of the fire in his aunt's sitting room, absorbed in accounts of battles and rebellions which, to most of his contemporaries, were only dates that had laboriously to be memorised.

Lord Ruffan spent the spring of that year in Barbados and Jamaica, so he did not come up for the fishing. Adam was now and then allowed to go out with the ghillies and, early in March, took great delight in landing his first salmon from the Helmsdale. But a month later a much greater excitement was in store for him. One evening he was looking through some of the older books in the library when out of a calf-bound folio volume there fell a discoloured parchment.

On examining it, he found it to be a letter from one Ian MacGilray—whose family had for many generations owned the Castle—to his wife. It had been written from Edinburgh in 1745, the year of Prince Charles Edward's attempt to regain the throne of Britain for the Stuarts. Hurriedly, it described the battle of Culloden in which the Pretender's forces had been defeated by those of the Hanoverian King. The Stuart cause was lost and MacGilray, with other survivors, was fleeing for his life, hoping somehow to get to France. It was now feared that King George's brutal English and German troops would overrun the whole of Scotland, paying special attention to the homes of Bonnie Prince Charlie's adherents and looting them of everything of value that could be carried off. Before leaving the Castle to join the Prince's army, as a precaution against defeat the MacGilray had hidden the family treasure, and there followed directions to his wife whence to recover it when the troubles were over.

The language was obscure and only someone who knew the estate well would have been able to interpret it, but after considerable cogitation Adam decided that the place where the treasure had been hidden must be under one side of the arch that spanned a small bridge over a tributary of the Helmsdale. He did not expect for one moment that the treasure was still there; yet, all the same, he could hardly contain his impatience to go and see what traces he could find of the cache that had once held the plate of the MacGilrays, and perhaps even gold and jewels. The hours of school next day dragged interminably. At last he was home, had bolted his tea and was free to hurry the mile to the little bridge.

The spot was a deserted one on the edge of a wood, and the bridge carried only a rough track used occasionally by farm carts and shooting brakes. Scrambling down the bank of the burn, he crawled under the low arch and looked about him, only to be disappointed. There was no romantic cavity in either wall and, as he peered in the semi-darkness at the moss-covered stones, he could see no unevenness suggesting that the hole had been hastily bricked up again.

It was not until two nights later that, thinking over the matter in bed, it occurred to him that several years had elapsed before the English had ceased to revenge themselves on the Jacobite nobility for the rebellion. During that time it would have remained unsafe to retrieve the treasure, and the MacGilray's wife might have died carrying the secret of its hiding place with her to the grave.

Going downstairs to the library in his night-clothes he hastily consulted the records of the family. Ian MacGilray had escaped to France and his wife had joined him there. He had been tried in his absence for taking up arms against his lawful Sovereign and his Castle and estates had been confiscated. The couple had never returned to Scotland and it was not until forty years later that a distant kinsman, who had married the daughter of a rich sugar nabob, had retrieved the estates for the family by purchase.

Again Adam had to disguise his excitement and impatience. It was not until Sunday afternoon that he could go to the little bridge. Kneeling on the narrow strip of dry earth, the sweat poured from him as he wielded a heavy hammer and a jemmy.

To prise free the first stone was far from easy; but once that was done, he was soon able to make an opening about eighteen inches square in the perished mortar. When he had found that, instead of earth, there was a hollow space behind the stones, his excitement rose to fever-pitch. Yet, on thrusting his hand into the hole it met only emptiness. For a further ten minutes he hammered away and wrenched out more small blocks of stone. Then his exertions were rewarded. Peering into the dark cavity he could make out a section of one side of a small, round-lidded, iron-bound chest.

Sitting back on his haunches he drew a deep breath and wondered what to do. Had his mother and father been alive he would have run to them with his amazing news. But Aunt Flora was another matter; so were the factor and the other men about the place. He had soon learned that they were suspicious of boys, regarding them as potential mischief-makers, and the reactions of these grown-ups were decidedly unpredictable. Swiftly he decided to keep his secret to himself.

It would not have been possible to get the chest out that day; so, reluctantly, he replaced the stones and returned to the Castle to clean himself up, eat his tea, then accompany his aunt to the Kirk for an evening service, of which he did not take in one word.

The next Sunday afternoon it poured with rain, so Aunt Flora would not let him go out. Somehow, he got through the following week. Then it was Sunday again and a fine afternoon.

To remove the stones was easy now, but when he attempted to pull the chest towards him the wood had become so rotten that it collapsed. Between the rusty iron bands at the nearer end there became visible a solid heap of precious objects: salvers, goblets and flagons of dull gold or silver, a jewel-hilted skirndhu, a necklace of small pearls and, from a burst bag, a trickle of gold pieces.

Adam examined some of them with awe, then put them back and replaced the stones that hid them from view. Again he wondered how he could best benefit from his wonderful find. If he took even a few of the coins there was no possible way in which he could dispose of them; and he felt sure that if he told his aunt about the treasure it would promptly be removed. He might be given a few pounds to put in his savings account and that would be the last he would hear of it.

During the next month he was able to spend three more Sunday afternoons under the little bridge, examining the treasure and packing it into small sacks. But he could still think of no way in which he could dispose of it to his own advantage.

Moreover, he felt certain that even if he could think of some means to sell it he had no right to do so. Obviously it was the property of the MacGilrays, if any of the family still existed, or, failing them, of Lord Ruffan as the present owner of the estate. Eventually he made up his mind that he must surrender it and hope that he would be treated generously as its discoverer.

Early in August, life at the Castle began to stir. Aunt Flora received a letter from His Lordship, with orders to prepare rooms for ten guests who would be arriving on the 11th for the opening shoot on the 12th. He would be coming up on the 7th, to ensure that all was in readiness for his house party. Late on the afternoon of the 8th, Adam saw Lord Ruffan for the first time. He was a big, heavy man of over sixty, with a bucolic but kindly face that betrayed his reputed fondness for vintage port. Adam, in his best suit, was duly presented by Aunt Flora and, carefully coached by her, said his piece about how grateful he was to His Lordship for having given him a home.

Adam was already tall for his age, well set up and, with his crop of red-gold curls, a fine-looking youngster. Lord Ruffan regarded him for a moment out of slightly protuberant eyes, then patted him on the shoulder and said:

'Glad to see you, young feller. Terrible thing about your family, but you're welcome here. What do you intend to do in life?'

It was just the sort of opening that Adam had been hoping for. Swallowing hard, he replied, 'Weel, sir. I . . . I've been wondering ef ye'd allow me te ask your advice aboot that?'

'Adam!' his aunt reprimanded him sharply. ''Tis no' for you to trouble His Lordship wi' such matters.'

But Lord Ruffan waved aside her protest. 'Easy on, Mrs. Inglis. I'd be glad to talk the boy's future over with him. As I shall be dining alone tonight, he can come in afterwards and keep me company while I drink my port.'

A few hours later Adam was reminded of a book that his mother had read to him shortly before her death. Its title was *Little Lord Fauntleroy*. The only likeness to the setting of the book was the richly-furnished dining room with its oil paintings of bygone Lords and Ladies on the walls, the big, mahogany table shining in the candlelight, the silver and cut-glass on it. Edward—known as Teddy—Chiswick, fifth Viscount Ruffan, bulky, red-nosed, semi-bald, lounging back in his elbow chair at the head of the table, did not in the least resemble the dignified Earl of Dorincourt; and Adam, years older than the little velvet-clad Fauntleroy, was no blood relation but came of common clay.

Yet there he was, sitting at the long table in this great room with the powerful owner of the Castle: the great Lord whose casual word could spell happiness or misery for scores of dependants scattered for miles round.

At a gesture from Ruffan, Adam had seated himself gingerly on the edge of a chair. To his surprise the red-faced master of the Castle poured him a glass of wine, smiled at him and said, 'Now, boy, drink that while you tell me about yourself.'

Adam gave a nervous smile and blurted out, 'Et's no me-self I wished to talk aboot, but I was agin saying so before the aunt.' Then he produced the MacGilray's letter, pushed it across the table and added, 'I come on this in ye'er Lord-ship's library.'

Taking the document, Ruffan read it through, laid it down and said, 'This is quite a find. Most interesting. Don't know much about such things myself, but it must be worth a few pounds.' He gave a sudden wink and went on, 'You're a smart boy to have brought it to me. Out to make a bit, eh? All right, we'll look on it as yours and I'll buy it from you, then send it to the Royal Stuart Society.'

'Aye, but that's not all,' Adam burst out excitedly, and he fished out from his trouser pocket a gold coin that he had taken from the hoard for such an occasion.

'God's boots!' exclaimed His Lordship, his brown eyes opening wide between their puffy rolls of flesh. 'You don't mean ... ?'

'Aye,' Adam nodded. 'The treasure's still there: cups and flagons made o' gold, some wi' jewels, lots o' siller, necklaces, rings an' the like—a whole chest of it.'

'Damn it, boy, this can't be true! You're pulling me leg,' declared Ruffan suspiciously.

'Nay! What'ud I gain by that?' Adam protested. ' 'Tis the truth. How else could I ha' come by this piece o' gold?'

Teddy Ruffan suddenly sat forward, his eyes narrowed and alert, 'And you've not told your aunt—nor anyone else?'

'Nay, not a soul. I'd a feelin' that ye'er Lordship might prefer it kept secret.'

'And you were right. I give you full marks for that.' For a long moment His Lordship stared at Adam in silence, en-deavouring to assess his character and wondering whether he could be trusted. The youngster's face was open and hand-some, but far from foolish, and held a hint of shrewdness; so he said:

'You've had the sense to hold your tongue about this. Can I rely on you to continue to keep it under your hat?'

'Aye,' Adam nodded vigorously. 'Ye'er Lordship kens best what's tae to be done, an' I'll no' breathe a word aboot the doin'.'

'Good. Listen, then.' Ruffan ran a pudgy hand over his thinning grey hair. 'The stuff is treasure trove. If the Mac-Gilrays who once owned this place had descendants I'd feel under an obligation to hand it over to them. But that branch is extinct; so as it's on my property I consider I've a right to it. There are laws about treasure trove, though. The government takes the stuff and the finder may get only a small percentage of their value. I'm not having that. We'll go along to this place tomorrow morning and collect the goods. Then I'll dispose of them privately—d'you see?'

Adam 'saw' and readily agreed.

'Now,' said His Lordship, 'help yourself to another glass of port and tell me what you want out of life.'

The generous wine loosened Adam's tongue. He made no mention of his occasional visions, but spoke of his wish to see foreign countries and of the books he had read to improve his education. Ruffan was much impressed, particularly with Adam's knowledge of early European history, about which he himself had only very sketchy ideas. An hour later he had decided that, the treasure apart, the boy would well repay looking after; and Adam, having skilfully evaded his aunt, made his way to bed, slightly muzzy but enormously elated at the outcome of his disclosure.

Next morning the beefy, bucolic-looking Englishman and the lithe, handsome Scottish lad made their way to the little bridge. While Ruffan sat on the bank of the burn, keeping watch in case anyone approached, Adam crawled back and forth bringing out the small sacks of treasure.

Ruffan examined each item. As he had anticipated, most of the articles Adam had taken for gold were only silver-gilt, while the gems were of indifferent quality and poorly cut; but, even so, owing to their age, they were collector's pieces and, he estimated, worth several thousand pounds.

When the last piece had been put back into a sack, His Lordship, in a high good humour, winked at Adam and said, 'Now, young feller, we've got to get the stuff back to the

Castle without some Nosy Parker spotting us becoming inquisitive. Early hours of the morning best time for that and to carry the lot I'll need your help. Think you can keep awake till one o'clock, then get dressed and join me down in the library without anyone being the wiser?'

'Aye.' Adam beamed with delight at the thought of this adventure with his new friend. 'I'll be there. Ye'er Lordship can count on it.'

The expedition went off without a hitch, and when the treasure had been packed away in the Castle safe the conspirators had a glass of wine together. While they were drinking, Ruffan said:

'I'm not as rich as people think, not by a long sight. Since the war these accursed taxes have made it devilish difficult for me to keep up this place, my home in Somerset and my flat in London. My heir won't be able to, that's certain. But he's a dreary fellow, so I'll never cut down to benefit him. Still, that's beside the point. As things are, this haul is a very welcome windfall and I want to show my appreciation of what you've done. Any ideas?'

Adam took a deep breath and replied, 'Could you run to a hundred pounds?'

His Lordship gave a cheerful laugh. 'I could, but I think you deserve more than that.'

To Adam a hundred pounds was an immense sum and he had hardly dare ask for it. His eyes widened with excitement as Ruffan went on:

'But there is a snag about my giving you a lump sum. As you are a minor we'd have to disclose it, and such a gift would be very difficult to explain. I've been thinking, though. You are a sensible chap and realise that a good education is the royal road to the trimmings that make life worth while. What do you say to my sending you to an English public school, then a university? No-one would question my doing that, because you're bright enough to warrant it.'

Overwhelmed at the new future opened up to him, Adam stammered his thanks.

'We'll have to play this carefully, though,' his benefactor resumed. 'Got to show people I'm taking an interest in you.

I tell you what. The guns arrive tomorrow for our first shoot
on the Glorious 12th. I'll take you out with me as an extra
loader, and later let you have a crack at the birds yourself.'

So, during the rest of August, Adam was skilfully established as a youngster of whom His Lordship thought a lot,
and early in September no-one at the Castle was greatly surprised when they learned that he was going to send him to
school in England.

When first making the suggestion Ruffan had counted on
the fact that his seat, Loudly Hall, was not far from Marlborough. As he was a Governor of that famous school, he
should have no difficulty in getting Adam into it; but he had
overlooked the fact that his protégé was over-age for entry.
However, Teddy Ruffan was not a man to be put off easily
and the headmaster was a broad-minded man with a very
natural desire to have scholars who promised to do his school
credit. In consequence, when he saw the excellent report sent
in by Adam's schoolmaster at Portgower, he was persuaded
to take the boy.

Thus, towards the end of September, happy, excited and
preening himself on the splendid new outfit with which His
Lordship had provided him, Adam travelled south to become
a denizen of an utterly different world from any he had known
or dreamed of. But very soon he was to rue the day he had
left his native Scotland.

It was not that his new companions deliberately bullied
him, but he was a fish out of water. His background, upbringing and accent were all different from those of his companions and, after he had fought and thoroughly beaten a
much older boy who laughed at his accent, he was regarded
as dangerous and unpredictable, so was left strictly alone.

He had been used to loneliness, but not loneliness among
a crowd of jostling, laughing boys; so for a time he was miserable. But at least there was one compensation; it threw him
back upon his work, and his masters found him to be their
star pupil. In addition, Marlborough has not only a truly
splendid library; it has been indexed so thoroughly that all
the ramifications of any subject can be found with ease. To
Adam this proved an abiding joy and he spent most of his

spare time there, reading voraciously: at first about the far-flung expeditions of the Norsemen and later about that other, tropical, country of which he still had occasional dreams. While looking through an illustrated *History of Early Civilisations* he had recognised this to be Mexico. In the library he also discovered Alexandre Dumas and Baroness Orczy and, between serious reading, he devoured their books with delight.

His visions of Mexico became ever more vivid. He saw it as a land of extraordinary contrasts: snow-capped mountains and rank vegetations only vaguely seen through the steam resulting from a tropical downpour; of architects whose mathematics were so exact that they could safely erect buildings the like of which had never been dreamed of in northern Europe; but which had still not devised the wheel that made many labours so infinitely easier; of a people to whom sunshine brought unbelievable plenty, yet whose hearts were filled with constant fear because it was an arid land and rain to make the crops grow could be bought only by the sacrifice of young men and virgins to the ferocious gods who, through their priests, ruled the country.

In spite of its sinister, fanatical and dangerous priesthood, this country of sunshine, music and brown-skinned women held for Adam much more attraction than the bleak, rain-swept northern lands with their people's primitive way of life and their long, dull winters; so he made up his mind that, as soon as he possibly could, he would visit Mexico.

It was in his second summer at Marlborough that he was quite suddenly pulled out of his lonely, studious life. There had been an epidemic in the school which had struck several members of the cricket First Eleven. The epidemic was over, but its victims were still convalescing and the match of the year was due to be played. Adam was a good bat, but a poor bowler and weak on fielding; so, in spite of his height and strength, he had got no further than doing well in the Third Eleven. But it was batsmen that were needed. The Games Captain took a chance and included Adam in the side.

He was put in sixth wicket down when already there seemed no hope at all of Marlborough's winning the match. Adam stayed the course, knocked up a hundred and five and carried his bat.

Towards the end of the match the excitement grew intense. Adam's last hit was a boundary, winning the match for Marlborough by three runs. The watching boys streamed on to the pitch, cheering like mad, seized Adam, hoisted him on their shoulders and carried him in triumph back to the pavilion. The Games Captain wrung his hand and told him then and there that he was capped. From that moment he was looked on as a hero.

At the beginning of his last year he received another distinction. Like other public schools, Marlborough has its Literary Society, but it differs in that there it is an élite. At most colleges any boy who is interested in books may join and listen to the talks given by well-known writers who are invited down to address the Society; at Marlborough the membership is limited to twelve senior boys, and only they may do so.

For some time past Adam had been contributing articles on sport to the school magazine, and it had never even occurred to him that he might qualify for this honour. Then, for his own amusement, he wrote three short stories about a Viking. To his surprise and delight, when the next vacancy occurred, he was invited to become a member of the Society. The double crown of his cap for cricket and membership of the literary élite, coupled with his cheerful character and good looks, made him immensely popular and during his last terms no youth could have had a happier life.

In the holidays, too, he thoroughly enjoyed himself, for Lord Ruffan's interest in him had continued. When in Scotland he took Adam fishing and shooting with him, and at other times had him to stay at Loudly Hall in Somerset; delighting to show him off to his friends as an example of what a public-school education could do.

He had changed during his time at Marlborough. His crop of unruly curls had been cut and coaxed into inoffensive waves, Ruffan's tailor had clothed him suitably and nothing remained of his broad Scottish accent but a pleasant burr.

All the rough corners had been rubbed off him and he felt at ease in any company.

Arrangements had been made for him to go up to Cambridge and, his ambitions having been fired by his membership of the Literary Society, he now hoped to become a professional writer, which would enable him to travel.

Then, three days after Adam left Marlborough for the last time, Teddy Ruffan had an apoplectic fit and died. Although it was not fully brought home to Adam for some days, for the second time the bottom had dropped out of his world.

. . . . .

Greatly stricken, Adam attended the funeral of his bluff patron and there, for the first time, met the heir. He was a distant cousin and had nothing whatever in common with his predecessor, who had disliked and ignored him. The new heir was in his fifties, married and with six children. He acidly informed Adam at an interview they had some days later that his late cousin had left his affairs in a scandalous tangle and it was now emerging that he had played ducks and drakes with the family fortune.

As Adam regarded the narrow, bony face opposite him, with its little, pursed-up mouth, he did not feel particularly sorry for its owner; but he did feel a sudden uneasiness on his own account, and, as he soon learned, with ample justification.

It transpired that his late benefactor had left him five hundred pounds in his Will, but had made no provision for the completion of his education. Aunt Flora was to receive the life tenancy of a cottage and a small pension, but the Castle was to be sold; so he was to lose what he had come to regard as his home.

The new Lord Ruffan went on to say with oily smoothness, 'On several occasions my cousin refused my pleas to help me with the education of my own children; so I am sure you would not expect me to pay for that of a young man like yourself who is not even a member of the family. It is regrettable that you may have to revise your plans for going up to Cambridge. But you have reached the age when you should have no difficulty in getting a job. I therefore suggest that you set about finding one without delay.'

So that was that. The legacy and a little nest-egg that he still had in National Savings Certificates would certainly not see him through three years at Cambridge. The social background he had acquired, as almost one of the jovial Lord Ruffan's family, had disappeared overnight. The only place that he might in future think of as home was the small cottage to be occupied by his dour Aunt Flora. He must try to get a job, and soon, but he had only the vaguest ideas how to set about it.

Sadly he packed his belongings and next morning said good-bye to Loudly Hall, where he had spent so many pleasant holidays, and went up to Scotland. Aunt Flora had received a letter from the Ruffan lawyers, but she was not unduly depressed. It seemed quite a possibility that whoever bought the Castle would be glad to reinstate her as housekeeper and she could then make a little extra money by letting the cottage. But Adam knew that with her limited resources there could be no question of her helping him to go through Cambridge.

Having assessed his qualifications for a job, he felt that he could almost certainly secure an appointment as a junior master in a private school. Then during the holidays he would have the time to write for magazines, and later start a novel; so he wrote to his ex-housemaster at Marlborough, stated his position and asked him to let him have testimonials to support an application for a post.

The housemaster replied cordially and sympathetically but, instead of enclosing testimonials, said that he was consulting the Head, as he thought they might find him something better than the sort of job he had in mind.

Then his lucky star moved into the ascendant once again. He received a letter from the Headmaster, who said they had been so concerned about his talents going to waste through not completing his education that they had persuaded the Dean of the University of Southampton to grant him a scholarship.

With no fees to pay, Teddy Ruffan's legacy and his own savings would just see him through. In new heart and determined to do well, Adam went south again towards the end of that September, to become an undergraduate.

His three years at Southampton were uneventful. The students at the University had much more varied backgrounds than had the boys at Marlborough. Some came from rich homes, but a high proportion had to be as careful of their money as Adam; so his limited means placed him at no disadvantage. He soon had a group of pleasant friends, entered into many of the social activities and fully justified his sponsors' expectations of him by achieving his B.A., and double Firsts in History and English Literature.

As a university student his call-up had been deferred, but after graduating he had to do his National Service and went into the Navy. Having completed his initial training he was posted to a minesweeper, where his cheerful willingness soon made him popular with both his mess-mates and officers. It was then that he grew his golden beard and was given the nickname of 'the Viking' but, although he enjoyed the life, he could not help feeling that he was getting nowhere with his ambitions to make a literary career for himself.

After a time he was given a course in W/T and became a proficient radio operator; then, for some reason he never discovered, he was transferred to Portsmouth and given a clerical job on the Admiral's staff. There he found the work easy and in his off-duty hours was able to take full advantage of the excellent recreation provided, including the Saturday-night dances held in the big N.A.A.F.I. hall.

Since Adam had lost his sisters he had had little to do with girls and had known none intimately. His holidays from school had all been spent in the country, where he had admired a few girls he had chanced to meet, but had had no opportunity to follow up the acquaintance, and at Southampton University he had deliberately avoided the many girls who endeavoured to attract his attention, because he could not afford to take any of them out regularly. In consequence, at twenty-two he was very much shyer than most young men of his age, and it was only with some difficulty that his mates persuaded him to accompany them to his first Saturday-evening dance.

When he entered the hall his fine 'Viking' head towered over those of his companions and, within a few minutes, bright eyes were fixed upon it from all directions. A score of pretty girls began to badger his friends for an introduction and, when he apologetically explained that he would make a poor partner because he had been to very few dances, several girls eagerly volunteered to teach him the latest steps. Among them was Polly.

She was a curvaceous blonde with a big mouth, rather full, highly-coloured cheeks, a tip-tilted nose and green eyes. Her father owned an ironmongery shop in which she worked, but only for part of the day, as her mother had died some eighteen months before and she had since kept house for her father in the flat above the shop. All this Adam learned during the three dances he had with her, and he thought her far more attractive than any of the other girls; so after their third dance, he asked if he might see her home.

Being as smitten with the handsome young giant as he was with her opulent charms, she readily assented and, ruthlessly cutting her obligation to the fellow who had brought her, suggested that they should slip away at once.

It was a fine, warm night and they walked through the almost deserted streets hand in hand, happily exchanging first confidences about themselves. In due course, to Adam's surprise, she turned out of the street into a long, narrow alley between high brick walls with, here and there, wooden gates outside which dustbins stood. She then explained that when the shop was shut she always used the back entrance; then, fifty yards along the alley, she opened a gate and drew him through it.

The faint moonlight showed him that they were in a back-yard, one side of which was stacked with corn-bins, chicken coops and other ironmonger's stock-in-trade; the other was a flower border and between the two there was a small lawn. No sooner were they inside the gate than Polly put her arms round Adam's neck, raised herself on tiptoe and kissed him on the mouth. Her warm, moist lips instantly aroused a fire

B

in him that had long been dormant. He responded avidly and for several minutes they clung together.

When at length, from sheer breathlessness, their kissing ceased, she whispered, 'It's early yet, let's make ourselves comfortable.' Then, breaking away from him, she walked over to a lean-to shed against the back of the house. There were some deck-chairs, two chintz-covered mattresses and half a dozen cushions in it. Grasping a mattress, she pulled it out. He took the other and they laid them side by side on the grass. As she began to arrange the cushions, he looked up a shade nervously at the blank, dark windows of the house and murmured:

'What about your old man? Say he hears us and looks out?'

She gave a low laugh. 'Don't worry, ducks, his room's at the front. Anyhow, he's as deaf as a post and we have no-one sleeping in. The char only comes in the mornings.'

During the hour that followed they lay closely embraced, exchanging fervid caresses in which Polly unashamedly took the lead. Adam had always supposed that nice girls gave themselves only when married or reluctantly seduced after most intense persuasion by their lovers; so Polly's willingness was a revelation to him. But his mind was in such a turmoil that he put aside all scruples and met her advances with equal ardour.

It was all over very quickly and afterwards she said, 'I . . . I'm afraid I excited you too much. Or . . . or could it be that you've never done it before?'

'That's right,' he admitted. 'I'm sorry if I disappointed you.'

'No.' She gave him a swift kiss. 'I'm not worrying about that, because I've really fallen for you. But you're such a handsome chap and you must have known lots of girls who would have been willing.'

Ashamed to tell her the truth, he murmured, 'Well, yes, but not one like you. Not one I liked enough. And how about you?'

She sighed with pleasure at the compliment. 'I feel flattered, then. About me—well, I was seduced when I was seventeen.

It wasn't very nice. Since then there have been two fellows.
I was in love with both of them. I wouldn't go with anyone
except a steady that I really cared about. But I fell for you
right away and . . . and I'll be your girl if you want me.'

'Want you!' he repeated, seizing her in his arms again.
'Of course I do! I think you're wonderful . . . wonderful.
And from now on I'm all yours.'

Adam's youthful virility swiftly reasserting itself, shortly
afterwards they again gave free rein to their passions, with
much greater satisfaction to both parties. A quarter of an
hour later they put away the mattresses and cushions, agreed
that he was to take her to a movie the following afternoon
and, after further prolonged embraces, parted. Adam walked
back to barracks on air, feeling as good as if he had suddenly
become a millionaire.

On the Sunday they held hands in the pictures and had a
meal in a café, where Adam stared gooey-eyed at his beloved
across the table, hardly able to believe in his good fortune.
Then they went out to the park and found a secluded spot
sheltered by bushes and, when darkness fell, again made hectic love.

But when it came to arranging their next meeting, Adam
was grievously disappointed. It suddenly emerged that Polly
was a member of a large and united family; and that it had
been a long-established custom for her to spend two or three
evenings a week with aunts, uncles and numerous cousins.
Still more surprising, he learned that she was a much cleverer
and more earnest girl than he had had reason to suppose.
The desire to improve herself had led her to attend courses
at evening school on Mondays, Wednesdays and Fridays and,
after each session, she had to put in two hours or more in
private study and writing up her notes, otherwise she could
not hope to pass her exams.

In consequence, he had to wait impatiently until, at last,
Saturday came again. They left the N.A.A.F.I. during the supper interval, Polly having assured Adam that her father was
an early-to-bed man and would be snoring by ten o'clock.
When they reached the backyard garden she pointed to a
window on the first floor and said :

'That's my room. We'll be much more comfy there. I'm going in by the door and up the stairs; but, deaf as he is, if he's not yet dropped off he just might hear your heavy tread.' She then pointed to a folding ladder that was leaning against the side of the shed, and added, 'If you go up that, you can easily reach my window from the roof of the shed. Soon as I get upstairs, I'll open it and you can climb in.'

His heart beating like a hammer, Adam followed her directions. As soon as he was in her room she pulled down the blind, switched on the light and began to undress. She had few clothes on and within a matter of minutes stood before him naked and smiling. It was the first time he had seen a girl in the nude and the sight took his breath away. With trembling hands he ripped off his own clothes and half carried, half flung her on the bed. They were both healthy, strong and twenty-two years old. Neither of them seemed capable of exhausting the other and, until the small hours, between intervals to whisper endearments, stroke one another, entwine and kiss, they hit the high-spots of ecstasy.

Apart from the terrible frustration Adam felt at being able to revel with his divinity in her bed so seldom, their affaire continued happily for six weeks. Now and then she let him give her a meal between her evening classes and returning home to study, and on Sundays they could spend from midday until six o'clock together; but after that there was always a family party that he could not persuade her to give up, so it was only on Saturdays that, on returning early from the N.A.A.F.I. dances, he was able to mount the ladder that led to his especial Paradise.

That she had had other lovers in the past did not unduly trouble him. He had learned from her, much to his surprise, that in these 'enlightened' times most girls took it for granted that they were just as much entitled to have fun as were men, and that if one came upon a girl who was eighteen and still a virgin there must be something wrong with her.

The main ingredient of the spell that Polly cast upon him was her splendidly healthy young body and unfailing willingness to let him assuage his desire upon it. To intelligent conversation she could contribute next to nothing, but she was never cross, difficult or demanding; on the contrary she was placid by nature, warm-hearted, kind and generous, so that he was always happy in her company. He failed to comprehend that she was in fact ignorant, shallow and showed little evidence of the courses she was taking. Indeed, he thought of her as an angel in female form, worthy of worship for the happiness she had brought him.

His belated introduction to the joys of sexual love so obsessed him that he began to count the hours until Saturdays came round. Then a Saturday came when he was on the roster for duty. A few days before it, he pleaded with her to get out of her Sunday party; but in vain. It happened to coincide with her 'Auntie Flo's' birthday party, so she could not possibly not be with them for that.

The thought of a whole fortnight having to elapse between his being able to clasp her yielding body in his arms was so devastating that, by Monday morning, exasperation had driven him to decide to pay her a visit that night; and to hell with her being too tired to make love after her evening class and work on her books.

Impatiently, he waited until well after ten o'clock then made his way to the yard-garden behind Polly's home. There was no light from her window, so he rather hoped that she was already asleep. Then, if he crept in, he could give her a lovely surprise by waking her with a kiss. The folding ladder was in its usual place; a minute later he was on the roof of the shed. It was a warm, still night. Her window was open and with one easy heave of his strong arms he pulled himself up, got a leg over the sill and, turning sideways, slid inside.

'Who's that?' came Polly's startled voice from the direction of the bed.

'It's me, Adam,' he replied in a whisper.

'Then, Adam whoever-you-are, get the hell out of here,' a gruff voice said, and, next moment, the bedside light was switched on. It revealed Polly, her eyes wide, her mouth agape, sitting up in bed and, beside her, a hairy-chested Petty Officer whose name Adam knew to be Grimes.

'So it's you, Viking,' Grimes said quite amiably. 'Sorry about your disappointment, but you've got your dates wrong.

Pretty Polly here always has a queue and I booked her for tonight a fortnight since.'

'I . . .' Adam stammered. 'I didn't know. I thought she was my girl. I . . . I love her.'

Grimes grinned. 'So she led you up the garden path, eh? I get it. You're her fancy boy and have your fun for free. Well, you've been darned lucky. To the rest of us she's "Polly up the ladder and two pounds a go".'

Polly gave a whimper, covered her face with her hands and, collapsing, buried it in the pillow.

For a moment Adam's temper boiled. He was seized with the impulse to grab Grimes by the neck, haul him out of bed and throw him naked out of the window. But the facts were all too terribly clear. Grimes was not to blame for being in Polly's bed and she made no attempt to deny that she was a whore. In that bed, where he had experienced such unalloyed delight, taking advantage of her father's deafness, night after night she gave herself to a succession of different men for money. Stifling a sob he turned away, stumbled to the window, got through it, reached the yard and, half blinded by tears, staggered out into the alleyway. Twice unforeseen circumstances had robbed him of his prospects of advancement and now this new world of love had collapsed about his ears.

. . . . .

Adam went no more to the Saturday dances and shunned his friends, suspecting that any or all of them were Polly's 'customers'. For a while his heartache was such that he could settle to nothing and was tortured nightly by visions of his ex-divinity doing with other sailors the things she had done with him: tall, short, young or horny-handed and hairy-chested like Petty Officer Grimes.

After a fortnight of this misanthropic existence he decided that he must either pull out of it or go mad; so he decided to divert his mind by writing a novel. Once he had forced himself to settle to this new occupation, he found it came easily. Soon he was immersed in his story and spent every free moment in the N.A.A.F.I. library, covering sheet after sheet of paper.

The book was about the adventures of a Sea King whom he called Ord the Red-handed, and the knowledge he had acquired through his dreams and the books he had read enabled him to describe the life of those days with uncanny verisimilitude. With feverish absorption he wrote one hundred thousand words in eleven weeks and his finishing the book coincided, within a few days, with his release from National Service.

Out of his meagre savings he paid for the manuscript to be typed, then sent it to a publisher who, from the advertisements in the *Sunday Times*, he judged to be the most likely to accept it. But he was now jobless and had, somehow, to support himself.

Now that he had his B.A., he had little doubt that his friends at Marlborough would be able to secure him a post as a master at a good private school; but he had never much fancied the idea of becoming a teacher and the more practice he could get at writing in any form the better for his ambitions as an author; so he made the rounds of the Portsmouth papers seeking an opening as a reporter.

The result was like a douche of cold water. Overworked and cynical editors told him that reporters were not just taken on because they had been members of the Literary Society of a snob public school; they had to graduate as copy-boys who mixed the paste and ran errands for all and sundry, on a pay-chit that would not keep a grown man in cigarettes and drink.

His head bloody but unbowed, Adam put his wits to work and his scruples aside. He telephoned an old friend of his, Mrs. Burroughs, the housekeeper at Loudly Hall, and, having learned that His Lordship was not in residence, said that he would come out there to spend a few nights. On Loudly Hall notepaper he then wrote to the editors of the two leading Southampton newspapers. To both he said that he aspired to a career in journalism and that Lord Ruffan had suggested that his connections might enable him to make a useful contribution to the paper's social column. His salary would be a secondary consideration, provided he was given reasonable expenses, as his main object was to gain experience. With both letters he enclosed the copies of *Marlborough College Magazine* in which his stories had appeared.

By return of post both editors said they would be pleased to give him an interview. Having talked with them he settled for a roving assignment on the *Hampshire Post*. His trouble then was that he knew no-one in Hampshire and only a few families in Somerset and Wiltshire. In each case the 'County' maintained its sublime exclusiveness. People 'belonged' by right of birth and long-owned estates, or they did not. Many of its members had abandoned their large houses for smaller ones in which they frequently did their own washing-up. But that did not prevent their firmly rejecting the overtures of the nouveau-riche who endeavoured to penetrate their circle. They were not intolerant and willingly accepted people who had distinguished themselves in government, science or the arts, whatever their origins, but they had an extreme dislike of publicity in any form, so, by becoming a newspaper man, Adam had automatically debarred himself from any participation in their activities.

It was not long before his editor realised that his contributions to the social column were limited to the doings of 'café society', who had week-end places in the country. But Adam's writing was definitely good and his editor was loath to get rid of him. As it happened, the chief crime reporter on the paper had to go into hospital for a serious operation; so the editor asked Adam if he would like to take over as understudy to the number two, who had stepped into the senior man's shoes.

Glad to be freed from the position he had obtained for himself on false pretences, and at this chance to gain experience in another branch of journalism, Adam readily agreed.

Apart from an occasional interesting assignment when his senior was otherwise occupied, he spent most of his time in magistrates' courts writing up cases that had any unusual features and, where many men would have found boring the long hours spent there listening to trivial misdemeanours, he felt that he was gaining valuable knowledge of human character and frailties which would later be useful for his books. Then, after he had been so employed for some months, he had a letter telling him that his novel *Across the Green Seas* had been accepted for publication.

The contract was not a very good one, as it had not even occurred to him to seek out a literary agent; so the publisher was taking twenty-five per cent of all subsidiary rights: serialisation, film, TV and foreign—if any. But several people in the office assured him that he was very lucky to have had a first novel accepted anyhow, before it had been sent to a dozen or more publishers; so he went happily about his work, only at times a little frustrated by the knowledge that it must be many more months before the book appeared in print.

It was in the following winter that he was suddenly given cause to worry. He was on friendly terms with the police and by then, having his ear well to the ground about crime in Southampton, had been able to give them a tip which led to the arrest and conviction of a scrap dealer who acted as a 'fence' for a gang of youths who made a living by stealing lorry-loads of old iron. After the trial he received a letter printed in capitals, which read:

'Us boys know you shopped old Fred. We don't like your face and won't have it round these parts. Unless you want it carved you'll get out of So'ton and quick.'

He showed it to his editor and the police. Both said in effect, 'It's an occupational hazard, chum. But if you keep your eyes skinned and don't go places late at night you ought to be all right.'

All went well for three weeks; then, at dusk one evening, as he was coming out of a pub in which he had been trying to get the lowdown on a safe robbery, the gang set upon him.

His size and strength saved him from the worst. He dealt with two youths who came at him with razor blades in a way that gave them cause to regret for many months that they had attacked him. But the others got him down and kicked him ruthlessly with their heavy boots until some sailors who were in the pub came to his rescue. He was still conscious and had succeeded in protecting his face and head; but his body was black and blue, two of his ribs were cracked and his right knee-cap so badly bashed that water on the knee resulted. For over a fortnight he was in hospital and before he was discharged he received another anonymous note:

'You got off lightly. Next time we'll do you proper. Get out of So'ton or else . . .'

During his vivid dreams when he lived the life of a Viking, Adam was a great fighter. Whirling aloft his mighty double-edged sword, he hewed his way with ferocious delight through groups of long-haired, skin-clad semi-savages striving to protect the coastal villages of Scotland and Ireland, or the better-clad but less warlike peasants of Romanised England. But he regarded these far memories as almost a form of fiction in which he was not responsible for the part he played, any more than a mild-mannered modern author who creates a ruthless secret agent. In his present personality he had inherited the gentle nature of his mother and abhorred all forms of violence. Occasionally his quick temper caused him to snap the heads off people who annoyed him, and once he had knocked down a fellow reporter; but he realised that his great strength could be dangerous and gradually learned to keep his temper under better control.

To be attacked by a gang was a different matter and he had the natural dislike of most men to exposing himself to injury if it could be avoided. So he went to his editor and said:

'This isn't good enough. I'm not prepared to remain here as a sitting duck for these young swine.' Then he handed in his resignation.

The editor endeavoured to persuade him to stay on in some other capacity, but he replied. 'No. They wouldn't know that I've ceased to be a crime reporter, and I like my face. So I'm quitting.'

While in hospital, his dreams had become more frequent and had all been of Mexico; so he was now eager to spend even a short time in that country. To go there as a passenger was far beyond his means, but he decided to work his way there and made the rounds of the shipping offices. His time in the Navy qualified him to go as a seaman; but he knew that would mean a rough life in the fo'c's'le and hoped, as an educated man, to get something better.

His enquiries were at first disappointing, as he found that no lines sailed direct from Southampton to Mexico. Then after a while he was offered a post as supercargo in a tramp that was sailing to Lisbon, the Canaries, Buenos Aires, then up to Rio, Recife, Caracas, Kingston Jamaica, Vera Cruz and New Orleans. The pay was modest and the ship shortly due to sail, so it was agreed that he should sign on only as far as Vera Cruz. From there he could pay his rail fare up to Mexico City and have enough money over to live modestly in the capital for a few weeks, or stay on longer if he could find a job. Two days later he had taken over the ship's manifest and was on his way.

The voyage proved a pleasant change; the ship's officers were a tough lot but friendly, and his duties of superintending the unloading and reloading of cargo in the ports light. In preparation for his stay in Mexico he had made up his mind to learn Spanish; so he had taken with him a small tape-recorder with a set of Spanish-teaching tapes, a Spanish grammar, a Spanish-English dictionary and copies of a novel by Ibañez in both English and Spanish. While at sea he was virtually a passenger; so he was able to spend many hours each day with his records and books, and by the time the ship reached Recife was confident that he knew enough of the language to converse on simple matters.

But at Recife, in Brazil, again the hammer of Fate fell. On going ashore the Captain was informed by the Company's agents that it had gone bankrupt. There was not even enough money to pay off the ship's company. Adam was left stranded, with only a little over fifty pounds in cash, no job and thousands of miles from either Mexico or home.

. . . . .

His weeks in Recife were some of the worst Adam had ever experienced. The shoddy port lies only eight degrees south of the equator. The moist heat is so terrible that a clean shirt is soaked with perspiration within a few minutes. People habitually carry towels with which to mop the sweat from their faces. The town is dreary beyond belief, its inhabitants Indians, the better-off having a dash of Portuguese blood, the majority ragged, dirty and half starving. After a week there

Adam would willingly have signed on as a seaman in any ship bound for Mexico or England, to get away, but the agents had said that funds to pay off the ship's company were being sent out, he had ten weeks' wages owing to him and he was loath to forgo the best part of two hundred pounds; so he stayed on.

Meanwhile, he lived uncomfortably in a squalid seamen's hostel, eking out his own money. That due from the Company still failed to arrive and, as time went on, he had to look at every *cruzeiro* twice.

He was near despair when one day he came upon an English newspaper. In it there was a review of *Across the Green Seas*, and it predicted a great success for the book. Realising that now his book had been published, he was due for the advance royalty on it, Adam used a good part of his remaining funds to send a cable to his publisher.

A week later an airmail letter reached him. The book was selling splendidly. To take advantage of its success it should be followed up with another next spring, so it was hoped that he had one well on the way to completion. His presence in England could be helpful in getting his name established. Money had been cabled to his credit at the American Express and he was urged to return home as soon as possible.

Overjoyed at this good news, Adam promptly moved to more comfortable quarters and booked a passage on a ship that was sailing for Liverpool the following week. Now he cursed himself for not having foreseen that, on the chance that his first book would do well, he ought to have another ready to send in; and for all the wasted hours he might have been working on it, instead of devoting his time to learning Spanish, then sitting about miserably in Recife.

Filled with enthusiasm, he went to work at once and roughed out a plot. It was based on his recent voyage and a love affair between a fictional First Mate in a ship and a young Brazilian girl passenger who was heiress to millions.

By the time he sailed he had written two chapters, and on the voyage over he wrote a further six. Well before he arrived in England he had decided there was no point in his returning either to Scotland or Southampton, so he would live in London. When he arrived there the rents appalled him, but he settled for a bed-sitter, bathroom and kitchenette, which he felt he could afford, in Wandsworth. Then, living on eggs, tinned food and frequent brews of tea, he renewed his literary labours, working twelve hours a day.

Soon after his return he was taken to lunch by his publisher, an elderly gentleman with a benign countenance but cynical turn of mind, named Winters. From Mr. Winters, Adam learned the hard facts of authorship as a career. It was the worst paid of all professions. He must not be misled by the incomes made by such writers as Agatha Christie, Somerset Maugham, Dennis Wheatley, Ian Fleming, J. B. Priestley, A. J. Cronin, Howard Spring and a few others of that kind They could be counted on the fingers of two hands. Over eighty new novels were published every week. Many of them had entailed two or three years' work but earned their authors only a few hundred pounds, because ninety per cent of their sales were to libraries, which meant that they received about two shillings' royalty on a book that would be read by scores of people.

There was also the matter of 'build-up'. However successful a first novel might be, unless it were filmed it would bring its author less than a leading barrister received for one case, or a Harley Street surgeon for two or three private operations. It was not until an author was established with eight or ten well-received books behind him, and a reasonable assurance that they would continue to be reprinted as paperbacks, that he could count on an income on the level of that of a bank manager in a not particularly rich suburban area.

Mr. Winters went on to advise that no author could count on a first success as a warrant for taking up full-time authorship. Far better get a steady job, even if it meant producing one book every two years, instead of two or three. Then, after a period, it would emerge whether the author was really a big-shot and could afford only to write for a living, or whether he was one of the thousands who gave all their leisure to providing entertainment for the public for a sum per book that could not have got them two minutes in a cinema.

All this was new to Adam, and he protested indignantly

that the reading public should be made to pay at least a half-penny per copy for every book they took out of the Free Libraries. Mr. Winters shrugged his shoulders, laughed and replied:

'A. P. Herbert and others have been trying for years to get a law to that effect through Parliament. But they are lone voices crying in the wilderness. The big-shot politicians don't give a damn for justice. All they think about is whether or not a measure might cost their party votes; and to make the British masses pay even a trifle for their reading would. So full-time authors, except those in the first rank, continue to eke out their existence on a few hundred a year, and most of our M.P.s couldn't care less. Now, my friend, *Across the Green Seas* has done exceptionally well for a first novel, but if you are wise you will get yourself a steady job.'

Considerably chastened, Adam returned to Wandsworth. On the voyage home he had had pleasant day-dreams of being received in England as a literary lion, invited here and there as the guest of honour and hearing his name on everyone's lips. Now it emerged that that did not happen after just one successful book, and he might even have to get some other form of regular work to support himself. But, apart from journalism, he had no experience or qualifications which could get him a reasonably well-paid post. Rather than become a drudge on a pittance, he decided to spend his days and nights flogging his talent for all he was worth.

Imbued with the new, fervid flame of creation he turned out story after story and scores of articles on topical subjects. Some were bad, some indifferent, but enough had something in them for several Fleet Street editors to become interested. Within three months he had established a connection and was earning just sufficient money to keep his head above water.

It was at that time that a new element entered his life in the person of Mildred Soames.

He met her at a party given by his publishers. Far from being the 'lion' at it, he was just 'one of our authors'. But Mildred had read his book and showed wide-eyed interest in him. She was a dark, slim, fine-boned young woman with small, well-chiselled features and would have been nearly beautiful in a classic way had it not been for her protruding teeth. Physically and mentally she was the very antithesis of Polly and the only attraction she had for Adam was her evident enthusiasm about his work. Pleasantly flattered as he was at finding her to be a 'fan', he did not take her praise very seriously until it emerged that her husband was the firm's representative in the northern counties, and that for some years past she had been reading manuscripts and advising on their acceptance or rejection.

Her husband was not at the party and she went on to convey that, as he had to spend the greater part of the year on his rounds of the booksellers in the north, she led a rather dreary life. This emboldened Adam to suggest that if she had no other plans she might care to go on somewhere with him to dinner. She accepted with alacrity and, when he confessed with some embarrassment that he knew very little about London restaurants, she suggested a place in Chelsea at which they dined snugly but inexpensively.

By the time they were having coffee the small, dark, intense Mildred was extracting from her large, shy, Viking-like companion full particulars of his ambitions, circumstances and present impecunity. Promptly she offered her assistance. She read not only for his publisher but also for several magazines, so was in a position to introduce his work to their editors.

This necessitated their meeting again on numerous occasions: at first over a drink or for dinner, then in her Chelsea flat. On the third occasion he went there he found that her husband had returned to London on one of his monthly visits to report sales. His name was Bertie and he proved to be a short, fat, jovial-faced man. Mildred had already told Adam that, as Bertie was seldom at home, he made no objection to her having friendships with other men; so he had heard from her all about her new 'literary discovery' and gave Adam a hearty welcome.

In fact Adam found it embarrassingly hearty, for the exuberant Bertie not only plied him with much more gin than he was used to, but slapped him on the back, referred to him as his wife's new 'boy friend' and proceeded to launch into his latest repertoire of questionable stories.

Mildred, failing to head him off, looked down her well-modelled little nose with obvious disapproval, and it was evident to Adam that any great affection that might once have existed between the couple had long since been dissipated.

At their next meeting, Mildred confided to Adam that she had good reason to believe that Bertie was unfaithful to her during his absences in the north and that they continued together only as a matter of convenience. He liked to be able to return to a comfortable home of his own to which he could invite his friends, while she was the gainer by the generous allowance he made her and by living in a better flat than she could otherwise have afforded.

Meanwhile, as the manuscript of Adam's second book had not yet gone to press she had been through it with a tooth-comb, cutting out many of the passages about the sea and expanding those concerning the love interest. He did not approve all her alterations, but accepted them because she assured him that she knew best. People, she said, did not want to read long descriptions of tempests and ill-feeling between ship's officers; they had, to her mind, a childlike absorption in sexual urges and the moves that eventually led to people getting into bed together.

Nine months later, owing largely to Mildred's connections, Adam was making quite a good income. It was not spectacular and, with Scottish caution, he refused to abandon his bed-sitter in Wandsworth for better quarters; but he had been able to refurnish his seedy wardrobe with new and smarter clothes and, more and more frequently, take Mildred out to dinner and a theatre or movie.

At last the big day came when *The Sea and the Siren* was published. That night, to celebrate, they dined and danced at the Savoy. Afterwards he took her back to her flat and went in for a last drink. It was a very long time since he had had his affaire with Polly and in recent months he had increasingly toyed with the idea of trying to find a girl whom he could care for and who would be willing to take him as her lover. Mildred had given him the impression that she despised that sort of thing, and he had never even kissed her. But that night both of them had drunk much more than they were accustomed to carry. On a sudden impulse he put his arms round her as they sat on the sofa. She protested, but only feebly. His caresses did not seem to rouse her and she refused his plea to undress and allow him to go to bed with her; but, eventually, still on the sofa, she let him have his way.

In the small hours of the morning he walked back from Chelsea to Wandsworth. He felt none of the elation he had experienced after his first night with Polly; only a relaxed feeling and a vague uneasiness about how the thing he had started might develop.

Next morning he sent flowers. Later that day Mildred telephoned her thanks and asked him to come in for a drink the following evening. By then he had recovered sufficiently to feel better about things. He thought it probable that Mildred's lack of enthusiasm was due to Bertie's having mishandled matters on their honeymoon, as it was said that many women suffered from a lasting reaction on that account. But he had again acquired a mistress, and one who shared all his interests, made a charming companion and had an apparently complaisant, virtually absentee, husband; so, given time and patience, he felt that the future could hold much happiness for them both.

When he arrived at the Soames' flat, Mildred opened the door to him. Her large eyes were intense, her prominent teeth flashed in a sudden, rather coy, smile and she said in a low voice:

'Come in, darling. Bertie's back from the north for a few nights, and I've told him about *us*.'

For a few seconds Adam did not take in the implications of what she had said. Then he was seized with an impulse to turn and run. But by that time he was inside and advancing towards the open door of the sitting room with Mildred blocking his retreat.

A moment later he was confronting the rotund Bertie, who gave him a look more of pain than anger, and said with a shake of his head, 'I wouldn't have believed it of you, young feller. You didn't strike me as that sort, and I thought Mil was content to go on as things were. I suppose it's largely my fault for not having insisted on her coming up to Manchester so that I could be with her much more frequently. But there it is. These things do happen, and Mil tells me that you've fallen for one another. Well, I'm not one to stand in the way of other people's happiness. She can have her divorce and I'm sure you'll do the right thing by the little woman.'

Swallowing a lump in his throat, Adam stammered, 'Yes . . . oh, yes. Of course.' Upon which Bertie suddenly became quite cheerful, began to mix Martinis for the three of them and declared:

'That's settled, then. I'm glad we can all remain friends. All we have to do now is to work out ways and means so that we can get things tidied up with a minimum of fuss and bother.'

It then transpired that Bertie was willing to give Mildred 'grounds' on the understanding that she made no claim for alimony and that, apart from her personal possessions, he retained the contents of the flat. He added, with disarming generosity, that until the divorce came through he would remain in the north, so Adam was welcome to move into the flat if he wished.

They then shelved the subject, made a determined pretence that it had never arisen and, with somewhat forced cheerfulness, dined together at a nearby restaurant.

Adam got away as soon as he decently could, and walked home with his mind in a whirl. Later, lying in bed, he made a fairly shrewd appreciation of the situation. The full-blooded and gregarious Bertie was thoroughly tired of his earnest and puritanical-minded wife; he had, therefore, jumped at this chance to be rid of her at no financial loss to himself. She, too, was thoroughly tired of him and, as his future held no particular promise, had seized on this opportunity to swap him for an author who was a potential best-seller and in due course, might become a distingushed and wealthy husband.

Much as Adam took pleasure in Mildred's company, he was not in the least in love with her and had no wish to be married to anyone. Yet it seemed that, like it or not, he had landed himself with her. Short of cutting loose and disappearing, he saw no way to evade the course that was being thrust upon him. She had become his main contact with the editors who provided him with a living. Moreover, having been taken off his guard, instead of having had the courage to make his feelings about her clear, he had rashly promised Bertie to do the right thing by the 'little woman'.

Greatly troubled, he eventually fell asleep, vaguely hoping that something might arise that would enable him to wriggle out of his obligation.

But next morning the ground was cut from beneath his feet. Mildred arrived at his lodging, kissed him with unexpected fervour and took charge of matters. She said that Bertie had gone, so Adam could move into her flat.

In vain he protested that to do so might queer the divorce and that her good name would suffer with her neighbours. Mildred replied that in these days there were so many divorces that the King's Proctor had not the means to investigate one per cent of them and that, as she and Adam were to be married as soon as the divorce was through, her neighbours were quite liberal-minded enough to look on them as turtle-doves rather than as adulterers. She then made Adam pay his landlady a week's rent in lieu of notice, packed his belongings for him and carried him off.

Once they had settled down, Adam was much happier than he had expected to be. He enjoyed many small comforts that he had previously lacked, and in bed, although she was no Polly, Mildred gave herself to him willingly. Having had little experience of sleeping with women he accepted it that her limitations were normal in contrast to Polly's, whose amorous abandon he now put down to her having been a nymphomaniac.

Nevertheless, after some months their initial contentment was to be marred by increasingly bad news from the literary front. Adam's second book proved a flop. It had been well subscribed; but the reviews ranged from indifferent to downright bad, and in its first three months it sold less than thirty per cent of the copies that *Across the Green Seas* had in the same period.

Mildred railed against the critics and remained convinced that Adam had the makings of a best-seller. Together they laboured on his third book in which, for background, he used his experiences as a crime reporter in Southampton. Again she insisted on inserting lush passages describing the hero's affaires with several young women. Reluctantly he accepted them, while marvelling that a woman who could write of sexual encounters with such gusto should, herself, be comparatively cold.

This was more than ever borne in on him after the divorce came through. They were married quietly a week later at Chelsea Town Hall, and moved to a smaller flat in the same neighbourhood which they had been decorating and furnishing as their new home. That night, although they had had only half a dozen friends in for drinks, she declared herself too tired to let him make love to her. And from then on their relations in that way steadily worsened.

Mildred began to suffer from migraines and backache. When Adam became sufficiently wrought up to press her she submitted; but reluctantly, and with the air of a martyr, so that he was left with the guilty feeling that he had behaved like a brute. Clearly she derived no enjoyment from it and for him it became only a hard-won temporary satisfaction. Bitterly, he came to the conclusion that she had exerted herself to give him pleasure before their marriage only to keep him on the hook. Twice when she flatly refused him he lost his temper, seized her with his big hands by the shoulders and shook her until her teeth chattered, then took her by force; but afterwards he was thoroughly ashamed of himself and begged her forgiveness.

A fortnight after he had sent in the manuscript of his third novel, Mr. Winters asked him to lunch at the Garrick, and there took him to task. Over the coffee he said:

'We are taking *After Dusk in Southampton* because the success of your first novel will still enable your name on a book to show us a margin of profit. But it's not going to get you anywhere. Now tell me, how much of it is you and how much is Mildred?'

Adam admitted that Mildred had had a considerable hand in it, particularly with the love sequences.

Mr. Winters gave his cynical grin. 'I thought as much, and to you as an author your wife is a menace. She is a competent reader and good enough to recognise the big stuff when she sees it; hence her appreciation of your first novel. But her real flair is for light romance: the triangle fiction that goes down well with young girls and frustrated spinsters. Its sales are entirely to the libraries and its authors are almost unknown. But the ones that Mildred picks always show a profit. Not much, but it is bread-and-butter publishing that helps to keep the firm going. Some writers are naturals at turning out such trash. But you are not, and your new book is neither flesh, fowl nor good red herring. Snap out of it, dear boy. Go home and tell Mildred to put her head in a pudding cloth, then sit down to it and write me a really good book.'

Adam knew inside himself that his publisher was right. When he got home he sugared the pill as well as he could, but gave Mildred an expurgated version of what Mr. Winters had said. The result was a blinding row. She accused him of gross ingratitude and added, he felt without any justification, that his failure to produce really good books was due to his obsession with lust.

They patched up their quarrel, but the rift between them widened. Mildred would let him sleep with her only when he had taken her out to dinner and deliberately filled her up with liquor until she was three parts tight. Meanwhile he set to work on another novel and refused to show her a page of it.

The new book was a sequel to *Across the Green Seas*. While writing his last two novels, and particularly since the beginning of his association with Mildred, his strange dream parade of life among the Norsemen had occurred only at long intervals; but now that his mind was once more engaged on the subject they again became quite frequent and proved invaluable.

The lofty barn-like house on the shores of East Gotland became as real to him as his Chelsea flat. It was one great room, the beams of the roof supported by two rows of tall posts. At one end there was a partition beyond which, through the dark cold winters, were housed the cattle; but only the prize beasts from which they would breed new herds. The rest were slaughtered in the autumn and salted or smoked

for the months when it was difficult to procure food. Round
the inner sides of the house there were stalls made from
wattle. In one, with a stone surround, was the fire that was
never allowed to go out. But there was no chimney to the
house, only a hole in the roof; and when a high wind was
blowing the smoke was beaten back, making one's eyes smart.
Another stall had a row of pegs on which to hang their furs,
although during the coldest months they never took them off.
There were no cupboards, but in one cubicle there was a row
of shelves to hold the cooking pots with their crude designs
and the drinking horns. In the place of honour, on the top
shelf, stood his glass mug; a thick piece with a design of a
strange animal men called a leopard miraculously depicted
on one side. It was said to have come from a great city far
to the southward on the inland sea, named Rome, and had
cost him twenty head of cattle. Apart from his great five-
foot-long, double-edged sword, which he had christened 'the
Avenger', the mug was his most precious possession.

So absorbed did he become by this transmission of far
memory that he could think of little else; so the book pro-
gressed most satisfactorily, but a price had to be paid for
that. During the past two years he had formed the practice
of writing alternately a chapter of a book, then a short story
or a few articles. Now he could not bring himself to break off
from his novel, with the result that after three or four months
his income began to fall off.

The advance on his last book had not fully covered the
furnishing of their flat. Many of the items had been obtained
on hire purchase and the instalments had to be met. Mildred
was still receiving her fees for reading manuscripts, but they
were sufficient only to pay for her clothes and help out with
the housekeeping. Neither of them had any capital or relatives who they could ask for a loan. Seeing the red light, she
both badgered and pleaded with him to put the book aside
and get down to more immediately remunerative work. He
knew that she was right, but he was now near to hating her
and her nagging brought out the obstinate streak in him.
With perverse pleasure, he flatly refused.

Then there came a bolt from the blue. Mildred, to her

fury, found herself to be pregnant. Adam did his best to console and comfort her, but she laid the blame on him and lashed him with her tongue until any pleasure he might have taken at the thought of becoming a father was destroyed by the knowledge that he was now tied to Mildred more firmly than ever. On top of that he was acutely harassed by the knowledge that having to maintain a child would prove an additional drain on their already strained finances.

His only consolation was that he had finished his book and was well on with revising it. Ten days later he was able to send it in and give his mind to devising plots for short stories. But writing the book had taken so much out of him that his imagination seemed to have dried up. He should, he knew, have had at least a fortnight's complete change and rest, but a holiday was out of the question: they could not possibly afford it. By driving himself mercilessly he succeeded in turning out about two thousand words a day, but he knew the writing to be of indifferent quality and was further depressed, although not surprised, that half the stuff he sent in was turned down.

The six months that followed were an ever-increasing nightmare. Mildred had a bad pregnancy and mounting fears of the ordeal she could not escape. Vindictively, she took it out of Adam, abusing him both as the cause of her sickness and about the sad falling off in the standard of his work. For as long as he could each day he now shut himself away from her, doing his writing at a small table in the bathroom, but they had to meet for meals and share their bed at night. In such an atmosphere his work deteriorated further. He found himself incapable of writing stories acceptable to good magazines and even from lesser papers the ratio of rejection slips for his articles steadily increased.

A time came when his bank manager refused him a further overdraft; so, in desperation, he asked Mr. Winters for an advance on his unpublished book. Winters pointed out that *After Dusk in Southampton* had proved an even worse flop than *The Sea and the Siren* and that both books had outstanding balances against them; so, with the firm, Adam was already well 'in the red'. But he admitted that his reader's

reports on the new book *Chronicles of Ord* were encouraging
and, somewhat grudgingly, let him have two hundred pounds.

In overdue hire-purchase instalments and other liabilities
the two hundred pounds melted away overnight. For some
time past Adam had been unable to take Mildred out to dinner or a movie, even once a week. They scraped and tried to
save by getting rid of their cleaning woman. The additional
work thrown upon Mildred made her still more shrewish;
although she hardly attempted to cope with it, with the result
that the flat became a pig-sty. Bills continued to roll in, but
only an occasional cheque for a few guineas from an editor,
and the bank manager became difficult, insisting that Adam's
overdraft must be substantially reduced.

By early summer the position had become desperate: the
grocer and Adam's tailor were both threatening to take proceedings unless their accounts were paid; he could not even
find the next quarter's rent. Worked out, harassed almost
beyond endurance, flagellated day and night by Mildred's
viperish tongue, utterly miserable, he realised that unless
something absolutely unexpected happened he would be
made bankrupt.

The absolutely unexpected did happen. Mildred was
knocked down by a car in the King's Road and killed. That
same afternoon, an hour before Adam learned that he was a
widower, Mr. Winters telephoned. He had sold the British
serial rights in *Chronicle of Ord* for a thousand pounds.

After that the thing snowballed. An American publisher
took the book, United States serial rights were sold for five
thousand dollars. When the book was published in the
autumn it went right to the top in the best-seller lists. It won
Adam the Atlantic Prize and was a huge success in the United
States. The film rights were sold and translation rights to
half a dozen countries; editors were begging Adam to let
them have at any price he liked to name the short stories they
had rejected. A year after Mildred's death a Company that
Adam had formed to exploit his copyrights had bought him
a Jaguar and paid for him to live in a suite at the Ritz.

Lucky Adam Gordon. He had survived when the rest of
his family had perished. Lucky Gordon, although the son of

a poor Scottish net-maker, he had been sent to one of England's finest public schools. Lucky Gordon, against all reasonable possibility at the time, he had been through a good university. Lucky Gordon, with his first book he had made a name for himself. Lucky Gordon, Fate had relieved him of a wife whom he had come to hate. Lucky Gordon, with his fourth book he had hit the high-spots and as an author was now the envy of the literary world. Lucky Gordon, that winter he was able to travel de luxe to Mexico, the warm, exotic, wonderful land of which he had for so long had dreams and longed to see.

But parts of his road to riches had been far harder than people knew, and several times it had seemed that his luck had deserted him for good. As he finished his daiquiri and his eyes again roved over the well-dressed men and lovely women dining in the roof restaurant of the Del Paseo, he wondered a shade uneasily for how long his present luck was going to last.

2

An Author in Search of a Plot

ADAM had flown out from England on New Year's Day
by the Qantas direct flight, touching down only at Bermuda
and the Bahamas. Soon after one o'clock in the morning the
aircraft had come in over Mexico City. Nearly six million
people lived down there in the broad valley so, on any cloud-
less night, countless twinkling lights could be seen; but, as the
Christmas decorations were still up, the great arena blazed
like a velvet carpet heaped with strings, loops and plaques
of precious jewels, making a never-to-be-forgotten sight.

Next morning he had slept late; then, after a breakfast-
lunch up in his eighth-floor bedroom, he got out a map and,
through the plate-glass that formed the wall of one side of
the room, he endeavoured to imagine the city as it had been
in the days of the Aztec Empire.

That proved impossible. Then it had consisted of a large
island in the middle of a great lake, to the shores of which it
was connected by three long causeways. A copy of a drawing
of it, attributed to Albrecht Dürer, that Adam had seen,
showed the island to have been entirely built over with many
fine plazas, palaces and pyramids. That was how Cortés and
his men had seen it on their arrival and reception by the Emperor Moctezuma. They had marvelled at the beautifully
carved stonework of the buildings, the scrupulously clean
markets and the balconies of the houses gay with flowers.

Moctezuma's intelligence service had been good. For years
past he had been receiving reports of the Spaniards' activities
in the Caribbean: of their ships as big as houses, their cannon
and muskets that could deal death from a distance by fire.

He had endeavoured to persuade his formidable visitors to go away by making them presents of many beautiful gifts and much gold. The Spaniards were few in numbers and after eight months, disgusted by his cowardice in submitting to their blackmail, his people had revolted, stoned him to death and driven the Spaniards out. In *la noche triste*, as that terrible night was called, many of them had been so loaded down with gold that while trying to escape they had fallen from the causeways into the lake and had drowned.

But Cortés, with the survivors and a host of Indian allies hostile to the Aztecs, had returned. Their last Emperor, Cuauhtémoc, had led a most courageous resistance, but in vain. Then, in revenge for the Aztecs' treachery, Cortés had razed the beautiful city of Tenochtitlán, as the capital was then named, to the ground. All that remained of it were many stones that the Spaniards had used when building a new and entirely different city.

An even greater change had been caused by the complete disappearance of the island. Late in the nineteenth century the great shallow lake had been drained, with the object of growing crops there. That had not proved possible because the marshland was strongly impregnated with salt; but ever-spreading suburbs had since been built on it, so that no trace remained of what had once been a tropical Venice set in the great fertile Anáhuac valley.

Yet, further afield, the scene was unchanged. On either side of the valley ranges of mountains, some with the sun shining on their snow-caps, dropped away into the misty distance. They were dominated by Popocatepetl, rising ten thousand feet above the city to seventeen thousand seven hundred feet.

Aeons ago Mexico had been split by a great rift running from Vera Cruz on the Atlantic to Cape Corrientes on the Pacific. The central plateau, on which Mexico City lay, had been heaved up and on both sides of it a belt erected eight hundred miles long by one hundred wide, dotted with innumerable volcanoes, many of which were still active. Once their lower slopes had been covered with dense forests of cedar; but, for building and fuel, the Spaniards had cut them down. The great ranges had since become a region of unbelievable harshness and desolation.

To the north of the rift lay many equally inhospitable areas of desert, and to the south of it, stretching away to Yucatán and Guatemala, vast tracts of low-lying land covered with jungle. Both could become unbearably hot and lack of roads rendered some parts so inaccessible that the Indians still lived in their villages in primitive conditions. So remote were they from law and order that if an aircraft had to make a forced landing in their neighbourhood they were still capable of murdering the passengers.

But during the past forty years enormous changes had taken place in Mexico. The land was incredibly poor and its agricultural value had been greatly reduced during the centuries by deforestation, which lessened the rainfall. Industrial development had attracted large numbers of the poverty-stricken peasants to the cities, many of which had quadrupled in size so that they now formed an extraordinary contrast to the barren lands scattered with miserable villages that surrounded them.

Mexico City itself was the *exemple par excellence* of this new age and when Adam went out that afternoon he was amazed by the grandeur of this modern metropolis.

Past his hotel ran the Paseo de la Reforma: a mile-long, six-lane highway that had been driven right through the centre of the city, with great skyscrapers of steel and glass rearing up on either side. Along it surged a flood of vehicles, the fast cars on the inner lanes speeding along at sixty miles an hour. In the side streets behind his hotel, where lay the best shopping district, there were jewellers, modistes, antiquiers and men's shops that were evidence of the riches of the Mexican upper classes.

In the evening he went out again to see the illuminations. The Reforma, and all the other principal highways, had chains of coloured lights across them at frequent intervals and, every few hundred yards, big set-pieces of Father Christmas in his sleigh, the Seven Dwarfs, groups of angels and big baskets of flowers. Skyscrapers, with every window lit, reared up towards the stars and downtown, in the old part of the city, the Plaza de la Constitution was a sight never to be forgotten. In it stood the oldest Cathedral in the New World, the National Palace and the two City Halls. Every facet of these huge buildings was lit with concealed lighting, making the square as bright as day and very beautiful. Nothing that Paris or London had ever shown could approach the magnificence of these illuminations and nothing could have more greatly impressed Adam with the wealth of modern Mexico.

As he ate his late dinner in the roof restaurant of the Del Paseo he thumbed through a guide-book to make plans for the following day, and decided that Chapultepec Park had places in it that were the most likely to provide him with ideas for the basis of a new book.

The one-thousand-three-hundred-acre park lies at the western end of the city and the broad boulevard of the Reforma continues on for two miles between its flower gardens, natural woodlands, lakes and recreation grounds; but next morning Adam's taxi turned off to mount the steep wooded hill on which stands Chapultepec Castle.

It had been built by one of the Spanish Viceroys in the eighteenth century and now contains a museum of arms, pictures and furniture; but its main interest was that it had been the residence of the ill-fated Austrian Archduke Maximilian. In the early 1860s Mexico's series of revolutions had so bedevilled her finances that the European Powers had decided to protect their interests by intervening. Napoleon III had offered Maximilian the support of French troops if he would go out, become Emperor and restore the stability of the country. He had ascended the throne in 1864, but reigned only for three years. A liberal-minded, kindly man who spent most of his time collecting butterflies, he had proved hopelessly incapable as a ruler. A Zapotec Indian named Benito Juárez had led a rebellion, the French troops had been withdrawn, Maximilian's forces had been defeated, he had been captured and executed by a firing squad.

There were still many relics of Maximilian and his beautiful Empress, Carlotta, in the rooms they had occupied. Adam found them pathetic, and their furniture hideous, but he had already ruled out the idea of using this period as the back-

ground for a book because their tragic story was so well
known.

That applied even more to Hernando Cortés; but in one of
the larger halls a spacious modern mural by Diego Rivera
greatly intrigued him. It portrayed all the rulers of Mexico,
from the Conquest on; and, among them, Cortés was shown
as a hideous, wasted, bandy-legged man with a head like a
skull.

Turning to his guide, Adam asked why the firm-faced and
virile Spanish hero should have been represented as such a
hideous creature.

The fat little guide sniffed and replied, 'To Mexicans he is
no hero. He brought to our people much suffering, and he is
so portrayed here because, when he died, he was riddled with
syphilis.'

'That is news to me,' Adam remarked, 'and I have read
pretty widely about him. What grounds have you for believing that he was a syphilitic?'

The guide then told him that in 1823, when the heroes who
fell in the War of Independence had been re-interred with
honour in Mexico City, the priests had feared that the Indian
mobs might desecrate Cortés' grave; so they had removed
his remains and secretly bricked them up in a wall of the
chapel of the Hospital of Jesus, which Cortés had founded.
Then in 1946 the finding of an old document had led to their
discovery. Mexican anthropologists had examined the four-
hundred-year-old bones and it was upon their assessment
that Cortés was now said to have been a syphilitic monstrosity.

Adam would have given long odds that this was a vin-
dictive libel arising from the intense hatred with which the
Mexicans had come to regard the Conquistadores; for he had
read every book about them that he could get hold of, and
knew that even Cortés' enemies who had known him in his
lifetime had written of him as a sombrely-handsome man,
with a body that was capable of almost tireless endurance;
although, of course, the popular belief that he had conquered
Mexico with five hundred Spaniards and sixteen horses was
a myth.

The fact was that during his campaigns he had had many

thousands of Indian allies. In 1519, when the Spaniards had landed at Vera Cruz, the Totonac *caciques*, who then ruled that part of Mexico, had received them with awe; then, when they had disclosed their intention of marching against the Aztec capital, willingly assisted them by supplying stores, porters and a great army of warriors.

There had been a very good reason for that. The Aztecs had appeared out of the north only two centuries earlier. Previous to that the Mayas and numerous other races who occupied different parts of the country had, from as early as 2000 B.C., built up splendid civilisations. They had achieved a high art: their engineers had constructed immense buildings and suspension bridges across the gorges in the mountains; their astronomers had produced a calendar that was more accurate than that then in use in Europe.

The Aztecs, on the other hand, had been fierce barbarians of an almost unbelievable cruelty. Having driven the inhabitants from the Central Plateau, they had established themselves on the island of Tenochtitlán then, from that fortress, sallied forth to conquer the whole of Mexico and turn its peoples into subject races. They waged war constantly, not alone for plunder but mainly to secure hordes of sacrificial victims with which to propitiate their blood-lusting god Huitzilopochtli. So it was no wonder that Cortés had found allies on all sides willing to aid him in destroying their Aztec overlords, and it was to his leadership that they owed their escape from this terrible tyranny.

He had on occasion acted with great harshness—as the only means of maintaining his extremely precarious authority —but he was not by nature a cruel man, and it is recorded that he threatened with death any of his own followers who were caught maltreating the Indians. Other Conquistadores, particularly Francisco Pizarro in Peru, and Nuño de Guzmán, who, after Cortés' retirement, became master of New Spain, disgraced themselves by inflicting senseless cruelties and forcing many thousands of the conquered peoples into slavery. But the Church sent violent protests back to Spain and soon received sanction to protect the Indians by setting up special Courts before which they could freely state their grievances.

It was, too, a remarkable fact that the Council of the Indies, sitting in Seville, whose authority was paramount in the New World, decreed the abolition of slavery in 1532—three hundred years before President Lincoln did so in the United States.

Great numbers of Indians unquestionably lost their lives as a result of the Conquest, but only a comparatively small percentage of their deaths was due to fighting the Spaniards. By far the greater part were carried off by smallpox, typhus, measles and other diseases previously unknown in the New World. Terrible epidemics ravaged the country, depopulating whole districts; but for that the Spaniards could hardly be blamed.

The Conquest, on the other hand, brought many benefits to Mexico. Before that the diet available to the Indians was extraordinarily monotonous. Even the nobles had lived almost entirely on maize cakes, fruit and a little fish. Wheat, rice, barley, lentils, onions and potatoes were unknown, the latter having been brought from South America. They had no cattle, pigs or goats; so had no milk, butter or cheese, no grease with which to fry and, only occasionally, the meat of birds and small animals. They had no carts, horses or beasts of burden; so the only transport for articles of commerce consisted of porters trained to the exhausting work of bearing on their backs for many hours a day sacks weighing up to a hundred pounds suspended from bands across their foreheads. They were excellent weavers and dyers, but had not invented the button; so their main garment was a square piece of material with a hole in the middle through which they put their heads and, as it could not be done up, it dangled awkwardly about them, exposing their lower limbs to the cold. They had neither windmills nor watermills with which to grind their maize, so had to pound it laboriously in mortars. They had no iron or steel, so had patiently to chip pieces of obsidian to produce a sharp edge for all cutting implements and weapons. For tilling the earth they had no ploughs; so to sow their crops they had to use a stout pointed stick and make thousands of holes into each of which a single seed was dropped.

Through disease and, at times, brutality, the Indians had certainly endured much suffering under their conquerors; but the belief that their Spanish masters had used them worse than had the British, French or Dutch the peoples of the countries they had colonised Adam knew to be untrue; and he thought it regrettable that, since the Mexicans had gained independence, their politicians should have indoctrinated them with their hatred of the Spaniards, to whom their country owed so much.

When he had done the museum, with its State coaches, cannon and mementoes of Maximilian's brief reign, his guide took him out on to the terrace of the Palace. Beneath, the wooded slope fell steeply, and above the tree-tops there was a fine view of the scores of lofty modern blocks that dotted the city. From among the trees in the near foreground there arose six smooth stone columns, about forty feet high with rounded tops.

His guide told him that at the time of the war between Mexico and the United States, which took place in 1846–8, the Castle had been a Military Academy. When the victorious American troops entered Mexico City they had demanded that the Mexican cadets should haul down their country's flag. The cadets had refused, and six gallant youngsters had defended the Castle to the end, dying there rather than surrender. The war had been lost. It cost Mexico her vast northern territories. The United States established her claim to Texas and acquired California, in which gold was soon afterwards discovered; but nothing could ever rob Mexicans of their pride in the six heroic boys whose monument was these six tall stone columns.

Returning to the city, Adam again walked round the best shopping area, looking for a place to lunch, and, from the dozen or more restaurants, decided on the Chalet Suisse. He made an excellent meal off a dish of huge Pacific prawns, a Cassata ice and a carafe of the local wine. Compared with what he would have had to pay for the same meal in a smarter restaurant, the bill was surprisingly reasonable and, although he had no longer to think about money, being a true Scot he made up his mind to return there frequently.

c

Adam hated sleeping in the afternoon, as if he did he always woke up with a headache; but, in accordance with ancient Spanish custom, everything was shut during the siesta hours; so he spent them reading on his bed, then again took a taxi out to the Park, this time to the new Museum of Anthropology.

It proved another revelation to him of the wealth and enterprise of modern Mexico, for it is the finest museum of its kind in the world. The roof of the vast central hall is supported by a single pillar, in girth as great as a three-hundred-year-old oak tree and eighty feet in height. It is carved with Maya glyphs and down it streams a cascade of water to splash on the stone floor thirty feet or so all round it. Outside the building, although it was early January, it was pleasantly warm; inside, this fountain in reverse made the hall very cold, but its function was to render the museum cool during the great heats of summer.

On three sides of the main hall there were spacious rooms with many exhibits of the numerous cultures of ancient Mexico, the earliest dating from a time when Hammurabi was ruling in Babylon: Otomic, Tepexpan, Huastec, Olmec, Maya, Chichimec, Toltec, Totonac, Mixtec, Tarascan, Zapotec and Aztec. All had individuality—there were the huge stone negroid heads of the Olmecs, crowned with helmets such as modern motor-cyclists wear; colossal columns representing Toltec warriors; slabs from temples carved by the Zapotecs with intricate geometrical designs; gold Mixtec necklaces of most delicate workmanship; images of Maya priests with flattened foreheads, great, curved noses and elaborate head-dresses; delightfully amusing Tarascan pottery figures; and big, wheel-like stones on which were carved the symbols of the Aztec calendar, the earlier cultures having contributed to the later ones. There were also papier-mâché models of ancient cities and, set in the walls, hundreds of coloured photographs lit from behind, showing archaeological sites.

Above these salons there was another range of rooms, demonstrating the life led in the Indian villages of the various nations. These contained figures of men, women and children, weaving, hunting, cooking, fishing, in open-sided huts and under groups of palm trees. There were arrays of bows and arrows, cases of coins and pigments, beautiful feather head-dresses and cloaks of many colours. Then, in a basement building, entered from one side of the ground floor, there was an exact replica of the famous tomb at Palenque, with the skeleton of the High Priest lying in it and, in a separate case, the fabulous jade death-mask that had lain on his dead face for many hundreds of years.

Adam was enthralled. He spent four hours in the museum and could happily have remained there for several days. The Aztec exhibits meant little to him, but he recognised a number of items from the older cultures and found himself speci-ally familiar with those of the Toltecs who had arisen about A.D. 200 and flourished until late in the tenth century. The latter was the period in Europe with which he was most fami-liar and he definitely made up his mind that he would set his novel in the Mexico of those days.

Before he left England, friends had warned Adam that the height of Mexico Cty might affect him, so he should be careful not to exert himself too much. But so far he had felt no ill-effects from the rarified air at seven thousand five hun-dred feet; so, as it was a nice evening, he decided to walk back to his hotel.

At intervals along the Paseo de la Reforma there are junc-tions each with a roundabout at which other streets enter it, several of them being the site of lofty statues. There is one to Columbus, another to Carlos IV—retained only because the Mexicans have an affection for El Caballito, his beautifully-modelled little horse—and a third to their national hero, the Emperor Cuauhtémoc. The westernmost of these great open spaces is at the entrance to the Park and has in its centre the Diana Cazadora Fountain. For strangers not yet familiar with Mexican traffic signals, these roundabouts are difficult to cross.

When stepping off the pavement towards the Fountain, Adam failed to look behind him, and a stream of traffic had just been released from that direction. The Mexicans are habi-tually fast drivers and, at the signal, three cars abreast shot forward. Too late, Adam realised his danger. The car heading for him had no room to swerve. He jumped towards the pavement, but the near mudguard of the car caught him on the thigh, bowling him over so that his head hit the kerb. Stars whirled before his eyes and next moment he was in another world.

3

The Man-God

ADAM was still in Mexico City, but it was an utterly different place from that in which his big body lay limp and unconscious on the pavement. The street he was in was narrow, most of the houses in it were not more than two storeys high. There were no cars, lorries, carts or even donkeys, but many people. They were bronze-skinned, had intensely black hair and eyes and were thickset but considerably shorter than Europeans, averaging only about five foot three inches in height. The men wore their hair pinned high on their heads and decorated with little mirrors; the women wore it in thick, plaited pigtails. All had on blanket-like garments, with geometrical designs of many colours. The better-dressed men had theirs suspended by a tie from two corners across the front of the throat so that they hung draped over the shoulders and backs; those of the others, and all the women's, simply had a hole in the middle through which their heads were thrust.

Suddenly, as Adam walked down the street, he became aware of three things: he was a head and shoulders taller than anyone within sight; he was playing a flute; and the people regarded him with reverence, but without fear. As he approached they all drew aside, backed against the walls, smiled at him, then bowed deeply and gravely. As he advanced, a litter carried by four bearers came towards him. The bearers promptly set it down. A young woman with a golden ornament entwined in her hair, gold bangles on her wrists and dressed in garments of such fine-spun cotton that they were almost diaphanous, stepped out and genuflected as he passed.

He, too, was dressed in a cotton cloak of the finest weave and below it wore, like the other men, only a breech-clout. But the sun was shining, the air balmy and he felt extraordinarily well. Instinctively he wound his way through several streets and crossed a number of small bridges over narrow canals which had gaily painted canoes passing up and down them. Ten minutes after he had come to his senses—in what he knew to be the city on the island in the lake that later was to become the Aztec capital of Tenochtitlán—he arrived outside a taller, much more imposing building. It was his own Palace. Still playing his flute, he entered it.

A porter salaamed to him deferentially as he walked into the lofty, pillared hall, the walls of which were covered with brightly-coloured murals. Without hesitation he went through a doorway that led on to a terrace. It was gay with pots of many exotic flowers and looked out on to the lake beyond which, in the far distance, its top shrouded in cloud, he could see the lofty volcano Popocatepetl.

Halfway along the terrace there was a pile of many-coloured cushions from which one could look out across the lake. Putting down his flute, he rang a silver hand bell. Within a minute a group of servants appeared: a man to supervise his service and half a dozen young women each carrying a tray. On a low table in front of him they set down an array of small silver bowls, a goblet, a flagon and a finely-woven napkin. One knelt beside him, holding a large, shallow silver salver that held scented water, with three hibiscus blossoms floating on the surface.

After dipping his fingers in it he began to eat, picking pieces from the little silver bowls. Several of them contained thin pancakes of maize rolled up with beans, chilies and other vegetables as a stuffing. Others held pieces of fish, a gamey meat that he could not identify, or slices of tropical fruit. The flagon held a delicious concoction of iced fruit juices which tasted like nectar on this sunny day.

He was vaguely aware that for many months past all his meals had contained a small quantity of some drug, and that it was this which caused his memory to be so hazy. But it did him no physical harm, so he had long since come to accept it.

While he ate, he looked across the lake to the vista of mountains in the distance. Only the tops of the tallest were obscured by cloud, the others standing out clear against a bright blue sky. Upon the lake there were many canoes and some slightly larger craft with sails. In the foreground, apart from a channel kept free from the Palace steps, the surface of the lake was hidden by vegetation. The land beyond the valley was, he knew, so barren that nothing would grow upon it; so to help feed their people the rulers had devised the idea of floating market gardens. Occupying a large part of the lake there were hundreds of reed rafts, about twelve feet by eight, and a variety of crops was growing on them.

Soon after he had finished his meal, his steward appeared and announced that the High Priest, Itzechuatl, had arrived and requested audience. He told the man that he was agreeable to receiving the High Priest and a few minutes later the steward led a small procession out on to the terrace.

It was headed by Itzechuatl, a formidable figure dressed in ceremonial robes, a huge feather head-dress that spread out like the fan of a peacock's tail, and with his face so heavily painted that it was difficult to make out his features. Yet at the sight of him Adam was filled with sudden fear and revulsion—black thoughts of a dungeon in the depths of a pyramid and friends sacrificed to evil gods. But the details of the past eluded him. Behind the High Priest sixteen brilliantly-costumed bearers carried four litters which they set down in a semi-circle in front of Adam.

The High Priest made a formal bow, then said, 'Exalted One, I bring you your four brides. I hope that they will please you.'

At a signal from him the bearers of the litters drew aside their curtains. Out of them stepped four young women. Under transparent veils they were nude, except for belts, breast ornaments and necklaces of gold set with precious stones. Their hair was elaborately coiffeured and set with ornaments glittering with jewels. From their ears, supported by short, very thin gold chains, dangled clusters of gems that made a faint, tinkling music as they moved. All four had superb figures but in different degrees of maturity.

One was a child of perhaps thirteen, with a boyish body and small, firm breasts; another, who may have been eighteen, was slim, straight-backed, svelte, with a suggestion of strength in her slender limbs; the third, a few years older, was voluptuousness personified, with hips and thighs the shape of an inverted pear, a narrow waist and breasts like the halves of small melons; the fourth was much taller than the other three. She had very broad shoulders from which rose a lovely neck and throat, her body was a poem of grace with, where it narrowed, an intriguing horizontal crease between her breasts and stomach; her arms and legs were long and beautifully modelled, her wrists and ankles slender.

Their faces were all beautiful, but again as different from one another as their bodies. The hair and eyes of all of them were black and their skins a pale, reddish brown, but their features suggested different races. The youngest had the narrowed, oriental eyes of a Chichimec; the second the slightly flattened nose of a Zapotec; the third had a rounded face, matching her curves, which proclaimed her to be a Maya. The fourth he could not place. She had a fine, broad forehead, magnificent eyes beneath eyebrows that turned up at their outer ends, a straight delicate nose, rather full cheeks and a generous mouth. Adam's interest was entirely concentrated on her. He thought her the most beautiful creature he had ever seen. Again his memory stirred. He had seen her before, during a great procession. She had been one of scores of lovely girls who had scattered flowers before him as he advanced along the Sacred Way of his old capital, and he had felt a passionate desire for her.

The High Priest remarked casually, 'They have been chosen for you to suit any man's taste. The two older have been carefully trained and are highly proficient in all the arts of love. The two younger are still virgins.'

Adam stood a head and shoulders above all the men on the terrace with the exception of the lean High Priest, who was exceptionally tall for an Indian. Next to him in height was the eldest girl and it was upon her that Adam's gaze was riveted. Physically she was the only one who, as a female, could come near matching his stature. But that was a minor

point; her body, with the crease above her narrow waist, was
perfection, her eyes held all the knowledge of the centuries,
yet there was still something almost childishly youthful about
her face that gave it an innocent, happy look. Making a slight
gesture towards her, he asked:

'What are you called?'

Her wide mouth opened in a smile, showing glorious teeth,
and she replied, 'Mirolitlit, may it please my Lord.'

Under its heavy layers of paint Itzechuatl's lean face also
creased into a smile and he said, 'I see that the Exalted One
has already chosen his favourite wife; but in twenty days he
will have ample time also to take his pleasure with his other
brides.'

Adam frowned. 'Twenty days? I do not understand. Why
only twenty days?'

The High Priest gave a slight shrug and raised his painted
eyebrows:

'The Exalted One's memory betrays him. It seems I must
refresh it. His year as a Man-God ends in twenty days. Then,
like all Men-Gods, he must die for the good of his people.'

On finding himself in the streets of this familiar city, Adam
had immediately accepted his present state without wondering how he came to be there. Now his memory suddenly func-
tioned. He was a Toltec, captured by the Chichimecs, a war-
rior nation which had recently emerged from the north,
defeated his own people and dispossessed them of their cities.
Itzechuatl was the Priest-King who had imprisoned him and
coerced him into agreeing to represent the God-upon-Earth
who was chosen annually then, at the end of his term, sacrificed. And it was at the ceremony of his 'Acceptance' that had
had seen Mirolitlit.

For over eleven months he had lived in luxury, with every
wish he had expressed instantly obeyed, except that he had
not been allowed to indulge himself abnormally in food or
drink lest the 'person of the God' should physically deteriorate. He had also been denied women, so that he should not
lessen his virility through excess. But for his last twenty days
of life it was customary that the Man-God should be given

as his brides four of the most beautiful girls that could be found in the city.

At the same moment there came back to him the resolve he had made to die fighting rather than submit to being sacrificed. Now he upbraided himself furiously for having allowed the drug he had been given in his food to lull him into a false sense of security and to forget his intention to escape.

But it was not too late. The sun was already casting long shadows on the terrace and about to set behind the range of distant mountains. If he acted swiftly and ruthlessly he might yet get away under cover of darkness and rejoin his own people.

He had no weapon but, springing forward, with one hand he seized Itzechuatl by the throat and with the other grasped the bejewelled hilt of the dagger at his girdle. Wrenching out the sharp obsidian blade, he lifted it high and struck with it at the High Priest's side. The point descended on a hidden buckle. The stone blade shattered into fragments, but the blow was so forceful that it drove the breath out of Itzechuatl's body. With a gasp, he lurched sideways and collapsed.

With cries of horror at this sacrilege, the bearers of the litters launched themselves on Adam. There were sixteen of them; but they were little men and Adam, by comparison, a giant. He seized the foremost by the hair and beneath one knee, lifted him high in the air and threw him into the midst of the others. Plunging forward into the gap in their ranks, he hit out right and left. Three of them went down under his blows; the rest, except for one, gave back.

That one still barred his path and had drawn a dagger. Adam could have feinted, as though to leap past one side of him, then dashed past the other; but there remained the danger that the man might swing round as he passed and knife him in the back. At that moment the tall girl, Mirolitlit, snapped the neck fastening of her transparent gauze cloak and cast the garment over the Chichimec's dagger hand, fouling it so that he could not strike.

Next moment Adam smashed his fist into the man's face and sent him reeling. Flashing a smile at the girl, which she returned with a shout of encouragement, he dashed forward in the direction of the steps that led down from the terrace to the water. Taking them three at a time he reached the stone landing stage. Seizing the painter of a canoe alongside, with brute strength he wrenched out the staple that held it. Before those of the bearers who had remained uninjured were half-way down the steps he was in the canoe, had grabbed the paddle and pushed off.

The sun had just gone down behind the mountains. Darkness was fast descending on the lake; but he knew that when he reached the shore he had hundreds of miles to cover before he could hope to reach the country near the coast, to which his own people had retired, and be safe among them. The Chichimec warriors were fast runners and they would soon be in pursuit. Kneeling in the canoe he drove the frail craft forward with frantic strokes across the lake. It was not until moments later that he realised it was to the Norse gods that he was praying desperately to save him.

4

A Girl with a Gun

WHEN Adam came to, he realised vaguely that he was leaning over sideways, embraced by the soft arms of a woman
and with his aching head pillowed on her breast. His dream
had been so vivid that he thought himself still in the past;
that somehow he had been knocked out and brought back
to the terrace of the Palace, and that it was the beautiful
Mirolitlit who was cradling him in her arms.

A moment later he opened his eyes, saw trees and traffic
through a window and realised that he was in the back of a
large car; yet the idea that he was being supported by Mirolitlit's arms still persisted.

Turning his head, he looked up at his companion and,
to his surprise, saw that she was not Mirolitlit. The only
resemblance between the two was that both had black hair
and copper-coloured skin. This girl had blue eyes and an
aquiline nose set between high cheekbones in a narrow face.
Her mouth was well shaped, but on the thin side, and her
chin showed great determination.

As he moved, she smiled. In repose her features had conveyed the impression that she was an autocrat: beautiful, but
self-willed and dictatorial. The smile was one of warm
friendliness. Her mouth opened, as though from constant
habit, to display two gleaming rows of even teeth; her eyes
radiated tenderness and concern. It was as though the sculp-
tured head of an imperious Indian Princess had magically
become alive, revealing a generous mind, responsive nerves
and a flow of rich blood from the heart.

She said in Spanish, 'We knocked you down and are taking

you to a hospital. I'm terribly sorry. I do hope that you are not badly hurt.'

Perhaps it was her voice, coupled with the entrancing smile; but Adam again thought of Mirolitlit. In spite of the difference in their appearance, the two women seemed to bear an indefinable resemblance to each other. It was something intangible: not of the body, but in the nature of an invisible aura or spiritual essence.

'*Muchos gracias, señorita*,' he muttered, endeavouring to sit up. But his head was aching atrociously and felt like a millstone. It rolled on his shoulders and he fell back. Then he managed to gasp, 'It was my fault. Sorry . . . sorry to be a bother.'

'Lie quietly now,' she said. 'We'll be there in a minute.' And shortly afterwards the car pulled up. Ambulance men appeared with a stretcher and Adam was carried into the hospital.

In a ground-floor room a doctor examined him. Meanwhile the man who had been driving the car stood nearby, looking on anxiously. His hair was thick but snow white above a square, forceful face, his brown eyes quick and intelligent, his clothes expensive and his air, as he questioned the doctor, that of a man used to being obeyed.

The doctor reported that Adam had sustained no injury except to his head, and that was not serious; but he would probably suffer from slight concussion, so it was advisable that he remain in the hospital, anyway for that night.

By then Adam had recovered sufficiently to give particulars about himself, upon which the other man said, 'Señor Gordon is to be put in a private ward and given every attention. I will be responsible for all expenses.' Then, turning to Adam, he added in halting English, 'Accept, please, my deepest regrets, wishes too for speedy recovery. As you are visitor here I hope you allow me to make reparation for the knocking down of you. Permit that I be of service to you during stay in Mexico City. I am named Bernadino Enriquez.'

Adam was then wheeled to a lift, put to bed in a pleasant room upstairs and given a sedative which soon sent him off to sleep. During the night he dreamed again and the lovely

Mirolitlit was the central figure in the dream, but it had no continuity and at times Mirolitlit turned into the girl in the car so that their personalities became inextricably mixed.

In the morning his head still pained him and he had a slight temperature, so, although otherwise he felt fairly well, it was decided that he should spend another night in the hospital. Soon after the doctor had left him, his day nurse brought in a huge bouquet of flowers and a basket of exotic fruit. There was a card with them inscribed, 'Bernadino Enriquez, Avenida Presidente Masarik 85', and an invitation to dinner two nights hence, the 7th January. Hoping that the intriguing lady of the car would be there, Adam promptly decided to accept, then asked his nurse if she knew anything about Bernadino Enriquez.

With a laugh she replied, 'But of course. He is the plastics king; and one of the richest men in Mexico.'

At that—the lady apart—Adam felt that his luck was in again; for it was well worth having been knocked down to have gained the acquaintance of a man who was in a position to give him considerable help in securing valuable data for the background of his book.

Next day, a Sunday, feeling none the worse for his accident, he returned to his hotel. There, to his surprise and indignation, he learned that, not knowing what had become of him, the manager had had his things packed up and his room let to someone else. Moreover, there was no other room free which he could be given. As he had booked accommodation there for this fortnight as far back as November, he was justifiably furious, lost his temper and proceeded to tell the management what he thought of their hotel in a mixture of Spanish and English through which came distinct traces of the Scottish accent he had had in his youth. An under-manager, who had been brought on the scene, only shrugged, said that they could let their rooms many times over, and that once a room had remained unoccupied for more than one night the booking for the whole period was regarded by them as cancelled. However, to pacify the outraged guest, other hotels were telephoned and, by luck, the El Presidente had just had a cancellation; so Adam's baggage was brought up and, vowing never again to enter the Del Paseo, he drove off in a taxi.

The El Presidente was only a few blocks away in the Hamburgo—the Bond Street of Mexico City. The greater part of the ground floor consisted of a lofty grotto, ending in a wall of rock down which water was splashing through growing ferns and creepers. Below it was an irregular-shaped swimming pool and, on the far side of that, tables, chairs and a small bar to enable people to enjoy their drinks while watching the bathers.

For the moment Adam was in no mood to enjoy this pleasant scene and went straight up to his room. He found it to be somewhat better equipped than the one he had had at the Del Paseo and, in addition, it had a balcony looking out over the roof-tops towards Popocatepetl; so, in spite of the bother he had been put to, he felt that he had benefited by the scurvy treatment the Del Paseo had meted out to him.

The remainder of Sunday and most of Monday he spent quietly; then, at nine o'clock that evening, dressed in his new Savile Row dinner jacket, he took a taxi out to the Avenida Presidente Masarik.

It lay north of the Park, in the best residential district, and No. 85 proved to be a block of flats, the penthouse on top of which was occupied by Enriquez. Adam was whisked up there in a lift and found it to be the finest private apartment that, in his limited experience, he had ever seen.

A white-jacketed houseman led him through a wide hall, where there were massed banks of flowers and orchids sufficient to stock a florist's shop, into a drawing room half as large as a tennis court. Three of the walls were of glass, beyond which lay broad stretches of roof shaded by awnings. Beneath them were swing hammocks, a dozen lounge chairs, a fountain and flowering shrubs in big pots. But neither in the big room nor out on the roof gardens was a soul to be seen. Adam had made the mistake common to visitors to Mexico. He had arrived at the time for which he had been invited, instead of half an hour or an hour later.

Against the one solid wall, which was panelled in natural wood, there stood a big bookcase and, after the houseman had bowed himself away, Adam spent a few minutes examining its contents. His attention was then caught by a painting further along the wall. It was a portrait of the girl in the car.

That made it probable, he thought, that she was Enriquez's daughter, or a relative, although they were not in the least like one another. As he looked at it he saw now that she must be tall and had splendid shoulders, which again recalled his memory of Mirolitlit, and he was more than ever intrigued by the subtle, if vague, resemblance.

Although the only words he had exchanged with the Indian girl were when asking her name, she had left an indelible impression on him; and he felt convinced that, given half an hour in her company, he would have fallen desperately in love with her. Uneasily he wondered if the girl in the portrait would have the same effect on him. She was equally beautiful, although hers was a different and much stronger face. Even so, the same indefinable personality seemed to radiate from it.

Ten minutes later, Bernadino Enriquez came bustling in, with profuse apologies for not having been there to receive his guest. Enriquez at first spoke in halting English, but Adam had brushed up his Spanish recently and found that, having spent so much of his time learning the language during his trip to Brazil, he could converse in it quite happily; so he set his host at his ease by replying in Spanish. He left the choice of drinks to him and was furnished with a delightful concoction of well-iced rum, lime and pineapple juice. Gesturing towards the portrait, he asked who the lovely lady was, and Bernadino replied promptly:

'My daughter, Chela. You have met her. She was with me in my car when I ran you down. Presently she will join us. But you know what women are. One hair out of place and they must spend another quarter of an hour at their toilette.'

The quarter of an hour went by while they talked amicably of Mexico, and Adam spoke enthusiastically of the wonders of the capital that he had so far seen; then, instead of Chela, the first guest arrived—a Canadian who, like his host, had big interests in plastics. He was followed by others until the room was half full of chatting people. Among them was a tall, pale-faced Englishman with a slight stoop. His fair hair

was thin, but he had a luxuriant moustache and was introduced to Adam as Wing Commander Hunterscombe.

Adam asked if he was still in the R.A.F., and he replied,
'No; got out years ago, soon after the war. Went into the
Foreign Service. I'm at the Embassy here. Not as a real diplomat, of course; just Cultural Attaché. That's how I came to
know your books.' He gave a rather vapid laugh. 'Got to,
you know, part of the job.'

In response to this somewhat back-handed compliment,
Adam said, a shade acidly, 'I hope you didn't find them too
boring.'

'Good Lord, no. Grand stuff. Have you signed the Book
yet?'

'Book?' replied Adam with a puzzled frown. 'What book
do you mean,'

'Why, the one at the Embassy, of course.'

'I didn't know that I was supposed to.'

'Oh, come. You're fooling. All British visitors are expected
to.'

'What's the idea?'

'Well, should any trouble blow up. Not that that's likely
here. But say it did, you'd be on the list of British visitors.
Then we'd get you on the blower and tip you off to scram
before things got worse. Besides, as you are a V.I.P., you'll
probably be asked along to the Residence for a drink. Or, if
H.E. has read your books and would like to see more of you,
he may ask you to lunch.'

Adam had not been a literary V.I.P. long enough to become blasé with the treatment and he had never been inside
an Embassy; so he told the languid, willowy Hunterscombe
that he would sign the Book the following morning.

It was just then that Chela Enriquez made her entrance
and, at the sight of her, a momentary hush fell on the room.
She was wearing a long, full-skirted gown of pale-blue satin
with a ruched 'V' neck, the point of which came down low
between her small but pouting breasts. The colour set off the
golden skin of her slender arms and splendid neck to perfection. Her height made her an impressive figure, but there
was nothing of the female Grenadier about her. The breadth

of her shoulders emphasised the smallness of her waist, her well-rounded hips and long legs. She carried herself superbly, her smile was dazzling and her movements a poem of grace as she acknowledged the greetings of those nearest her and walked straight over to Adam.

When he had assured her that he had fully recovered, she asked him how long he had been in Mexico, how long he meant to stay, whom he knew in the city and what he had so far seen in it.

He told her that he had come without introductions, meant to remain in the country, for several weeks anyhow, then enthused about the Christmas decorations and the new Museum of Anthropology.

She said that, as he had no friends in Mexico, they must look after him. Then, seeing that his glass was empty, she took it herself to the drinks table, brought it back refilled and said with a smile, 'You must excuse me now. I have to look after our other guests; but we will talk together again later.'

As she moved away, a short, tubby, bald man came up to Adam and asked what he thought of Mexico City. Again Adam enthused about the fine streets and buildings and the wonderful illuminations.

His companion made a wry grimace. 'Those lights cost us taxpayers a pretty penny; electricity is terribly expensive here.'

Adam raised his eyebrows. 'You surprise me. From such vast quantities of it being used, I thought it must be quite cheap. Why does your government go in for such extravagance?'

'To please the masses. It is their policy to keep the people happy with bread and games.'

'Is there no control over that sort of thing then?'

'None. Here we live under a dictatorship. Since 1920 we have had a one-party government. It is now called the P.R.I. —*Partido Revolucionario Institucional*. They decree everything and, short of another revolution, we'll never get them out.'

'The last revolution was a Communist one, wasn't it?' Adam asked. Then, gesturing round the big room, he added with a smile, 'Although from this, one would never think it.'

With a shrug the bald man replied, 'It was thought in Europe to be Communist because Alvaro Obregón, who led it, made use of the grievances of the masses. Mexico has never been truly Communist; only, if you like, very much to the Left. For example, our government was intensely anti-Franco during the Spanish Civil War. But we benefited from that. When Franco won, his opponents of all kinds were encouraged to emigrate and settle here. That brought us many thousands of valuable citizens of the type we badly needed as a nation whose general standard of education was very low—doctors, lawyers, scientists, writers, publishers, artists, mechanics and technicians of all kinds. It is largely owing to them that Mexico has made such antonishing progress in the past twenty-five years.'

'Then, judging by results, it doesn't seem that you have much to complain of about your government.'

'On the face of it, no. They are shrewd enough to let us capitalists alone, because we are the geese that lay the golden eggs, and security of capital encourages foreign investment, which we badly need. But living under a totalitarian government has its drawbacks. Anyone can be arrested here and held incommunicado for seventy-two hours. And, of course, there is no security of tenure of property. If it is decided to make a new road which cuts off half your garden, workmen arrive and get on with the job overnight.'

'In that way things aren't much better in England now; although the owner is notified first and can appeal, and is paid compensation.'

The fat man laughed. 'Oh, he is paid compensation here, then charged three times as much for the benefit he is supposed to derive from the new road. Talking of roads, recently Mexico started to manufacture cars. They are by no means bad but very far from being either the best or the most economical to run; yet a law has been passed prohibiting the import of all foreign cars, and we are having to give up our Rolls and Mercedes. That is part of the price we have to pay for the security we enjoy under our present government.'

It was half past ten before a move was made. Then the whole party descended in the lifts and piled into a fleet of cars, which carried them along to the centre of the Park, where they alighted at a new restaurant called El Lago.

The place was another revelation to Adam of the wealth and luxury of Mexico City. It resembled a theatre and along its wide curve there was tier upon tier of balconies upon which the tables were set. All of them looked out upon a lake from which rose a wondrous fountain, at times jetting its water a hundred feet in the air, at others spreading it out like a huge fan. Coloured lights played on the water, turning it to rainbow hues, and its movements were timed to coincide with the tempo of the band.

They sat down sixteen to dinner and, to Adam's delight, he found himself placed next to Chela. During the meal she asked him innumerable questions about himself that were probing and intelligent, listening to his replies with absorbed interest.

When they reached the dessert, a fantastic creation of icecream, candied fruits and meringue decorated with orchids, she said:

'As you have no friends here, my father wishes me to be your guide and take you to all the interesting places in the city that a professional guide might not show you.'

'I can think of nothing more delightful,' he smiled, 'but isn't that a bit hard on you? I mean, you must have dozens of friends and be booked up with any number of engagements. I wouldn't like to be a nuisance and interfere with your usual activities.'

She shrugged and returned his smile. 'I can see my friends at any time. And Jeremy Hunterscombe tells me that you are a famous author. I love books, and must read all yours. We shall find lots to talk about and I shall look upon showing you the city as an honour.'

When coffee was served she lit a small cigar then, after she had smoked for a while, smiled at him and said, 'Aren't you going to ask me to dance?'

'I should love to,' he gave her an uneasy glance, 'but I'm afraid I'm not a very good dancer.'

'I wonder. Have you ever danced with a girl as tall as I am?'

'No, I don't think I have; not that I can remember.'

'Then that may be the answer. Come on; let's try.'

Chela proved right. Adam was so tall that almost invariably when he was talking to his dancing partners he had to stoop awkwardly over them, which made it difficult for him to steer. But he could hold Chela firmly while still remaining upright and, as they went smoothly round without bumping into people, he really enjoyed a dance for the first time in his life.

Afterwards, out of politeness, he danced with several of the other women in the party; but with them, as usual, his height proved a handicap and both he and his partners were relieved when he could take them back to the table.

Later, he danced with Chela again and when the band stopped she said, 'It's a lovely night. Let's go out for a stroll in the park and look at the stars.'

With a happy laugh he agreed then, after a moment, said a trifle hesitantly, 'But would it be safe? I mean, in London I wouldn't take a girl for a walk in Hyde Park after dark. Too many hoodlums about who might cause trouble.'

She smiled at him. 'With anyone else I would think twice about it. But gangsters keep to their own quarters of the city. At worst, we might come upon some poor wretch made desperate by hunger, and he would not dare attack a big man like you. Wait for me at the entrance while I go to the cloakroom and fetch something to put round my shoulders.'

When she rejoined him he had expected that she would be wearing the beautiful chinchilla coat in which she had arrived at the restaurant. Instead, she had draped round her a voluminous wrap of fine muslin spangled with gold signs of the Zodiac.

'What a lovely thing,' he remarked.

'Yes, isn't it?' she laughed. 'It's not mine, though. It belongs to one of my friends. I borrowed it because I thought my coat would be too heavy.'

Outside, the night was dark but the sky clear and the stars brilliant. For a while they walked almost in silence, exchanging only an occasional remark. They had taken a side path that wound its way among trees and bushes. Adam could feel his heart hammering. Chela's hand lay lightly on his arm, he was breathing in the heady scent she was wearing and was intoxicated by her nearness. They had met no-one and the place was so deserted that they might have been alone in another world. He felt an almost irresistible desire to take her in his arms and kiss her. That she had suggested the walk could possibly be taken as an invitation to do so. But until that night they had hardly known each other. Mexicans' ideas about behaviour might be different from those current in England. Perhaps she looked on him only as a new friend who could be trusted. If he took advantage of their being alone together she might resent it intensely. Then there would be a premature end to this wonderful companionship. He dared not risk that. Yet if he did not seize this chance she might think him only half a man, lose interest in him and never give him another opportunity.

He was still wrestling with the question when he heard a rustle in the bushes behind him. He had only half turned when a ragged figure sprang out with a knife raised high to stab him in the back.

Chela had turned at the same moment. In one swift movement she pulled the muslin wrap from her shoulders and swept it forward so that it entangled the knife and the arm of the man who had been about to stab Adam. Leaping back a pace, Adam raised his fist, lunged forward and hit the man hard in the face. With a loud moan he went over backwards, dropped his knife, rolled sideways, scrambled to his feet and made off into the bushes.

Adam took a stride to go after him, but Chela grabbed his arm and pulled him back. 'No!' she exclaimed. 'Let the poor devil go. If I had been with any other man he would only have demanded money from us. It was because you are so big that he hadn't the courage to face up to you.'

A little reluctantly Adam said, 'All right then. But he might have given me a nasty wound. I owe it to your presence of mind that he didn't, and I'm very grateful. But for that I might now be lying here a bloody mess while you were being raped by that desperado.'

She gave a low laugh. 'I don't think so. You see, I was rather hoping that something like this might happen, just to find out how you would behave. And as I had decided before we left the apartment to take you out for a walk, I came prepared for trouble.' As she spoke she lifted one side of her long, full, satin gown, displaying a lovely, long leg up to the thigh. Strapped to the outside of it was a blue velvet holster containing a small, flat automatic.

'Good Lord alive!' Adam exclaimed. 'Do Mexican girls usually tote guns?'

'They do when they expect to find themselves faced with unpredictable situations.'

He grinned. 'I've come across ladies who carry guns only in thrillers, and they always keep them in their handbags. I'd have thought they were easier to get at quickly than under a skirt.'

'On the contrary.' She had let her skirt fall. Now she slid her hand through a placket hole in its folds above her hip. In a second she had whipped out the small pistol and had him covered with it. Giving him an amused smile, she said, 'You see. That's much quicker than having to open a bag.'

He willingly conceded the point, at the same time thinking, 'What a wicked piece of loveliness. She could have done that before, but she wanted to show me that glorious leg.'

Slipping the pistol back, she went on, 'Our men nearly always keep a pistol in their cars. Tempers here are quick and there have been occasions when a dispute about the right of the road has been settled by an exchange of bullets.'

With a smile he said, 'I see I've a lot to learn yet about Mexico.'

She made a graceful curtsey. 'It will be my pleasure, sir, to be your instructress. And now, I think, we will go back to the restaurant.'

Retrieving the long muslin wrap, Adam disentangled the knife from it and put it in his pocket as a souvenir. Then, as he draped the wrap about her, he planted a light kiss on one of her splendid shoulders. She took no exception to that, but at once set off at a walk and began to talk about places she meant to take him to. A quarter of an hour later they rejoined her father's party.

It was nearly four o'clock in the morning before Adam

got to bed. Snuggling down, he sighed with contentment. It had been a marvellous evening, and what a girl Chela was. He had not meant to let himself become entangled again with a woman, but he knew he had fallen for her, hook, line and sinker. Recently he had thought a lot, with nostalgic longing, about Mirolitlit. But she had been dead for close on a thousand years, whereas Chela was here in Mexico City, alive, warm flesh and blood, and had not disguised her desire to see a lot more of him.

But there was more to it than that. He knew now that, although the physical appearance of the two girls was so different, the indefinable likeness he had sensed between their personalities was not a coincidence. The gesture that Chela had made with her wrap to save him from being knifed was precisely the same as that Mirolitlit had made when saving him from the knife of the Chichimec bearer. Now he had not the least doubt that Chela was a reincarnation of Miro-litlit.

5

Out of the Past

IN SPITE of the late hour at which Adam got to bed, he had
had himself called at nine o'clock because it had been
arranged that Chela should call for him at eleven. A swim in
the pool on the ground floor of the hotel thoroughly revived
him and he breakfasted heartily off an omelette, delicious hot,
white rolls and tropical fruit. Then, dressed in a smart grey,
lightweight suit of terylene and worsted, he went down to face
the day, bursting with renewed vitality.

Chela was only half an hour late. She arrived in a long,
low, open car, dressed in primrose tweeds and wearing over
her hair a bright-red scarf, the ends of which streamed out
behind her. As he climbed into the car, he said gaily:

'I hope you've got your gun; because I've a hunch that you
plan to drop me off among a gang of Mexican bandits, just
to watch my reactions, and I'm not used to dealing with that
sort of situation.'

'Not today,' she laughed. 'We'll save that for later, when
you are a little more acclimatised.'

Turning out of the Reforma, she took another six-lane
motorway, the Avenida Insurgentes, which led south to Acapulco. Adam had never owned a car until two months earlier
he had bought his Jaguar and hired a chauffeur-valet to
drive it. That had been a very pleasant experience; but here,
in the centre of Mexico City, he found driving with anyone
terrifying. Unlike many modern cities, it did not consist
mainly of parallel streets enclosing square blocks, but had
many focal points from which, like the rays of a star, the
streets led in all directions, cutting across others at sharp

angles. There were innumerable traffic lights, the working of which it was difficult to decipher, and, very frequently, the Mexicans ignored them. They seemed, too, to be a speed-crazed people; for, in their determination to get ahead, they constantly left one line of traffic without warning, to cut in across the front of a car in another. The number of cars with bent bumpers and dented sides testified to the very real danger of entering this packed mechanical jungle.

Wedged in the fast-moving stream, his fear tempered only by admiration, Adam sat tight as Chela drove with superb self-confidence, at never less than forty and sometimes up to eighty miles an hour, past heavily-laden lorries and other less speedy vehicles. Then, as they approached a great complex of lofty buildings, she slowed down and said:

'This is our University City. It occupies five hundred and fifty acres of what was formerly waste land; over a hundred and fifty of our best architects and engineers worked for four years to build it, and it cost three hundred million *pesos*.'

Adam could well believe that, as they ran slowly past block after block of steel and glass suspended, apparently miraculously, on rows of tall, slender concrete pillars. Facing the campus was the fifteen-storey administrative building, to one side of it the thousand-foot-long Arts Centre and on the other the huge library, its solid walls covered in intricate designs in colourful mosaic, symbolically depicting the rise of Mexican culture from the earliest times. There was a vast stadium, squash and tennis courts, swimming pools, car parks to hold thousands of vehicles, all interspersed with gardens, lakes and wooded areas.

'Your students are lucky,' Adam remarked, 'and with their every need catered for like this, they can hardly fail to do well.'

Chela made a grimace. 'They could, if they gave all their time to study; but like students everywhere these days they waste a large part of it getting themselves steamed up about politics.'

'I'd have thought that, with a one-party government, that would not have been allowed. Or are a lot of them anti-the-bomb-ers?'

'No. The bomb has not yet become a sufficient threat to Mexico for them to concern themselves about that. I was referring to university politics. You see, in 1929 the passion for making everything democratic led to a decree that half the governing body of the University should be elected by the faculty and the other half by the students; and the governors were given the power to hire or fire any professor. That meant that all the professors became dependent on the goodwill of their students. If one of them was accused of inefficiency by a pupil he had to defend himself; and if he wanted promotion he had to go canvassing. Naturally, some students favoured one prof. and others another. Every time there is an election books are thrown aside, scores of impassioned speeches are made and the campus often becomes a battlefield.'

While Chela had been talking she was driving north-eastward away from the University and soon they entered the district of El Pedregal. It was an area many square miles in extent that, until quite recently, had been entirely desolate: old lava flow. Now its uneven waves of stone had disappeared, large quantities of it having been cut into blocks to build several hundred houses. But this was no ordinary housing estate. Each house differed: some were in the old colonial style, others of the large villa type and others again fantastic creations by the most advanced architects of the day. All stood in at least an acre of garden that had been expensively landscaped, had swimming pools, sun parlours, tennis courts or rockeries and were gay with newly-planted flowering trees and shrubs. Adam estimated that in England these delightful properties would have cost their owners anything from thirty to sixty thousand pounds.

'Here,' Chela remarked, 'you see how some of our rich live. Later, I will take you to see where the poor struggle to survive.'

Her tone was decidedly acid and Adam was both interested and a little surprised to find that the lovely, wealthy playgirl should concern herself with such matters. After a moment, he said:

'I had the idea that Mexico was a Welfare State?'

'In a way it is; but only in a way that our clever government has devised to keep itself in power. There are other housing estates unlike this one. They are only row upon row of little four-room bungalows, but they have electricity and modern sanitation, so they are palaces compared to the places in which most of the people who have them used to live. Many of them —families of six or eight—used to be crammed into a two-room tenement without even water laid on. The people who get these bungalows pay only a nominal rent, so they are in clover. But they are very carefully selected, and it is no use applying for one unless you are a white-collar worker, a trade-union official or a schoolmaster. Can you guess why?'

'I think so,' Adam replied. 'It is because it is always the underpaid Civil Servants, self-educated mechanics and that type of man who create revolutions.'

'You've got it. The really poor and the ignorant masses are helpless without leaders; so the government suborns the class that might give them trouble by pandering to it.'

'That is certainly a cynical attitude, but I don't suppose they could afford to house anything like the number of families that need better homes. And at least it is a start in the right direction. Things will improve as time goes on.'

She shrugged. 'I doubt it. Mexico has always been a land of extraordinary contrasts. Vast areas of barren useless land and occasional valleys rich in fertility. The very rich and the very poor. In the cities there has never been such wealth as there is today, but in purchasing power the peasants earn less than they did a generation ago. Their state is pitiful; but they will never be better off until they have been organised to bring about a real revolution.'

The car had been heading back westwards towards the University City. Passing through its northern outskirts, Chela drove on into an entirely different district of narrow, cobbled lanes and big old houses behind high stone walls.

'This,' she said, 'is San Angel. Many wealthy families of Spanish descent have had their homes here for generations. I'm taking you to an old monastery which is now a restaurant. It is very good and lots of people drive out here for lunch.'

A few minutes later they pulled up and went into the building. The spacious restaurant was crowded with well-dressed people and a big centre table was loaded with cold dishes and delicacies of every kind. They went through to a court-yard, the walls of which were covered with jasmine, passion-vines and bougainvillaea, had drinks there and afterwards ate a meal the cost of which would have fed a poor family for a fortnight. As Adam paid the bill he wondered if Chela ever gave such extravagance a thought. But he was enjoying him-self too much to concern himself about that.

Afterwards she drove him back to his hotel, dropped him there and said that she had engagements she had made before they met for that evening, but would call for him at the same time the next day.

That evening he went again to the Anthropological Museum, which was open until ten o'clock, and gazed fas-cinated at a number of the ancient Toltec exhibits that seemed so familiar to him; then he had a light meal in the hotel and went early to bed.

The following morning Chela drove him northwards through the city to show him one of the government housing estates, then on for twenty-odd miles to Teotihuacán, the ceremonial capital of the Toltecs, from which they had been driven late in the tenth century.

It was the largest centre of religion that the world has ever known: eight square miles of courts and pyramids dominated by those of the Moon and the Sun, the latter being in bulk and area even larger than the great pyramid of Egypt.

They parked the car outside the museum with its adjacent wings of shops that sold every variety of Indian antique and souvenir, then spent two hours walking round the ruins. Up to the Pyramid of the Moon there was a broad, mile-long open space with rows of ruins on either side, from the steps of which many thousands of spectators must have watched the colourful processions of befeathered priests and nobles.

Grouped about the foot of the big pyramid were several smaller ones, connected by little courts and passages. At the entrance to this maze they engaged a guide who explained to Adam that the pyramids consisted of many layers; as their builders had believed that every fifty-second year the world entered a new cycle, they had encased the pyramid in a new covering of stone blocks, making its area and height ever greater.

On one side of the pyramid an excavation had been made showing all these layers and, descending a ramp, they passed through a narrow gallery off which there were a number of small, dark rooms deep in the base of the giant structure. The guide said that they had been used for storing treasure, but, as Adam peered into one of them, he was suddenly almost overcome by an attack of nausea. He felt certain they were cells and that in an earlier incarnation he had been imprisoned in one of them. The memory of the fears that had afflicted him during that terrible experience brought him out in a cold sweat. Half choking, he muttered to Chela that he was suffering from claustrophobia; then pushed past her, stumbled up two flights of broken stone stairs and out into the sunlight. It was not until he had been breathing in the fresh air for some moments that he ceased trembling and managed to pull himself together.

As they strolled back along the broad processional way, Chela said that he ought to go up to the top of the Pyramid of the Sun, as from it on all sides there was a splendid panorama. Her suggestion held no terrors for him, so he agreed. Then she announced that she would not go with him, as it was a tiring climb. Instead, she would collect the car and bring it round to the far side of the pyramid, where there was another, nearer, car park.

When they came opposite the Pyramid of the Sun he left her to walk on and, as there was no direct path to the pyramid, turned off to cross the quarter of a mile of tumbled ruins that separated him from it.

Until the excavations of comparatively recent times the whole area had been covered with earth blown there during the centuries. Only the more important ruins had been stripped and, in places, repaired; so the ground he was crossing consisted of uneven mounds of coarse grass with, here and there, blocks of stone protruding from them. Some of the mounds rose to fifty feet with, between them, deep gullies round which he had to make detours.

To his annoyance, when he arrived quite close to the base

of the pyramid he found himself separated from it by one of these lower levels that had, perhaps, once been a court. Its floor was some twenty feet below him and the side of the mound was too sheer for him to scramble down. He could see no way round unless he retraced his steps for a considerable distance, so he walked along the edge until he found a break by which he could get to within eight feet of the floor. Below that there was a large, smooth stone slab embedded in the mound at a sharp angle. Believing that if he jumped down on to it he could, with one foot, push himself off and land safely, he let himself go. His foot slipped on the stone, he hurtled through the air and, his arms outstretched, hit the ground with a terrific smack, flat on his face. The breath was driven from his body and his mind blacked out.

.   .   .   .   .

It was pitch dark and very cold. He knew himself to be in the cell down in the bowels of the Pyramid of the Moon. He knew, too, that he was the King and High Priest of the Toltecs, whose army had been defeated many weeks earlier while attempting to defend Teotihuácan and that he had been taken prisoner by his enemies. Apart from that, his memories of the past were dim and vague. But he was more certain about his immediate situation.

It was Itzechuatl, the King and High Priest of the Chichimecs, who had taken him prisoner, and his captor had offered him a choice. Either he could remain where he was indefinitely until he died or, by a great ceremony, divest himself of his magical powers in favour of his captor. Death, if he refused the latter choice, would not come quickly, because he was to be well fed and cared for; so he might remain there for years in the cold and darkness, afflicted by cramps and rheumatism until he eventually expired. On the other hand, only by dying could he pass his magical powers on to another. So the choice really lay between a prolonged, lingering death and a swift one as a human sacrifice.

He was not afraid of death, but he was of pain, and for seemingly endless days he had been haunted by the thought

of Chac-Mool. This was a stone figure of a man, his knees
and back raised so that his lap made a valley. The idol's head,
on which there was a flat, brimless hat, was turned sideways;
the fat face expressed indifference. But it was upon the lap
that the sacrificial victim was thrown down on his back, then
the priest slit his breast open with an obsidian knife, plunged
a hand into his body, wrenched out the warm, bloody, still-
palpitating heart and offered it to the gods.

For the victim, the agony of those moments must be in-
tolerable, and any man might long hesitate before deciding
to face them. Yet Adam, in the person of the Toltec ruler,
had at last decided to do so, rather than continue for weeks,
months, years, in this pit of black despair.

When the guards next brought him a meal and a three-
inch-long flickering torch of resin, that would last only ten
minutes, to eat it by, he told them of his decision.

There followed a timeless interval, during which he was
brought six more meals; then they led him out and to an upper
chamber. At first he was so unused to daylight that he could
hardly see, but gradually he made out Itzechuatl and his
entourage. All of them were dressed in gorgeous garments
and their faces were so heavily painted as to be hardly recognisable. The Priest-King said to him in Nahuatl, which
was their common language:

'I am glad that you have at last become sensible and regret
the two days' delay that have been necessary to make our preparations, but all is now in readiness.'

Four of his retainers then came forward, painted Adam's
face and decked him out in ceremonial robes: a loincloth of
the finest linen, a belt and sandals of gold, blazing with precious stones, a cloak of many colours, and a huge head-
dress from which waved the magnificent plumes of the Quetzal bird. His toilette completed, two nobles took him by the
elbows and, as though supporting him, led him out of the
pyramid to the Sacred Way.

Massed on either side of it on the mile-long tiers of steps
were many thousands of people. His appearance was hailed
with a thunderous roar of greeting; automatically he raised
his hand in acknowledgment of the multitude's salutation,

squared his shoulders and began his slow, dignified walk to the place of sacrifice.

Itzechuatl walked just behind him, accompanied by scores of other priests and nobles. Behind them marched a band that played weird, but to him familiar, music on strange instruments. In front of him there danced a hundred or more beautiful maidens, each holding a basket of flowers which they scattered in his path as he walked.

His eyes focused on one of them, a very tall girl with magnificent shoulders, a wasp-like waist and long, beautifully-shaped legs. Their glances met; hers held admiration and compassion. Momentarily his fears of the terrible death ordained for him were submerged in sudden passionate desire for her.

At last they reached the base of the Pyramid of the Sun. There, bearers were waiting with elaborate carrying chairs. The chairs had short legs in front and longer legs at the back, so that at times they could be rested upright on the ascending steps of the pyramid. Adam was eased into the foremost and most decorative by his attendant nobles, then the ascent began.

The slow and dignified progress brought him at length to the top of the pyramid. It was flat and about half an acre in extent. From the centre rose a flat-roofed, one-storey temple, in front of which reposed the gruesome figure of Chac-Mool. As Adam's chair was turned round and set down he was brought face to face with the brilliantly-clad figures which had followed him in the procession. Itzechuatl and his principal dignitaries had been carried up the pyramid in chairs; the rest had climbed it and most of them were breathing heavily.

Among the latter he caught sight of three of his Captains who had been captured with him. They were naked to the waist and their hands were tied behind them. As they came opposite him, each of them made a low obeisance, but all of them avoided his eyes. He knew why. They were deeply ashamed not to have died fighting, instead of having allowed themselves to be taken prisoner. To lighten their distress he called to each of them by name and spoke kindly to him.

When the last in the procession had reached the broad

D

platform in front of the temple, Adam could see right down it. He had hoped for another sight of the tall maiden; but the dancing girls had come only part of the way up the pyramid to the highest of three terraces that broke its slope, and were now assembled there. On the lower terraces and below it, in solid masses, stood the great multitude of people, presenting a sea of unidentifiable upturned faces. Beyond, in the far distance, a chain of mountains stood out against the azure sky.

Adam sat with his hands tightly clasped. His face did not betray the fears that racked him, but his heart was pounding furiously as he prayed for the business to be over swiftly.

Itzechuatl came forward to the edge of the terrace and raised his arm. The murmur that had been coming up from the vast crowd ceased and, in a ringing voice, he addressed them:

'O people! Our august captive has agreed to accept the fate that I believe the gods to have decreed for him. We shall now make sacrifice to learn if he is in truth acceptable to them.'

Out of the corner of his eye, Adam saw his three Captains led away behind him. Guessing that they were to be sacrificed before he was, he called out to them to have courage. To his immense relief the chair in which he was still sitting had been set down facing outward, so his back was to Chac-Mool and he would be spared the horror of seeing his men murdered. To plead for mercy would have been useless and escape impossible. All three of them were brave warriors and he knew that they would go to their deaths without any futile struggle.

There fell an utter silence that seemed to last an eternity, then a long, low moan, followed a moment later by a ghastly scream of agony as the priest tore the heart from his first victim's body. As he held it aloft a thunderous roar surged up from the multitude below.

The palms of Adam's hands were damp and he was thankful that his face had been painted, for he knew that the blood had drained from it, leaving it chalk white.

A moment later the victim's bleeding body was carried

past Adam by four priests and thrown outward with all their force. With whirling arms and legs it hit the steps of the pyramid and tumbled grotesquely down them, to be seized on by other priests and borne away.

There was silence for some minutes, then again came the wailing groan, the agonising screech and the great shout issuing from the throats of the thousands of spectators. And, again, the body was heaved down the pyramid.

For the third time there fell the nerve-racking silence, to be followed by the sounds that seemed to pierce Adam's own racing heart, and the third sacrifice was completed.

His turn had now come. The sweat was pouring down his face and his nails were biting into the palms of his hands. In vain he strove to force from his thoughts a mental picture of the sharp knife being driven high up into his chest and ripping down it, then of his ribs being forced apart and his heart being dragged from the bloody cavity.

Another tense silence, longer than those that had preceded it, followed the immolation of the third victim. Unseen by Adam, the priests behind him were examining the hearts of their victims to judge their mystical significance. Although now almost petrified by fear, he cursed the delay in facing his ordeal; for he was striving to comfort himself with the belief that once it was over his spirt would be released and happiness await him in a reunion with friends already dead who would be waiting to welcome him.

At last a noble appeared on either side of him, took him by the elbow and raised him to his feet. He expected them to turn him about and lead him the few paces to the Chac-Mool. Determined to make an end befitting a Toltec ruler, he mustered all his courage, rose to his full height, pushed them aside, turned and took a step towards the now blood-soaked idol. Quickly they seized him by the arms and turned him about again.

As they did so, he saw Itzechuatl raise his arm high, enjoining silence on the great assembly. Next moment his voice rang out:

'O people! Our gods are kind. The hearts of those sacrificed to them show that they accept our august captive as a

Man-God who will bring victory and prosperity to our nation.'

A burst of cheering came from the priests and nobles up there on the top of the pyramid. Its significance was caught by the multitude below and within a minute it was drowned by the deafening applause of the people.

As it subsided, Itzechuatl made a low obeisance to Adam. One after another the other priests and nobles followed suit. His escorts then lowered him again into the elaborate carrying chair, the bearers picked it up and began the descent of the pyramid.

For some moments he could hardly grasp that he was to be spared. Overwhelmed with relief he was only vaguely conscious of being carried through the masses of men and women who, section after section, ceased their cheering as he approached to do him homage by falling to their knees and lowering their foreheads to the ground.

Subconsciously he took in the fact that he was being taken not to the Pyramid of the Moon but towards the Palace which lay on the far side of the Pyramid of the Sun. Until his captors had defeated the Toltecs and driven them from Teotihuacán it had been his Palace, and he had always resided there when conducting the great religious ceremonies of the year.

When they reached it and he was escorted inside he was pleased to find that it had not been looted. Instinctively he walked towards the suite of rooms he had occupied. As he entered it the nobles withdrew and were at once replaced by servants who deferentially unrobed him, washed the paint and sweat from his face and bathed him in the sunken, silver-lined pool.

As soon as they had dried him he dismissed them and, wrapped in a light gown of the finest cotton, he walked through to his bedroom. There, utterly exhausted, he flung himself down on the leather-strap-sprung bed. After a few moments he turned over and caught sight of his reflection in a highly-polished stone mirror that hung on the wall.

With a start he sat up and stared at himself. As a Toltec Prince he had naturally supposed that he would resemble other Indians in features and colour, but the face he was looking at bore no likeness to any that he had ever seen. Instead of being a reddish brown, the skin was pale pink, the eyes, instead of black, were blue, the lower part of the face, instead of being hairless, was covered with a thick, curly beard and, most staggering of all, both beard and hair, instead of being black, were a rich red gold.

Utterly bewildered, he fell back on the bed and lay there striving to think of an explanation. But his tired brain could take no more and, after a few moments, he fell asleep.

6

The Eavesdroppers

WHEN Adam came to, he was lying on his face with his arms outstretched. Picking himself up he found that the palms of his hands were grazed, his knees bruised and that his wrists, from having taken most of his weight as he hit the ground, ached painfully; but otherwise he was uninjured.

Ruefully he saw that one leg of his brand-new suit was badly torn at the knee. That, and the fact that he was covered with dust, was ample evidence that he had had a nasty fall, but he had not yet climbed the pyramid. To rejoin Chela and admit that he had funked the climb just because he had fallen down would, he felt, be a shocking loss of face; so, although he was feeling rather groggy, he pulled himself together and walked slowly towards it.

As he did so, it entered his still hazy mind that he might have been unconscious for a considerable time. If so, Chela would already be wondering what had become of him and he ought to rejoin her at once. But a glance at his watch showed him that he could not have been 'out' for more than a few minutes, which he found surprising.

Starting up the first staircase, he pondered his vivid memories of the shattering past experience he had just relived. It explained much that had been obscure to him about his vision after he had been knocked down by Señor Enriquez's car, and he was now able to co-ordinate the two.

In this recent vision he had relived a period of time that had preceded the other by very nearly a year. It was clear now that after he had succumbed to Itzechuatl's pressure and gone through the ceremony of 'Acceptance' on the Pyramid of the

Sun, he had been consistently drugged, so that he should appear among the people as entirely carefree and, presumably, happy in the knowledge that when his time as a Man-God was up he was to give his life so that they might prosper. In addition, the drug had served Itzechuatl by dulling his prisoner's faculties, so that he would forget the fate awaiting him and not attempt to escape. But he had escaped.

At least, so it seemed; although he could not be certain that he had got away from his pursuers. He was strongly under the impression that he had succeeded and hoped that in another vision he would learn what had happened to him after Mirolitlit had enabled him to get away in the canoe; yet, at the same time, he dreaded a further revelation, as it might prove that he had been captured, in which case he would have to go through the horror of being ripped apart by Itzechuatl's sacrificial knife.

The thing that puzzled him most was why, in this land of brown-skinned Indians, he should have seen himself as a golden-haired white man and, when he prayed for help to escape across the lake, it should have been to the Norse gods.

The Pyramid was built in four stages separated by broad terraces. Its steps were not very deep and the slope comparatively gentle; so Adam found it easier going than he had expected. In a quarter of an hour he reached the summit.

When starting up the pyramid his mind had been greatly disturbed by the terrible experience that he had so recently relived. But the bright sunshine, clear air and the exertion of climbing soon brought him back to normal. It was only with curiosity that he looked at the spot where the Chac-Mool, on which he had feared he would pour out his life-blood, had once stood. He could visualise the scene but it was as though it had been only an act that he had seen in a play.

Unlike the Egyptian pyramids, those in Mexico do not rise to a point; they are truncated and the flat surface at the top of this, the largest of the Mexican pyramids was, perhaps, as much as a quarter of an acre in extent. But it looked very different from when Adam had been there 'before'. Then the whole of the centre had been filled by a great, flat-roofed temple. Only the broad terrace surrounding it remained unchanged. The temple had been destroyed by the Spaniards and was now just a tangled heap of broken stones.

Slowly he walked right round the terrace. In the clear air he could see for many miles across the Anáhuac valley to the great ranges of volcanic mountains that enclosed it. Having enjoyed the wonderful panorama, he began the descent and found going down more trying than coming up, for there was no guard rail and one false step would have sent him rolling from that dizzy height to end up a bundle of broken bones, and probably dying, at the bottom.

Chela was sitting in the car reading a book and smoking a cigar. She exclaimed at his dishevelled state, then commiserated with him on his fall; but, although his wrists were still paining him badly, he assured her that he was unhurt. They drove to the restaurant near the museum where he was able to tidy himself up, and lunched there off *Tacos*, a very popular Mexican dish consisting of maize pancakes, called *tortillas*, stuffed with pork, onions and tomatoes, then rolled up and fried.

On leaving the restaurant they found that quite a strong wind had risen, creating a minor dust-storm. Each gust lifted little clouds of sand from the ground and blew it most unpleasantly into their faces. As they walked towards the car park, Adam commented that they were lucky it had not been like that in the morning during their long walk round.

Chela agreed, then added, 'But this is nothing to what we sometimes have to put up with in the spring. Such a great part of the land is barren and dried up that the high winds collect huge clouds of dust which blow right into Mexico City. Everyone who can afford to leaves the capital and goes down either to Cuernavaca or Acapulco. That reminds me. We usually go down to our house at Cuernavaca at week-ends and father wished me to ask you if you would like to come down with us on Friday.'

Adam happily accepted, then they got into the car and wound up all the windows.

When they had covered only a few miles on the way back, Chela turned off the smooth, broad motorway on to a bumpy gravel side road that was full of potholes. Ten minutes later they entered a small town and, as she pulled up in the little plaza, she said:

'You have been to some of our luxury restaurants in Mexico City, seen the lovely homes out at Pedregal and one of the housing estates for the favoured white-collar workers; now I want to show you the wretched state in which our rotten government still leaves by far the greater part of the people to live.'

She made no move to get out of the car and they sat in it for a quarter of an hour while Adam took in the scene.

The plaster was peeling from the houses round the square, few of them had windows and the roofs of several were either broken or unskilfully patched. A few bedraggled palm trees threw patches of shade on broken paving and a rusty iron rail. Evidently it was market day, as there were many people about, some leading cows so emaciated that their ribs showed through their hides, others carrying several undersized chickens by a string tied round their legs. There were a few battered cars of ancient vintage, loaded to the roof with fruit and vegetables; but most of the traffic consisted of rickety carts drawn by painfully thin mules or, quite often, a sweating peasant. The people were scantily clad, the colour in the women's dresses long since faded, the once-white cotton suits of the men grey with grime, their straw hats frayed and sometimes brimless. Many of them were in rags and the younger children playing in the dirty gutters were naked.

In the centre of the square there was a statue that had lost an arm. Below it there was a single water faucet at which a small queue was waiting to fill battered two-gallon jerry-cans. It was composed mostly of children and Adam saw one little boy who could not have been more than seven stagger away with his filled can on his back, supported by a piece of rope that crossed his forehead, his eyes starting from his head.

'Poor little devil!' Adam exclaimed. 'It's terrible. After seeing Mexico City I would never have believed it.'

Chela gave a bitter laugh. 'I could take you to scores— no, hundreds and hundreds—of little towns and villages like this. And do you know what they live on? *Tortillas* and a few vegetables and fruits. They are lucky if they see meat once a month. It's *tortillas* for breakfast, *tortillas* for dinner and *tortillas* for supper. And they haven't even got mills to grind the maize. The men go out to work in the fields while the women pound the maize with a pestle and mortar; then, as they have no electricity or gas or wood, they have to blow their lungs out fanning into flame a miserable little heap of charcoal on which to cook it. Three times a day they do that, and it takes up most of their waking hours. Can you wonder that there are Communists?'

Adam gave her a questioning look. 'From the way you speak, one might imagine that you are one.'

Opening the door of the car, she replied cryptically, 'Christ was a Communist, wasn't He? Come on, let's go to see the church.'

They walked a short way down the dusty road on one side of which there was a line of stalls selling cheap cotton garments, luridly-coloured soft drinks, piles of dangerous-looking, home-made sweets and preserved fruits, upon which hordes of flies were feasting.

The church was a fairly large one. Adam was surprised to find it crowded, and that there were as many men as women in it. It was very old and the interior a strange contrast of the beautiful and ugly. The ceiling was a gem of intricate carving, although most of the gold that must once have made it dazzling had flaked away. There was a row of saints in niches, some of which were works of art; and one, he saw with interest, was black, with the features of an Indian. In contrast, grouped round the altar, there were other, smaller, modern figures of saints: cheap, gaudy and with garishly-coloured robes. But before all of them were pyramids of thin, lighted candles, which were constantly being added to by the poverty-stricken worshippers, paying a *peso* or two for them out of their hard-won earnings.

Chela made her genuflection, then knelt in silent prayer. While she was doing so, Adam saw that people were queueing up in front of the altar and he was quite touched to see a peasant, evidently the father of two small boys, who made them kneel beside him, then sprinkled their heads with Holy Water.

To Adam's surprise Chela remained on her knees for a good ten minutes. As they left the church he said, 'I had no idea you were so devout. In people who lead the sort of life you do, that is unusual in these days.'

'It so happens that I am deeply religious,' she replied seriously. 'But even if I weren't, I should give all the support I could to the Church, because it is the only body that strives to better the lot of our down-trodden peasantry.'

In his youth, having been brought up as a Presbyterian, Adam had often heard it said that Catholic priests battened on their flocks and extorted the last *sou* from them to build grandiose churches or send as tribute to the Pope; so he remarked, a shade cynically. 'That may be so here; but in Catholic countries in Europe the Church hasn't a record it can be very proud of. For centuries it has deliberately kept its followers in ignorance and played on their superstitions to wring money from them.'

'That is not true,' she retorted sharply. 'Religion is a very necessary discipline. Its acceptance prevents the break-up of families and enables people to resist many temptations from which, if they gave way to them, crimes would result. The teachings of the Church are based upon a combination of divine revelations and immensely long experience. Therefore, to allow them to be questioned is not for the common good. As for the money side of it, the poor have few pleasures and one of them is attending the great feasts of the Church. Their impressive pageantry must be paid for and the people make their contributions willingly. Anyhow, in Mexico, ever since the Conquest, the Church has done nothing but good.'

'How about the Inquisition? You must have had that here.'

'For a time there were *auto-da-fè*, just as there were in Spain, but on nothing like so great a scale. Its only victims in the New World were Portuguese Jews and other European heretics. The Indians benefited so greatly under the rule of the Fathers that the vast majority of them accepted Christianity willingly, made it the focus of their lives and became, in their own way, very devout. Mentally, though, they were and are like children and not fully responsible; so the Church decreed that the Inquisition should not apply to them.'

'I find it surprising that the Indians should have given up their old gods so readily.'

'Well . . .' Chela hesitated. 'They didn't exactly. The Church was clever about that. Just as happened in Europe hundreds of years earlier, it allowed its pagan converts to identify the more beneficient of their gods with Christian saints. That is why you often see statues of saints with Indian features and brown faces in the churches here. But there is no harm in that since their devotees practise the Christian religion.'

By half past three they were back in the city. Chela dropped Adam at his hotel and that evening took him to a party given by one of her friends. There he saw unmistakably that he was by no means the only pebble on her beach. Two good-looking Mexicans and an American pursued her with unflagging ardour and she flirted outrageously with all three of them. Adam cut in whenever he could, but they were older friends of hers than he was, and he could not help wondering whether she was having a serious affaire with one or other of them. He tried not to show his jealousy, but doubted if he succeeded.

At this party he met a couple who invited him to one they were giving the following night and, on learning that Chela was going to it, he happily accepted. The following day he did not see her until the evening; so he spent the time visiting the Cathedral and the Museum of History.

On the Friday morning Chela called for him again and they set off for Cuernavaca. It lay some thirty miles away and the road took them up into the highlands south of Mexico City. They climbed to ten thousand feet through grasslands and, even at that height, occasional woods of pine and casuarina trees; then they descended the steep slope to five thousand feet and entered the city.

It, too, was on a steep slope and very different from the capital. There were few big modern buildings, the streets were narrow and the houses mostly very old. That of the Enriquezes was near the castle-like residence that Cortés had had built and lived in during his declining years. From the street the house appeared tall, narrow and by no means impressive; but it had great depth, with fine, lofty rooms inside, the furnishings of which contrasted strongly with those of the penthouse in the Avenida Presidente Masarik. Here there were Old Masters and fine tapestries on the time-darkened wood-panelled walls, Indian woven mats on the polished floors, chairs, tables and commodes that had belonged to Spanish hidalgos long since dead; so that Adam felt as though he had entered the house of a nobleman living in an earlier century.

Alongside the house and beyond it there was a charming garden with a large, irregular-shaped swimming pool, across a narrow neck of which was a broad wooden bridge supporting a summer-house. As it was a lovely day, they decided to refresh themselves with a swim; so they changed into swimsuits at once and, for the first time, Adam saw Chela almost naked. Never, he decided, had he seen a girl with a more beautiful figure and, from the way she narrowed her eyes slightly as she looked at him, he inwardly rejoiced at the thought that, almost certainly, she was admiring his own splendid proportions.

After their swim they sunbathed for a while then, still in their bathing things, lunched under an awning in the garden. It was then time for the siesta, although Adam begrudged the hours that he would be deprived of the sight of the lovely Mexican girl who had so swiftly become his divinity.

At five o'clock they met again downstairs and soon afterwards four other week-end guests arrived, all young people who were friends of Chela's. The introductions were barely over when her father joined them. With him he brought a handsome, well-set-up man with dark, wavy hair and lustrous brown eyes, who looked to be about thirty. He had a strong likeness to Bernadino Enriquez, and Adam was not surprised when it transpired that he was Chela's half-brother.

On seeing him she exclaimed, 'Why, Ramón, what are you doing here? Why have you left Washington?'

Laughing, he kissed her. 'I got in on this morning's plane. A big deal connected with plastics is being negotiated with

the United States government, and our Ambassador thought
it would be a good idea to send me down to discuss it with
father.'

'I should have thought the United States have enough
plastics of their own,' she remarked.

'Oh, it's not a deal in that sense,' he replied lightly. 'It's a
matter of exchanging information on certain secret processes.'

After they had had drinks under the awning where Adam
and Chela had lunched, all of them except Ramón and his
father went up to change into bathing things. When they came
out of the house Adam saw that father and son had settled
themselves in the summer-house on the bridge over the neck
of the pool and were in earnest conversation. But he gave
them only a glance, as his eyes were all for Chela.

For a while the six young people dived, laughed and
plunged about in the broader end of the pool then, after a
long swim under water, Adam surfaced to find that Chela
had disappeared. Momentarily he was seized with an awful
fear that she had perhaps dived in where it was too shallow,
hit her head on the bottom, knocked herself out and failed
to come up. Grabbing the diving board from below, he pulled
himself out of the water, threw a leg over the board and swung
himself up on to it. From there he could see the whole of that
end of the pool. It was lined with blue tiles and the water
was clear, but Chela was nowhere to be seen.

He realised then that she must have swum away under the
bridge to the far end of the pool. Diving in, he set off after
her. A minute later his swift crawl brought him under the
bridge and there she was, her back turned to him, not floating
or treading water, but hanging with both hands to one of the
cross-beams supporting the low bridge. Her face was turned
upward and she appeared to be listening intently.

At the sound of his approach she swung round, let go
with one hand, frowned at him and gestured him to remain
silent. Catching at another cross-beam he hung there a few
feet away from her.

As the water he had churned up ceased to swish, he caught
the sound of voices coming down through the floorboards of
the summer-house. He could not hear all that was said but

enough to get the gist of the conversation. The Mexican Ambassador in Washington had been tipped off by the F.B.I. that a revolution was brewing in his country. As security man at the Embassy, Ramón had been sent back to alert his government; but he had come first to inform his father, who was greatly worried at this news and very glad of the warning, as it would enable him to put certain people on guard against possible trouble.

After a few minutes Chela let go her hold on the beam, slid under water and swam away to the narrow end of the pool. Adam promptly followed and they surfaced face to face some fifteen feet on the far side of the bridge.

When she had shaken the water from her face, her wide mouth opened in its dazzling smile and she said, 'Wicked of me to eavesdrop, wasn't it? But I love learning other people's secrets, and as Ramón has nothing to do with commerce, I felt certain his unexpected return was not connected with plastics.'

Adam grinned at her a little awkwardly. 'Well, as I eavesdropped too, we are birds of a feather. Do you think it likely, though? I mean, the possibility of there being a revolution?'

She shrugged her splendid shoulders. 'I doubt it. There are plenty of people both rich and poor who would like to see the present government overthrown and some of them are indiscreet enough to say so. But talk is one thing and action quite another. I shouldn't think this is more than a baseless rumour that some eager-beaver American agent has picked up. Best forget it. Come on. I'll race you back to the other end of the pool.'

As she struck out, Adam gave her a good start, caught her up, then took things easily, gallantly letting her win by a head and shoulders.

When they had all dried themselves and were drinking their first cocktail, a visitor was brought out of the house. He was an elderly, thickset man, with long, lank, silver hair that turned up at the ends and strangely contrasting bushy black eyebrows, beneath which were a pair of curiously dead-looking black eyes. His sallow complexion and hooked nose suggested a dash of Indian blood, although he had the haughty look of a pure-bred Spaniard. He was dressed in a dark suit of gabardine. Bernadino and Ramón were still in the summer-house but the others all stood up as the visitor approached and greeted him with deference. It was not until Chela introduced him as Monsignor Don Alberuque that Adam realised that he was a prelate.

As Adam met the glance of those cold, fish-like eyes, he felt certain that he had looked into them—or a pair extra-ordinarily like them—somewhere before; but he could not re-member where. He was, too, suddenly conscious of an in-stinctive feeling of mingled fear and hatred of their owner, although the Monsignor gave him no grounds whatsoever for such a reaction. On the contrary, he could not have been more polite and charming as he questioned Adam about his impressions of Mexico and offered to do anything in his power to make his stay more enjoyable.

He had a deep, sonorous voice, a ready smile and an agile mind. Tactfully he drew one after the other in the little circle into the conversation, asking after their parents and their recent doings. He drank his martinis with evident enjoyment and, without any trace of the coy wickedness adopted by some priests, conveyed the impression that he was a broad-minded man of the world.

Some quarter of an hour after he had joined them he said to Chela, 'My daughter, I feel sure your friends will forgive me if I deprive them of you for a few minutes, so that we may have a short private conversation.'

As she stood up he added with a smile to the others, 'Dear Chela is invaluable to me in my work, and I called to solicit her aid in smoothing out an unhappy dissension between two members on the committee of one of our many charities.' Then he took her by the arm and led her away towards the other end of the garden.

By then dusk was falling; so the others finished their drinks and went up to change for dinner.

They assembled again at half past eight, the men in dinner jackets, the girls in long dresses as fashionable as any that could have been seen in Paris. Another hour of drinks and laughing chatter followed, during which Don Alberuque rejoined them. Then, an hour earlier than they would have done in the capital, they went in to dine.

The meal was of six courses, all carefully chosen, and better, Adam thought, than could have been got in most expensive restaurants. The wines had been shipped from Europe: a Manzanilla with the soup, a Montrâchet with the fish, a château-bottled Lafitte with the roast, champagne with the sweet and a Beerenauslese hock to finish up with. Again there came into Adam's mind the little boy staggering under the weight of the jerry-can of water, and the appalling contrast with this feast which, he felt sure, had not been put on simply for him but was an everyday occurrence in this millionaire's household.

When the girls left the men at table, Alberuque at once moved down next to Adam and buttonholed him. In spite of his sudden and instinctive dislike of the Monsignor, the man's mind was so lively and his interest in Adam so evident that it would have been churlish not to respond pleasantly.

To begin with he questioned Adam about his books, his other interests, his early life and, with urbane tact, his religion. To the last Adam replied that he had been brought up as a Presbyterian, then took a slightly cynical pleasure in repeating what he had said to Chela about the Roman Catholic Church keeping its followers in ignorance in order to retain its power over them.

Alberuque shook his massive head. 'You are wrong about that, my friend. All through the Dark Ages in Europe it was the Church alone that kept the flame of learning alight. And if we do not allow our people to question the tenets of the Church, that is for their own good. And, religion apart, the Church has played a part unrivalled by any other body as a civilising influence.'

Greedily picking a couple of muscat grapes from a nearby dish, he popped them in his thin-lipped mouth, chewed them and went on, 'Here in Mexico the Church has saved the people from generations of suffering. The Dominican Fathers, who were the first to arrive here, fought the Conquistadores tooth and nail to prevent them from exploiting the Indians. In those times priests were the only lawyers. The Dominicans controlled the Council of the Indies and they appointed the three members of the *Audiencia*, the Supreme Court here, which had powers even greater than those of the Viceroys. The Fathers' object was to erect a 'City of God' in which all men, irrespective of their colour, would be free and able to secure justice. It was the Church that forced through the laws restricting the *encomiendas*.'

'What were they?' Adam enquired.

'Soon after the Conquest, the Spaniards divided the country into districts, making themselves feudal lords on the same pattern as the nobles in Europe. They looked on the Indians on their great estates as serfs, and compelled them to give their labour without payment. The Church could not altogether abolish these *encomiendas*, as they were called, but it did persuade the King of Spain to agree to a law that after "two lives" the exploiters should have to surrender their right to use the Indians as slave labour.

'Of course, there were evasions. Many of the Spaniards continued to exploit the simple Indians by selling them goods at exorbitant prices for which they could not pay, then making them continue to work against debts that they could never hope to wipe off; so the *encomiendas* were not finally abolished until Mexico achieved independence. Even so, the law did result, two generations later, in great numbers of Indians becoming paid workers instead of slaves.

'Then there came the Franciscan friars. They did not concern themselves with the law but were simple missionaries and, like all missionaries, they were aware that the quickest way to convert the heathen was to work for his health and happiness. Three of them walked barefoot all the way from Vera Cruz to Mexico City, and that made an immense impression. Later the Franciscans spread all over the country, often penetrating to places in which no other white man had ever been. They led frugal, pious lives, teaching the Indians such arts as they knew, and acting as righteous judges in all local and family disputes; so that they became greatly revered.

'As in Spain, these friars organised their parishioners into guilds, each with a devotion to a certain saint. On the Saint's day his guild put on a play in which angels and devils, knights and Moors fought battles; always, of course, ending in the triumph of Christianity. To be given a part in these spectacles was thought a great honour and to be debarred from participating in them a terrible disgrace. They became the most important thing in village life and in that way the friars were able to exercise great influence for good over the social as well as the religious lives of the people.'

Snatching another couple of grapes, Alberuque ate them quickly, spat out the pips and, before Adam could think of any remark, resumed :

'Before the coming of the Spaniards, the peasants had enjoyed a form of Communism, by which the land surrounding each village was held in common and plots were allotted to families in relation to their capacity to work them. The Church insisted on the maintenance of that system and forbade white men or half-castes to live permanently in the villages, to prevent their setting up shops and tempting the Indians to impoverish their food supply by exchanging produce for tawdry goods. It was such measures that caused those who lived in the villages to give absolute obedience to the friars; not because they feared them, but because they really looked on them as representatives on earth of a benign God.

'The health of the people was also cared for, both individually by the secular priests and nationally by the Church. For example, as Mexico is such a mountainous country a great difference exists between the climate and the density of the air at different levels. On average the temperature in Mexico City is twenty-five degrees lower than that at Vera Cruz. In consequence, it was found that if Indians were taken from the highlands to work in the lowlands, and vice-versa, great numbers of them died from respiratory diseases. The Spanish settlers were interested only in getting cheap labour, but the Church insisted on strict laws being passed to prevent the transfer of workers from their own districts. Of course, in those days, and for several centuries, the Church here was virtually the State. Her power was paramount. It was always exercised for the good of the people, and it still is.'

Adam nodded. 'From all you tell me, I appreciate that the Church must have done a lot of good in the old days. But today I imagine it is almost moribund, as it lost all its power when Mexico became independent.'

'By no means,' Alberuque replied quickly. 'There have been periods when it has suffered persecution under atheist governments; but the people have always realised that it is their only protection against exploitation and so remained loyal to it. Do you realise that Miguel Hidalgo, the first man to lead a serious revolution, was a priest?

'For just on three hundred years Mexico had been the milch cow of Spain. The greater part of the silver coinage of today came originally from Mexico. Over four billion dollars' worth of it was sent to Europe. But the Spaniards were not content with that. Thousands of them came here to make fortunes, then went home again. They were known as *gachupines*—wearers of spurs—and they were given all the most lucrative jobs, both in the government and in the Church. The Creoles—that is, Spaniards who had been born in Mexico—they regarded with contempt, and the Indians as cattle.

'Miguel Hidalgo was a Creole. Owing to that he had no hope of ever becoming a Bishop and he intensely resented the privileges that the Spaniards enjoyed. To protect Spanish interests the inhabitants of New Spain were not allowed to cultivate grapes or olives or to deal in salt or tobacco, or in the ice brought down from the mountains. The Indians were not even permitted to ride a horse, carry arms or work in specialised crafts. But Hidalgo was a born rebel. He did many of these illegal things, read forbidden books and, as the shining light of the Literary Society of Querétaro, he brought to its members the doctrines of the French Revolution. Then, with the cry of "Mexico for the Mexicans", he urged his parishioners to revolt.'

'I've read about that,' Adam put in. 'But in the rebellion he led he made a hopeless mess of things and countenanced an appalling massacre of government troops who had surrendered at Alhóndiga.'

'It is true that he was no general; that in the end he was defeated, captured and executed. But the fact remains that all over the country people rose in their thousands to support him; and the reason for that was not only a political one. It was largely because he took as his banner that of Our Lady of Guadalupe, and it is this small-town priest whom all Mexicans now honour as the Father of Independence.'

'But that was way back in 1810. Religion was still a great force everywhere.'

'In Mexico it has remained so. Of course, there have been periods when the Church has suffered severely at the hands of her enemies. Under the Constitution brought in by Benito Juárez in 1857 the Church was deprived of all her immense properties, the privileges of the clergy were abolished, priests and nuns were permitted to renounce their vows and education was taken out of the hands of the Church to be conducted by atheist schoolmasters. But persecution only strengthened the ardour of the faithful and their numbers were so great that for three years there was civil war in which they put up a desperate resistance.

'The war disrupted the whole country to such an extent that Porfirio Díaz, who afterwards ruled Mexico for so long, had to make peace with the Church and again allow her to acquire property.

'The Presidents who succeeded Díaz were again of the Left and endeavoured to force their atheism on the country, especially by the new Communist-inspired Constitution of 1917. With the Pope's blessing, our Archbishop repudiated the Constitution. The government retaliated by expelling all foreign-born priests and nuns, and again closed the parish schools. The Church fought back by ceasing to hold religious services for three years. By 1928 the masses became so desperate at being denied the consolations of religion that they again rose in revolt. The rebellion was called the War of the *Cristeros*, because the insurgents went into battle against the forces of the atheist President Calles with the cry of "Long live Christ the King".

'Six Bishops were exiled and the government troops carried out a brutal scorched-earth policy in the western provinces where the *Cristero* rebellion had originated. But the country continued to be in such a state of anarchy that Alvaro Obregón, who was running as Calles's successor, got himself elected only by promising to amend the Constitution in favour of the Church.

'Most unfortunately, before he could take office he was shot by a fanatic. That resulted in a wave of anti-clericalism and further persecutions. But the Catholic faith was so widespread and so strong that the atheists found it impossible to suppress. For over ten years a struggle for the restoration of the Church continued; then, at last, in the 1940s, President Camacho publicly admitted that he was a Catholic and brought about a compromise.

'There are still anti-clerical laws in force which enable the provinces to limit the number of priests in them, forbid the wearing of clerical garb in public, curtail Catholic education and activities, and no member of the Cabinet is allowed to attend Mass while holding office. But the government recognises the P.A.N.—that is, the *Partido Acción Nacional*— a Catholic party that sends to the legislature delegates who are allowed to put the views of the Church to the Assembly. And ninety-five per cent of the people are still practising Catholics.

'So, you see, you are quite mistaken in thinking that the Church has lost her power. An overwhelming majority of the people would obey their priests if another Miguel Hidalgo appeared and called on them to take up arms against the government.'

At this point Bernadino, who had been talking to his son and the two younger men, broke up the party. When they went upstairs to join the girls, Adam saw that the servants had cleared the drawing room of most of its furniture. A hi-fi radio was turned on, to which they danced. There was more champagne and at one o'clock silver salvers of split rolls appeared, upon which had been spread lavish portions of imported foie-gras, caviare and smoked salmon. At dinner none of them had drunk more than one glass of each of the wines but, with the cocktails that had preceded the meal and champagne afterwards, they had all consumed enough to make them carefree and merry. A little before two o'clock they gaily exchanged good-nights and went happily to bed.

It had been a much longer day than Adam was accustomed to; but, even so, he could not get to sleep. His mind was filled with mental pictures of Chela—swimming, dancing, gravely consulting with Don Alberuque, laughing with her friends, and eavesdropping under the bridge.

Suddenly he caught himself thinking of asking her to become his wife. He thrust the idea aside as absurd; yet it brought home to him how completely he was fascinated by her. He recalled his former resolution—not to become embroiled with any woman again until, much later in life, he really felt like settling down; now he was contemplating marrying one whom he had met barely a week before.

There was, of course, her intangible resemblance to Mirolitlit, which had convinced him that she was a reincarnation of the long-dead Chichimec beauty. But he had seen Mirolitlit only twice and had exchanged no more than a dozen words with her and, although he had now spent several days in Chela's company, he knew about her only that she was a bundle of contradictions: a devout Christian who held Communist views; a rich man's daughter who indulged herself in every extravagance in spite of the distress she displayed at the poverty of the Indians; a Roman Catholic who connived at the Mexican country folk continuing to worship their pagan gods; apparently a playgirl concerned, apart from her religious activities, only with the social round, yet so interested in political secrets that she would play the spy in her own family. What, he wondered, really went on behind the big, blue eyes in that narrow, but splendid, aquiline Aztec head?

As had been the case with Mirolitlit, Chela's physical attraction for him had proved so strong that he had at once felt a craving to possess her; but, still influenced by the rigid morality of his Scottish upbringing, he had instinctively assumed that an unmarried girl of her class would still be a virgin. Again his thoughts turned to asking her to marry him. That she was attracted to him both mentally and physically he felt sure. But, even if she was willing, what about her father? By British standards, Adam was now very well off, but the money he earned was a pittance compared to the great wealth of Bernadino Enriquez. He would almost certainly expect his only daughter to marry another millionaire. And even if to please her he consented to the match, Adam was plagued with doubts about whether he could make Chela happy for long. She was accustomed to so much. Her clothes alone must cost a fortune and he could not count on his present success continuing. To an industrialist or the owner of a chain of shops many ways were open by which he could retain a large part of the profits in his business, but that did not apply to authors. If they had a bumper year they were allowed to spread their royalties for tax purposes over two years, but no more; so the government took the lion's share earned by any single best-seller. Then, if future books flopped, the author could find himself back earning less than a lorry driver. If that happened, how could he possibly maintain a wife like Chela?

Turning from side to side in the big, canopied bed, he wrestled with the problem, then endeavoured to think of other things. The conversation he had overheard between Ramón and his father had been most intriguing. Had the F.B.I. stumbled on a mare's nest or was a revolution really brewing?

If so, what section of the people was planning to attempt a *coup d'état*? Certainly not the Army or the, traditionally Liberal, white-collar workers. Both were too pampered to desire a change. Then it must be either the peasants or the capitalists. The former, neglected and half starved, had abundant reason to desire a different state of things; the latter bitterly resented the Socialist restrictions that prevented them from amassing still more wealth. Yet a peasant *jacquerie* was hardly possible. The Indians formed a brainless mass and, without leaders to inspire them, must remain impotent. The capitalists, on the other hand, had the brains to plan and the money secretly to import weapons with which to arm their workers who, promised sufficient inducements, might form a formidable army. Bernadino had warmly expressed his appreciation of the news his son had brought him and had spoken of warning 'certain people' that they should guard against possible trouble. Those 'people' must be other big industrialists and key men in his employ who were in the plot and prepared to lead the workers when he gave the word.

That seemed to be the answer, but it was no concern of

Adam's. His concern was Chela and again his mind became absorbed by thoughts of her.

The night was thundery and the atmosphere heavy. The window of his room was wide open, but he still could not get enough air. His throat was parched and, owing to the rich spices with which some of the dishes he had eaten at dinner had been seasoned, he felt thirsty. He thought of going into the bathroom to get a drink of water, but decided not to, in case the tap water there was not safe to drink. It then occurred to him that if he went downstairs to the dining room there were several half-filled decanters on the sideboard; so he could quench his thirst with a glass of wine. Afterwards he could take a walk round the garden, which would clear his head and later give him a better chance of getting off to sleep.

Throwing back the bedclothes, he rolled out of bed, put on his dressing gown and, moving very quietly so as not to disturb other people who were asleep, tiptoed down to the ground floor. Strong moonlight coming through the tall windows enabled him to see his way without difficulty. At the bottom of the staircase he was about to turn left towards the dining room when he caught sight of a streak of light coming from a slightly ajar doorway on his right.

The door led, he knew, to a small library and for a moment he thought that the light must have been left on by mistake; so he moved in that direction to switch it off. Then he heard low voices coming from the room. His curiosity aroused about who could be there in the middle of the night, he tiptoed forward. His soft bedroom slippers made no sound on the polished parquet. Holding his breath he advanced to the door. Turning sideways he squinted through the narrow opening between the door and the wall. In a mirror he could now see that the occupants of the room were Monsignor Don Alberuque and Chela.

They were standing near the centre table. On it there was a briefcase which Adam recognised as the one that Ramón had brought with him. It was open, so it seemed obvious that Chela had purloined it and that they had either picked or forced its lock.

Alberuque was putting some papers back in it as he said:

'There is nothing here, dear child, to cause us undue anxiety; but you did well to get hold of it for me so that I could have a sight of the Ambassador's report. Upon the other matter the Good Lord will reward you for your excellent sense. That this stranger should have been sent to you at this time is a certain sign that our endeavours have the blessing of the Holy Spirit. I cannot stress too greatly the importance of inducing him to give us his willing aid; so you must secure and bind him to our interests, whatever the cost.'

Pausing, he made the sign of the Cross on her forehead and went on, 'From whatever sins you may have to commit in order to achieve this end, I hereby promise in advance to absolve you. With him in our midst as a sign of God's intent, we cannot fail to triumph. You are now, my child, a chosen vessel and I know you will not fail me.'

Withdrawing from the door without making a sound, Adam tiptoed back up the stairs, his mind in a whirl. What were the two of them planning? Had it to do with this rumoured revolution? That seemed hardly likely, yet the Church and the wealthy formed alliances against Communists and atheists. But Chela was, apparently, a Communist of a sort, so that did not make sense either; and she had obviously got hold of her brother's despatch case without his knowledge. Then—greatest conundrum of all—could it be he to whom Alberuque had referred?

He was no saint or holy man whose participation in some crusade could influence the people, so it seemed most improbable. Yet who else could it be? No other stranger had suddenly come into Chela's life so that it could be said of him that he had been 'sent'. Utterly mystified, he got back into his bed, lay pondering for a while, then fell asleep.

7

'Our Man' in Mexico

IT WAS nine o'clock when Adam was roused by a soft-footed valet pulling open the slats of the venetian blinds so that sunlight streamed into the room. As Adam sat up, the man made a low bow, wished him a smiling *beunos dias*, then wheeled a breakfast trolley into the room.

On the trolley there was coffee, some strips of paw-paw, pineapple, mango and apple, known in Mexico as a 'fruit plate', and a basket holding little sweet cakes and crisp white rolls. After a good drink of coffee Adam made a dead set at the rolls, for the white *bolios* of Mexico had been one of his discoveries. In Europe and the United States the refinement of flour and modern baking methods have in recent times rendered bread almost tasteless. But for Mexicans to have wheat bread in their houses, as well as maize cakes, is a status symbol and they insist that the wheat should be undiluted and hand-baked. The result is a revelation to visiting foreigners and Adam had found the rolls so delicious that he would willingly have made a main meal of them alone.

As he ate, the events of the previous night gave him plenty to think about. Why, he wondered again, should Monsignor Alberuque be so anxious to know what the F.B.I. had found out about a possible revolution that he had induced Chela to steal temporarily her half-brother's brief-case for him? For it seemed evident that that was what he had done.

The obvious inference was that he, as well as Bernadino, was involved in the conspiracy. It was always in the interests of capitalists to secure cheap labour; but the Church, as the protector of the poor, should be opposed to that. There could, though, be another angle to it. Alberuque was no village priest. As a Don he must be of noble descent and as a Monsignor a minor Prince of the Church. In every country such worldly prelates had often ignored the well-being of the masses if by so doing they could get for themselves rich benefices and great estates. And the lower orders of the clergy were bound to obey their superiors. Perhaps, therefore, the capitalists and the Bishops had made a pact. Yet, if that were so, why had not Bernadino told Alberuque what was afoot or, when Chela had reported to the Monsignor what she had overheard, had he not asked Bernadino about it, instead of coming in the middle of the night to examine the contents of Ramón's brief-case?

Finding no answer to this puzzle, Adam's mind turned to the other. For the past five days he had been almost constantly in Chela's company, he had now met most of her closest friends and she had talked freely to him about them. If some man who particularly interested her had recently come into her life surely he would have been at one of the parties to which Adam had gone with her or, at least, she would have made some mention of him. But there had not been the least indication that such a man existed; so it seemed inescapable that Adam was the 'stranger' to whom Alberuque had re-ferred. Yet how could he possibly be of any value to them as the figurehead in a revolution? The very idea was absurd.

There must then be some other explanation. Perhaps the 'stranger' was someone right outside Chela's social circle: a man her father and friends knew nothing about. If that was so, and the 'stranger' was a clandestine acquaintance, that would account for her never having mentioned him.

At this idea Adam was seized with sudden perturbation. He had had ample evidence that half a dozen men were in eager pursuit of Chela, but she had seemed indifferent to all of them. This might explain that. This new supposition made it probable that he had a rival, and a really dangerous one, for if there was a man that Chela was meeting in secret that would make him all the more interesting to her. It might even be that she was already in love with him. Still worse, Alberu-que had as good as ordered her to use her charms to secure his aid in their plans and, by giving her absolution in advance, clearly indicated that, if need be, she should give herself to him.

Mentally, Adam began to writhe. If she was willing, to lose her to another would be bad enough. But it might be that she was not, yet would obey Alberuque and sacrifice herself as a martyr to her cause. It was as well for the Monsignor that he was not then in the room for, at the thought, a fierce surge of anger ran through Adam. Had he at that moment had the chance, he would have used those great hands of his to choke the life out of the unscrupulous priest. As it was, he could only relieve his feelings by a flow of curses, consigning the priest to an obscene hell, and when he grew calmer determine to do everything possible to thwart his designs.

Yet how he could set about that was another problem. To disclose to Chela that he knew she had enabled Alberuque to read the despatch for which her half-brother was responsible would embarrass her so much that a breach between them was certain to result, and there seemed no other way in which he could lead her to talk of her secret activities. All he could do, for the time being, was to talk to her casually about the Monsignor, in the hope of picking up some clue, and weigh every word she said, on the off-chance that she might give some indication of the identity of the man upon whom Alberuque had ordered her to use her wiles.

Chela had said that she would take him that morning to see Cortés' palace, which was now a museum. It was not a very large building, but occupied one side of the main square. Many of the rooms were now used as offices of the City Council, but the chapel contained some splendid frescoes and most of the first floor consisted of an open terrace arcaded on both sides. Adam visualised the great Conquistadore, as an old man, sitting there sheltered from the midday heat, while looking out towards the nearest mountains in the vast country that, backed on landing only by a handful of adventurous Captains and a few hundred desperadoes, he had not only conquered but pacified with such wisdom that the people had come to regard him as their protector from injustice.

After their visit to the Palace, while walking back down the steep streets, Adam brought the Monsignor's name into the conversation. Showing no trace of uneasiness, Chela at once responded by going into raptures about him. He was, according to her, everything that a good priest should be: wise, pious, tolerant, with a great understanding of the human heart and an untiring zest for fighting the battles of the oppressed who came to him with their troubles. All of which got Adam nowhere.

On their return they found the rest of the house-party assembled round the pool, so they changed into bathing things and went in with them. Lunch was a cold collation taken in the garden where they helped themselves from a table carrying a score of delicacies which would have been sufficient to feed a whole platoon of hungry soldiers. The day then followed the pattern of Friday: more bathing and laughter, cocktails, a lengthy gourmet's dinner, then dancing until two o'clock in the morning.

On Sunday the routine differed only in that all the women and the three younger men went to Mass, leaving Adam and his host sitting together in the summer-house over the pool.

After they had been talking for a while Adam, keeping his voice casual, said, 'All the people I have talked to here say it's most unlikely there will be a change of government in the foreseeable future. D'you agree about that, sir?'

Bernadino gave Adam a swift, sideways glance, masking it by a pull on his cigar, then he replied, 'I should say they are right. The government is far too firmly seated to be overthrown at all easily. But one never can tell. People often take their characteristics from the land in which they live. Mexico is a land of many volcanoes; like them its people are given to sudden violent eruptions.'

'There is something to be said for a government that keeps the peace,' Adam hazarded. 'Even if it is a dictatorship.'

'I agree.' Bernadino nodded his white head. 'Revolutions have been the curse of Mexico ever since she gained independence. Except during the thirty-four years that old Porfirio Díaz was our President, hardly a year passed without either some ambitious General making a *pronunciamiento* or there being a *tumulto*, as we term riots, in Mexico City. As a youngster I can remember them, and they were quite alarming. In those days, and all through the past century, the streets were infested with hordes of beggars called *leperos*. Most of them were fake cripples. Any sort of excuse was good enough for them to throw away their crutches and rampage through the town in big mobs, looting, burning and murdering. For a day or two all decent people had to barricade themselves in their houses and have their firearms ready. At least our present government has put a stop to that sort of thing and has cleared the streets of such dangerous vagabonds.'

'You were saying, sir, that Porfirio Díaz succeeded in remaining President for thirty-four years. How did he manage to do that?'

Bernadino gave a low laugh. 'Because he had the sense to see on which side his bread was buttered. Like all these Generals, he came to power by inciting the Indians to revolt with the promise that the lands should be restored to them. Like all the others, he ratted on his promise. But, unlike them, he did not then try to rule only through his army. He made allies: the great landowners, such as my own family in those days; the Church and, shrewdest move of all, the Americans. With their help he pulled the country's finances out of the incredible mess they were in and encouraged foreign investment. What is more, he restored order throughout the whole country. For over half a century it had been plagued by hordes of bandits. Díaz enlisted all the gangsters in the cities, put them into smart uniforms and sent them out to clear the country up. They were called *Rurales* and had orders to shoot on sight. The Socialists, of course, paint him as a bloodthirsty tyrant who ground the faces of the poor; but that is not altogether true. For the first time since Independence, Mexico began to prosper and soon commerce was booming. Property and the lives of the law-abiding were secure. The taxes were heavy but there was money to pay them, and even the poorest people fed better than they do now. That is why from the late seventies until 1910 is known as Mexico's "Golden Age".'

'Would you say that things were better here then than when Mexico was a Spanish colony?'

'Oh no, I would not say that.' Bernadino smiled and waved his cigar airily. 'You British pride yourselves on having been the best colonial administrators the world has ever known—except perhaps for the Romans. But I do not think you can rival Spain's achievements in that field. We Spaniards—I use the term because I am descended from one of Cortés' Captains, although as for many generations my forbears have been born here I am actually a Creole—we Spaniards developed this country and ruled it for close on three hundred years. That is twice the length of time that the British were paramount in India. For three centuries our Viceroys, assisted by a Council called the *Audiencia* and wise decrees from the Council of the Indies that sat in Seville, kept the peace here, introduced every form of agriculture and bred vast herds of cattle. We also became the staging post for the enormous wealth in silks, spices, ivories and many other things that Spain imported from China and her possessions in the Far East. Under the Bourbon Kings of the seventeenth and eighteenth centuries Mexico was one of the most prosperous and well-governed countries in the world.'

'Why then,' Adam asked, 'did the people revolt and drive the Spaniards out?'

Bernadino sighed. 'It is a sad story; for from security and riches it reduced the country to chaos, brigandage and poverty for the best part of a century. I suppose the ideas emanating from the French Revolution were the initial cause; but it was Napoleon who upset the apple cart. You will doubtless recall that early in the last century he imprisoned King Carlos IV and his heir Ferdinand, then made his own brother, Joseph Bonaparte, King of Spain. That caused a schism among the ruling caste here. Some were for acknowledging the usurper Bonaparte; others supported the imprisoned King and wished to establish a Regency until he should be restored to his throne. Others again, particularly the Creoles, who had always resented being ruled by Spaniards sent out from Spain, urged that the time had come for Mexico to throw off the Spanish yoke and declare herself a sovereign nation. There followed violent disputes, *tumultos* and sporadic civil war that went on for several years. The result was that in 1810, when the renegade priest Hidalgo led the masses in a rebellion, the government was in no state to cope with it. Seeing their danger, the Spaniards and the Creoles sank their differences and, in due course, defeated him. But it had started something that could not be stopped. From then on Mexico was desolated by almost ceaseless civil wars and, after her break with Spain, became the body on which a long line of unscrupulous dictators gorged themselves.'

When Bernadino ceased speaking he sat smoking in silence for a few minutes, then changed the subject and spoke to Adam about his plans. He said that now Adam had seen most of the sights in Mexico City, he must spend a few days in other places of interest. In recent years archaeologists had discovered no fewer than ten thousand sites scattered over Mexico where there were remains of the ancient civilisations. It would probably take a century to excavate them all, but in the past fifty years a number of the finest had been cleared of jungle and restored. Oaxaca was one centre from which some of the best could be visited and Mérida, down in Yucatán, was another. Both could be reached with ease, as there were daily services of aircraft to them.

For several days past Adam's mind had been occupied mainly by thoughts of Chela; but this recalled to him the fact that his reason for coming to Mexico had been to collect material for another book and, loath as he was to leave her, he was eager to see these other great monuments of the past.

It was therefore decided that he should go down to Oaxaca on the coming Thursday, to do so sooner being ruled out by his having accepted an invitation from one of Chela's friends to dine on the Wednesday. Bernadino said that his office would get a seat for him on Thursday's aircraft and arrange accommodation for him in the Victoria Hotel at Oaxaca; then he airily waved away Adam's protests that he must pay for the trip himself. Adam could only thank him and again think how lucky he had been to be knocked down by the car of a generous millionaire.

On Monday morning they all returned to Mexico City. At the El Presidente Adam found waiting for him an invitation to lunch the following day at the Residence of the British Am-

E

bassador. The *grande-luxe* life led by the wealthy Mexicans had amazed him, as he had had no idea that anywhere in the world there still existed people who were served like feudal nobles. But this was another thing. It was an honour earned by his own achievements. At once he wrote out an acceptance and took it across the Reforma to the British Embassy in the Calle Lerna.

That night he and Chela had been asked to dine with some friends of hers at the Rivoli restaurant. He had had little experience of such places, but the perfect service of the well-groomed waiters and the décor of the place, with the wall cabinets filled with Sévres china, made him doubt if there could be a better restaurant in Paris. Afterwards they went on to the Jacaranda to dance and he thoroughly enjoyed another happy evening.

Next day, at two o'clock, he had a taxi take him out to the Residence. Their Excellencies received him most kindly. They had read, and praised, his latest book. The Enriquezes were well known to them and they congratulated him on his accident's having brought him into contact with people so well able to give him a good time while he was in Mexico.

A cocktail session lasted until a quarter to three, then they went in to lunch. Fourteen sat down to table. The majority were Mexicans, but they all spoke English; so Adam had no need to resort to Spanish, in which practice during the past week had enabled him to converse very freely. His neighbours were delighted when he expressed his admiration for their city, and when he said that he was going down to Oaxaca they plied him with information about things he must not fail to see while he was there.

For coffee and liqueurs they moved into a long drawing room which, as the building was a modern one, had one wall entirely of glass, through which the pleasant garden could be seen. Soon after they had settled down, Jeremy Hunterscombe joined them. Languidly the tall Wing Commander stretched himself out in a chair next to Adam, talked to him for some minutes about what he had been doing, then said:

'I've a little project I'd like to have a word with you about,

Gordon. Do you happen to be free for lunch tomorrow?'

When Adam replied that he was, Hunterscombe went on, 'Then come and have a bite with me at the Ritz.' With a grin he added, 'Sounds terribly posh, doesn't it? But actually it's just an old-fashioned hotel downtown in the Calle Madero. Not the sort of haunt for rich authors, but it suits chaps like me and I'll guarantee that the food's good.'

Adam thought the comparison in rather bad taste and swiftly replied that, until recently, he had often made his dinner off sandwiches at a coffee-stall; then they agreed to meet at the Ritz at two o'clock.

That evening Adam took Chela to the ballet, downtown at the Palace of Fine Arts. He was not a balletomane, but the performance had been cracked up to him so he expected something exceptional. In that he was disappointed. The first ballet he enjoyed, because it was a most colourful spectacle of Aztecs in their gorgeous robes and wonderful feathered head-dresses. But the others were only folk-dances of the previous century, which he found trite and boring. Afterwards they went on to dance at the Via Fontana.

On the Wednesday Adam stood for some while on the pavement of the Reforma endeavouring in vain to get a taxi. Then, to his surprise, in response to his upraised arm, a small yellow car pulled up in front of him, which already had two people and the driver squeezed into it. After a hasty exchange with the driver Adam learned that it was one of a fleet of such vehicles which plied up and down the main thorough-fare of the city, picking up and dropping single passengers wherever they liked along the route for the modest sum of a single *peso*.

As he clambered into the remaining free seat he thought it a splendid idea, and what a benefit it would be to Londoners if a similar service were instituted from Marble Arch along Oxford Street to the City and from Knightsbridge up Piccadilly through the Strand and Fleet Street to St. Paul's. A *peso* was only sevenpence, and for a shilling such a run would be cheap.

The communal taxi decanted him opposite the spacious Alameda Square, with its palm trees, gardens and the huge Centre of Culture which had window displays of books in every language. From there it was only five minutes' walk to the Calle Madero and he found the Ritz without difficulty.

It was far from pretentious, as to enter it one had to walk through a short arcade with shops displaying Mexican craftwork and souvenirs; but it had a comfortable cocktail lounge in which Hunterscombe was waiting for him.

During the hour that followed Adam grew to like the Ritz more and more. It had a pleasant old-fashioned air about it and a regular clientéle of well-to-do business men. The tables were set well apart, most of the waiters were of the friendly old-retainer type and the food was excellent; although, as he saw from the menu, the prices were reasonable.

It was not until he was enjoying a Mexican pudding of preserved pears, meringue and short pastry that their conversation became of any particular interest, and he unconsciously led up to it himself by asking if his host knew Monsignor Alberuque.

Hunterscombe gave him a swift glance and replied, 'Yes, slightly. What do you make of him?'

'I've met him only once and he gave me the shivers,' Adam said frankly. 'Why, I don't know, but those dead black eyes of his put my hackles up.'

'That rather surprises me, for he has tremendous charm. But he is certainly a queer fish and, curiously enough, to ask you what you knew about him was one of the reasons I asked you to lunch.'

'It surprises me that you should even have known that I'd met him.'

'Elementary, my dear Watson. You were down at Cuernavaca last week-end, and he is as thick as thieves with Chela.'

'I saw him only during one evening, so I know hardly anything about him,' Adam lied glibly. 'But why are you interested?'

Hunterscombe took a long pull at his cigarette. 'Look, old boy. You'll treat what I am about to say as confidential, I'm sure. The fact is we have reason to believe that there is trouble brewing in this country, and that Alberuque has a big finger in it.'

'What sort of trouble?'

'Possibly a revolution.'

Greatly intrigued, Adam began to fish for information by saying, 'I thought revolutions in Mexico were a thing of the past.'

'Most people do, but they are endemic here. It's in the blood of the people. Do you know much about Mexican history?'

'I've read quite a lot about the ancient civilisations and the Conquest, but I haven't bothered to go into all the complications since Independence.'

'Then on account of what I want to talk to you about, I must give you a short résumé.' Hunterscombe tapped out his cigarette and lit another. 'Apart from a few Indian risings, there was no serious trouble until Hidalgo led the rebellion of 1810. He made a mess of things; but one of his followers, José Morelos, took over and more or less got the better of the Spaniards and Creoles, who hated each other but teamed up to defend their wealth and privileges.

'Morelos as good as had the country in his hands, but he made the mistake of calling a Congress to proclaim a Republic. His preoccupation with the future led to his being caught napping and executed; so it was not until 1821 that Mexico actually gained her independence.'

'I know that much and quite a bit more,' Adam remarked.

'Maybe you do, chum,' replied the Wing Commander, brushing up his long moustache. 'But to make my point, I want to refresh your memory about what has been going on in this country for the past one hundred and fifty years. To continue. It was upon Morelos's programme that all the revolutions that followed were based. He proposed to confiscate the great estates of the rich and the Church and restore the land to the Indians. A royalist Colonel named de Iturbide, who had put paid to Morelos, took over; but he ratted on his Spanish pals and had himself proclaimed as Emperor Agustín I.

'In due course Iturbide was overthrown by an extraordinarily shifty customer, one Antonio de Santa Anna. He was like a cat with nine lives, or rather eleven, for between 1833 and 1855 there were eleven periods when he was master of Mexico. To get the masses on his side he started off by being very much to the Left; but he didn't give a damn for anyone but himself, and gradually watered down all the reforms that had been set in motion until the masses were back pretty much where they had started, with the rich and the priests jumping on their necks.

'The Texans didn't like him, so they decided to break away. That led to a civil war which ended in his defeat and capture by a lad named Sam Houston. He then bought his own freedom by giving Texas independence.

'The Mexicans did not like that and, in 1846, reasserting their claim to Texas led them into a war with the United States. They lost it, and it cost them not only Texas for good but also California—the best part of a million square miles of territory. In addition to that, when Santa Anna got into power again he was feeling hard up, so he sold a large part of Arizona and New Mexico to the Yankees for three million quid.'

Adam smiled. 'Then, by and large, he proved a pretty expensive President.'

'He certainly did. In eighteen years he reduced Mexico from the fourth largest country in the world to less than half its original size. Anyhow, the people were not only fed up about that, but because he had let the rich and the Church get back on their necks again. Then there emerged an extraordinary fellow named Benito Juárez. He was a full-blooded Zapotec Indian, one hundred per cent honest, a first-class General, a great law-giver and a puritan ascetic.

'Juárez led a successful rebellion against the reactionaries and brought in the Constitution of 1857. It went even further than the programme of Morelos. Not only was the Church forbidden to own property and priests and nuns were freed from their vows, but all privileges were abolished, it gave freedom to the Press and decreed free education for the children of all classes.

'The Church and the Conservatives weren't standing for that, so it resulted in a most bloody Civil War. Juárez won through but, by the time he had, the country was so disrupted that it was bankrupt. As French, Spanish and British investors could not get their money, their governments decided to intervene. Napoleon III sent out the Archduke Maximilian, backed by a French army, to become Emperor. Well, you know what happened to that poor well-meaning poop. Three years later Juárez did a magnificent job of work. It was he who created modern Mexico, and in 1872 he died in office. He was followed by one of his generals, Porfirio Díaz. Under him the pendulum swung back again. In his way he, too, was a patriot, but he was no believer in democracy. He ruled Mexico for thirty-four years—from 1876 to 1910. During his Presidency he spent Lord knows how many millions on ornate buildings and extravagant ceremonies, his idea being to make Mexico appear great in the eyes of visiting foreigners. But, of course, the money was squeezed out of the wretched people and, as from top to bottom his officials were open to bribery, the rich and the top priests again lived like fighting cocks. Under Díaz, Mexico became a Police State, and to pay for his ostentatious frivolities he played ducks and drakes with the nation's property. To his pals he sold at peppercorn price one-fifth of all the land in Mexico. One lucky boy acquired seventeen million acres, and another twelve million.

'The modern side of the picture is that he gave the cities modern drainage, drove broad avenues through their slums, created harbours that would take deep-sea ships, built railways and made the trains run on time. He played it skilfully with the Great Powers, too, by giving their industrialists concessions and exempting them from taxes; so that in his last eighteen years in office foreign investments here more than doubled.

'But it was a grim time for the masses and in 1910 a chap named Madero started agitating against him. *Tumultos* followed all over the country. The most successful risings were led by the ex-bandit Pancho Villa and a peasant named Emiliano Zapata. Old Díaz was forced to resign and went into exile.

'Madero succeeded him but he was an impractical idealist and did not last long. Naturally the Church and all the boys who had had such a good time under Díaz didn't want their lands taken from them and given to the peasants; so they ganged up against him. Mexico City itself became a battleground, with both sides shelling it to pieces. The Whites got the upper hand and Madero was arrested. He resigned in exchange for a promise that his life would be spared; but a drunken old Indian General, Victoriano Huerta, betrayed him, had him shot and went over to the other side.

'Believing that they were on to a good thing, his new pals made Huerta President; but he turned out to be a Mexican Nero, left the country to run itself and spent all his time as Master of Ceremonies at drunken orgies.

'That was in 1913. For the next seven years Mexico was in a state of anarchy and there were ten Presidents, one of whom held the job for only forty-six minutes. Villa fought Carranza, Obregón fought Villa, González fought Zapata, Calles fought Maytorena, Obregón fought Carranza and Carranza fought Calles. The lawlessness and slaughter was appalling. Mexico's then population of fifteen millions was reduced by a million dead.

'At last Alvaro Obregón got the upper hand. It was he who was mainly responsible for the new Constitution of 1917; but the struggle between the peasants trying to get a fair deal and the rich attempting to hang on to what they'd got has never really ceased, only gone underground. Just like Mexico's volcanoes, it erupts now and then, as in the Church-inspired rebellion of the Cristeros in 1926. So you can take it from me that after this long period of comparative quiet, as the majority of the people are still poverty-stricken, there may at any time be another eruption.'

For a moment Hunterscombe paused; then he concluded, 'The reason I've bored you with all this is because I want to bring home to you that every one of these eruptions has resulted in years of civil war and desperate unhappiness for millions of people.

When Hunterscombe ceased speaking, Adam remarked, 'I give you full marks as our Cultural Attaché, for being well up in the history of this country; but it strikes me as a little strange that you should be so concerned about the political situation.'

The lanky Wing Commander's bright-blue eyes held Adam's with a steady stare, then he said in a low voice, 'Look, pal. We are both Britishers so I can talk turkey to you. The

job of Cultural Attaché sometimes covers a multitude of—
well—other things. In my case, collecting info' for a certain
office not far from Whitehall. We get along pretty well with the
present government here and, anyway, the devil you know
is better than the devil you don't. So it is up to us to help in
any way we can to prevent another revolution in Mexico.'

After a moment he went on, 'Not only on account of our
interests here, but because we know what a revolution would
lead to. Judging by the horrors that took place in the Spanish
Civil War, the Spaniards have a pretty unpleasant reputation
for cruelty and there is a lot of Spanish blood in this country.
But the Spaniards are gentle little lambs compared to the
Indians. The sort of parties that took place in the free-for-all
that preceded 1920 are almost unbelievable. Captives had
the soles of their feet sliced off and were made to run across
open country until they were shot down. In one case, a sportsman who prided himself on his marksmanship had two hundred of them released just for target practice. Some were
forced to dance for hours until their hearts gave out. Others
were buried up to their necks then ridden over by cavalry.
Others again were tied to horses' tails and dragged at a gallop
until they became bleeding pulp. Scores of prisoners had their
ears lopped off and plantation foremen were nailed to the
doors of their homes, then left to die of thirst. We don't want
that sort of thing to happen again, do we?'

'My God, no!' Adam gave a shudder. 'But I don't see
how I can help to prevent it.'

'Oh yes, you can,' Hunterscombe replied quietly. 'You are
right in with old Enriquez, and the capitalists have plenty to
gain if the reactionaries came to power. What is more, you
are the lucky lad who has become the Señorita Chela's latest
boy-friend. We are convinced that she is in this thing up to the
neck, and that their contact is Alberuque. If you play it gently
you are in a position to win her confidence and get the lowdown on the tie-up between the Church and Bernadino and
his pals. That is what I want you to do, then report to me
every damn' thing you can get out of her and her family so
that we can turn it in to the Mexican government.'

Into Adam's mind there flashed a vision of his beautiful

Chela, arrested, being tried for treason and then condemned to spend the best years of her life in some awful prison.

Suddenly, seething with rage at the idea of being asked to betray her, he came to his feet and said icily, 'Thanks for the lunch. But what is going to happen in Mexico is not my problem. As for spying on friends who have been extremely kind to me, I'll see you in hell first.'

The Wing Commander appeared mildly amused by Adam's outburst. He said, 'Hold it, dear boy; hold it. Even if you haven't the undiluted patriotism of a pukka sahib, I'd be grateful if you'd refrain from making a scene in my favourite restaurant.'

Feeling rather foolish, Adam subsided and Hunterscombe went on, 'I accept your decision. All the same, you are wrong about it's not being your problem. God knows there is enough trouble in the world today and each area that blows up lessens the stability of others. If you are not interested in the welfare of your own country, that is reason enough for refusing to help me protect British commercial interests in Mexico. But there is another side to it which is the problem of us all. That is to do everything we can to prevent wars and civil wars from breaking out, in which many thousands of innocent men, women and children die violent deaths or have their lives ruined by some ghastly wound. We'll leave it at that, and I'll only suggest that you think it over.'

'I see your point,' Adam agreed. 'But I'm not going to involve my friends in trouble.'

Hunterscombe nodded. 'That's understandable. Now I'll revert to my official position as Cultural Attaché. It's part of my job to run the Anglo-Mexican Society. We meet once a week and get some visitor to give us a talk. He may be a visiting M.P., an economist, a man who has travelled a lot or a well-known sportsman. Authors, and particularly best-selling authors, are especially welcome. Can I persuade you to oblige?'

Adam had soon learned that he was not one of those fortunate people who can be interesting and amusing for three-quarters of an hour without first thinking out what he was going to say, making copious notes and rehearsing his speech;

so it would mean a full morning's work. He had often done it when he needed the publicity. Now he didn't; but, all the same, he felt it a duty to provide an evening's entertainment for British people living abroad, so he replied:

'Right ho! When is it to be?'

'We meet on Tuesday evenings. I've got a chap for next week; an engineer who builds bridges. How about the following Tuesday?'

'Fine. That's all right by me.'

'Thanks, chum. I'll drop you a line about time and place. Now, if you will forgive me, I must get back to the Embassy. But I can give you a lift up town.'

Twenty minutes later they parted with no unfriendly feelings.

After his lunch with 'our man' in Mexico, Adam pondered the situation very seriously. For the under-cover agents of both America and Britain to have got on to it, there could be no doubt that real trouble was brewing. It being reasonable to suppose that the Mexican security people were not a pack of fools, it could be assumed that they had, too. Anyhow by now they would know about it as, short of abandoning his career as a diplomat, Ramón could not evade turning in his report.

Bernadino had said that he meant to warn his friends, which implied that the Enriquezes, father and son, still had time to pull out and put themselves in the clear. But Adam knew to be wrong Jeremy Hunterscombe's assumption that Chela was acting as liaison between her family and Alberuque. Both parties might be involved in the conspiracy but, for some reason he could not fathom, on different levels. Bernadino had seen the red light; but even after reading the despatch that Ramón had been carrying, Alberuque had shown no uneasiness. That meant he and Chela would continue their subversive activities and would remain liable to be caught out.

During the siesta hours Adam tossed restlessly on his bed wondering whether he ought now to come clean with Chela and tell her that he had been a witness to her midnight meeting with the Monsignor and warn her of her danger. At length he decided that, if a suitable opportunity arose, he would; but otherwise, as it seemed that the conspiracy was still in its infancy, he would leave the matter until his return from Oaxaca.

At the party that night he was twice on the point of broaching the subject to her; but their conversation was interrupted by other good-looking gentlemen eager for Chela's company, so, none too happily, he left things as they were.

Next morning he was up early, had himself driven to the airport and took the seat that had been booked for him by Bernadino in the aircraft that left at 8.15 for Oaxaca. It was a flight of only an hour and a quarter. Not long after taking off, the plane flew right over Popocatepetl and he was able to stare down into the crater of the great volcano. Then they passed out of the Anáhuac valley to enjoy a vista of other mountains in the distance.

At the small, trim airport at Oaxaca he found that a car had been ordered for him. He was whisked away through the city and up a mile-long slope on its far side to the Hotel Victoria.

The hotel intrigued him, as he had never before seen one like it. Instead of being rectangular, it was round. The ground floor was a circular, open space from which one could see right up to the roof. Rising from this lounge, a broad, spiral staircase led to three upper floors of bedrooms. Adam was given one facing east. It looked down on a big swimming pool framed in banana palms and a variety of trees in flower. But it was the far view that entranced him. The hotel, set high on a slope, looked straight down a seemingly endless valley between two ranges of mountains. This splendid stretch of country had once been Cortés' estate, and from it he had taken his title, 'The Marquis of the Valley'.

Seeing that it was only a little after eleven o'clock, Adam descended the spiral staircase and had himself driven into the city. His driver spoke fluent English and, having parked the car in the palm-shaded square, accompanied him as his guide.

One side of the square was occupied by a long arcade above which rose the Governor's Palace and another by a still older Palace, both in the Spanish style. The latter was now a museum, its interior courtyard containing a number of stone images. Having seen so many in the museum in Mexico City, Adam went straight upstairs to see the antique jewellery, which the guide had described as fabulous. The finest of the items had been discovered in Tomb 7 at Monte Albán, which lay only a few miles away, and they were indeed very well worth seeing.

There were necklaces, ear-rings, breast ornaments, also elaborately chased axes, spear-heads and sceptres inlaid with gold, which were triumphs of the goldsmith's art, and a superbly engraved crystal cup.

They then visited the Cathedral and the Church of St. Dominic, which Adam found much more impressive. Over the entrance of the broad porch there was a brilliantly coloured and gilded carved ceiling, among the elaborate embellishments of which were the life-size faces of the leading Conquistadores. Along niches in the sides of the church there were many figures of saints, several of whom had Indian features; and one, with an ebony face, was obviously a Negro.

When Adam remarked on this, his well-informed guide told him that as the Spaniards had found the Indians a comparatively feeble people, incapable of prolonged heavy work, many thousands of Negroes had been imported who, on being given their freedom, had intermarried with the Indians, and this accounted for many modern Mexicans of the lower classes having negroid features.

Afterwards they walked back through the square and down a street to one side of the Governor's Palace, where there was a market. There were scores of stalls selling cotton garments, plastic goods and toys. Of the last there were such great quantities that Adam marvelled that the stallholders could make a living by selling them; but, as they obviously did, it argued that the Mexicans must be loving and generous parents.

Further down, on the right of the street, was the market proper: a great, high-roofed building along the narrow alleys of which hundreds of people were pushing past one another. The contents of the meat stalls looked revolting; but Adam was interested in the fish, many kinds of which he had never before seen. The fruits and vegetables were even more varied.

There were great piles of every kind known to Europe and the tropics: the largest oranges Adam had ever seen and mandarins as large as ordinary oranges.

When Adam commented on this abundance, his guide said, 'How our people would live without fruit and vegetables I do not know. But in that, God has been kind to Mexico. The land is so mountainous that fruits ripen in the lowlands many months before they do in the highland valleys, so we never lack for most kinds of fruit all the year round.'

Back at the hotel Adam had a late lunch, his siesta, then went downstairs for a swim. The floor below the big central lounge was occupied by a roomy bar and restaurant. After reading for a time while consuming a couple of Planter's Punches, he went in to dinner. As at lunch, he found the food passable but quite unpredictable. Sole Colbert was on the menu but, when it arrived, instead of being a whole fried sole split down the middle, with a big dab of parsley butter between the rolled-back sides, it was bits of some unidentifiable fish with a white sauce, served in a small round pot.

After his long day he went early to bed and by eleven o'clock was sound asleep. Shortly before midnight, he was roused by the opening of his door. Quickly switching on the light, he propped himself up on one elbow. To his amazement Chela, clad in a flowered silk dressing gown, was standing in the doorway.

For a moment he thought he must be dreaming. But she closed the door behind her, undid her dressing gown and let it fall to the floor. Standing there now only in a transparent nightdress that revealed her magnificent figure, she smiled at him and said:

'I've come to keep an appointment that we made only with our eyes nearly a thousand years ago.'

8

The Sweet Cheat Gone

In a second Adam was out of bed and had her in his arms. He had never known such bliss as he experienced during the quarter of an hour that followed. Chela was not a virgin. Far from fearing his embrace, or displaying any false modesty, she met him eagerly, yet unhurriedly, in a prolonged loving, the mounting pleasure of which carried them out of this world to a superb and utterly satisfying climax.

For a while they lay silent, his arms still about her and his head pillowed on her shoulder. At length he murmured, 'My beautiful, my wonderful one, how do you come to be here?'

'I drove down in my car,' she replied with a little laugh.

'But your father and family. Where do they think you are?'

'Here, although not for the special purpose of being with you. That our visits to Oaxaca should have coincided will be accepted as just a pleasant coincidence.'

'How clever of you, my sweet, to think of a plausible reason for your visit. Are you supposed to be staying with friends?'

They sat up and, after he had kissed her breasts, both lit cigarettes. Then she replied, 'Darling, you really know very little about me. I'm not altogether the playgirl that you must imagine me to be. Had it not been that we are in the school holidays I wouldn't have been able to give you so much time, because I am a teacher.'

He looked at her in amazement, and she laughed at him. 'Not a professional one exactly; but in term time, three times a week, I take classes in English and in Mexican history.'

'Well, I'll be damned! But that doesn't account for your being here.'

'No, there is another side to my voluntary work. I am one of the Board of Education's Inspectors and go to all parts of the country to report on conditions in the schools; so father is quite used to my going off for several days on my own. The reason I gave for making this trip was that I had been asked to inspect the schools in Oaxaca.'

'I take off my hat to you for giving your time to such work. Very few girls in your position would.'

'You are wrong about that. Several of my friends take junior classes two or three times a week; although as they haven't quite my—er—qualifications, they are not also Inspectors. You see, education in Mexico is terribly important, because such a large percentage of our people is hopelessly backward. It's so important that, a few years ago, the government made an appeal for everyone who was literate to teach at least one other person to read and write. That helped, of course, but we are still tragically short of trained schoolteachers.'

Adam then put the question he had been burning to ask. 'But tell me, beloved; how and when did you realise that we had known one another in a previous incarnation?'

'Immediately we got you into the car after we had knocked you down. Father is ordinarily so absorbed in his business affairs that he would have simply ordered that you should be given every care, sent you a fat cheque as compensation, then forgotten all about you. It was I who suggested that, instead of money, it would be better to give you an interesting time here. The moment I set eyes on you, I recognised you as Quetzalcoatl.'

He turned his head to stare at her. 'But Quetzalcoatl was a god.'

'A Man-God,' she corrected, 'and you must know his story. He is said to have been a golden-haired white man who arrived on our coast about A.D. 960. He travelled inland to Tula, which was then the great capital of the Toltecs, and ruled there as Priest-King for twenty years. Then the Toltecs were driven from Tula by my people from the north, and

Quetzalcoatl migrated with his warriors down to Yucatán. After that he went back to the sea, sailing to the west on a raft composed of snakes. But he promised to return; and ever since the Indians have been hoping that he would, to become again their leader and King.'

Adam nodded. 'Yes, I know. And when Cortés landed, as one of his Captains—Pedro de Alvarado I think it was—had a golden beard and hair, the Indians thought he was Quetzalcoatl and fell on their knees and worshipped him.'

'That's right. But they soon found out their mistake and they are still hoping that the real Quetzalcoatl will return to them.'

'But I thought that for a long time past all but a very few of the Indians had become Roman Catholics.'

Chela hesitated. 'Well . . . as I told you on the day we drove out to the pyramids, from the beginning they identified many of their gods with Christian saints. For example, St. Patrick is always represented with a snake at his feet and, as one of Quetzalcoatl's many attributes was power over snakes, they assume that the two were one and the same. But that doesn't matter in the least. What does is that they are deeply religious and observe the ceremonies of the Catholic Church.'

After a moment's silence, Adam said, 'From my childhood I have had dreams and visions of my previous incarnations, both as a Viking in Norway and as a Prince here in Mexico; but they are always disconnected episodes, so I really know very little about the life I led. It would be wonderful if you could fill in some of the gaps.'

'My returns to the past have been very patchy too, and there is really not much that I can tell you. I was the daughter of a Prince and became a priestess. The first I heard of you was that you were the King of Tula. My people defeated yours in a great battle outside Teotihuacán and you were captured. Weeks later the whole nation was mustered to witness a great ceremony. You were brought out from the Pyramid of the Moon, and I was one of the priestesses who scattered flowers in front of you. At the sight of you I nearly fainted. I had never seen such a wonderful man and I wanted to fall flat on my face at your feet.'

'Oh darling, did you?' Adam gave her a long kiss. 'And I felt just like that about you. In all my life I had never seen such a beautiful girl. And, although your features are quite different now, the same beauty radiates from you. But you didn't appear to be at all distressed that I was on my way to be sacrificed.'

'You weren't.'

'I believed I was. I thought my last hour had come and they were going to tear the living heart out of my body. My God, I was terrified!'

'Then you showed tremendous courage. You didn't look the least frightened. You kept on smiling at me and I was thrilled to death.'

'It was looking at you that helped me keep my courage up.'

'What an awful ordeal it must have been, walking all that way while believing you were going to be slaughtered. We, of course, all knew that it was only a ceremony to ask the gods whether they were willing to accept you. When they did, the jubilation was immense, and afterwards there was feasting for days.'

'My vision came to an end before that. Do you know what became of me then?'

'Only vaguely. When a Man-God was discovered by the priests, he was kept alive for a year after his ceremonial acceptance and lived in the greatest luxury, but was allowed no women until twenty days before the end of that year. Then he was given four brides with whom to enjoy himself until the twenty days were up. Having planted his sacred seed, as it was hoped, in all four so that they had children, one of whom might in due course prove acceptable as another Man-God, he went willingly to be sacrificed. I have no memories of what happened towards the end of that year, although I have an idea that I schemed like mad to be selected as one of your brides. The next thing I remember was being presented to you.'

'It wasn't till then I had an idea that they intended, after all, to sacrifice me. When I found out, I decided to make a fight for it. But I would never have got away if you had not thrown your shift over that bearer's dagger. You saved my life.'

'Knowing I had done so was worth it. That was the only thing I had to cling to when they took me to little bits afterwards.'

'Oh my darling, how awful!'

'Fortunately, I don't remember much about it, as I passed out soon after they started on me. But what happened to you?'

'I don't remember anything after I got away in the canoe. When I came to, I was lying in your arms in the car. For a few minutes I didn't realise I was Adam Gordon, and thought you were Mirolitlit. If the legend is right, I suppose I somehow managed to get back to my own people on the coast.'

She turned and kissed him. 'I'll tell you one thing, though. I was terribly disappointed to miss those twenty days. I'd made up my mind to tear those other girls' eyes out, so that I could have you all to myself.'

With a low laugh he pulled her to him. 'Then now's our chance to make up for lost time.'

When they had rested after another glorious bout, Chela said, 'I'm hungry.'

'So am I, and thirsty,' he agreed. 'It can't be much after one o'clock so there must still be people about. You pop into the bathroom, my sweet. Then I'll ring for the floor waiter and see what can be done.'

As Chela slipped out of bed and stood up, Adam for the first time had a full view of her without a stitch of clothing on. 'Stop!' he cried. 'Don't move. No, turn round. I want to look at you.'

As she stood there smiling at him, he took a deep breath. Then he whispered, 'Darling, you're marvellous. Many girls have pretty faces, but I would never have believed that any woman could have such an absolutely perfect figure. The legs of most girls are too short for their bodies, or their shoulders are too narrow for their busts. Some are spoilt by thick hips and fat bottoms; others are so stupid that in some way they manage to make their breasts stick out so much that it ruins their curves. But you! My God! In you I could believe that Venus has come to earth again.'

'For your especial pleasure, my dear Lord,' she laughed.

Scrambling out of bed, he took her hands, raised, dropped them and slid his down the satin of her sides and hips; then he closed his eyes, drew her to him and kissed her, meanwhile endeavouring to register the fact that he was the luckiest man in the whole world.

In due course the waiter brought Adam a bottle of champagne off the ice, some slices of galantine of chicken, white rolls and a plate of fruit. Laughing, they shared the single glass and fed one another with bits from the fork and spoon.

What Chela had said about Adam being a reincarnation of Quetzalcoatl had given him plenty to think about; for he saw now how his resemblance to the semi-mythical Man-God might be used to stir up a rebellion. But he did not believe for one moment that Chela had come down to Oaxaca and given herself to him on that account; so he was loath possibly to spoil things by telling her that he knew of her secret relations with Alberuque.

Instead, he put that out of his mind and surrendered himself to pure delight in her lovely presence, the feel of her smooth skin against his and the rich tones of her low voice.

They made love again, then slept; but Adam did so only fitfully, to rouse now and then and enjoy the sublime satisfaction of feeling Chela's warm body in his arms.

When first light came through the curtains he woke her to tell her that she must soon go back to her own room. Only half awake, she clung to him, glued her mouth to his, then murmured that she wanted to stay there for ever. Gently he turned her on her back and brought her to full consciousness by making love to her again. Afterwards, with happy sighs and many endearments, she slid out of bed, put on her night-dress and dressing gown and left him.

A few minutes later he decided to have an early swim. As he walked downstairs, his body seemed to him to have an unusual buoyancy, almost as though it could float. Mentally he was on top of the world and felt as though he owned it. To use a phrase, 'he would not have called God his uncle'.

It was still early, only about half past six, but the waiters were about; so, after his dip in the pool, he ordered an enormous breakfast. On going back to bed he kissed the pillow where Chela's head had lain, then buried his face in it and drew in the scent of her that lingered there. Soon afterwards he dropped off to sleep. When he woke he thought he had had a wonderful dream. As he turned over he saw the empty champagne bottle on the bedside table. His heart leapt with elation. It was no dream but had really happened. He then saw that it was twenty minutes to eleven. They had agreed to meet down in the lounge at eleven o'clock and Chela was going to drive him to Mitla. Jumping out of bed, he hurriedly shaved and dressed.

Down in the lounge, Chela greeted him, for the sake of appearances, with apparent surprise and they had a cup of coffee together before going out to her car.

Mitla was about an hour's drive away and they took the road that led straight as a die down the long, fertile valley. It was a section of the two-thousand-mile-long Pan-American highway, which runs from the United States frontier through Mexico City and right down to Guatemala. There was little traffic and the road was broad and smooth, so they made good going. On either side there stretched fields of maize, clumps of castor-oil plant with occasional coconut palms and paw-paws.

About halfway to Mitla they pulled up outside a church that had several enormous trees near it. Chela said they were water cypresses and that the largest was reputed to be three thousand years old. Getting out, they walked round the tree and estimated its gigantic trunk to be not less than a hundred and fifty feet in circumference.

The village nearby was the source of Mexico's famous black pottery, and in a rickety shed they watched an old crone make a perfectly symmetrical vase out of a lump of greyish clay. The people there still scorn the potter's wheel and she made the vase from long serpentine coils of clay, which she twisted between her hands. From her incredibly wrinkled face she looked to be a hundred, but when Adam asked her age she said she thought she was about sixty.

To reach Mitla, they took a side road for the last few miles. The village stood on a slight rise. Beyond it was a large church built, as was the custom of the Spaniards, on the site of the principal temple pyramid, when such pyramids were not too big to pull down. Two hundred yards in front of the church was the best-preserved of the three great square courts they had come to see. The sides of all of them consisted of masses of stone with some thirty steps down to the court, in the centre of which was a low, square, sacrificial platform. On top of these thick ramparts were the priests' quarters. The buildings were only about twelve feet high but had lintels above the doorways weighing perhaps twenty tons and their walls appeared to be magnificently carved in geometric designs.

Waving towards them a cigar she was smoking, Chela pointed out that they were not carvings in the ordinary sense, but a vast number of thin stone bricks with different-shaped ends; so that when built up in layers they formed intricate patterns. They were the work of the Zapotecs and no other remains at all like them existed in Mexico.

Back at the Victoria, they lunched, lazed away the afternoon, bathed, dined and went early to their rooms. Soon afterwards Chela came along to Adam's, and again they took wonderful delight in each other.

For a good part of the day Adam had been wondering how best he could broach the subject of the revolution to Chela without mentioning his knowledge of her secret association with Alberuque or breaking his implied promise to Jerry Hunterscombe, and at length he had decided that he would do so while keeping Hunterscombe's name out of it. So when they had settled down he said:

'You know, I lunched the other day at the British Embassy. A chap who was there gave me a rather alarming bit of news. Of course it may only be a baseless rumour, but he seemed convinced that a revolution is brewing. Have you heard anything of the sort?'

He feared she might say 'no', which would make it difficult

for him to reopen the matter; so he was greatly relieved when she replied :

'Darling, I can have no secrets from you. What he said is true. And, as the subject has come up, I may as well tell you that I am one of the people who want to bring about a revolution. For over four hundred and forty years the people to whom Mexico belongs have been little better than slaves. Governments come and governments go. Many of them have promised reforms, but nothing really gets done, and today the peasants are worse off than they have ever been. A few days ago you asked me if I was a Communist. Well, I suppose I am—a Christian Communist.'

'Christ preached resignation and Karl Marx advocated the use of violence, so their doctrines are incompatible,' Adam remarked.

'That may be. I want the Indians to own the land, the mines, the banks, everything, and before long they are going to.'

'I recall your telling me that revolutions were always led by the white-collar workers and that the government had succeeded in muzzling them and the trade-union bosses by making this a Welfare State for that class. That being so, how can the Indians hope to overturn the government, without intelligent leaders?'

'By sheer weight of numbers. Besides, they will have leaders. They will be led by the priests.'

That was what Adam had come to suspect, and he said, 'Then that explains why you regard the movement as Christian-Communist. But it will mean that the priests must abandon their Christian principles. Because there is bound to be bloodshed and lots of it. There will be another Civil War, and think of the horrors that took place in the earlier ones.'

She shook her head. 'There will be no Civil War, because the masses will rise as one man. It will all be over in twenty-four hours.'

'You seem to have forgotten that the government have an army and will not scruple to use it.'

'Darling, if you knew more about Mexico you would realise that, in one way, we are a very lucky country. Anyone who tried to invade Mexico would have our good neighbour Uncle Sam down on him like a ton of bricks. So by comparison with other nations our Defence Budget, per head of population, is minute. We have an army, but it is only a tiny one for show purposes. By far the greater number of men who could put on a uniform are the militia. They do only an hour or two's drill on Sunday afternoons. But they have weapons that they could use if need be and, as they are peasants for the rest of the week, they will be on our side.'

'I see,' said Adam thoughtfully. 'And when is this party due to take place?'

'I'm sorry, dearest, but I'm under oath not to disclose that. It will before very long, though, and I'll be in the forefront of the battle.'

For a few moments Adam remained silent, wearing a worried look, then he said, 'Must you? Why should you be? From what you've told me, it is clear that you are taking part in organising this thing. Isn't that enough? I understand your sympathy for the poor down-trodden Indians, but it is unreasonable that a girl like you should go to the length of making yourself one of their leaders. Being mixed up in a revolution can be damn' dangerous. You might easily get killed or, if things went wrong, be sentenced to spend the best years of your life in prison.'

'That is a risk I must take. And just now you said "a girl like you". How very little you know about me, darling. To start with, my father was not married to my mother and the odds are that Bernadino is not my father. I'm almost certainly a bastard and quite certainly a Mestizo with lots of Indian blood in me. There is more to it even than that. Last week, in the village I took you to, you saw that poor little boy humping a great jerry-can of water. Well, when I was his age I lived in an Indian village. Barefoot and clad in stinking rags, I did that many a time myself. That's why I mean to fight for my people.'

Adam turned to stare at her in astonishment and she asked with a little smile, 'Are you shocked at finding me after all to be only a tart's by-blow?'

'Good Lord, no! That makes you no wit less adorable.

And what does it matter who your mother was? It's your own personality that counts, and you created that yourself in your past incarnations.'

'Of course that's so. I was only pulling your leg.'

'What, about the whole thing?'

'Oh no. It wasn't until I was ten that I became the Señorita Chela Enriquez.'

'There must be an extraordinary story behind all this. Do tell it to me.'

'I'd like to, because I want you to know everything about me.' After lighting a cigarette, Chela went on, 'I'm twenty-six, so it must have been some twenty-seven years ago that Father—or Bernadino, as I suppose I ought to call him—was living in Monterrey. That was before he had increased the fortune he inherited to millions, but he was already very well-off and the managing director of a big company there.

'My mother was a hostess in a night club; and you know what that meant in those days. She must have been very lovely as a girl, although, as I remember her, she had sadly gone to seed. Anyhow, he took her out of this dive, made her his mistress and set her up in an apartment. Three months later Bernadino formed an amalgamation with some other companies, moved his office to Mexico City and paid mother off with quite a nice sum of money.

'A month or so after Bernadino left her, mother found that she was pregnant; but it may not have been with his child because, knowing that the money he had given her would not last indefinitely, she had begun to use her pleasant apartment to receive gentlemen on a cash basis. All the same, she attempted to father me on to him.

'Bernadino would not be where he is today if he were not a tough egg, and he wasn't falling for that one. His reply to her letter was to send one of his people down to see her and tell her that if she persisted in this nonsense he would have her put in prison. In Mexico, you know, rich men used to be able to get that sort of thing done to people without influence, on a trumped-up charge, for the price of quite a moderate bribe.

'Naturally, mother drew in her horns and for a while I

believe made quite a good thing out of whoring. But a few years later she was fool enough to fall for a brute of a man. He drank like a fish and spent all her money. The time came when she had to sell her apartment and move from one place to another till they were living in the slums, and he drove her out every night to work as a street-walker.

'From the age of seven I can remember the ghastly life we lived: the man always stinking of drink and beating up mother if she did not bring home enough money; never enough food to eat and the place filthy from neglect. The end came when I was just over nine. The man was more than usually drunk one night and tried to rape me. Mother hit him over the head with the pestle with which she ground our maize. Whether she killed him we'll never know. I hope she did, but I doubt it.

'Anyhow, she thought she had; so she jammed our few belongings into a wicker basket and we beat it back to the Indian village where she had been born. When she had been moderately prosperous she had never sent her family any money; but the poor are always generous, so her people took us in. After that we lived like pigs. Six of us sleeping on the floor in a tumbledown shack. But at least people were kind to me and we were free of the man.

'Mother was already ill with an awful hacking cough and it turned out that she had consumption. The hospitals were only for the better-off, so nothing could be done for her and she died just before my tenth birthday. But before she died she made an attempt to save me from the usual fate of a wretched Indian child.

'She had secretly kept one quite good ring. With the money it fetched, she bought me a pretty dress, shoes, stockings and had my hair done. Then she wrote a letter and sent me with it to Bernadino.'

'What, on your own at the age of ten!' Adam exclaimed.

'Yes. Children who have lived as I had are far more grown-up at that age than children of the upper classes when they are fourteen. All I felt was intense excitement at going for the first time on a train, and amazement when I saw the great buildings in Mexico City. But everyone was kind and helpful.

They gave me sweets and sandwiches and a kind old lady found out for me where Bernadino's office was and took me there from the station.

'When I got there I was a bit scared, and going up in the lift frightened me out of my wits. But when the receptionist wanted to take the letter from me I clung to it and insisted, as I had been told, that I must give it to Bernadino personally. Fortunately he was in, so I was taken through to him.

'He read the letter and asked if I knew its contents. "Yes," I said. "I am your daughter and mother wrote it when she was dying. She says that for old times' sake you must take care of me."

'Then he sat there staring at me. For how long I don't know. It seemed to me to be for hours, but I am sure it was for a good ten minutes. During that time I suppose he made up his mind that he would like to have a girl, because his wife had given him only a son—Ramón, who was then twelve years old—and had died when he was only an infant.

'At last he smiled at me and said, "Yes, you are a pretty little thing, and you are my daughter. Your name from now on is Chela Enriquez. Remember that—Chela Enriquez. You must do your best to forget the past. Never, never mention it. When anyone asks you about yourself you are to tell them I married your mother in Monterrey eleven years ago, but that shortly afterwards we secured an annulment. Since then you have lived with her there in moderate comfort. Now, what would you like best of all things in the world?"

' "A plate of roast pork, please," I burst out.

'He roared with laughter and said, "From now on you shall have roast pork every day, if you wish. And as many sweets as you can eat and all the toys that money can buy. Because you are my daughter, Chela Enriquez." Then his eyes hardened and he added, 'But should you forget that, and ever tell anyone of the life that I gather from your mother's letter you have been leading, it will be as though an evil fairy had waved her wand. For you, the good things of life will vanish overnight and I will send you back to that squalid Indian village."

'He had me taken to a convent and there I was given special

tuition. Being fairly intelligent, I soon caught up on the schooling I had missed. From time to time Bernadino came to see me and brought me wonderful toys. At the age of seventeen I became a member of his household. He had skilfully prepared the way and everyone accepted me as his daughter by a second marriage that had not succeeded. I think he even put it about that he had become infatuated with an Indian woman then, realising the damage having married her must do him, quickly got rid of her. Anyhow, I'm happy to think that I've never given him cause to regret having made me what I am today.'

When Chela had ceased speaking, Adam murmured, 'What an extraordinary story. Oh darling, how I feel for you at having been through the horror of those early years.'

'No,' she replied, 'you needn't. I've no doubt that my mother was paying off a most unpleasant time that she had given that awful man in a previous incarnation, and that the time had come for me to learn what it is like to suffer dire poverty in childhood. Anyhow, I've no regrets about that. It was a valuable experience. But you understand now how deeply I feel for the sufferings of my people.'

'Of course I do.'

'Would you,' she asked, 'be willing to give your help in the attempt that my friends and I are about to make to redeem them?'

It was the question that Adam had been expecting and he had already made up his mind to refuse. 'No darling,' he said gently. 'If you personally were in danger, I'd willingly risk my life to save you. I'm sure you know that. But to become involved in a political showdown that is none of my business is quite another matter. I'm afraid, too, that you are being over-optimistic and that your attempt will end in a blood-bath. I sympathise with the hard lot of the Indians, but in this affair I'm going to stand on the sidelines. Then, if things do go wrong, I'll still be on hand to do my damnedest to get you out.'

She gave a heavy sigh. 'I'm sorry you feel like that, because I'd rather counted on you. Still, there it is. Let's forget it for the moment and make love again.'

Grateful that she had not pressed him, he readily agreed and, without further serious conversation, they spent the rest of the night much as they had the previous one.

Next morning they drove to Monte Albán. It was much nearer than Mitla and the way led in snake-like bends up a steep hillside. When they reached the top, Adam found the ruins and their situation overwhelming. They occupied a long, broad plateau, several hundred feet in height, enclosed on every side by deep valleys and, beyond them, great ranges of mountains. Pyramids had been constructed which framed an oblong area two hundred yards wide and half a mile long. Some were still grass-covered, others had scores of steep steps leading down into the arena. It dwarfed any modern stadium and, when fully occupied, could have held countless thousands of people.

At the far end of it Chela showed Adam a row of flat, carved stones about five feet high, which had been set into the base of one of the low pyramids. On them were carved figures with a variety of features. One was obviously a Negro, another a Chinese, others clearly types of European, Asiatic and Indian. They represented a prehistoric gallery representative of a United Nations; but how an artist of that remote era could ever have known and portrayed such a variety of races seemed to Adam a mystery, and he exclaimed:

'But this is extraordinary! The archaeologists say that this place was founded about 500 B.C. Another two thousand years elapsed before Cortés and his Spaniards arrived here. These are totally different types of men—white, yellow and black—so how could the early Mexican Indians ever have known about them?'

Chela smiled. 'It is accepted now that Columbus did not discover America. He only rediscovered it after the appalling black-out of knowledge that descended on the peoples of Europe during the Dark Ages.'

'Yes, that's so. The Norsemen explored part of the North American coast, established colonies there and called it the Vineland. But that was not until the tenth century, only five hundred years before Columbus, and there is not even a suggestion that they knew of the existence of Mexico and South America.'

'But other people did, and hundreds of years earlier. In the time of Minos, the Cretans were a great sea-faring people. It is quite probable that they crossed the Atlantic. That would not have been anywhere near so great a feat as that of Pharaoh Necho's sailors who sailed right round Africa and came home up the Red Sea. It is as good as certain that, long before Christ, the Phoenicians established trading posts here, because their alphabet and the Mexican had definite similarities. Then, much later still, but a thousand years before Columbus, there were the Irish. They colonised parts of the Amazon and it is said that tribes of white Indians still living there in the jungles are their descendants. The Norsemen, too, went right up the Amazon to Peru, then ventured on across the Pacific. It is recognised now that the Polynesians in Tahiti and other islands owe their fair skins and the roots of their language to them. So, you see, it is not really surprising that here on Monte Albán you should see the carved portrayals of many different races.'

Adam shook his head. 'It is quite enough that you should be so beautiful. To be erudite as well is almost overdoing it. If Athene had been a man, I'd say he'd had a roll in the hay with Venus and you were the result of it.'

They passed the rest of their lovely day swimming, sun-bathing and endlessly discussing the fascinating subject of their past lives. After they had dined she said to him, 'I have some work to do, so I'm going up to my room. I'll be seeing you.'

For a while he read in the lounge, then he too went up-stairs. In bed he lay forming exciting mental pictures of her with glowing anticipation of another glorious night of love-making. Time passed, eleven o'clock, twelve, but still she failed to join him. At last, overcome with impatience, he got out of bed, put on his dressing gown and tiptoed along to her room.

Aghast and shattered, he found it empty and with no trace of her. Hurrying downstairs, regardless of what the night clerk might think, he verified the number of her room. He had been to the right one, but the desk clerk said, 'The Señorita Enriquez left in her car for Mexico City an hour and a half ago.'

She had said 'I'll be seeing you', but not when; so had practised a cheat upon him. Furious and inconsolable, he had to accept that, for the time being at least, he had lost her.

9

A Dark Ceremony

IN THE morning, as early as he thought permissible, Adam telephoned the penthouse in the Avenida Presidente Masarik, only to be told that Chela was not there. Then, as it was a Sunday, thinking she might have gone to the house at Cuernavaca, he tried that, but with the same result. This led him to suppose that she had broken her journey to pass the night somewhere on the road, would attend Mass in the morning and would be back in Mexico City at latest by the afternoon.

On enquiry he found there was no morning flight to the capital, so he would have to take an evening plane. In an endeavour to distract his mind, he spent a couple of hours mooching round the town, bathed twice and tried in vain to settle down to a book; but the day seemed interminable. Hour after hour he badgered his wits for an explanation of Chela's extraordinary conduct. He could think of only one, and that made him utterly miserable.

She had asked for his help in the coming revolution and he had refused it. Bitterly he recalled the midnight meeting between her and Alberuque and overhearing the Monsignor speak of the 'stranger' who could prove such a great asset to their cause, and how she must secure his help even if, by inference, she had to sleep with him. That he was that 'stranger' he no longer had a shadow of doubt. Chela's revelation, that in his Mexican incarnation he had been Quetzalcoatl, was ample proof of that. They meant to use him as a figurehead with which to rouse the passions of the Indians. The sight of him, a near-giant, with his red-gold hair and beard, when presented to an already prepared mob, would send them into battle howling with fanaticism.

Yet it seemed impossible to believe that his beautiful Chela, who had given herself to him with such passion, was cold at heart, really cared nothing for him and had just allowed herself to be used as the tool of a scheming priest. There was, too, their wonderful link from the past. Their miraculous coming together again after nearly a thousand years. Surely that unique experience must mean as much to her as it did to him? Nevertheless, she had abandoned him without even a word of farewell, and on the evening after he had refused her his help; so what other explanation for her behaviour could there possibly be?

At last he was in the aircraft on his way back to Mexico City. As soon as he reached his hotel he telephoned the penthouse again, but she had still not arrived. On the chance that he might get news of her he asked to speak to either Bernadino or Ramón, but both were away and were not expected home until the following morning.

After another night of misery he rang up again. This time Ramón came on the line. He had just returned from spending the week-end at Cuernavaca. No, Chela was not there and they were not expecting her. She was away on one of her tours inspecting schools, so might now be in any one of half a dozen towns. Then he asked, 'Do you happen to be free for lunch today?'

When Adam replied that he was, Ramón said, 'Then come and lunch with me at the Bankers' Club. It's on the top floor of the Bank of Mexico building. That is just past the Palace of Arts and the entrance to the Avenida de Mayo. I'll be expecting you at about two o'clock.'

Thankful that he would have something later in the day to distract his mind and, perhaps, learn something of Chela's movements, Adam mooned away the morning. He arrived at the Bank of Mexico absurdly early; so on seeing that there was a Sandborn's next door, to kill time he went in to buy himself a drink.

There were a number of Sandborn restaurants in the city and he had heard them likened to Lyons in London,

F

although, in addition to being restaurants and selling food, Sandborn's did a big trade in picture postcards, patent medicines, beauty preparations and numerous utility lines. This downtown one was a fine, lofty old building, the interior walls of which were lined with colourful patterned tiles, and it had a minstrels gallery. The waitresses were mostly Indian girls; all of them were dressed in national costumes with big bows on their dark hair and long streamers down their backs. The place was packed with people, and Adam did not wonder after he had found a seat and had a look at the menu, for it offered a fine choice of dishes and the prices were most reasonable.

A quarter of an hour later he walked into the big, marble entrance hall of the bank and was whisked up to the top floor in a lift. From what he had already seen of the way rich Mexicans lived, he had expected the club to be luxuriously equipped, and he was not disappointed. Elegance and comfort could hardly have been better combined. Ramón was there and greeted him cheerfully, then they sat down to drinks.

Adam saw no reason why he should not disclose that Chela had been down in Oaxaca at the same time as himself, but his hope of locating her through Ramón was disappointed. Apparently she went off on these trips fairly frequently and on this occasion she had said she would be away for about ten days; usually she left a note of her itinerary so that letters could be forwarded but, apparently, this time she had forgotten.

Adam guessed that to be because she had intended to spend several days with him at Oaxaca, but that was now no consolation. Their talk then turned to other matters and, halfway through an excellent lunch, Ramón asked about his guest's future plans.

'I really haven't made any,' Adam admitted. 'My object in coming to Mexico was largely to gather background material for a new book. Of course I shall go down to Yucatán and, perhaps, Palenque. Are there any other places that you think are particularly worth seeing?'

'Yes, plenty,' came the prompt reply. 'You should certainly see Taxco, the centre of our silver industry, and the beautiful old churches at San Miguel de Allende. Why don't you hire a car with a driver-guide and make a round trip? You could go north to the picturesque old Spanish town of Querétaro, across to San Miguel, then to Guanajuato, where there is a lovely eighteenth-century theatre, on to San Diego then down to Morelia. From there it is a delightful drive through San Luis Caliente which would bring you round to Taxco in the south, then back to Mexico City. None of these places is much more than a hundred miles from the next, so you could make the trip easily in a week and have plenty of time for sight-seeing.'

The ancient ruins were of much more interest to Adam than Spanish architecture, but, as Chela had not returned direct from Oaxaco to the capital, it now seemed unlikely that she would be back for another week, and the suggested trip would keep him occupied; so he agreed that it was a good idea.

Ramón promptly volunteered to send him an itinerary, arrange about hotel accommodation and engage a reliable driver-guide. Then, after hesitating for a moment, he gave Adam a quick look and went on, 'I suppose that, as an author wanting to get as much information as possible, you talked to the guides you had down at Oaxaca not only about the sights they were showing you but about all sorts of other things: the conditions they live under, education, politics and so on?'

As Chela was supposed to have been inspecting schools, Adam naturally refrained from saying that he had had a professional guide only for his first morning, and thought it easiest to reply, 'Yes.'

'Did any of them happen to say anything about unrest among the Indians?' Ramón asked casually.

It was a subject which now deeply concerned Adam, so he was glad that it had been brought up. With the object of drawing his host, he replied with a smile, 'I take it you would not ask unless you believed there to be.'

Ramón was silent for a minute while he ran a hand over his crinkly hair, then he said, 'I see no reason why I shouldn't tell you. My job at our Embassy in Washington is Security. The F.B.I. picked up some indications of possible trouble and I was sent back to inform the Minister. When I got here I found that our own people were on to it that there is something brewing. They wouldn't be much good at their job if they hadn't. Anyhow, I was ordered to remain here for a bit and lend a hand collating such information as can be picked up.'

Adam was wondering how much Ramón knew about Chela's activities and if he would in due course try to pump him about her. Smiling again, he asked, 'Is that why you asked me to lunch?'

'Gracious no!' Ramón's surprise appeared quite genuine. 'It was my offer to get a good guide for you that led me to ask you about the ones you had at Oaxaca. You see, people of that kind often let off steam about the government to foreigners in a way they never would to anyone like myself, and I just thought you might have heard something.'

To draw Ramón further, Adam had to play a card; so he said, 'As a matter of fact, I did. I gather that the peasants have been disappointed time and again about promises that they should be given the land, and they have become so fed up that they are likely to rise in a mass and take it.'

Ramón nodded. 'That's it. Was any mention made of the Church?'

'No. Is it involved in this?'

'Yes, up to the eyes. The Church was sitting pretty as long as the Spaniards ruled the roost here. It ran a virtuous sideline of protecting the Indians from exploitation and in the meantime accumulated enormous wealth. But after Independence it was forced to disgorge, and ever since it has been our nigger in the woodpile, continually inciting trouble in the hope of getting its ill-gotten gains back.'

'I see; and it is able to make use of the peasants because the great majority of them are such devout Catholics?'

'Devout Catholics! Don't you believe it. At heart they are every bit as pagan as they were a thousand years ago. They attend the ceremonies of the Church, of course, but only because all pagans believe that any god may play them a dirty trick if they fail to propitiate him. And to them the white man's God must seem pretty powerful. When they show particular devotion to a Christian saint they are really asking some favour from one of their own deities with whom they have identified him. What is more, most of them come to Mass on Sunday morning after having participated in a good old-fashioned blood sacrifice of a cock and a hen the previous evening. The priests know that perfectly well and make no effort to stop it. All they care about is the hold they have over the people.'

'I must say I find this a bit surprising.'

'It's common knowledge. Ask anyone. The Indians are so riddled with paganism that they don't even bother to hide it. Right here in the middle of Mexico City there is a Witches' Market.'

'Oh, come! You're pulling my leg.'

'I'm not, I assure you. I'll take you to it after lunch if you like.'

'I'd be most intrigued. But what do you deduce from all this?'

'That the Church is planning the overthrow of our agnostic government by inciting the peasants to rise in a *jacquerie*. If it succeeds, all hell will be let loose. The Indians and Mestizos have always hated our guts. By "our" I mean Mexicans of pure Spanish descent and the many Americans and Europeans who live here for business reasons. Perhaps one can't blame the Indians, but they are not a pleasant people. Most of those in central Mexico are descended from the Aztecs and they were about the cruellest race the world has ever known. If they did get the bit between the teeth there would be whole-sale arson, pillage, rape; and anyone who had any money would be hideously tortured to make him hand it over.'

'What are the chances of nipping this threat of revolution in the bud?' Adam enquired.

'It's hard to say. The damn' thing is so nebulous. So far we have not got a line on any of the leaders. It seems to be like a sort of epidemic and is a general movement right through the country. I suppose it might be stymied if we pulled in all the priests and put them behind bars. That has been done before—in part at least. On one occasion when the Jesuits were getting above themselves their quarters were simultaneously surrounded and every single one of them was arrested overnight. But an operation of that kind now could prove the fuse to set off the dynamite and launch ten million Indians on the warpath.'

For a few moments Ramón's brown eyes were lowered, as he stared unhappily down into his balloon brandy glass; then he said, 'I suppose the chaps you talked to down at Oaxaca didn't mention any names?'

Adam shook his head. 'No, it was just general grumbling about the awful conditions in the small towns and villages, and the sort of vague, sullen threats of the discontented that one does not take very seriously.'

Ramón looked up. 'But it is serious, believe me. That's why I have decided to ask your help. It only occurred to me a while back when we spoke of this week's tour you have decided to do. As I mentioned, the ordinary people are very cagey with anyone they feel might report what they say; but they talk pretty freely to foreigners. In the evenings you will be sitting about in cafés and, no doubt, talking to people. You might pick up quite a lot. Should you hear anything worth while, I'd be awfully grateful if you'd let me know.'

Adam considered the matter for a long moment. When down at Cuernavaca, while eavesdropping under the bridge, he had assumed that Bernadino was involved. That night, the fact that Chela had purloined Ramón's briefcase to let Alberuque see his papers had indicated that, although the capitalists and the Church might both be planning a revolution, they probably had different aims and were certainly not working hand-in-glove. Yet Hunterscombe had been of the opinion that both were involved and had asked him to spy on Chela, Alberuque and Bernadino. But now, from what Ramón had just said, it was clear that Hunterscombe was mistaken. The capitalists might not like the government, but regarded the Church and the Indians as a menace, so would do all they could to maintain the *status quo*. Therefore, when Bernadino had spoken of warning certain people, he had not been referring to fellow conspirators but, most probably, telling the principal executives in his organisation to keep their eyes open for signs of coming trouble. This new assessment put the Enriquezes, father and son, in the clear; but it still left Chela vulnerable if the part she was playing was discovered.

He had never subscribed to Chela's belief that if the masses rose everywhere the government would be overwhelmed in a matter of hours. The Mexican regular army might be small, but it had tanks. There was, too, an air force that would probably obey orders to machine-gun mobs, and the police could be counted on to use their pistols and tear gas. Against even a small minority so equipped, the largest force of malcontents could not swiftly prevail. Ferocious fighting must result. Many thousands of innocent people caught up in it would lose their lives or have their property destroyed.

All that Hunterscombe had said supported that belief, and Adam now decided that he could not possibly refuse to do what he could to prevent such tragic happenings. As far as Chela was concerned, he thought it highly improbable that during his proposed trip he would meet anyone who had even heard of her and, should her name be mentioned in connection with the conspiracy, he could suppress it.

Ending his long silence, he said, 'All right. I don't suppose there is much chance of my picking up anything of value, but I'll keep my ears open and get in touch with you on my return if I have anything of importance to report.'

'Many thanks,' Ramón smiled. As by then they had finished their coffee and liqueurs, he added, 'Now let's go to see the Witches' Market.'

Adam had expected the market to be hidden away in some building and that they would be questioned by watchers before they were allowed to enter it; or, at least, that it would be in some narrow street in the heart of a noisome slum. On the contrary, although it was in a poor part of the city, it faced on to a broad boulevard and several cars were drawn up in front of it.

The market consisted of two avenues lined with, in all, some thirty or forty small shops. In front of each was an array of a score or more sacks open at the top to display a variety of dried herbs. Beside each array of sacks sat a witch. Most of them were fat and elderly, but none of them looked particularly evil, and with cheerful greetings they cried their wares.

But it was the windows of the shops that at once caught Adam's eye. They were filled with grotesque masks, dried bats, rats and other animals, the bald, fleshless heads of vultures; toads and newts in jars of spirit, rosaries made from the skulls of small animals and glass bottles partly filled with most sinister-looking concoctions.

'Apart from practising witchcraft,' Ramón told Adam, 'these old beldames do a big trade in herbs. Most of us tend to forget that nearly all modern medicines are derived from herbal remedies of the distant past. Many, too, have never been studied by our research chemists, so are not available to qualified practitioners. For example, you see that pile of nuts over there. If you always carry two of them—a male and a female—in your pocket, should you be a victim of piles you will never suffer from them again.'

'Thank goodness I don't. But is that really so?'

'Yes; many people swear by them. A European Ambassador who left here some months ago found them so efficacious that he recently wrote to a chap in our Foreign Office asking to have half a dozen pairs sent him for friends of his who were sufferers.'

Adam pointed to a string, from which dangled several vegetables looking like carrots, but having roughly the form of a man, with legs ending in points. 'I imagine those are mandrakes. What do they use them for?'

'Oh, they grind them up with other horrors to make potions. For quite a small sum they will sell you a concoction that will bring your rival out in boils; and under the counter they keep stuff that, if you pay them well enough, will ensure your old aunt's dying a pretty painful death, apparently from natural causes, so that you can inherit her money.'

'But do they really cast spells?'

'Indeed they do. As I've told you, the mentality of the Indian peasants has hardly advanced at all since Cortés arrived here. They are so devil-ridden with superstition that if they think they have been bewitched they develop the ill that they have been cursed with. There is no scientific explanation of how such physical changes take place, but there is no doubt that they do.'

Ramón dropped Adam at his hotel and that evening sent him several pages of typed notes, listing the hotels into which he had booked him and places of interest he should not fail to see during his trip. Next morning a cheerful-looking Mestizo, who introduced himself as Felipe Durán, arrived with a car and they set off.

They reached Querétaro soon after midday; so Adam was able to have a good look round the old Spanish town before lunch, then do the forty miles on to San Miguel de Allende where he was to stay that night. In the fine church there he got into conversation with an elderly priest. Secretly amused by the thought that he was now an unofficial secret agent, Adam entered on his new role and asked him about his work.

The priest said that there was always plenty to do but, unfortunately, never enough money to do it with. As in most parishes, they had many old and ailing for whom the State did nothing, and the Church was hard put to it to give them even a modicum of the attention they needed.

Taking the hint, Adam produced a hundred-peso note as a contribution to the poor-box. The priest, from being merely polite, became quite cordial, showed him the treasures of the church, asked him to what other places he had been and, when he learned that Adam was gathering material for a book, said, 'I hope that when you write it you will not, like most foreign authors, tell only of the modern Babylon that Mexico City has become, but also describe the real Mexico and the harsh life led by her people.'

'Is their lot a very hard one?' Adam enquired naively.

'Deplorable,' replied the priest with a shake of the head. 'When I was a younger man I had a parish up in the Sierra Madre Occidentale. It covered eight hundred and fifty square miles. In it there were over thirty villages and I was the sole stay of their inhabitants. To many of the villages there were no roads, only mule tracks. I spent my life riding from one to another, ministering to the bodies as well as the souls of my wretched parishioners; for no doctors ever go to those places. Tuberculosis, malaria, dysentery and rickets due to malnutrition are rife in such sparsely-populated areas; so a medicine chest is a part of a priest's equipment and he does what little he can to relieve the afflicted. He is also their counsellor in family disputes and all matters concerning the commune. Their poverty is such as to wring the heart. They are truly devout and willingly give what little they can to support their priest; for he, too, must live, albeit on a pittance. But so near the starvation line are they that in some cases the only church they can afford is a single room with not even a confessional in it. Write of these things, I pray you, señor, for if the rich were made more fully aware of the miseries the Indians suffer, they might prove more charitable.'

Much moved, Adam said good-bye to the old man, whom he could not possibly believe was involved in the conspiracy. But it did strike him that peasants leading such a grim existence, and with nothing to lose but their lives, would prove easily inflammable material if called on to right their wrongs by a priest who was a firebrand.

That evening, instead of drinking and dining at his hotel, he visited several cafés and ate in a small restaurant. The people to whom he spoke were invariably most courteous and talked with him on a variety of subjects, but he picked up no information of interest. Early next morning Felipe drove him the few miles to Guanajuato.

There he looked in at the charming little horseshoe-shaped theatre with its tiers of gilded boxes. At the church he got into conversation with a younger priest, a gloomy dark-skinned man who evidently regarded him with suspicion and, as soon as he mentioned the poverty of the Indians, shut up like a clam.

Early in the afternoon he reached Irapuato, where he was to spend his second night. At the church he could not find a priest; but he passed his evening scraping acquaintance with people in the cafés and, when he had his dinner, shared a table with a commercial traveller who sold patent medicines. He was an urbane type, full of information, but not of the sort that Adam was seeking. With pride he talked of Mexico's industrial revolution. New factories were going up everywhere. Production had tripled in the past quarter of a century, and was still increasing at the rate of seven per cent a year. He knew little about the Indians and cared less.

On the Thursday, Adam went on to Morelia. The town was situated in some of the loveliest country in Mexico. He found the Hotel Mendoza there much superior to those he had stayed in earlier during his trip, so he was glad that he was to remain two nights. But he spent most of his time out and about talking to people who were sitting alone outside the cafés.

As had been the case in the other towns, nearly all of them were drinking *tequila*, the national spirit made from cactus, and, at intervals, sucking a piece of lemon sprinkled with salt. Adam did not much care for *tequila* but, to be sociable, he always ordered it, although in the form of a *tequila* Collins, as drinking it with ginger ale made it more palatable.

Nearly all the people he talked to turned out to be small townsmen, so from them he did not learn much. Most of them were of the opinion that the Indian peasants had never been far above the level of slaves and, until education became more general, would remain in that condition. But a few said that it was believed they had recently been forming some sort of organisation to better themselves.

That evening, as a change from the fiery curries with which he had had to make do in small restaurants, he decided to dine at the Mendoza and, after dinner, he had a chat with a man who introduced himself as Don Augustin Flores. He was the owner of a big estate and gave Adam the opposite side of the picture he had been given by the commercial traveller.

Don Augustin said that Mexico was heading for ruin owing to the drift of the peasants to the cities during the past two decades. The deforestation of the land by the Spaniards had greatly reduced the conservation of water, with the result that many areas that in the old days had borne crops had deteriorated into arid wasteland. In consequence, for centuries there had been barely enough food to feed the population. Since the end of the Second World War the situation had further deteriorated because, tempted by the higher wages—although, owing to the high cost of living in the cities, they were little better off—great numbers of peasants had left the land to take jobs in industry as unskilled workmen. The result had been a further great reduction in the area of land cultivated and a steady decline in the amount of food produced.

Don Augustin predicted that if this drift to the cities continued, as it almost certainly would, within a few years the price of food, whether home-grown or imported, would become so high that the peasants would not be able to pay it, and they would then begin to die like flies from starvation or, in desperation, rise spontaneously and march on the cities with the intention of bringing about a revolution.

Adam was deeply interested in all this. Ramón had told him that Mexico was already importing large quantities of food, with the result that prices had risen. Evidently this was one of the causes of the peasants' discontent; although apparently Don Augustin was unaware that a revolt was already in the making.

The following day Adam enjoyed a most picturesque drive to Pátzcuaro, near which there was a beautiful lake. Then, in the evening, back at Morelia, he met another interesting character, a retired schoolmaster named Juan Padilla.

The Señor Padilla was a fiery Liberal. He had spent his life in schools and agitating for more of them. It was his belief that education was the panacea for all ills and he was full of praise both for the government's endeavours in that direction and the people's willing acceptance of them.

He conceded that there were many thousands of villages which still had no schools at all, or ones housed in old, decaying *haciendas*. But he said that this would soon be remedied. For some years past the Ministry of Education had been providing prefabricated schools and teachers for them. In the villages the peasants welcomed them with enormous enthusiasm, willingly gave their free time to erecting the schools and, when classes had started, the adults would often cluster round their open windows to absorb the lessons being taught to the children.

However, he admitted that there were two great factors that retarded the speed of education. One was that, for a good half of the year, the peasants would not allow their children to attend school, because for many generations they had been accustomed to have the use of them, however small, to play some part in sowing and harvesting; and, as there were three crops a year in the fertile valleys, this seriously interfered with the school curriculum. The other was the terrible shortage of teachers. Although they were emerging from the universities in much greater numbers than in the past, their ratio was far exceeded by the increase in pupils, owing to the fact that the advance of medicine in the cities, and to some extent in the country, had resulted in a population explosion with which it was impossible to cope.

Saturday morning Adam went on to San Luis Caliente, a smaller town a few miles off the main highway. There he visited the church and found the priest to be a sallow-faced man with the receding forehead and fleshy, hooked nose of an Indian. He proved both talkative and very bitter about the conditions in which his parishioners lived. As Adam led him on, it soon emerged that he had Communist leanings and was a true militant. He dogmatically asserted that Christ's teachings were basically Communist, and even went on to say that in the Middle Ages many Bishops had taken up arms on behalf of their beliefs; so there was no reason why, should the occasion arise, priests like himself should not lead their people in an attempt to overthrow tyrants and establish a truly Christian community. On leaving him Adam felt no doubt at all that he was playing an active part in the conspiracy.

Adam took his evening meal at a small café-restaurant in which about a dozen people were eating or just sitting drinking. He was wondering if he dare finish up with an ice and, as he had been taking two Enterovioform pills every morning since his arrival in Mexico as a precaution against typhoid, he had just decided to risk it, when a tall Indian with a long, droopy moustache appeared in the doorway. As he stood framed in it, several of those at the table lifted their hands in greeting. The man then said, 'We eat pork tonight,' turned, and went out.

The incident passed almost unnoticed by Adam, as he assumed that the man was inviting his friends to an anniversary feast or some other celebration. Although it was winter, the evening was by no means chilly and, as was customary in such small towns, the square was crowded with people slowly strolling to and fro beneath the palm trees, or squatting in the dust with their backs against walls, smoking cheroots. In one corner there was a small group clustered round a man who was strumming on a guitar. Adam joined it and stood there for a time. Then his attention was caught by a tough-looking Mestizo pushing his way into the crowd. Next moment the man said, 'We eat pork tonight, pass the word.' Then he pushed his way out again.

This gave Adam furiously to think. Evidently the announcement did not refer to a family celebration, but was a password that would summon the initiated to some secret meeting. Edging out of the crowd, he looked round for the Mestizo, caught sight of him and kept him under observation. The man moved slowly down that side of the square, pausing briefly here and there at other groups, presumably saying his piece, then walking on.

The thought that he was now really on to something filled Adam with excited satisfaction, and he at once made up his mind to try to find out where the meeting was being held, then spy on it. Recalling the sallow-faced priest with whom he had talked of Communism, it seemed almost certain that he would be mixed up in this; so Adam made his way to the church.

It was situated in a side street among the older houses of the town, which stood in their own gardens. Full darkness had now come, the thoroughfare was badly lit and there were few people about. But the church was not entirely deserted. Dim light came from the windows at one end of it, although no service was being held; neither were people coming in that direction.

Entering the graveyard, Adam stood there in the shadows for half an hour. By then he was beginning to fear that his hunch about the priest had been a wrong one. But he could think of no other line to follow and decided to remain there for another ten minutes or so. His patience was rewarded. A door of the church opened and a small procession came out. It was headed by the priest, carrying what Adam felt certain was the Host. Two acolytes accompanied him and half a dozen men, some of whom were carrying lanterns, followed.

The fact that the priest was carrying the Host made Adam again think that his hunch had been wrong, for it seemed hardly possible that he would be taking it to a political meeting; and more likely that he was on his way to give Extreme Unction to someone who was dying. Then, as Adam crouched down behind a tombstone while the procession passed, a swinging lantern momentarily lit the face of one of the men. It was the fellow with the long moustache. Adam drew a quick breath. His hunch had been right, after all.

When the little group had moved off down the road he emerged from his hiding place and followed at some distance. Soon he realised that they were heading out of the town and ten minutes later they were on an open road, lit only by the stars.

When they had covered about a mile, he saw ahead, rising from the flat countryside, a mound about thirty feet in height and recalled that he had passed it on his way into the town that morning. It was one of the innumerable small pyramids that are scattered over Mexico and have not yet been fully retrieved by the archaeologists. He remembered that the greater part of it was still covered with grass. Only the steep flight of steps leading up to the flat top had been cleared and repaired.

It stood about a hundred yards from the road and, as Adam came nearer, he could make out a considerable crowd of people squatting in front of it. At the approach of the priest they all came to their feet. As they turned towards him, Adam glimpsed the white blur of their faces. Fearing to be discovered he promptly threw himself down into the ditch at the roadside.

Cautiously raising his head, he watched the proceedings. The people received the priest in silence, except for a queer low grunting, and for a few moments he disappeared among them. Then, by the light of the lanterns, he became visible again as he and his companions climbed the steps of the pyramid. When they reached the top, Adam could see that a stout table had been carried up there to serve as an altar, as it was draped in cloth and a crucifix stood on it.

Turning to the congregation, the priest began to intone. Adam was too far off to catch his words; but the loud responses of the people told him that a service was being held in Latin, and he guessed that a Mass was being celebrated. In due course the little bell tinkled, the crowd went down on their knees and the Host was elevated.

No partaking of Communion followed. The priest disappeared down the far side of the pyramid for about ten minutes. During this time there came again the strange grunting. The priest reappeared wearing a feather head-dress and clad in Indian robes. Then he addressed the people in loud, harsh tones and, from their cadence, Adam guessed that he was now speaking in Nahuatl. In his dream-visions of his incarnation in Mexico, Adam had spoken and thought in that language; but to his present life he had brought back only a partial understanding of it and, in any case, he was too far off to hear distinctly. As the priest continued, now and then with violent gestures, the crowd became more and more excited, occasionally giving vent to loud shouts of approval. Suddenly he ceased speaking. For a moment there was silence, then a tremendous burst of cheering *'Olé! Ole! Ole!'*

The crowd did not disperse and from its centre there came murmurs and movement. Some minutes later Adam learned the cause and that of the grunting he had heard. At the base of the pyramid there was a large crate containing several pigs. Four men, each holding a leg of one of the pigs, were lugging it up the broad flight of steps. It was, like all native-bred pigs, not a large animal and, without difficulty, they got it to the top. There they lifted it on to the altar and held it down on its back.

The light from a lantern shimmered on a knife the priest had drawn as he raised it then struck downward. The pig gave a hideous, high-pitched squeal, then went on squealing. The priest had not cut its throat but ripped open its breast. A moment later he had torn out its heart and was holding it on high for all to see. The crowd went nearly mad with excitement.

As the *Olés* died, the four men swung the now dead pig by

its legs and pitched it on to the top of the steps. Spurting blood, it rolled over and over to the bottom, to be seized on eagerly by others who carried it round to the rear of the pyramid. From there a lurid glow had arisen, of the significance of which Adam had no doubt. A big fire had been lit to roast the sacrifice. 'We eat pork tonight.' They would soon be tearing at the hot flesh with their bare hands and gorging it.

A second pig was sacrificed in the same manner. Then, when its body had been carried away, there was a sudden commotion among the spectators. A third pig had escaped when being taken from the crate. Mad with fear, it charged through the people, knocking down several of them. Only seconds later it emerged from the crowd and headed straight for the place where Adam was crouching in the ditch. Almost as one man, the crowd turned and came streaming in pursuit of it.

Aghast at the certainty of discovery, Adam came to his feet and turned to run. In getting out of the ditch he stumbled and fell. He had only just picked himself up when there came screams of 'A spy! Seize him! A spy! A spy!' Next moment the crowd was upon him and he was fighting for his life.

10

A Ghastly Ordeal

FOR the first time since, when a crime reporter in Southampton, Adam had been attacked, he used his great strength to the full. Lashing out right and left with his big fists, he felled two of his attackers, then seized a third round the waist, lifted him high in the air and flung him into the crowd. His whirling body knocked down three more; but the crowd seemed as though possessed by a demon. Screaming with hate, their dark faces transformed into hideous masks, they trampled over their fallen comrades and came at him again.

His arms shooting out like piston rods, he met the attack. Nearly all of them were small, short men, so his height gave him a big advantage and blows from his fists sent one after another reeling. Yet their fanatic urge to pull him down was so strong that, as each of his victims gasped or moaned and toppled over, others took his place.

Breathing hard now and sweating from his exertions, he knew that, unless he could succeed in getting away, his death was certain. They would tear him limb from limb or, perhaps, lug him up to the top of the pyramid and sacrifice him to their evil god, as they had the pigs. But if he ceased to face them, even for a second, and turned to run, they would leap upon his back and hurl him to the ground. So far the fight had lasted barely a minute, but several of them beyond the reach of his punches had run round behind him. At any moment he expected to receive savage blows from them or, worse, the sharp stab of a knife as it was thrust into his back.

In desperation he sprang forward, seized one of them by his long hair, pulled him off his feet and swung him breast high in a scythe-like sweep. The man's heavy boots tore great gashes in the faces of the two nearest men. Yelling with pain they went over backwards. For the moment Adam's front was clear. Lifting the man again, he repeated the movement, at the same time swivelling on his heels. He was only just in time. The man's legs smashed into the body of another actually in the act of jumping. Struck in mid-air, he curved over sideways and hit the earth with a heavy thump. Behind him were four or five others. Letting go of the screaming man he had used as a weapon, Adam charged them. One got a fist full in the face, another a blow on his Adam's apple, which made his eyes start from his head. He lurched away, vomiting. The others, momentarily cowed as the golden-haired giant rushed upon them, panicked and sprang aside. Suddenly Adam realised that he had fought his way free and, with overwhelming relief, raced off down the road as fast as his long legs could carry him.

Howling with execration, the murderous mob streamed in pursuit of him. He had a lead of only a dozen yards, was gasping for breath and aching from a score of blows that had landed on his body; but his stride being so much longer than that of the Indians, he had good hopes of increasing his lead until they tired and he could get clean away.

His heart hammering in his chest, he pounded on, fear lending him new strength. The trampling of a hundred feet behind him made a continuous roar, broken every few seconds by shouts and curses. After two minutes they sounded a little fainter. But he was now streaming with sweat and his lungs seemed near to bursting. Grimly he realised that he could not keep up that pace and that many of his pursuers who had not participated in the fight were fresher than he was. If they continued the chase they must wear him down.

Almost blinded by the sweat that was running down into his eyes, he was following the road and had not even given a glance at the terrain on either side. A swift turn of his head to find out how far ahead of the mob he was showed him that he had entered an area of bushes and small trees. Suddenly it came to him that by diving in among them he could elude the howling human pack. Swerving, he jumped the roadside ditch and dashed into the undergrowth. Next moment his foot caught in a root, he pitched forward and his head hit a rotting tree stump.

Half stunned, he lay where he had fallen. A good half-minute had gone before he was sufficiently recovered to stagger to his feet. Once more, in desperate fear for his life, he began to thrust his way through the bushes. But the fall seemed to have driven the last strength from his body. He had not stumbled ten yards before he heard the cracking of small branches in his rear. His brain was in a whirl. It was much darker there than out on the open road. He could no longer see his way and felt utterly exhausted. Brought up short by a small tree, he staggered and fell again. In a matter of seconds, with exultant shouts, the mob was upon him.

A dozen hands grabbed at his clothes, his arms, his hair. With kicks and curses they dragged him to his feet, then pushed and pulled him back towards the pyramid; but their progress was slow because they were as breathless as he was. Dimly he realised this and for the next few minutes the thought that it might give him another chance germinated in his mind. To recruit his strength, he began to take long, deep breaths.

They had nearly reached the place where he had been attacked when he made his effort. Two men were holding each of his arms but, compared with him, they were puny creatures. Suddenly coming to a halt, he tensed his muscles, threw his weight backwards and wrenched himself free. Seizing the two nearest Indians by the neck, he banged their heads together, then began to strike out, first to one side then to the other.

His blows no longer had their former strength, but several of his captors staggered back from them. Others cannoned into one another in the wild scramble to seize him again. The greater part of the crowd had been shuffling along in his rear and his sudden attack now gave him the chance he had prayed for. To his right front no-one barred his path. Drawing a deep breath, he launched himself forward.

He had covered no more than ten feet when something hit him lightly on the head and slid down over his face. It was a rope. Suddenly it jerked tight round his neck. With an agonised gasp, he came to an abrupt halt. A muleteer in the crowd behind had lassoed him.

Half choked, he grabbed the noose with both hands to save himself from being throttled. He had barely succeeded in loosening it a little before he was again surrounded and seized. His last hope of escape was gone.

Jostling and shouting, his captors pushed him along the road, then across the coarse grassland towards the pyramid. It was now deserted, but they took him round behind it. There, as he had supposed from the bright glow he had seen, a big fire of brushwood was burning. Above it, spitted on long poles supported by trestles, the torn carcasses of the two pigs were being roasted. Beyond the fire stood a long, low barn and Adam was taken into it.

Evidently it was there that the priest had changed into his Indian robes and feathered head-dress. Still wearing them, he and several older men who had not joined in the chase were in the barn seated at a rough table drinking *tequila* from thick tumblers. As Adam was dragged in front of them they rose to their feet and glowered at him.

During the past few minutes he had again recovered his breath and, although his body was bruised all over, he had suffered no serious injury. Owing to his height none of the blows aimed at him had reached his face and, as he had hit the tree stump with the side of his head, his features remained unmarred. A loud grunt caused him to glance towards the corner of the barn from where it had come. Like himself, the pig had evidently been recaptured, as a man stood there holding it by a rope round its neck.

As he faced his captors, Adam felt sick with fear. There could be no disguising the fact that he had been a witness to the abominable rites that had been performed not much more than a quarter of an hour earlier. Although he was not a Catholic, the celebration of a Mass as a prelude to a pagan sacrifice had seemed to him a most appalling sacrilege. They must assume that even an accidental spectator of such a scene would report it, which must lead to the high authorities both of the Church and the police taking drastic action. Therefore, they could not possibly afford to let him go. For their own

protection they must silence him, and the only certain way
to do that was to kill him.

Their faces dark with anger, the priest and his companions
stared at Adam from time to time while arguing in low voices.
From the few words he caught, he realised that they were
divided. Some of them were set upon his death; the others
were fearful of killing him because he was not simply an
uninitiated citizen of San Luis Caliente but obviously a
foreigner and probably a tourist; so his disappearance was
certain to result in an investigation which might prove their
ruin.

At length they decided to take a vote, whether he should
be killed there and then or made to swear the most awful
oaths to keep their secret, with the threat that, should he afterwards betray them, he would never escape their vengeance.
At that he took new heart, feeling fairly confident that they
would not dare risk a police enquiry. But his relief was short-
lived. Each of them had scribbled on a scrap of paper torn
from a single sheet, then passed it to the priest. Having sorted
them into two piles, he said in a hoarse voice, 'Four for re-
prieve, seven for death.' Then, addressing the men who were
holding Adam by the arms, he added, 'This is an opportunity
to show the gods our complete faith in them. Take him up to
the top of the pyramid.'

Adam went as white as a sheet. He had all he could do to
prevent himself from trembling. But in that moment inspiration came to him. So far he had not spoken. Now, half-for-
gotten words of Nahuatl suddenly flowed into his mind.
Drawing himself to his full height, he frowned and said:

'What folly is this to which I have listened with patience?
Kill me and your cause is lost. I came here only to assess the
loyalty of my followers. Without warning I was attacked. Being now in the form of a human being I was forced to defend
myself. Otherwise I would have been sent back prematurely
to the place whence I come to lead again my people out of
bondage. Do you not recognise me? I am Quetzalcoatl.'

Sitting back, they gasped and stared at him. With new per-
ception they took in his height, his red-gold hair and beard.
After a moment of tense silence the priest stammered:

'It must be. . . . Only a week back I received word that the Man-God had returned to us . . . was here in Mexico. . . . Come again to give us joy and prosperity.'

Standing up, the priest came round from behind the table, followed by his companions. Kneeling, they prostrated themselves before Adam. The men who had been holding him had swiftly stepped away and were now also on their knees, banging their foreheads on the ground.

There followed an awkward silence. Adam was terribly tempted to say, 'Now, for God's sake, let me go. Get me a car if it's possible or, failing that, I'll walk back to San Luis.' But he dared not. He could only await developments and hope to reap the best advantage from them.

At last the priest raised his head and said, 'Mighty Lord, the third pig was caught. I beg that you will not refuse us the honour of sacrificing it in the presence of us, your slaves.'

A lump rose in Adam's throat, but he saw no alternative to agreeing, and gave a silent nod.

Taking off his rich garments, the priest humbly offered them and Adam put them on. Messengers were sent out to reassemble the congregation and the pig was led away. During the quarter of an hour that followed, those who remained in the barn stole covert glances in Adam's direction and were evidently too filled with awe to dare address him. He maintained an aloof silence, his stomach rising at the thought of having to slaughter the pig; but he feared that if he failed to go through with it they might decide that he was an impostor, which could yet cost him his life. His limbs were aching, he felt very tired and would have given a lot to sit down. But he decided that, as he was supposed to be a god, he must show no sign of weakness.

At last the men who had left the barn returned. The priest, now again in his clerical garb, made a deep obeisance and said, 'Exalted One, I pray you to precede me.'

Leaving the barn, Adam led the way up the grass-covered rear slope of the pyramid. As he appeared on the top, there came a low murmur from the congregation down below, then a hushed silence. The priest addressed the people but spoke only a few sentences, his harsh voice now betrayed his agitation. Again there came the murmur as the people went down on their knees, then lowered their faces to the ground.

From their midst emerged four men who had remained upright. Each holding a leg of the pig, they lugged it up the steps of the pyramid, lifted it on to the altar table and held it there on its back. With a bow, the priest handed Adam the sacrificial knife.

He was already feeling nausea from the smell of the blood of the pigs that had been slaughtered there half an hour earlier. For a moment he shut his eyes and swallowed hard. With a great effort he pulled himself together and stepped forward.

As he raised the knife he was terribly tempted to plunge it hard into the breast of the pig, so as to put it swiftly out of its agony; but he knew that to be the one thing he must not do. Exerting all his will to make his arm obey him, he stuck the knife into the pig's belly, and drew it upward. The blade was as sharp as a razor, so the skin and flesh parted easily.

The minutes that followed exceeded the horror of any nightmare he had ever experienced. The animal squealed and squealed on a high-pitched note that resembled the screams of a human in the utmost agony. Somehow, Adam forced himself to thrust his hands into the cavity he had made and, as the blood spurted out up to his elbows, fish around until he found the heart. Now obsessed with the thought of getting the awful business over as swiftly as possible, he tore at it frantically, lugged it out and held it aloft.

His gesture was followed by a thunderous roar of applause from the congregation. Crazy with excitement, they shouted themselves hoarse and were still doing so as Adam was solemnly escorted down the far side of the pyramid. Then he was led back to the barn and bowed to a seat at the head of the table. His urge to get away from the evil men who surrounded him was almost uncontrollable. But he fought it down because he felt sure that the diabolical ceremony would not be completed until they had feasted on the sacrificed pigs and that, to play out his role, he must participate.

By then the two first pigs had been roasted and the man with the long moustache came into the barn carrying an earthen platter with a portion of the cooked meat on it. The priest took the platter from him and, kneeling, presented it to Adam.

With renewed disgust he saw that he was expected to eat the pigs' testicles. His stomach almost revolted, but he fought down his nausea. Then, with sudden inspiration, he leaned over, took the knife from the priest's sash, cut off only a small portion of the meat and put it in his mouth. To his surprise, the taste was very pleasant. Having swallowed the piece of flesh, he stood up and said:

'It is enough. I have many other places to visit; so I go now, and I desire no escort to accompany me back to the town.'

No-one attempted to stay him. They all went down on their knees. Swiftly he discarded the Indian robes which he had put on over his own clothes, and threw them on the table. Then, with a dignified step, he walked unhurriedly out of the barn.

The scene outside was like a witches' sabbath, except that all the participants were male. They were crowded round the big bonfire over which the pig he had slain was still roasting. The other two pigs had been torn in pieces. Groups of men held lumps of the hot flesh in their bare hands as they gorged themselves on it, and gulped down from raised bottles draughts of *tequila* or the raw, local wine.

Within two minutes of leaving the barn Adam was back on the road. His relief at having regained his freedom had caused his tiredness to drop from him. His mind still filled with the revolting scenes he had witnessed, he hurried towards the town.

In less than twenty minutes he arrived there. He felt as though many hours must have passed since he had left it, so he was surprised to find a number of people still sitting about in the square; but it was only a little after midnight and, as his hands were dyed red with blood, he was thankful not to have to knock up someone to let him into his hotel.

Putting his hands into his trouser pockets, he went straight up to his room and scrubbed them again and again until he had got the last trace of dried blood from under his finger-nails. By then reaction had set in and he again felt so exhausted that he could not raise the energy even to ring for a drink or have a bath. Pulling off his clothes, he flopped into bed and, five minutes later, was sound asleep.

When he awoke he could hardly believe that he had not had a ghastly nightmare; but there were bloodstains on the shoes beside his bed and, as the ceremonial robe had been much too short for him, also on the lower part of the legs of his trousers. Realising that he really had been through that seemingly incredible experience, he fervently thanked God that he was still alive.

As he sat up in bed, he gave an 'ouch' of pain and his body began to ache all over. That made him wish that he could stay in bed all day to recover from his beating-up, but he had already decided to get away from San Luis Caliente as soon as he possibly could, in case the evil priest came round and sought to involve him in further horrors.

The mirror in the bathroom down the passage showed his body to be black and blue, and one of his ribs pained him badly; but, in view of the ferocity of the attack on him, he considered that he had got off lightly. Bathed, shaved, dressed in clean clothes and after a hurried breakfast, he felt somewhat better. By nine o'clock he was on his way down to Taxco.

It was again a Sunday and, on arriving at the famous silver town, he found the shops that sell beautiful silver-work shut. He was not sorry about that, as he felt like anything but going sightseeing. On the contrary, he was a little concerned about his rib; so, after he had lunched, he went to bed and sent for a doctor. The doctor told him that his rib was only strained or, at the worst, slightly cracked, so it was nothing to worry about, and advised him to spend the rest of the day in bed. He charged the equivalent of three pounds for his visit, which Adam thought excessive, but he gladly took the advice.

During his trip Adam had spent most of his waking hours talking to scores of different people. That had helped to keep his mind off Chela, but it could not prevent him from thinking about her during his drives in the car from town to town, when he woke each morning and before he went to sleep every night.

Those two nights they had spent together at Oaxaca had

been a truly wonderful experience for him. In his mind's eye he could still visualise her lovely, laughing face and faultless body. Without effort he could recapture the rich tones of her voice and the satin texture of her skin. Added to all this, there had been the perfect ease with which they could communicate their inmost thoughts to each other, or just remain silent side by side in absolute contentment. He felt certain that in this life he would never meet another woman to compare with her. Yet she seemed horrifyingly unpredictable and, after one lightly-spoken sentence deliberately calculated to deceive him, had left him flat.

As he lay in bed, turning over from time to time to ease his bruised body, he wondered what to do about her. He had long since given up puzzling over her reason for having abandoned him, bitterly accepting that the only possible explanation was his refusal to help her in her crusade. And now, with ample cause, he was more opposed than ever to doing so. The ten days she had told her family she would be away had expired on Saturday. As they spent every week-end at Cuernavaca, the odds were that she would now be there and back in Mexico City on the following day, Monday.

Unhappily, he faced the possibility that, having made her attempt to secure his help and failed, she might refuse to have any more private meetings with him. But, in view of their powerful attraction for each other and, even more, the strength of the past link between them, he thought that unlikely. It would be against any passionate woman's instincts to allow a political difference of opinion entirely to override her physical desire; and there could be no doubt about Chela being a passionate woman. It therefore seemed well on the cards that he could win her back, and even possible that, after their separation of ten days, she was looking forward eagerly to resuming their affaire immediately she got back to Mexico City.

His intention had been to return there himself the following morning after a quick look round Taxco. But it now occurred to him that, if she was expecting him to be waiting on the mat for her, it might be no bad thing to disappoint her, leave her kicking her heels for a couple of days wondering what had become of him, then reappear and tell her that he had not hurried back because he regarded their brief affaire as finished.

The inference that he had already got her out of his system might make her more eager; on the other hand, she might resent it so strongly that he would lose her for good. As that was the last thing he wanted, he decided not to risk it, but to stay in Taxco only over Monday then, when he did get back, leave it to her to make the first move. Or, anyhow, wait until he could bear no longer the suspense of not knowing how she felt towards him.

He spent the next morning making the rounds of the silver-smiths, admiring their beautiful work. Somehow, he got through the rest of the day and returned to Mexico City on the Tuesday. He had left the bulk of his luggage at the El Presidente and was considerably relieved to learn that the rooms he had reserved there for his return had not been let to someone else.

No message from Chela awaited him at the desk, but there were two letters sent round from the Del Paseo.

One was from his Aunt Flora. It was to thank him for his Christmas present to her, although in somewhat austere terms. Having been busy with preparations for his trip to Mexico, he had jibbed at racking his brains for a present that would please her, so had sent her a cheque for fifty pounds.

In her letter she remarked that, while money was always acceptable, the greatest pleasure lay in receiving a gift in the selection of which the giver had expended thought. She added that the size of the sum gave her reason to fear that Adam's good fortune had led to his becoming reckless about money. This she urged him to guard against seriously, as she found it hard to believe that anyone could continue to live as he was doing simply by writing novels. She had, therefore, spent only five pounds on some new linen and had put the remainder aside against a day when he might need it. There followed news about a few of her neighbours and a report that a Jewish gentleman from the Midlands—said to have big interests in television—was negotiating to lease the Castle.

Aunt Flora's letter carried Adam back to a different world —a sane and real world inbred in his very being; so that for

a moment it seemed that all that had befallen him in Mexico
—his affaire with the lovely but strange and unpredictable
Chela and his terrible experience at San Luis Caliente—could
not really have taken place. Yet the slight pain that he still
felt in his bruised rib was ample evidence that they had been
no dream.

On opening the second letter he found to his consternation
that it was from Jeremy Hunterscombe, giving particulars
of the meeting of the Anglo-Mexican Society that evening.
Adam had entirely forgotten about it, and it was already
four o'clock. With a groan, he forwent a belated lie-down
and set about composing his speech.

He had been working on it for about half an hour when the
telephone rang. As he picked up the receiver, his heart gave
a violent lurch. It was Chela calling him.

'So you're back,' she said. 'Ramón told me that you had
gone off on a tour, and when I called up this morning I was
told that you had not yet returned. I've been trying to get
hold of you for the past three days. Come round here for
drinks this evening, then we'll go out to dinner.'

Her opening to renew their affaire warmed him, but
strengthened his resolution to play hard-to-get; so, tempted
as he was to start saying endearing things to her, he steeled
himself to reply in a rather off-hand manner, 'I'd love to,
but I can't. I have to give a talk to the Anglo-Mexican Society
this evening.'

'Oh!' She hesitated. 'But that will be over by about half
past ten. You could take me out afterwards.'

'No,' he said firmly. 'That's not on, either. Jerry Hunterscombe is running this show and he is expecting me to dine
with him afterwards,' which was the truth.

'Oh, damn Jeremy!' she exclaimed angrily. 'Tell him you
can't. Put him off.'

Her eagerness to see him further strengthened Adam's feeling that he was taking a sound line, so he replied, 'Sorry; I
wouldn't like to do that but . . .' He had been going to suggest
their making a date for the next day, but got no further because she had hung up on him.

Afterwards he wondered whether he had gone too far, and

had half a mind to ring her back. But he resisted the impulse and returned to writing his speech; although, with visions of Chela now occupying the greater part of his mind, he found it extraordinarily hard to concentrate on it.

At half past seven he went over to the hall in which the Society held its meetings. In a private room Jeremy and other members of the committee fortified him with drinks, then escorted him downstairs. As usual, on such occasions, he felt rather nervous; but the audience was large and gave him an encouraging reception. Hunterscombe introduced him in a brief, flattering and well-thought-out speech. Then Adam said his piece.

As had always proved the case with him, 'everything was all right on the night', and when he ended he received enthusiastic applause. There was then a half-hour of questions, a sequel to which he rather looked forward, as it often gave him a lead to air his views on a variety of subjects. Then followed a vote of thanks and a few words with friendly people in the audience, after which Hunterscombe carried him off in a car.

They dined at a small restaurant which had a French cuisine and a French chef to see to it that the dishes were truly à la française, so the food was excellent. Halfway through the meal, Hunterscombe said :

'You were telling me that you've been on a trip. During it did you think any more about the subject we talked of when we lunched together? You know, old boy. I mean the off-the-record stuff.'

Adam nodded. 'Yes, I did. And I have no doubt now that you were right. There is plenty of trouble brewing. The Indians really are still primitives, and in some places the priests are playing on their superstitions to encourage them to revolt.'

'Can you give me any particulars?'

Before going to the meeting Adam had carefully considered how much he should say if Hunterscombe raised the subject again; and he had decided to say very little because the Wing Commander suspected Chela. So the less he was told about what was going on the better, just in case some item of information enabled him to confirm his suspicions definitely.

'No,' Adam lied glibly. 'But I can tell you one thing. You were wrong in believing that the Enriquezes are involved. Bernadino and his capitalist friends have no tie-up with the Church, and they are all against anything which might upset the *status quo*. I learned that from Ramón, and I'm certain he wasn't fooling me.'

The Wing Commander brushed up his fair moustache. 'But how about Chela?'

'Oh, Chela!' Adam shrugged. 'I haven't seen her since I last saw you. Undoubtedly she is an idealist and Alberuque's pet, or he hers. But that doesn't add up to much, now we know that she is not acting as liaison between the Monsignor and her father.'

'Could be you're right, chum,' Hunterscombe admitted. 'If she is a dead end, there is no point in wasting further time on her.'

Adam felt that he had handled the situation as well as possible, but he was not fully convinced that the Wing Commander believed him. There was a quality about him that was difficult to assess. On the face of it, he was almost a Wodehouse character and Adam would not have been at all surprised to be addressed by him as 'old egg' or 'old bean', or to hear him speak of 'cads' and 'rotters'. But there seemed to be an underlying shrewdness about him, and Adam had heard it said more than once that apparently 'silly-idiot' British agents were the cleverest in the world.

To his relief Hunterscombe made no further reference to the subject during the latter part of their pleasant dinner, nor while taking him back to his hotel.

Next morning he rang up Chela, with the intention of putting matters right with her, but she had already gone out and it was not known when she would be back. He then asked for Ramón and, when he came on the line, asked him to lunch. Ramón would not hear of it. In Mexico the term 'visitor' is synonymous with 'guest'. He had an engagement but that could be put off. He was anxious to see Adam and would expect him at two o'clock at the Bankers' Club.

Adam again made his way downtown, but this time not

too early for his appointment. Ramón received him cordially and at once asked how he had enjoyed his trip.

'I had a most interesting time,' Adam grinned, 'and damn' nearly got my throat cut.'

Ramón raised his dark eyebrows. 'The devil you did! I can't wait to hear about it.'

Over lunch Adam gave a full account of his week's tour, ending up with a graphic description of his shattering experience at San Luis Caliente.

'That is the sort of Saturday-night gathering we have had reason to believe is taking place,' Ramón said. 'But this is the first actual description we have had of one, and I'm extremely grateful to you for having obtained it for us. I give you full marks, too, for pulling the bluff on them that you were Quetzalcoatl. What gave you the idea?'

'Chela,' Adam replied promptly. 'She told me that I look exactly like the description of him in the legends.'

'That was lucky for you. She is a born romantic, which accounts for her having always championed the Indians. In view of what is going on at the moment, it is unfortunate that her feelings for them are so strong. Just between us, since you have been away we have found out that she is taking an active part in fermenting this rebellion.'

Adam's face showed quick concern, although Ramón did not realise the shock that their discovery that Chela was involved had given him; and he went on quietly, 'She has been acting for Don Alberuque, as his go-between in the towns to which she has gone recently to inspect schools.'

Striving to hide his acute alarm, Adam asked, 'Is . . . is it likely that they will arrest her?'

'Oh, no. We shan't arrest that priest at San Luis Caliente either; nor any of the others we have a line on—yet. It is much sounder to let them have plenty of rope, then there is a good chance that they'll lead us to the big-shots who are directing this damnable affair. We can afford to wait for a week or two before we pounce.'

'But then? What then? If Chela is proved to have been one of the ringleaders, she . . . they'll put her in prison.'

'I don't think for a moment that she is, or that she realises the full implications of what she is doing. In her devotion to the poor she is almost a saint, and I am sure she would swallow any line that smarmy devil Alberuque cared to sell her.'

'But she could be in deeper than you suppose,' Adam persisted.

Ramón gave him a friendly smile. 'I hadn't realised that you were one of the many who have fallen for Chela.'

'Well, er—I certainly find her very attractive and she's been extremely kind in taking me about to places; so it's natural that I should feel anxious about her. I should have thought you would be, too.'

'I'm not.' Ramón shook his dark head. 'And you needn't be either. Even if they worked on her to the extent of persuading her to throw a bomb at the President, we'd get her off. Money counts in Mexico. It might cost my father a million *pesos*, but he'd see to it that at worst she would have to spend a few months in a nice comfy home for neurotics.'

Immensely relieved, Adam was able to enjoy the rest of his lunch. He then returned to the El Presidente and lay down on his bed with a book, as he had decided that it would be better not to ring Chela again until after the siesta. Half an hour later he had dropped off to sleep.

He was roused by a loud knocking on his door. As he had hung up the 'Do not Disturb' notice outside it, he called out '*Entrada*' in a far from pleasant frame of mind. But the knocking continued and he then remembered that he had turned the key in the lock. With a scowl on his face he slid off the bed, walked over and opened the door. Chela, dressed in a gay, flowered spring frock, and looking radiant, was standing there.

'Well!' he exclaimed with an angry expression, still half asleep and caught off his guard. 'It seems you mean to make a habit of invading my bedroom.'

Pushing past him, she shut the door behind her, then turned and gave him a puzzled look. 'What's the matter with you, darling? I simply thought that as the mountain wouldn't come to Mohammet, I'd . . . But you don't seem at all pleased to see me.'

Recovering himself, and now elated that his stratagem of

G

playing hard-to-get had worked, he said quickly, 'Yes, I am.
I really couldn't back out of my talk and dinner last night.
But I phoned you this morning and was going to again in an
hour or so's time.'

At that she gave her dazzling smile and held out her arms.
Seizing her in his, he crushed her to him and gave her a long,
rich kiss. As their mouths parted, she murmured, 'Oh my
brave, foolish one. How I adore you; and how proud I am of
you.'

'Eh?' Releasing his hold on her, he looked down in surprise
into her big, limpid dark eyes and said, 'I'm afraid I don't
get you. What have I done that you should regard me as a
hero?'

'Why, darling, declaring yourself and performing the sacrifice at San Luis Caliente, of course,' she laughed.

'How did you come to hear about that?'

'From Don Alberuque. He had it through our grapevine
and was overjoyed. For persuading you to take the part of
Quetzalcoatl, he has given me ten thousand years' exemption
from Purgatory. And, fool that I was, I thought that I had
failed him.'

Adam frowned. 'Then you did leave me in the lurch at
Oaxaca because I said I wouldn't play?'

'Well, it wasn't altogether that. I would have had to leave
you the next morning anyhow. Three days was all I could
possibly squeeze out of my commitments to inspect schools,
and other things. I didn't lie to you when I said that I had
work to do. But I did decide to leave overnight because I
believed that you truly loved me and would miss me so much
that you would think things over and make up your mind to
do as I asked. But, of course, even if you hadn't, I couldn't
possibly have given you up. I've wanted you desperately
ever since; I want you now, this moment. Let's get our clothes
off and hop into bed.'

Intoxicated by her presence, Adam gave her another long
kiss, and cried, 'My sweet, I'll race you to it.' Then, laughing
like happy children, they began to fling their garments on the
floor.

A quarter of an hour later they were sitting up in bed. He

had his arm round her shoulders and she had just lit a cigarette. As she lit one for him, she said:

'Tell me, darling. Why on earth didn't you disclose yourself to Father Miguel when you saw him at the church, instead of going to the ceremony unaccompanied, and nearly getting yourself killed?'

Having had time to decide on the line he should take if she asked him that question, he replied with a smile, 'I discovered only by chance late that evening that a ceremony was to take place, and I felt that I must see what form it took.'

She gave a happy sigh. 'Now you know, and have accepted the role as Man-God, it will be very different next time. You will be escorted to the place of sacrifice in dignity and with every honour.'

'I'm afraid there is not going to be a next time,' he announced quietly.

'What!' she exclaimed, jerking her head round to stare at him with anxious, distended eyes. 'You can't mean that! You can't possibly!'

He gave her a quick kiss on the forehead. 'I'm terribly sorry to disappoint you, beloved; but I do.'

'But why? Why? Why?'

'Because I thought the whole business pretty beastly. I hated having to slaughter that wretched pig and the sight of those men guzzling its flesh afterwards was revolting.'

'One must follow the ancient ritual,' she protested. 'And what is wrong with those poor, half-starved Indians being given a meal of roast pork?'

'Maybe; but that was not the only part of the ceremony that I took exception to. I'm not a Catholic; but holding a Mass before the pig-killing episode, and bringing the Host to such a party, struck me as the most appalling sacrilege.'

'No, darling, no! There are many roads to Heaven, and I've told you before that the Indians are a mixed-up people. For centuries they have combined Christianity with their own religion. As long as they are believers in intercession through the saints and the mercy of our Lord, there is no real harm in their practising their ancient rituals.'

Suddenly she flung her arms round him and burst into tears.

As he tried to comfort her, she sobbed out, 'But, Adam, you must go on! You must! Surely you realise that the news of your appearance at San Luis has now spread all over the country? Thousands of poor people are looking to you as the Man-God, whose light and power will enable them to escape from their wretchedness to better, happier lives. You can't let a whole people down like this. Even if you don't really love me, you must think of them. But you do love me, don't you?'

'Of course I do, my sweet,' he assured her.

'Then do it for my sake, if not for theirs. And I'd planned things so beautifully. About a fortnight is still needed until everything is ready for the great day. My work is finished. There is no more I can do until I bring you, as I've promised I would, to the place of Recognition.'

After several loud sniffs, she sat up and went on, 'I've told my family that in a few days' time I have to make another round of school inspections. But I've a tiny villa down at Acapulco, which no-one knows anything about. It has a little oratory in it and I bought it so that I could go to live there while I was doing retreats, and wouldn't have my mind disturbed. Although I'll confess that I have used it for other purposes as well. The sun and the sea in that beautiful bay are heavenly, and I had planned that we should spend ten days there. Just the two of us on a sort of honeymoon before, before . . .'

Again she began to cry. His heart aching, Adam let her go on until her sobbing eased; then he said gently, 'Darling, I hate to put it to you so bluntly. But are you telling me that unless I agree to play the part of Quetzalcoatl there will be no honeymoon at Acapulco?'

Drying her eyes, she murmured, 'I didn't mean quite that. I love you so much that I'll spend those ten days with you anyway. But they won't be the same as I'd expected them to be. All the time I will be thinking of my failure to persuade you, and how everything may go wrong because of that.'

Miserably Adam heard her out, then he said, 'For your sake, sweet, I think I could face up to the primitive barbarity of these ceremonies, but there is another side to it. Whatever you may think, this is not going to be a walk-over for your people. The government is not going to throw in its hand without a fight. It will have the support of the wealthy and the new, well-to-do middle class, who are quite certain to meet force with force, rather than see themselves robbed of their possessions. Your Indians will be armed only with old-fashioned rifles, a few revolvers, knives and sabres. The other side will have tanks, machine-guns and tear gas. I know you put your faith in holy banners and that sort of thing, but they are not going to prove of any value against fire-power. You may be right that, in the end, you will win owing to the fanaticism of the Indians and sheer weight of numbers. But, believe me, if you do launch this crusade, thousands of people are going to die in agony before it ends. And I can't bring myself to be a party to starting it.'

With a sigh, she said, 'No; I understand. And I suppose you are right. There is bound to be opposition and it may not be easy to overcome. I have always believed that faith can work miracles; but several of our people have told me recently that we must be prepared to sacrifice many lives in order to win through. But we must go on; we must. It's too late now to draw back. We must put our trust in God and, with or without your help, somehow destroy the tyrants.'

For a time they lay silent, then she leaned on an elbow and looked straight into his eyes again. 'Darling, let's agree that you are right, and that there will be terrible fighting. I'm not quite so besotted about my people as to think them saints. They have a savage streak in them that will come out when they see their friends shot down. Many of them will go berserk, give no quarter and behave with terrible brutality.

'If you were paramount among them you could prevent that. As the Man-God, whatever you decreed would be scrupulously obeyed. Not one of them would dare disobey your divine commands. If you decreed that there must be no burning, no looting, no killing of prisoners, you could save many lives and an infinity of misery. Had you thought of that?'

Adam had not. She had presented to him an entirely new aspect of the part he could play in the coming struggle; and she was obviously convinced that nothing could now stop it

from taking place. Knowing that the authorities were on to it,
he doubted that; but she might be right. Greatly as he sym-
pathised with the wretched lot of the Indians, he still felt that
it was up to him to do what he could to prevent a revolt, and
to accept the role of Quetzalcoatl could only stimulate it.

On the other hand, as Quetzalcoatl he would learn the intentions of the conspirators. He would then be in a position
to pass on such information to Ramón, and so give the Ministry of Security a much better chance to prevent the rebellion
by arresting the leaders just before they intended to start it.

Mentally he squirmed at the thought of playing such a role.
It would mean betraying in the basest manner the woman
who had given him her love. He already realised that, behind
her noble profile and high, narrow forehead, there lay the
mind of a fanatic, and a confused mind at that. In some
strange way she reconciled a fervid belief in the Roman Catholic Faith with a contemptuous disregard for its moral pre-
cepts—for she had made no secret of it to Adam that from
the age of seventeen she had had a succession of lovers. Again,
by some inexplicable mental gymnastic, she could see nothing
contrary to the principles of Christianity in permitting the
Indians to couple in their thoughts their pagan gods with
Christian saints, and to perform blood sacrifices in immediate
succession to the celebration of the Mass. Perhaps the strangest contrast of all was that for one half of her life she was an
elegant, beautifully-gowned leader of Mexico's wildly extravagant young socialites who drank and danced till dawn, and
for the other half she was a teacher and conscientious Inspec-
tor of Schools, working for an agnostic government that she
detested. Yet all this made it no less the fact that, should he
do as she wished and pass on to Ramón the knowledge of
the conspiracy he gained thereby, he would be qualifying for
a new nickname—'Judas' Gordon.

They were lying embraced. Suddenly he freed himself from
her arms, sat up in bed and said, 'Darling, I've got to think.
Stay where you are. I won't be long.'

Getting out of bed, he went into the bathroom. He much
preferred baths to showers, but realised that now a shower
would serve him better. To start with, he turned the water

on lukewarm, then he increased the cold flow until it became icy and he was shivering. Turning off the water, he stepped through into the bathroom, dried himself, then sat down on the edge of the bath and once more grappled with his problem.

If he stood aside, it seemed unlikely that the Ministry of Security would secure enough information during the next ten days to prevent an outbreak of violence. If there was an outbreak, it was absolutely certain that many innocent people would die or suffer before it could be suppressed. If he took on the role of Quetzalcoatl, there was a good chance that he could enable the Ministry to prevent a rebellion from starting. If, even so, it did occur, and the Indian masses succeeded in overwhelming the forces of the government, as the Man-God his powers would be immense. He could prevent excesses during the conflict and, after it, become the Protector of the defeated. His mind was no longer clouded with doubt. However heavy the burden on his own conscience of betraying Chela, his duty lay in endeavouring to save the thousands of innocent people from the blood-bath of a revolution.

Returning to the bedroom, he smiled at Chela and said, 'You win, darling. I'll do as you wish.'

He little knew what he was letting himself in for.

11

The Stolen Honeymoon

NOW that the die was cast, Adam put the future out of his mind and Chela's happiness was unalloyed. Time drifted by unnoticed as they talked, laughed and delighted in one another. It was not until they felt hungry that they looked at the time and found it to be half past eight. Rather than dress and go out or to the restaurant, they decided to dine there and studied the elaborate room menu together. Chela collected her clothes from the floor and took refuge in the bathroom, while Adam rang for the floor waiter and ordered double portions of everything; which, as he towered over the man by a head and shoulders, did not seem to surprise him.

When the meal had been wheeled in, Chela put on one of Adam's pyjama jackets which, tall as she was, came down to her knees. Giggling, they shared the glass and Adam cut up the food, feeding her with the fork. Replete with champagne, a truffled omelette, lobster and strawberries, they went back to bed; but as they had decided to make a fairly early start the next morning and Chela had to pack, she dressed before midnight and, after many kisses, left him.

At nine o'clock the following morning, Adam rang up the Enriquezes' penthouse and, using an assumed name, asked for Ramón. His intention was to report that he had accepted the role of Quetzalcoatl with the object of finding out the conspirators' plans, but Ramón had already gone out.

At ten o'clock Chela arrived in her car and they set off on their two-hundred-and-sixty-mile drive. The way out of the city lay through a seemingly endless suburb, towards the end of which Adam noticed that at the roadside the small houses and shops had numbers over five thousand. But, at last, they were clear of the built-up area and out on the fine motorway to the south.

It was the road on which lay both Cuernavaca and Taxco, but by-passes took them round those cities. By that time they had come down several thousand feet, it was much hotter and the vegetation gave ample evidence of the difference in temperature. They had left behind the almost barren mountain slopes upon which little but occasional groups of firs and casuarinas grew. The hillsides were now more thickly wooded, there were many palms and, here and there, clusters of spiky euphorbias, some looking in the distance like irregular patches of straight poles from twelve to fifteen feet in height and others like giant hands with many prickly fingers.

For the whole of the way from Mexico City to Acapulco the road was fenced on both sides, to prevent animals from straying on to it and becoming a danger to the traffic, and the surface was so good that, along straight stretches, they were able to travel at ninety miles an hour. Patches of cultivation were few and far between but, after Taxco, every half-mile or so beyond the wire fence there were groups of from twenty to forty square-topped, gaily-painted beehives, and the country became much more picturesque. The last forty-odd miles of their drive was alongside a wide, but almost dried-up, river bed. Wooded mountains rose on every side, the road curved sharply every few hundred yards to run up steep gradients then plunge down again, and, beyond the heights in their immediate vicinity, there was always a vista of blue mountains in the distance.

It was four o'clock when they entered Acapulco, with its beautiful mountain-surrounded double bay. After all that Adam had read about Mexico, he expected to see some evidence of the ancient glories of this city which, in the seventeenth century, had been the largest port on the Pacific in all the Americas.

Spanish expeditions had sailed from it to establish new colonies as far south as Chile and as far north as San Francisco. It had also been the Spaniards' base for trading with their settlements in the East Indies and Manila. Since their rivals, the Portuguese, had denied them a peaceful passage home by the western route via Ceylon, the Spaniards had sent all their rich cargoes of spices, silks and ivories from the East to Acapulco, had them carried by thousands of native porters overland to Vera Cruz, then shipped again across the Atlantic to Spain. The Philippines had, in fact, been ruled from Mexico, which is why today their culture has no resemblance to that of their Asiastic neighbours, but is entirely Spanish.

But, except for a double-domed cathedral facing the little square, not a building was left from the days when great fleets of unwieldy galleons, caravels and pinnaces had sailed from Acapulco harbour. In recent years it had become a holiday resort of the first rank, rivalling Juan les Pins or Miami Beach for luxury and high prices.

Chela turned left along the great sweep of the southern-most bay. Interspersed with lines of palm trees, there reared up huge, many-storeyed hotels of glass and concrete. On the inland side of the road were more modest buildings: restaurants, airline offices, cafés, motels, tourist agencies, night clubs and garages, eager to supply every facility for the enjoyment of this sunny playground. After some two miles they gave way to another two miles of private villas set in spacious gardens; then, when the car had reached the far end of the bay, facing the town, Chela turned off the coast road to take one that wound up a steep hill.

'This,' she told Adam, 'is the Las Brisas estate. It is mainly occupied by an hotel which is unique. I don't think there is another quite like it in the world.'

Craning his neck, Adam looked up the wooded eight-hundred-foot-high hillside they were climbing. Between the trees, and what looked like croton hedges, he could see scattered about quite a number of small, flat-roofed villas but no building of any size, and he asked:

'Where is the hotel? All I can see is scores of little bungalows.'

She laughed. 'They are the hotel. Each consists of a big double bedroom and bathroom. In each there is a fridge containing soft drinks and a big dish of fruit, and above it there

is a bar carrying a selection of a dozen wines, spirits and
liqueurs. Outside is a terrace with a private swimming pool,
chairs, tables and lilos, which cannot be overlooked from any
of the other little villas. Every morning one of the hotel boys
comes up, cleans the pool and scatters a hundred or so hibiscus blossoms on it, while another leaves a set of thermos con-
tainers outside the door, so that you have only to take it in and
have a hot breakfast at any hour you wish. The hotel owns
over a hundred jeeps. Look, there is one with its red and
white striped awning. If you wish to go to the restaurant,
halfway down the slope, you have only to ring up for one.
Or they will take you right down to the shore, where there
are several big enclosures for swimming, protected from
sharks, speedboats for water ski-ing, barbecues and bars. So
you can take your choice: either join the merry throng along
the beach, or telephone down for your meals to be sent up to
you and live like sybaritic hermits in your private heaven.'

Adam turned to smile at her. 'How absolutely marvellous.
But you told me you had your own villa, so I take it we will
have to fend for ourselves.'

She shook her head. 'No, darling. There are quite a number
of villas on the far side of the estate that are privately owned
but enjoy the service of the hotel. I have one of them and we'll
soon be there.'

Ten minutes later they arrived. Chela had telephoned in
advance, so they found everything ready for their reception:
the bar re-stocked, blossoms floating on the surface of the
oval swimming pool, big bath towels laid out on the lilos, and
flowers on the altar of Chela's little chapel.

As Adam entered the spacious, air-conditioned bedroom,
he had not failed to notice that, instead of twin beds, it contained the largest double bed he had ever seen. Chela had
made no secret of it that she had used this luxury hideout before for purposes quite other than periods of solitary religious
contemplation and, as she went into her oratory to say a short
prayer of thanksgiving for their safe arrival, he marvelled
again at the complexity of her nature.

The villa was four hundred feet up the hillside and from
the terrace there was a magnificent vista across the great bay,

but it was extremely hot. As soon as they had got their suitcases from the car, they stripped and swam naked in the
pool. Afterwards, wrapping Chela in one of the big bath
sheets, Adam carried her into the bedroom then, laughing
with joy, they made love on the huge bed.

The eight days that followed were undiluted bliss for them.
There were no telephone calls or post to distract them. On
most days they never left the villa, but on one occasion they
drove in to have a look round the town and lunched in the
garden of the Hilton, after having drinks at the great, circular,
thatched bar which stands in the middle of the huge swimming pool. On another day they had cocktails on the seaside
terrace of the El Presidente, with its tropical trees and the
rocks below them lit with red floodlights. Afterwards they
dined at La Perla, on the north side of the peninsula that
separates the two bays. The restaurant there is built out in a
series of semi-circular terraces, suspended one hundred and
thirty feet above a cove only fifteen feet wide, bordered by
treacherous rocks. For the entertainment of visitors, courageous young Mexicans dive from one side of the chasm, nearly
one hundred and fifty feet into the wildly-foaming sea below.

While Adam was applauding this audacious feat, Chela
stubbed out her cigar and said angrily, 'Just think of it! Those
young men risk their lives every night for a mere pittance,
when they should have land enough to live out their lives in
prosperity and safety.'

Her bitter comment brought Adam sharply back from the
halcyon existence he was enjoying, to the fact that he had
pledged himself to play a leading role in a most dangerous
undertaking, and that in a few days' time he might have to
face the awful situation that, greatly as he loved Chela, it was
his duty to betray her.

Those last few days sped by more swiftly than a few hours
spent on uncongenial tasks and, all too soon, their glorious
honeymoon was over. On the evening of the second Friday
after their arrival, Chela broke it to Adam that they must
leave on the following morning to go down to Yucatán; but
beyond that she could tell him nothing, as not until they got
there would she receive further instructions. After a last

hectic night in the little villa they reluctantly drove back to Mexico City. On the way they stopped for an hour to look round Textla, then lunched at Taxco, so it was not until half past five that Chela put Adam down at the El Presidente. As she did so, she said :

'You won't have any too long to rearrange your packing, because I put off leaving Acapulco until the last possible moment, and we have to fly down to Mérida on the seven-thirty plane. Take only your lightest things, darling, because it will be very hot down there. I'll call for you in a taxi in an hour.'

While down at Acapulco, Adam had had no possible opportunity to get in touch with Ramón; so the first thing he did on entering the hotel was to ring up the penthouse, but it was Saturday and Ramón was spending the week-end at Cuernavaca. As Adam had stayed at the El Presidente and intended to return, the management courteously placed at his disposal a room to change in and promised to have the luggage he had left there sent up. As soon as he reached the room he put through a call to Cuernavaca, only to learn that Ramón had gone out.

To write him a letter seemed too dangerous, for Adam had heard it said that security officers carried out spot checks on Mexican mail. That might not be true; but if the letter did fall into wrong hands, some officious person might make a lot of trouble for Chela and himself before Bernadino or Ramón could intervene on their behalf. Moreover, Ramón had particularly stressed the importance of no action being taken against the conspirators until the leaders were in the net, so to commit anything about it to paper was obviously most undesirable. While he was re-packing he decided that there was, after all, no real urgency about the matter, since as yet he had no definite information about the conspirators' plans that he could report.

It was only twenty minutes' drive to the airport, so they were in plenty of time to catch their plane. The aircraft was comfortable and their flight of one and three-quarter hours uneventful. When they arrived at Mérida they were met by

a porter from the Pan Americana Hotel and taken there in
the hotel bus.

As Mérida was a provincial city, Adam had not expected
the accommodation there to be superior to that of the Victoria at Oaxaca, so on entering the Pan Americana he got
quite a surprise. It had a spacious entrance hall, where a
dozen lofty columns surrounded a pond out of which grew
tall tropical trees and flowering shrubs. Beyond it was an
even larger courtyard open to the sky, on the far side of that
a cocktail lounge in which a dance could have been given for
two hundred people and, above it, a restaurant that looked
out on to a big swimming pool.

He was delighted to learn that Chela had booked adjacent
rooms for them by telephone from Mexico City and, as there
were no instructions awaiting her they would, at least for a
day or two, be able to continue their 'honeymoon'. The bedrooms and bathrooms were spacious, with air-conditioning
and every comfort; but they were very tired after their long
day so, for the first time since they had been together, they
slept apart.

Next morning they hired a car to take them to Chichén
Itzá, where there is the greatest area of Maya ruins in Yucatán. By daylight Adam saw that, although Mérida had two
hundred thousand inhabitants, it showed no signs of modern-
isation or prosperity, as was the case with the capital. The
buildings were old and low; the streets narrow and dirty. As
a precaution against motorists speeding and endangering the
lives of the townsfolk, every few hundred yards there were
rows of studs the size of half-footballs, that drivers either had
to slow down to avoid or risk their cars being thrown out of
control by a violent bump.

On their way out of the city, Chela pointed out to him a
large, plaster elephant, a jaguar and other animals on the
roofs at street corners and told him that they had been put
there to identify the streets for people who could not read, just
as painted swinging signs had been used in mediaeval London
and Paris. She also pointed out to him a large but decayed-
looking palace. It was the 'Town House', to which Indians
coming in from the country with their produce could bring

their hammocks and sleep free for the night.

The road led dead straight through the flattest country imaginable. For miles on end at either side of it were fields of sisal—a spiky cactus from which rope is made—almost Yucatán's sole industry. Here and there cut bundles of the leaves lay waiting to be collected. Very occasionally there were patches of maize and dumps of charcoal, the making of which further impoverishes the fertility of the country by reducing its wooded areas, but which is the only fuel available to the Indians.

The land looked incredibly poor. There was little soil and everywhere rocks protruded from the surface. The villages were about fifteen miles apart. The dwellings in them were mostly one-room about fifteen feet by eight, oval in shape, the walls made of mud plastered on to a frame of cane and with openings both at the back and the front. In their dark interiors could be glimpsed native women with sagging breasts, naked children, goats and scrawny hens. About them grew a few mango, breadfruit and paw-paw trees, but there were no flowers or cultivated plants.

About halfway on their two-hour drive they passed out of the vast sisal area and jungle took its place at the roadside. But it was like no jungle that Adam had ever imagined. The soil was so poor and rocky that, but for an occasional palm, there were no trees over thirty feet in height. It was solid bush, low but dense, largely composed of mimosa, with here and there a kapok or bean tree. To a depth of about forty feet either side of the road it had been cut down, and they passed several groups of Indians at this work, dispiritedly wielding what appeared to be long swords. Adam had read that in the jungles of Yucatán there were to be seen many beautiful birds, but the only birds he saw were long lines of horrid-looking black buzzards perched on the low stone walls.

By the time they reached Chichén Itzá it had become very hot; but they decided that, instead of going into the hotel for a drink, they would do the ruins first, before it became still hotter. The ruins covered an area even larger than those at Monte Albán, the greater part of them being on the left of the road. It took them over two hours just to walk to each pyramid in turn and go up the largest one.

It had ninety-one steps on each side, approximating to the three hundred and sixty-five days of the year, and corners in thirteen stages to represent the fifty-two weeks. On the top was a low, flat-roofed temple; inside, at the back, was a three-foot-high stone platform upon which the Vestals had danced before one of them was chosen for sacrifice.

Behind the great pyramid was another called that of the 'Warriors'. Alongside it was a vast, now roofless, hall, from the floor of which rose a thousand stone columns. In it stood an altar on which new fire had been created every fifty-two years. A lower pyramid had been named after Venus, because of the star upon it. Beside this was a path that had once been a fine, paved way. Following it through the jungle for half a mile they came to a huge, natural well. It formed a crater some hundred yards in diameter and a hundred feet deep. The chosen Vestal Virgins had first been drugged and then thrown into it to drown and become brides of the Rain God.

Facing the great pyramid, but a quarter of a mile away across the flat surface of the ground, was a colonnade with a fresco of skulls. Behind it was the largest of the seven Ball Courts. There the Mayas had played some game of still unknown religious significance. It was two hundred feet long by forty wide. On either side it had raised walkways below high walls. Halfway along both walls, a large stone ring stood out through which the ball had had to pass to score a goal. It was said that in this sacred game there were seven men a side. They were not permitted to touch the ball with their hands or feet, only with their hips or elbows, and the captain of the losing team paid for defeat with his life. This appeared to be borne out by a carving in stone inserted into one of the low walkways under the tall walls.

They lunched at the hotel then, in the intense heat of the early afternoon, made a round of the ruins on the right side of the road. To reach them they had to walk half a mile along a twisting jungle path. In that area lay the Pyramid of the Brothers, the Nunnery, which was pure early Maya architecture, and a circular Maya observatory to which the Toltecs had later added a square top. Another early building consisted of a series of 'corbelled' arches, formed by each layer of stone on both sides protruding a little beyond that below it until the gap was closed and they met.

Looking at them, Adam remarked, 'I've seen photographs of Minoan buildings with arches exactly like these, and they are said to be the earliest form of arch devised by man. Of course, it might be just coincidence, but it does support the possibility that the Cretans did cross the Atlantic and founded colonies here.'

Chela squeezed his arm and laughed. 'Poor Christopher Columbus. How upset he would be if he knew that people are beginning to believe that the ancients beat him in his discovery of America by two thousand years.'

Adam found these vast remains of a long-dead civilisation fascinating. Although he had had no definite revelation, seeing the ruins of Chichén Itzá convinced him that he had succeeded in escaping from the Chichimecs and rejoined his own people there. He had a strong impression that they had found it already abandoned by the Mayas, restored it, added to it and made it their new capital.

Tired out and dripping with perspiration, they had long drinks at the hotel, then returned to their car. As it had had the sun beating on its roof for several hours, the interior was like a furnace. When, with all the windows down, it moved off, they were incredibly grateful for the small breeze.

Fitfully, they dozed on the way back to Mérida but, on arriving there, they had a dip in the pool and afterwards felt much refreshed. Chela then told Adam that she had found a letter awaiting her with orders that next day they should move on to Uxmal; so they telephoned for rooms at the Hacienda Hotel there. By dinner-time they had recovered from their fatigue and, this being the last night they might have together for some time, they made the most of it.

Next morning they were driven in their hired car the one and a quarter hours' run to Uxmal. For the first hour the road was again dead flat, then the car ascended a slight rise. At the top they stopped the car to get out and look at the view. It was unlike any that Adam had ever seen. For as far as he could see the flat, brownish-green landscape continued in

front and to either side, unbroken by a single low hill or
building of any kind.

At Uxmal he again found the hotel much more attractive
than he had expected. It did not compare with the Pan Americana at Mérida, but was a two-storey building, three sides
of which enclosed a swimming pool, arching over which there
were trees from which birds with colourful plumage flew to
and fro, and beyond which there was a well-cared-for two-
acre garden.

Again they had adjoining rooms, which were not air-conditioned but had wire screens to keep out the mosquitoes
and were pleasantly cool after the intense heat in the open.
When their bags were brought along, the porter was accompanied by a waiter, bringing them tumblers of iced pineapple
juice, with the compliments of the management. Although
their journey had not been a long one, the car had been like
an oven, so the iced drink went down like nectar.

Changing at once into bathing things, they went out to the
pool, which was partly shaded by the trees on its far side,
spent half an hour there then, in their wraps, drank Maya-
land cocktails sitting outside the bar.

There were not many people in the hotel and most of them
were elderly Americans. That had been the case in all the
larger hotels at which Adam had stayed and, as he lounged
in this perfect holiday setting, he thought how sad it was that
so few young people had the money to travel to distant places
and stay in such delightful surroundings.

About the three-sided Hacienda, with its interior surround
of covered walkways outside the ground-floor bedrooms, the
pool dappled by sunlight coming through the leaves of the
trees, the stillness broken only by the cawing of the brightly-
hued birds and the occasional movement of servants or visitors, there was such an air of peace and normality that Adam
could hardly credit that he had involved himself in a dangerous conspiracy. But he was soon to have evidence of it.

As they went in to lunch, a short man in dark clothes, with
a round, pink face, half rose from his table and bowed to
Chela. She acknowledged his bow but did not stop to speak
to him. The lunch proved excellent, the main course being

duck, and they were given one apiece. They were quite small, but did not taste like wild duck, and Adam demolished his with gusto. Down here in the hot lands there was a greater variety of fruit than Adam had ever before seen. For dessert a big basket was placed before them, in which were heaped mangoes, figs, guavas, apricots, pomegranates, mammees, tiny red bananas and zapotes. The last were green, peach-shaped fruit with black flesh, and he found their flavour unique.

On leaving the dining room they found the short, round-faced man waiting for them and Chela introduced him in a low voice as Father Lopéz. He did not extend his hand to Adam, but made him a grave bow then said:

'I am honoured, señor. May I request a short conversation with you? It is a private matter, so perhaps it would be best if we took a walk round the garden.'

This request by a priest jolted Adam back to the unpleasant reality that his glorious, unofficial honeymoon was about to come to an end and that he would soon be called on to carry out his promise to Chela. As he assented, Father Lopéz murmured with a smile, 'We have no secrets from the Señorita, and I should be happy for her to accompany us.'

For a few hundred yards the three of them walked in Indian file along a winding, concrete path bordered by banana palms, frangipane trees and clumps of flowers. The path led down a slope and when they came to an open, circular space at the bottom, where several paths met, the priest said:

'We must not stay long under the blazing sun, so I will be as brief as possible. There will be two ceremonies at which the presence of the Man-God is required: one here, and a second in another place. The first will be that of Recognition. Participation in the sacrifice at San Luis Caliente was un-heralded and the congregation there consisted almost entirely of people of little importance. It is, therefore, necessary that the Man-God should appear to the leaders of our sacred move-ment from all over the country. They will then be able to vouch to their followers that the return of Quetzalcoatl is no idle rumour, but that they have seen the Man-God with their own eyes. To that end they will assemble here.'

'When?' Adam asked.

Father López spread out his plump hands. 'Many of them must come from distant places. The ceremony cannot take place until they have all arrived. But most of them are already in hiding in the neighbourhood and the rest should soon complete their journeys; so it will not be long.'

'And the second ceremony?'

'Again, I cannot say. Time must be given for the leaders to return to their districts, and further time for them to spread the word so that it reaches even the remotest villages.'

'What is to happen then?'

'The Man-God will appear again to a chosen congregation. That will be the signal for five million men to rise, proclaim their faith and launch the crusade that is to drive the wicked from the seats of power. But let us return to the immediate future.' Drawing a sheet of paper from his pocket, Father López went on:

'It is known that the Man-God can speak Nahuatl, but that, although understood by a greater number of our Indians than any other, is only one of scores of languages that are their only tongue in many parts of the country. Indeed, tens of thousands of them are still so backward that they can comprehend only their own dialect. In what language the Man-God should address the congregation that is to assemble here has, therefore, been a problem.'

'So I am expected to speak,' Adam said, a shade dubiously.

'That is essential. And as we are in Yucatán, where the Man-God was last seen in his earlier incarnation, it has been decided that he should speak in Maya.'

Adam frowned. 'But that is impossible. I don't know it.'

'No matter.' The priest handed him the sheet of paper. 'Here is the speech. It is quite short, so can be learned by heart without difficulty. I speak Maya fluently, and my services as a coach in pronunciation will be available.'

Taking the paper, Adam quickly ran his eye down it. There were only some twenty lines of Maya typescript and beneath each was another, giving the phonetic pronunciation of the words above. As he stared at it, he suddenly realised that some of the expressions were familiar and that during his dreams he must at times have spoken Maya as well as Nahuatl.

'Very well, Father,' he said, pocketing the paper. 'Perhaps we could try it over after dinner tonight.'

The priest bowed. 'I should be honoured to be of assistance.'

There seemed no more to be said; so they walked back up the slope to the hotel and, perspiring from the heat, went to their rooms for their siesta.

Sitting on the edge of his bed, Adam read through the speech more carefully. After reading it three times he could make out its sense. In effect it said:

'In my person is reincarnated the Man-God Quetzalcoatl. A thousand years ago I left your ancestors to sail away to the east. But I promised that I would return and I now redeem that promise. In the past I brought you rain to ensure you good harvests every year. I gave you wise laws and kept the peace among you. In those days the fields and the fruits of the earth were yours. You have been wickedly dispossessed of a great part of them and I have grieved for you. Now I am come again to restore to you all that you have lost. The day is not far distant when I shall call upon you to rise in your might and destroy the evil-doers. Have no fear. Obey your priests, have faith in the Holy Virgin and our Lord Jesus Christ, whose representative I am, and you cannot fail to triumph.'

Again Adam's mind turned to Ramón and that he ought to be informed of what was afoot. But to get in touch with him was not going to be easy. In Mexico long-distance calls often took an hour or more to get through and in no circumstances must Chela become aware that he was secretly selling out her friends to her half-brother. If she learned that he had put through a call to Mexico City she would want to know why. And what explanation could he give? But during the siesta he might get a call through without her knowledge.

Making up his mind to risk it, he put on his shirt again, with the intention of going along to the office. As he was doing so, the communicating door leading to Chela's room opened and she came in. With a smile she said:

'Hello, darling. I'm afraid it's too hot for us to lie embraced, but as there is a double bed here I thought I'd come and lie down beside you.'

That, for the time being, put an end to any possibility of Adam's telephoning Ramón. Before he was much older he was to have cause to rue it.

12

At the Pyramid of the Magician

IN THE cool of the evening, they walked the half-mile to see the Uxmal ruins. Unlike those at Chichén Itzá, these were on hilly country; they did not cover so great an area, but were almost as impressive. The sight of them again stirred memories in Adam, and he felt certain that some important event in his past life had occurred there.

The nearest to the road was the Pyramid of the Magician. It was very high and the steepest in Mexico. The flat-roofed temple on the top was only partly in ruins, and the lintels over the doorways were huge balks of wood, showing it to be pure Maya and very old.

Down in a hollow, some way behind it, there was a large, square court, on all four sides of which there were long buildings about twenty feet in height. They faced inward, stood on terraces well above the level of the court and had a number of doorways and beautifully-carved façades. The Spaniards had christened this well-preserved ruin 'The Court of the Nuns', because the stonework in the upper half of one of the buildings has been carved in the form of a grille; but Adam knew it to have been the university at which Maya priests were educated in the mysteries.

On much higher ground, a third of a mile to the left of the pyramid, stood another long and quite lofty building, known as the Governor's House, because it was the biggest of its kind in Mexico. Over each of the doorways and at the corners there were many carvings, several times larger than life, of the 'Plumed Serpent'—a man's head looking out from the distended jaws of a crested snake—which was Quetzalcoatl's symbol.

Behind the Governor's House, the ground fell away sharply, almost in a precipice, and across the valley from it stood another large building, now a ruin. The upper structure consisted of a row of gables, which gave it the appearance of a thick-toothed comb. In the gables there were many square holes which had purposely been left unfilled, to let in air. For this reason it was now called 'The House of the Pigeons'.

Scattered about in the area there were several other ruins and fallen monoliths which Adam could recall in the days of their splendour as temples and palaces with crowds of brightly-clad priests and warriors moving about among them.

The sun was just setting as they returned to the hotel, but it was still blissfully warm; so they again swam before dinner. Afterwards they went out into the garden with Father Lopéz, and Adam recited his piece.

The priest was far from happy about Adam's rendering of it and declared that, as pronounced by him, it was hardly recognisable as Maya. Adam thought he knew the answer to that. Every language is constantly changing. When practising that afternoon, he had ignored the phonetic spelling under the typed sentences and, as more and more of his past acquaintance with Maya returned to him, said the speech over as he would have done a thousand years earlier.

Obviously it was pointless to address an audience in a speech which none of them would understand; so, without arguing about the matter, Adam submissively allowed Father Lopéz to coach him in modern Maya, repeated the speech sentence by sentence after him three times, and agreed to have another session with him the following morning.

Next day, as there was nothing whatever to do at Uxmal except laze in the hotel or walk round the ruins, Adam and Chela made a second visit to the ancient temple-city before the sun became too hot. Rambling about there aroused in Adam many vague memories of people and ceremonies. He described them to Chela, but she reluctantly admitted that, like Chichén Itzá, Uxmal recalled nothing to her, so it was unlikely that she had ever lived in either.

On returning to the hotel they found Father Lopéz impatiently awaiting them. By then the sun was well up in the heavens, in the garden there were no great trees that would give shade to several people, and he was naturally reluctant to give Adam further instruction in the pronunciation of his speech anywhere where they might be overheard. In consequence, the garden it had to be. As Adam had practised the speech several times early that morning with Chela, after a few minor corrections the pink-faced priest said he thought it would pass; but they must have another session after dinner that evening.

Adam and Chela swam, lunched, had their siesta together, swam again and, in due course, went in to dinner. Several times during the day he had been worried by the thought that he really ought to let Ramón know what was going on, but he was never out of Chela's sight for more than a few minutes. For his continued failure to contact Ramón he comforted himself with the thought that the first ceremony was to be one only of 'Recognition'. There must then elapse a period of at least ten days, possibly a fortnight or three weeks, before he was to make another appearance somewhere else that would trigger off the rebellion. When they had returned to Mexico City with, he expected, many days to go it seemed certain that plenty of chances would occur for him to get in touch with Ramón and put him in the picture.

After they had dined, Father Lopéz invited them to have coffee and liqueurs with him. Adam once more recited his speech and it was finally approved; then they settled themselves at a table in a corner of the bar and talked of a variety of subjects.

It emerged that the little priest was an authority on Mexico's ancient civilisations. Adam, owing to his visions, had a considerable knowledge of a people whom he had recently realised were the Toltecs and some knowledge of the Mayas, but only during the tenth century AD. Apart from that, he knew only what he had acquired from books; so he asked:

'Can you explain the cause of the Maya migrations? From what I have read, over a period of two thousand years they developed four separate capitals, many hundreds of miles apart, all having great pyramids and other buildings; here, at Palenque, in Honduras and in Guatemala. Yet there is no evidence that they were driven from one to another by war. Every five hundred years or so they just abandoned everything, made a great trek and started somewhere else from scratch.'

Father Lopéz nodded. 'That is so, and it is most unlikely that they were forced by enemies to abandon their cities. When Cortés landed, the Maya civilisation had existed for over three thousand years, yet they had not become decadent and showed greater courage than any of the other Indian nations. Cortés destroyed the Aztec Empire in two years; it took his lieutenants, the de Montejos, fifteen to defeat the Mayas, and another half-century was to elapse before the Spaniards were fully masters of Yucatán. No; the only possible explanation for the Maya migrations is the poverty of Mexico's soil.

'The Indians lived almost entirely on maize, fruit and vegetables, as indeed the majority of our people still do today. And the cultivation of maize spells death to the land. The earth here is a thin layer of decomposed limestone. After two years' cropping, its fertility is exhausted, then the peasants must clear new areas of jungle. As time went on, these *milpas*, as they are called, had to be further and further from the centre of the civilisation; and, at last, so distant from it that the time and labour given to bringing the maize to the capital did not leave long enough for the peasants to cultivate their plots. Famine must have ensued and year after year become worse until eventually the Maya rulers were forced to order the whole nation to march out into the wilderness in search of another great area of virgin land.'

'Then that would account for Mexico's having, for its size, so little land suitable for raising crops.'

'That is the main cause, but it was unwittingly aggravated by the Spaniards. Before their arrival, the Indians used a pointed stick to make holes in which they planted each grain separately. By that method the subsoil was not disturbed; but the Spaniards introduced the plough. That resulted in the destruction of the root fibres which held the earth together. When the heavy rains came there was nothing to prevent the soil from being washed away, or, in the long, dry season, strong winds whipping it up and whirling it off.'

'I see. So that is the explanation for the dust-storms that plague Mexico City and other places. I have been told that the Spaniards also did an immense amount of damage to the land by cutting down the forests in order to make the thousands of beams they needed for building their towns and churches.'

'True,' the priest agreed. 'But it should not be forgotten that the Spaniards brought great benefits to Mexico; first and foremost, the Christian Faith. Then they imported sheep and bred them in vast numbers, so that the export of wool became second only to that of silver as Mexico's source of wealth. For that, the establishment of a sugar industry and many other profitable ventures, the great Cortés was responsible.'

'Yet I gather that today his name is hated here.'

'You are right. They even carry their hatred to Doña Marina, the clever young woman who was given to him as a slave and remained for many years his devoted mistress. She spoke two Indian languages and quickly learned Spanish; so as an interpreter she was invaluable to him. The Aztecs gave her the name of "Malinche", which means "the Tongue". Now that word has a double meaning. If you wish to say that a person is a traitor you term him a "Malinche".'

Father Lopéz paused to sip his brandy, then went on, 'But this abuse of Cortés is most unjust. He was not only a great soldier and shrewd statesman. After the conquest he became a great administrator and adopted a wise policy of conciliation towards the conquered. He resettled the Indians who had been dispossessed of their lands, relieved the *caciques* of all taxes and made them magistrates over their own communities, appointed many Indians to high office and, as far as he possibly could, protected the lower orders from being exploited by unscrupulous fortune-hunters. So beloved was he that they christened him "Mighty Father" and, when he at last retired to Spain, the whole populace was stricken by a great grief.'

'You surprise me,' Adam remarked. 'I had no idea that Mexico owed so much to him.'

Chela frowned. 'Perhaps to him; but think of the brutal way in which most of the other Conquistadores treated the people.'

'More is made of that now than the facts justify, my child,' Father Lopéz said mildly. 'From the beginning the great Dominican, Fra Bartolomé de las Casas took up the cudgels on behalf of the Indians. His furious diatribes to the Council of the Indies in Seville, denouncing those Conquistadores who despoiled the Indians, soon resulted in Holy Mother Church intervening on their behalf.'

Adam smiled. 'Yes, I've read his work, and Bernal Díaz's wonderful descriptions of the marvels of art and architecture here that, in their different way, could rival anything produced by the Renaissance. But I must say, Las Casas struck me as prejudiced. He seemed a little too vitriolic against the soldiers to be painting quite a true picture.'

'Perhaps; but by repetition he made his point. And he was far from being alone in his determination to secure for the Indians equal rights with their conquerors. The first two Viceroys, Don Antonio de Mendoza and Don Luis de Velasco, also played a part that cannot be praised too highly. Both were humanitarians of the highest principles and would suffer no wrong to be done to the Indians. Between them, in fewer than thirty years, they brought order out of chaos, and made Mexico a land good to live in. The high standard they set was followed by many of their successors; and it should not be forgotten that for the three hundred years that Mexico was ruled from Spain, while the European nations were almost constantly at war, the people here enjoyed peace and security.'

'That's true,' Adam agreed. 'The Pax Española in the New World lasted nearly twice as long as the Pax Britannica in India and the East. I imagine that few people in Europe, outside Spain, realise that.'

'Yet it is so. Our troubles began only when the so-called "yoke" of Spain was thrown off, and the Church deprived of much of her power to ensure that the people did not become the victims of their baser instincts. Since then it has been one long tale of self-seeking, injustice and bloodshed.'

Breaking off, Father Lopéz looked at his watch and exclaimed, 'Dear me, I have been talking too much! It is a quarter to eleven and we are due at the pyramid at eleven o'clock.'

Startled, Adam sat up straight. He had assumed that the ceremony would not take place for another day or two, and that he would be given warning of it. This pleasant talk about the Conquistadores had lulled him into a false sense of security. Uneasily he turned and looked at Chela. She was just lighting a second cigar. Smiling at him, she said:

'Women are not permitted to be present at such ceremonies, darling; so I can't go with you. But I know that you will acquit yourself nobly.'

Reluctantly, but putting the best face on the situation that he could manage, Adam said good-bye to her and accompanied Father Lopéz out of the hotel.

The night was warm and the garden scented by moonflowers. On leaving it they followed the road for some distance, then the priest turned off it and led the way along a bridle path. It was densely wooded on either side and it was not until they emerged from it, a quarter of an hour later, that Adam realised that it by-passed the Pyramid of the Magician to bring them out opposite the Court of the Nuns.

During their walk Father Lopéz had made light conversation, to which Adam had replied only in monosyllables, as he was grimly wondering what form the ceremony would take. Now, as they approached the building, the priest addressed him formally:

'From now on, throughout the ceremony, it is required that the Man-God should utter no word, except to make his declaration to the people, and return no obeisance that is made to him.' In silence, side by side, they walked the last few hundred yards.

From the Court there came a faint glow and, as they

emerged on to one of the terraces, Adam saw that there were lights and people in some of the rooms that opened on to it. As he passed one of them, he glimpsed several priests in their surplices kneeling in prayer, and in another a set of gorgeous Indian robes arranged on bamboo frames. Halting at the entrance of the third room they came to, Father López stood aside and signed to Adam to enter.

Five or six priests were in the room, all clad in rich vestments. Among them Adam instantly recognised Don Alberuque. All the other priests were Indians or Mestizos. Again, as Adam met the glance of the Monsignor's black, lustreless eyes, he felt that he had known him somewhere before. He still could not think where, but his instinctive feeling of dislike for the man was stronger than ever. At Adam's appearance, they all genuflected, then Alberuque said to him:

'In the name of an oppressed people, I welcome you, Exalted One. Our Lord Jesus has sent you to be their saviour. Your name has been revered by them for countless generations. In the future it will be accounted blessed.'

Adam's face remained expressionless and, in accordance with Father López's instructions, he did not reply. All the priests genuflected again, then Alberuque said, 'Be pleased, Exalted One, to accompany Father López.'

Turning about, Adam rejoined the little priest outside and was led back along the terrace to the chamber in which he had noticed the robes. Four Indians in semi-clerical attire, whom he took to be deacons, were there. After going down on their knees before him, they stood up and set about robing him.

The garments were similar to those that Father Miguel had transferred to him before he had sacrificed the pig at San Luis Caliente, but infinitely more splendid. The long cloak was of fabric upon which had been stitched thousands of small feathers of many colours, arranged in intricate patterns. There was a breastplate, knee guards, anklets and wristlets of solid gold, set with many precious stones that glittered in the light from the lanterns. The sandals were of soft, gilded leather and the shield of tough hide, the latter having a zigzag design formed by hundreds of turquoise studs and a fringe of quetzal feathers sewn all round the edge. Round his neck they put seven necklaces from which hung dozens of tiny gold bells and from the lowest of them depended a wonderful carved jade cypher. The enormous helmet was a magnificent affair, composed of gold, gilded leather, jewels and a huge plume of feathers. It was so tall that, had Adam worn it in the room, the feathers would have brushed the ceiling; but his attendants were too short to crown him with it and looked uneasily at Father Lopéz. The priest spoke to them in Maya, then said to Adam in Spanish:

'It is desired that the people should see the Man-God's golden hair, so he will carry his head-dress slung to his shield.'

When it had been fixed securely, Adam was handed a seven-foot-high staff, the top of which was crowned by a plumed serpent made of jade and gold set with jewels, which he recognised as the symbol of power.

During his robing he had been speculating unhappily on what form the ceremony would take. It seemed probable that it would follow the same lines as that at San Luis Caliente: a Mass followed by the sacrifice of several pigs. To have to witness the sacrilege of a Mass combined with pagan rites was bad enough, yet he was even more revolted by the thought that he would again have to tear the heart out of a live pig.

But he was committed now. Not only had he given his promise to Chela, but in retaining the goodwill of Alberuque lay the best chance of sabotaging the conspiracy and preventing a bloody civil war. So, hateful as his part would be, he knew he must go through with it.

As he stood there, miserably contemplating the hour or more that lay ahead, he heard footsteps ringing on the stone terrace outside. A moment later, the head of a procession came into view. It consisted of some twenty priests, all Indians and Mestizos, with the exception of Alberuque. Many of them were carrying banners upon which Christian saints were depicted and, in their midst, Alberuque was bearing the Host. As it passed, Father Lopéz and the deacons went down on their knees and Adam bowed his head.

When the last of the priests had passed, Adam instinctively

took a step towards the doorway, intending to follow; but Father López whispered, 'The presence of the Man-God is not yet required. He will show himself to the people only at the end of the ceremony.'

Adam's heart lightened a little then. The end of the ceremony must surely mean not only after the celebration of the Mass, but also after the sacrifice; so he could now hope to escape having to perform that horrible rite.

While the minutes ticked by, his mind turned to Chela, by now probably in bed. But it could not yet be midnight, so other guests at the Hacienda would still be up and about. It was easy to picture the handful of rich, elderly Americans, sitting over their Bourbon on the rocks, or J. & B. 'Rare' whiskies, telling new acquaintances of other trips they had made in recent years, of their young people at the universities, of their summer places at Cape Cod and winter ones in Florida. Pleasantly courteous to one another, laughing quietly now and then; entirely normal citizens of the modern world.

They were less than a mile away; and here was he, separated from them in time by a thousand years, decked out in a costume and accoutrements that, if sold at Christie's, might fetch a hundred thousand pounds, and about to play the role of a Man-God to an assembly of pagan fanatics. The whole idea was fantastic—unbelievable. For some minutes he persuaded himself that this was one of his visions, but one such as he had never had before, in which his past incarnation was somehow mixed up with his present one.

At last, Father López said, 'The time has come, Exalted One. Be pleased to follow me.'

With an effort Adam came back to earth. This was no dream but really happening. Adam Gordon, the poor Scots lad who, through a number of strange vicissitudes, had made good, become a best-selling author and flown out to Mexico in search of a background for a new book, had got himself caught up in a conspiracy to overthrow the government and, dressed in the costume of a Toltec Prince, was about to present himself as a Man-God to scores of credulous people. It was absurd, ridiculous—but a fact.

Father López preceding him and the four deacons following behind, Adam, towering above all five of them, walked at an unhurried pace to the rear of the Pyramid of the Magician. At its base there were some half-ruined arches that formed an arcade. For a few minutes he waited there with his attendants, while Father Lopéz stood beyond the furthest arch, looking up the steep slope of the pyramid. Suddenly, he called:

'The signal has been made. The Man-God is summoned to ascend.'

Stepping out into the open, Adam began to climb the steep staircase of broken steps. Weighed down by the mass of gold upon him, he found it hard going. Looking upward he could see the partially-ruined temple on the top, but no human figures were outlined against the starlit sky. By the time he had accomplished two-thirds of the ascent he was breathing heavily and looking down at his feet as he put them in turn on each succeeding step.

It was then he heard footfalls and glanced up again. Now he could see a massed body of men. Alberuque and his escorting priests had come round from the front of the temple and were just beginning the descent of the pyramid. As they approached he saw that they were coming down one side of the broad flight of stairs, leaving the other free for him. When he came abreast of him they halted, turned and bowed to him, then went on. Two minutes later he reached the summit. Behind him Father Lopéz said in a low voice:

'From here the Man-God proceeds alone.'

As Adam walked along the broad ledge round the side of the temple he expected to smell blood, but the night air was clean. That seemed a sure sign that no sacrifice had yet been made. Perhaps, then, he was expected to slaughter not only one pig, but many. He had nerved himself to go through the nauseous business again of tearing the heart out of one animal, but the thought of having to repeat the process was almost too much for him. He was seized with a sudden urge to turn about, throw his hand in and refuse to have anything more to do with Alberuque and his fanatical followers.

Chela would be bitterly disappointed and be justified in reproaching him for going back on his word. It might mean a

H

quarrel; but he felt sure that, loving him as she did, she would understand and forgive him.

It was at that moment that he turned the corner of the temple. No hideous image of Chac-Mool reposed in front of it, awaiting the slaughter of a warm-blooded animal in its stone lap. Nor was there any other altar upon which a sacrifice could be made. The priests must have removed the one at which the Mass had been celebrated and put it inside the ruin. The terrace was now entirely bare and he was alone upon it. Evidently, for some reason, Alberuque did not consider a sacrifice desirable at this ceremony of 'Recognition'. Immensely relieved, Adam drew himself to his full height and walked to the centre of the terrace.

Looking down, he could make out a sea of white faces turned up towards him. Suddenly a searchlight was switched on from below. It wavered for a minute, then fixed him in its glare, completely blinding him. From the crowd of two or three hundred people massed below a vast sigh of wonder ascended to him. In some mystic way it seemed to lift him so that his body became almost weightless and he felt as though he was floating upright far above them.

Automatically, in ringing tones, he began his speech. Then a strange metamorphosis engulfed him. While he was still speaking, his mind was elsewhere. It had gone back to an earlier time when he had addressed a great multitude from the top of the Pyramid of the Magician. He was again Quetzalcoatl making his farewell speech to his people.

But he was not only Quetzalcoatl. He was also Ord the Red-Handed, and it was revealed to him how he came to be there.

As Ord the Viking he had voyaged many times to Scotland, Ireland and England on plundering expeditions. He also knew Iceland well, and its inhabitants were akin to his own people. There he had heard stories of a land to the west of the northern ocean. It was said to be rich and fertile, and grapes, such as were to be found in Spain, grew there; so it was known as the Vineland.

He had determined to go there, and one spring set sail with his hardy *jarls*. But they had met with storms that had driven them hundreds of miles to the southward. The voyage had lasted many months. On scores of occasions they had landed, terrified the inhabitants of those unknown lands by their size and ferocity, taken such supplies as they needed and sailed again. Time after time they had set and attempted to maintain a course to the northward; but, again and again, after a few days, storms had forced them to furl their sail, and great seas swept them down into hotter climes. The end had come, as Adam realised now, somewhere in the Caribbean. A hurricane had cast their galley up on to a reef. Except for Ord, those of his crew who had survived the terrible voyage had been drowned. He alone had been washed up, still alive, on the shore of Mexico.

When the natives had come upon him, half drowned, they had marvelled at his tall stature, white skin and golden hair and beard. With superstitious awe, they had tended and revived him. Once he had recovered he was able to repay them a hundredfold, owing to his knowledge of many things about which they knew little. So they soon looked upon him as a worker of miracles—a being sent to them by a dispensation of heaven.

As he acquired their language, they told him of rich cities that lay many miles inland. His instinct, as a born freebooter, had nagged at him until he became determined to raid them. He had had no difficulty in raising an army, because the people were by then confident beyond all doubt of his power to lead them to victory.

With his army he had marched three hundred miles to the great city of Tula. After only a feeble resistance the Toltecs, whose capital it was, had fallen down and worshipped him. Before that he had been known as Acatl Topeltzin. It was they who gave him the name of Quetzalcoatl, and recognised him as a Man-God.

Beloved by all, he had reigned in Tula for twenty years. Then the semi-barbarous Chichimecs had swept down from the north. There had been a terrible war, in which his Toltecs had been defeated, had lost their great, sacred city of Teotihuacán, with its pyramids of the Sun and the Moon, and he had been taken prisoner.

His captors had also regarded him as a Man-God, and he had lived among them for close on a year. Towards its end he had been told, without warning, by the High Priest Itzechuatl that he was to be sacrificed. But, owing to the intervention of Mirolitlit, he had succeeded in escaping and rejoining his devoted Toltecs. Having lost their capital and most of their lands, they were in sore straits. But he had put new heart into them and led them in a great trek down to Yucatán.

There they came upon both Chichén Itzá and Uxmal, abandoned by the Maya hierarchy many centuries earlier, but still having considerable numbers of Maya people scraping a living for many miles round. Their *caciques* too had accepted him as a God, and he had set them to work on restoring and embellishing their sacred buildings. Much of the land round about had been fallow for so long that it had again become fertile, so he had decreed that his Toltecs should settle there and become one with the Mayas. But he was by then well on into middle age and more and more had begun to long for his bleak northern homeland.

That he had sailed away on a raft of snakes was a legend. Actually he had supervised the building of a small Norseman's galley, the prow of which, instead of having a bird or beast as a figurehead, had been fashioned as his own emblem —a great serpent with head drawn back and wide-open jaws framing a man's face.

His people had been most reluctant to allow him to leave them, so he had promised to return. Then, from the top of the Pyramid of the Magician, he had made his farewell speech. From that point on, his memories again became vague. He could not recall whether or not he had taken with him a crew of volunteers or had sailed alone. He was only aware that he had never reached the lands in which he had spent his youth and early manhood. The galley had gone down during a hurricane and he had drowned, presumably somewhere in the Caribbean.

During those minutes of dual consciousness Adam was aware that he was delivering the speech he had learned by heart. As he ended, there came, as from a great distance, the sound of thunderous applause. Then the shrill blowing of whistles impinged on his mind. The spotlight that blinded him was suddenly switched off. For a moment, standing there in total darkness, he had no idea where he was. A voice behind him brought him back to reality. It was that of Father Lopéz, who had emerged at the corner of the temple. He was shouting:

'We are betrayed! But God will protect His own. There is still time to escape. Run, Exalted One! Run!'

Afterwards Adam realised that Lopéz had meant him to turn and run towards him. But, instinctively, he jumped forward and began to descend the pyramid, taking two of the deep steps at a time. Still half blinded from the spotlight, he was only vaguely aware of what was happening below him. There was some shouting and movement, like a troubled sea. As he ran down towards the crowd, the greater part of it seemed to disintegrate and fan out in all directions. But a small compact group formed at the base of the pyramid.

Suddenly, to his horror, he realised that the impetus with which he had launched himself forward had now become too great for him to control his speed. His feet were flying from step to step. In vain he endeavoured to check his wild career down the steep slope. He kept his balance only by a miracle. As he neared the bottom he could see the group that waited below more clearly. They were not a part of the congregation. They wore uniforms. They were police.

Utterly unable to check his flying legs, he hurtled towards them. Another moment and he was within seconds of crashing into the group. Fearing that he would bowl several of them over, the men in his immediate vicinity sprang back, leaving him a gap to pass through. Aghast, he saw that, with nothing to act as a brake, he must land with a bone-breaking crash on the ground just beyond them. But two of them grabbed at his cloak as he shot past, lay back on it and brought him up with a frightful jerk. His shield, feathered head-dress and staff of authority were jolted from his hands. His cloak ripped away from those who were hanging on to it and he staggered on a few paces. But the police did not mean to let him escape. One of them sprang after him and hit him on the back of the head with a truncheon. His knees buckled under him and he slumped to the ground unconscious.

When he came to, he was sitting in the back of a car; his chin on his chest, his head lolling forwards. As he opened his eyes, an excruciating pain shot through his head. Then he saw that his wrists were handcuffed.

13

The Road to Prison

ADAM closed his eyes again and tried to think. Between stabs of pain the events of the past few hours came back to him: Father Lopéz springing his surprise after dinner that the ceremony was to take place that night; accompanying the priest along the path through the jungle from that normal, modern world of rich, travelling Americans at the Hacienda to enter another world of unbelievable fantasy, in which he was the ruler of the Toltecs; then the sudden realisation that things had gone wrong, that Alberuque and his followers had been betrayed; his plunging at breakneck speed down the steep pyramid and the blow from a truncheon that had knocked him out.

His mind then switched to the vision he had had while automatically making his speech. He had always accepted that his incarnations as a Viking and as a Toltec Prince had been different lives; now he knew them to have been one and felt that he should have realised that before. The history of the Norsemen, in which he had steeped himself during his teens, had left him in no doubt that, as a young man, he had started to rove the seas about A.D. 950, and the date given for Quetzalcoatl's arrival in Mexico was in the 960s. Obviously he could not have lived two different lives at the same time, and the fact that the legend that Quetzalcoatl had come up from the sea in the form of a giant white man, with golden hair and beard, fitted perfectly with his having been a Viking.

So much for the past. What of the present? Grimly he contemplated his situation. His handcuffs made it plain that the police regarded him as a criminal and would bring a charge against him. Captured as he had been, just after making his speech and rigged out in all his gorgeous plumage, it was going to be difficult to refute an accusation of subversive activities. His only hope lay in Ramón, and he cursed himself now for not having let him know, somehow or other, that he had agreed to play the role of Quetzalcoatl. He would then have been in the clear. Still, Ramón could at least vouch for it that he had reported the ceremony at San Luis Caliente, and had promised to do his best to provide the authorities with further information.

He wondered then what had happened to the others. Still half absorbed by his vision and blinded by the spotlight, he was far from clear about what had taken place. Everything had happened very quickly. Not more than a minute had elapsed between the first shrilling of whistles and Father Lopéz calling to him from the side of the temple to run. Yet when he had reached the bottom of the pyramid the congregation had vanished, to be replaced by the group of police. From the one glimpse he had had of the group as he hurtled downward, he thought there could not have been more than a dozen of them and he had heard no sounds of fighting further off; so it seemed that no attempt had been made to arrest as many as possible of the fleeing crowd.

But what about the rear of the pyramid? Although it had not been surrounded, another group of police might have arrived there, or seen the glow of light coming up from the Court of the Nuns and been in time to arrest Don Alberuque and his confederates before they could get away. There was only one thing Adam could be thankful for: that Chela had remained at the hotel, so she could not be caught up in this catastrophe.

The pain in his head had eased a little and he wondered where he was being taken. Probably, he thought, to Mérida, as that was the only place for many miles round large enough to have a police headquarters. He noticed then that the car was going downhill. If he was right about the direction in which it was heading, that meant that it had not yet reached the long, flat stretch through the jungle; so he could not have been unconscious for many minutes—probably only long enough for them to carry him to the car.

The thought crossed his mind that, if the car pulled up, he might perhaps make his escape; but he quickly abandoned that hope. A policeman was sitting on either side of him. They would almost certainly be armed and, although they were both small men, he was handcuffed; so any attempt to overcome them must prove hopeless. Miserably, he resigned himself to spending the rest of the night in a cell, being taken ignominiously back to Mexico City, then spending several days in prison before Ramón and Chela could procure his release.

The car had just passed through a large village and was entering the flat lands when it slowed down. The driver sounded his horn urgently, ran on another fifty yards, then pulled up. Peering forward through the windscreen, by the light of the headlamps Adam saw the reason. Lying down across the road and completely blocking it was a huddle of a dozen or more Indians.

He and the policeman sitting with him had hardly taken in the fact when a tremendous shouting broke out and two other much larger groups of Indians emerged from the jungle on both sides of the road. In a human wave they threw themselves at the car and wrenched open the doors.

The two policemen had drawn their pistols. Before they had time to raise them, rough hands seized them, the driver and an officer who was sitting in front, by the arms and legs and dragged them out on to the road.

For a moment Adam remained where he was, dazed by the suddenness of the attack. Quickly recovering his wits, he shuffled his way out. Two other police cars had been following. They, too, were almost submerged under mobs of Indians. A single shot was fired, but no cry of pain came to tell that a bullet had found its mark. A solitary policeman succeeded in getting away into the jungle, then it was all over. As an ambush it had been a complete success.

Feeling slightly ridiculous, Adam stood in the middle of the road arrayed in his finery. The fighting had ceased, the Indians were binding the police hand and foot, then lifting them into the back of a lorry that had just driven up. A voice said behind Adam:

'Exalted One, permit me to introduce myself. I am Father Suaréz, and your humble servant.'

Turning, Adam saw that he had been addressed by a man who did not look at all like a priest. He was a big, burly, red-faced Mestizo with broken teeth. Adam began to stammer his thanks for having been rescued; but Father Suaréz waved them aside, led him some way down the road, then along a cart track off it that ended after a hundred yards at a small, square, one-roomed house.

It was empty except for a chair and a small table on which there were a candle, a bottle of *tequila*, a glass and a platter of fruit. The priest apologised for not taking him to his own dwelling, on the grounds that even the glimpse his people had caught of Adam would have made them tremendously excited, and he was anxious to avoid a demonstration in the village which might arouse from their sleep a few untrustworthy people who lived there. He then said that he must despatch a messenger to let Adam's friends know that he had been rescued, but would return as soon as was possible, with a file, so that Adam could be freed from his handcuffs.

Left on his own, Adam clasped the bottle of *tequila* with both hands and awkwardly poured some into the glass. He did not much care for its flavour, but he badly needed a drink. Taken neat it was fiery stuff and, as it went down, he gasped and spluttered; but it warmed his stomach and soon afterwards he felt the better for it.

Sitting down, he began to speculate on what was likely to happen as a result of the new turn events had taken. Wryly he recalled his nickname of 'Lucky' Gordon, and supposed that he was lucky to be sitting there a free man, instead of being still on his way to a cell in a police station. But for how long could he count on his luck holding?

It seemed obvious that his rescue could have been ordered only by Don Alberuque or Father Lopéz, so either or both of them must have escaped arrest; although how they had managed to arrange so quickly for the ambush was puzzling. Any-

way, it could be assumed that they would soon be on their
way to pick him up.

What would they have planned to do with him? It was
hardly likely that they would take him back to the Hacienda.
There must still be police at Uxmal trying to find out all they
could about the ceremony, and some of them might be questioning the staff at the hotel. The most likely alternative was
a return to Mexico City, via Mérida. But that, too, could be
dangerous. It might be hours before the policeman who had
escaped into the jungle could reach a telephone or find some
motor vehicle to take him in to Mérida; on the other hand,
he might already have done so and be on his way there.

Once news of the ambush reached police headquarters,
they would establish road blocks in the hope of recapturing
the man who had played the part of Quetzalcoatl, and
Adam's height, features and hair would make him easily iden-
tifiable to anyone who had his description. To keep him where
he was would be even more risky as, by morning, it was
certain that the village and its neighbourhood would be
swarming with police trying to find out where he had got to.
At length he decided the most likely possibility was that they
would spirit him away to some other hideout deep in the
jungles of Yucatán.

The prospect was anything but pleasant, as he might have
to remain there for weeks before it was safe for him to emerge.
Almost it seemed better to give himself up and rely on
Ramón to get him out of trouble. But to do that would also
entail a nasty risk. The authorities might prove indifferent
to anything Ramón had to say and, as a matter of policy,
put Quetzalcoatl on trial, then award him a long prison sentence. In what better way could they knock the bottom out
of the conspiracy? It was possible that if he turned 'King's
Evidence' they might let him off. But in that case what about
Chela? If he gave her Monsignor away and utterly wrecked
her hopes of bettering the lot of her beloved Indians, would
she ever forgive him?

It occurred to him then that perhaps her hopes were already
wrecked. Ramón had said that the authorities would not
pounce until they knew who the leaders of the conspiracy

were; yet they had struck that night. Possibly Don Alberuque was only one of the leaders and there were bigger fish in Mexico City who were not prepared to show themselves until the revolt actually started. If the government was now on to them the whole project was already a busted flush.

Adam sincerely hoped it was. If so, and the police could pull in and put on trial a number of prominent Mexican churchmen and Indian *caciques*, they might not greatly exert themselves to catch the unknown man who had been used to play Quetzalcoatl simply because he had the right figure and colouring. Then, if he lay low for a while, once Chela had recovered from her disappointment they might go again to her little villa at Acapulco and resume their wonderful honeymoon, with this nightmare business no longer looming over them.

By the time Father Suaréz returned Adam, although still greatly worried, was in a slightly happier frame of mind. The priest brought a file with him and set to work on the handcuffs. While he filed away, Adam asked him how it had been possible to prepare the ambush so quickly, and learned that he owed his liberty to the Father.

Suaréz had been present at the ceremony. When the police had come on the scene he had not panicked but kept his wits about him. There had not been many police—only three car loads of them—although it was possible that others whom he had not seen had arrived simultaneously at the back of the pyramid. In any case, it had at once been obvious that the police were not sufficiently numerous to attempt anything against the congregation, but had come to arrest the principal participants in the ceremony. Having taken cover among the only group of stones in the immediate vicinity which, Adam recalled, were a dozen or so waist-high phalli, the Father had seen him come plunging down the pyramid and realised that his capture was inevitable. Without losing a moment, under cover of darkness he had run the quarter of a mile to the place where he had left his motor-cycle, jumped on it and driven, all out, back to his own village. There, feeling certain that if Adam survived his perilous descent the police would take him in to Mérida, he had aroused his congregation and, only just in time, prepared the ambush.

Having thanked him for the initiative and courage he had displayed, Adam said, 'I am worried, though, Father, about you and your people. When the authorities learn what happened it is certain that the police will return to your village and make things most unpleasant for all concerned. It might lead to you and a number of your parishioners being thrown into prison.'

The bulky priest shook his head and displayed his broken teeth in a grin as he replied, 'I thank the Exalted One for his concern, but it is needless. While the scrimmage was taking place, your servant kept under cover so cannot be connected with the ambush. As for my people, everything took place so quickly, and in semi-darkness. I feel sure that none of the police would be able to swear to the identity of any of the men who attacked them. They cannot even prove that it was the men of this village who laid the ambush. It might have been others summoned from their huts in the jungle by the mystic powers that many of our people still possess. At worst, too, the police have only been made fools of; and that they will keep to themselves. No harm was done to them. They have been taken by lorry and laid out on the roadside about fifteen miles away; when they get free of their bonds they will find their cars parked on the edge of the jungle quite near them.'

By this time Father Suaréz had filed through one of the links that held the handcuffs together, so Adam was able to separate his hands; but the file was not strong enough to cut through the wristlets and he had to reconcile himself to continuing to wear them until a hacksaw could be procured.

About ten minutes later there came a knock on the door of the little house. The priest opened it to disclose an Indian. Behind him were Chela, Father Lopéz and two other Indians, carrying suitcases. Entering the room, they all went down on their knees before Adam, and Father Lopéz said a prayer of thanksgiving in Latin for the Man-God's restoration to them. When he had finished Chela looked up, her dark eyes swimming with tears of joy. As Adam stretched out his hands and raised her to her feet, he could sense that she was longing to throw her arms round his neck; but in the presence of others it would not have been seemly for her to do so.

When she and Father Lopéz had thanked Father Suaréz for the great service he had rendered their cause, the Indians retired and the two suitcases were opened. The smaller belonged to Adam and contained a set of his own clothes; the larger was empty and had been brought to hold his robes. Chela retired while the two priests reverently divested him of them and assisted him to change into his well-tailored suit.

While they were doing so he learned that a second group of police had appeared in the rear of the pyramid. It was seeing them that had caused Father Lopéz to shout a warning to Adam. The small, plump priest had then made his escape by sliding perilously down the side of the pyramid, and had reached the bottom with nothing worse than some painful bruises. He had not since seen Don Alberuque or any of his confederates but, as no sounds of strife had come from the Court of the Nuns in which they were then disrobing, it was as good as certain that they had got safely away.

Adam then asked somewhat testily why, since there were comparatively few police and such a large congregation, no attempt had been made either to prevent his arrest or rescue him.

Somewhat shamefacedly, Father Lopéz excused the congregation on the plea that they had been taken by surprise and could not know that many more police were not about to arrive on the scene. Moreover, they had been given strict orders that, in the event of police intervening in any secret gathering, they were to offer no resistance and at once disperse, so as to avoid a clash and bloodshed.

When Adam had changed, the bull-necked Father Suaréz led them back along the cart track to the road. A car with an Indian driver was waiting there. Having said good-bye to Father Suaréz, they got into it. As the engine started up, Adam asked:

'Where are you taking me?'

'Why, back to the Hacienda, of course,' Chela replied.

'But, surely, that would be dangerous?' he protested. 'The police are certain to have made enquiries there. If anyone has given them a description of me they will have tumbled to it that I am Quetzalcoatl. The odds are they wouldn't expect me to be daft enough to go back there; but, all the same, it's a good bet that they will have left a couple of men on the look-out to arrest me in case I was so rash as to attempt to collect my belongings.'

Chela shook her head. 'If the police had meant to pay the Hacienda a visit they would have done so before Father Lopéz and I left it. But they didn't, because they wouldn't expect the sort of people who stay there to have any connection with ancient secret rites. That also applies to you. It would never enter their heads that Quetzalcoatl was a British visitor.'

'The Señorita is right,' Father Lopéz said. 'Among the police we have a number of secret adherents from whom we receive information. Through them we know that the authorities believe that the Man-God who appeared at San Luis Caliente was a tall, pale-skinned Mestizo wearing a fair wig and false beard.'

That did not square with the fact that Adam had told Ramón about his having had to save his life at San Luis by announcing that he was Quetzalcoatl; but it was possible that, for the present, Ramón had kept that to himself in order to ensure that no over-zealous Police Chief interfered with Adam's movements and that among the force the belief just stated by Father Lopéz had become current.

Adam was still far from happy at the idea of returning to the Hacienda, but as no other plan had been thought of, there seemed no alternative; so he reluctantly allowed himself to be persuaded to agree.

Twenty minutes later the car set them down within a few hundred yards of the hotel. They walked down a slope that brought them to the bottom of the garden, then came up through it towards the hotel. It was then getting on for three o'clock in the morning and, except for a single light over the swimming pool, the hotel was in darkness. Chela went ahead to make certain that no-one was about and a few minutes later returned to report that the coast was clear. Tiptoeing past the pool, they exchanged whispered good-nights and went to their rooms.

Tired out from the strain he had been through, Adam threw his empty suitcase on the floor, pulled off his jacket and sat down heavily on the edge of his bed. He had hardly done so when Chela came in from the adjoining room, ran to him, flung herself into his arms, smothered his face with kisses and, between them, gasped :

'Oh, my darling! My beloved! My treasure! What a ghastly night it has been. When Father Lopéz got back here and told me that you had been arrested I thought I'd die. I've never spent such a terrible hour in my life as I did from then until Father Suaréz's messenger arrived to let us know that you had been rescued. I spent the whole of the time on my knees, beseeching the Blessed Virgin to restore you to me.'

Adam returned her kisses only half-heartedly and gave a rueful grin. 'Well, maybe your prayers helped, my sweet. Anyhow, my luck was in again. I had some pretty nasty moments, though, and I'm feeling dead beat.'

'Of course, my precious. You must be,' she soothed him. 'Let me help you get your clothes off, then you can flop into bed and get right off to sleep.'

Wearily he stood up and began to unbutton his trousers while she knelt down and untied his shoe-laces. With a sigh he said, 'Well, thank God this awful business is finished now, and in future we'll be able to lead a normal life.'

Looking up, she asked in a surprised voice, 'What do you mean?'

'Why, that there'll be no more of this dangerous tom-foolery. The police appearing on the scene tonight made it as clear as crystal that they've got the lowdown on your friends. By this time they will have pinched the Bishops and all the other high-ups who were to lead the rebellion and have thrown them into jug.'

Chela's eyes widened and she shook her head. 'Darling, you are quite mistaken about that. The Bishops are playing no part in this. They don't even know of it. Neither do all but a very few of the white clergy. They wouldn't approve. We wouldn't dare trust them. Our strength lies in the Mestizo and Indian priests, who form the great majority and are the true leaders of the people. In them, and a handful of white Fathers who are devoted to our wonderful chief, Don Alberuque. No-one in Mexico City will have been arrested tonight, because all our regional leaders were gathered here for the ceremony of "Recognition". Now they have actually seen you, they will return to their people and redouble their faith in our cause.'

'Don't you believe it,' Adam retorted. 'Some of them must have seen me arrested and lugged off by the police. The news of that will spread like wildfire and soon put a damper on their enthusiasm. Real Men-Gods aren't taken into custody like common felons. They'll realise that I'm a phoney.'

'But you are not, darling! You're not! You really were Quetzalcoatl and you are Quetzalcoatl returned to us today. If the police had got you in prison that might have made a difference. It might even have been disastrous if they were able to bring you to trial and sentence you, and it appeared in all the papers. But that can't happen now. The police won't dare admit to the Press about how they were ambushed and you were rescued. Our position now is stronger than ever. Tomorrow our grapevine will spread it all over the country that you were arrested, but the police were incapable of holding you and you made a miraculous escape. We have only to wait now for another ten days or a fortnight and . . .'

Suddenly Adam lost his temper. Scowling at her, he cried, 'If that's what you think, you can think again! I'm through with this mumbo-jumbo—through with it for good and all. At San Luis I near as damn it lost my life, and to save it was forced to the revolting act of tearing out the heart of a pig. Tonight I'm lucky not to be locked up in a cell and awaiting a trial that could land me in prison for the best years of my life. God knows I love you as a woman; but to hell with your scheming priests and barbarous, bloody-minded Indians. The lot of them can rot as far as I am concerned.'

Slowly she came to her feet. The blood had drained from beneath her coffee-coloured skin. For a moment she could not find words, then she gasped :

'I can't believe it! You promised! You can't go back on your word.'

'I can,' he retorted harshly. 'And I mean to. I've never approved of this business. It can bring only death and misery to thousands of people. You are crazy to believe otherwise. I'm through, I tell you. Through! Now leave me to get some rest.'

Large tears began to seep from her eyes. Without another word she turned on her heel and, with faltering steps, stumbled away to her room.

In the morning he woke, to find her standing beside his bed. She looked thoroughly washed out and very sad. In a low voice she said, 'Darling, I want to talk to you.'

He sighed and replied, 'Yes, I suppose you do.' Then he raised one of his hands that still had a handcuff encircling the wrist. 'But first I'd like you to find some way of getting these things off me.'

She nodded. 'Yes; but to do that I'll need a hacksaw. I doubt if they would have a tool like that here. If not, I'll have to get a car to drive me into Mérida and buy one. That will take me the best part of three hours.'

'Thanks, my sweet.' He took her hand and kissed it. 'I'm afraid that's the only thing for it. But I can do with another nap.'

She kissed him on the forehead and said, 'I'll be back as soon as I can.' Then, with a pale smile, she turned and left him.

He dozed for about an hour, then was roused by a sharp knock on the door. Thinking it was probably Father Lopéz, he called 'Entrada'. The door opened and three police-men marched in.

Adam's brain instantly began to seethe with apprehension. Had the police got on to him, or was this only a routine en-quiry to find out whether the guests at the hotel could furnish any information about the doings of the previous night?

The officer who led the party asked abruptly, 'You are Señor Gordon?'

Raising himself on one elbow, Adam replied, 'Yes; yes, I am.'

'I have authority to question you. Please answer promptly. Are you of British nationality?'

'Yes.'

'How long have you been staying at the hotel?'

'Two nights.'

'From where did you come?'

'From Mérida.'

'Did you arrive alone?'

'No, with a lady.' Adam's mind became a shade easier. Evidently they could not know much about him or he would not be asked such routine questions.

'Her name?'

'The Señorita Chela Enriquez.'

'While here have you talked with any of the other visitors?'

Adam swiftly decided that it would be inadvisable to mention Father Lopéz; but he and Chela had dropped into conversation with some Americans in the bar, so he was able to reply truthfully, 'Yes, a few.'

'Name them.'

'Sorry; I can't. I suppose we did exchange names, but they often don't register when making casual acquaintances.'

'What time did you go to bed last night?'

'A little before midnight.'

'And the Señorita?'

'About the same time.'

'Did you sleep together?'

'No! Certainly not!' Adam flared. 'And what the hell has that to do with you anyway?'

The officer shrugged. 'In Mexico, when a gentleman travels alone with a single lady, it is customary for him to sleep with her. Where is her room?'

'Next door,' Adam admitted grudgingly.

'Is she there now?'

'How should I know?'

His heavy boots smacking loudly on the floorboards, the officer marched over to the communicating door, found it unlocked, turned to grin at Adam and flung it open.

'No, she is not there. Very well. You will now get up, dress yourself and come with us.'

The order was so ominous that it caused Adam sudden renewed alarm. Were they on to him after all? Was his rescue by Father Suaréz to prove of no avail? Endeavouring to mask his acute anxiety by an angry frown, he shouted, 'Why? What right have you to make me leave this room?'

'It is because your appearance tallies with the description of a man who last night masqueraded as the Man-God Quetzalcoatl; and we wish to question you further.'

The blow had fallen, but Adam burst out, 'What nonsense! I am a British visitor to Mexico. A score of people will vouch for my bona-fides.'

'That we shall see,' said the officer harshly. 'Get up.'

'What if I refuse?' Adam demanded truculently.

The only reply the officer made was to draw his pistol, point it and repeat, 'Get up.'

Adam was near panic, but he knew that his only hope was to remain where he was. Feeling confident that the officer would not shoot him where he lay, he stuck out his bearded chin and cried defiantly, 'I'm damned if I will. Go to hell.'

With a sweep of his pistol the officer signed to the two men behind him and barked, 'Get him up.'

One of the men stepped forward, grasped the single sheet under which Adam had slept and wrenched it off. He was lying at full length, clad only in his pyjama jacket, and the sleeves were not long enough to hide the tell-tale handcuffs that proclaimed his guilt.

The officer grinned. 'So we were right. Señor Gordon, I arrest you for subversive activities.'

14

A Living Nightmare

IN UTTER desperation Adam decided to resist arrest. All three policemen were small men. With three blows of his great fists he could knock them out. They were so close to him that they had no room to manœuvre. Only the officer had drawn his pistol and one of his men now stood between him and Adam. The man could be smashed back on to him, with luck the gun would be knocked from his hand. The third man would receive the second blow before he had time to draw his weapon. Taken by surprise all three could be overcome in a matter of seconds.

Swinging his legs off the bed, Adam came to his full height. His fists clenched, then relaxed. Suddenly he sat down again. It could have been done and with little risk of a bullet. But what then? He was nearly naked and it would have been madness to leave by the window like that. He would have to bind and gag them all, dress and collect his money before making his escape. The fight would cause a racket; before he could gag them it was certain that one or more of them would be yelling for help. Even if their cries did not bring a crowd of other people on the scene, where could he go once he had left the hotel? He would only get himself hopelessly lost in the jungle.

Glowering at the officer, he said, 'All right. I'll come with you. But first I must have a bath.'

'No time for that,' came the sharp reply. 'Get dressed at once, or I will take you as you are.'

Ignoring the command, Adam walked over to the basin, cleaned his teeth and washed. Then he began to dress. Meanwhile the two policemen were packing his other clothes and belongings into his suitcases. As soon as he had finished dressing, one of the men snapped another pair of handcuffs over his wrists.

'How about paying my bill?' he asked.

'The manacles will not prevent your signing a traveller's cheque,' was the reply. Ignominiously they led him along past the swimming pool and the curious stares of other guests to the office. There he asked for Chela's bill as well as his own and paid both.

'So you knew that the Señorita had left the hotel?' the officer remarked.

'Yes,' he admitted. 'Where are you taking me?'

'To Police Headquarters in Mérida. Do you wish to leave a message for her?'

'No. She will not be coming back,' Adam lied. But he had achieved his object. The desk clerk had heard the conversation and would pass it on to Chela.

The officer shrugged. 'Whether she returns or not, we'll soon pick her up.'

Adam's heart sank still further on learning that Chela was to be pulled in, and he wondered whether they knew how deeply she was involved in the conspiracy. Even if her father could later arrange for her release, it looked now as though she would have to spend some time in gaol and the thought of his beautiful beloved confined, ill-fed and treated as a convict, depressed him unutterably.

Outside, a police car and chauffeur were waiting. The officer put him in the back between himself and one of his men; the other man was left at the hotel, presumably to arrest Chela if she returned there.

Twenty minutes later they passed through the village near which the ambush had taken place, but this time there was no ambush. As against that, there were no signs of anything unusual having occurred there that morning; so it looked as though the police had realised the futility of carrying out an investigation among its inhabitants. For their sakes and that of the courageous Father Suaréz, Adam prayed that might be so.

At the Police Headquarters in Mérida general particulars about him were entered in a register and he was then locked in a cell. It was reasonably clean, but starkly comfortless. In the early afternoon he was brought a meal of *tortillas* and chili-peppers which were so fiercely hot that he could hardly get them down, and in the evening another meal of *tortillas* and beans. Otherwise he was left there all day, with nothing to occupy his mind except his gloomy thoughts.

Soon after eight o'clock he was called out of his cell and, with an escort of the officer who had arrested him and another policeman, taken to the airport.

When he had arrived there with Chela five nights earlier they had been whisked away so efficiently by the porter from the Pan Americana that Adam had not realised what a miserable little place it was. Although the city of Mérida had two hundred thousand inhabitants to Oaxaca's seventy-five thousand, the airport at the former was less than one-third the size of that at the latter. It was now packed with people, nine out of ten of whom must have been killing time by seeing off the limited number of people who could travel by the evening plane.

Adam estimated that there must be at least two hundred men, women and children jammed into the small waiting hall, and it had only three chairs. Under the electric lights it was intolerably hot, everyone was sweating freely and numerous mosquitoes were pinging and stinging about people's faces and necks. Every time one of the little pests settled on Adam he was unable to disturb it without displaying his handcuffs and, as he was so much taller than his neighbours, he soon became the fascinated focus of most pairs of eyes in the room. His efforts to get at the back of his neck caused great amusement and the little Indian children were held up by their elders to join in the fun. If anything could have possibly added to his misery it was an announcement, made after he had been standing pressed in the smelly crush for some twenty minutes, that the aircraft had been delayed and it would be another hour before it took off.

The natives did not appear at all concerned, but seemed to welcome the information as extended time for a social gathering. They continued to chatter away happily and laugh hilariously each time a local humorist displayed his wit at poor Adam's expense.

At last this taste of what the Black Hole of Calcutta must have been like came to an end. Almost in a state of collapse, Adam was led out to the plane. To gasp in the clean night air was an incredible relief. But the plane had no heating and he was dressed only in tropical clothes; so, soon after it had taken off, he was shivering with cold. It struck him that he might get pneumonia, but by then he was too weary to care. With wry humour it occurred to him that if he ever got round to writing his book with a Mexican background he would be able to portray a very different side of it to such places as the luxury of the El Presidente Hotel. A few minutes later he fell asleep and did not wake until they reached Mexico City.

As they had arrived on an internal flight, there were no formalities at the airport and Adam's suitcases were identified and handed over to his escort without delay, whereas had he been on his own he would have had to slip the baggage man ten *pesos* as the only alternative to kicking his heels for a quarter of an hour. He was then taken to Police Headquarters, a drive of little more than two miles from the airport, as it lay in the Plaza de los Presidentes on the eastern outskirts of the city.

There he was duly checked in and locked in a cell. By then it was close on midnight. The previous night he had not got to bed until past three in the morning; the strain of the long, anxious day and the nightmare he had gone through at the Mérida airport had left him like a limp rag, and his hour's sleep in the plane had done nothing to refresh him. Regardless of the brick-like pillow, he gratefully stretched himself out on the truckle bed and pulled the solitary, tattered blanket over him.

But he was not to be allowed to occupy his hard couch for long. He had been asleep for less than a quarter of an hour when the steel door of his cell was thrown open with a clang and he was ordered out. A brawny warder with the face of an ex-pugilist took him up some stairs to an office which had the appearance of being occupied by someone of importance. Behind a big desk sat a squat, bald man who, from his uniform and several rows of medal ribbons, Adam judged to be a Police Chief. With him was a younger man with a very sharp nose, dressed in plain clothes: evidently a detective.

The Police Chief told Adam to sit down opposite him and opened the proceedings by saying, 'Señor Gordon. We know all about you, so it would be pointless to tell us any lies. If you speak the truth we will make things much easier for you. Now I want you to give us in your own words an account of everything you have done since you arrived in Mexico on January 2nd.'

Adam had known that, sooner or later, he would have to face an interrogation, but he had had ample time while sitting in the cell in Mérida to think out the line of action he would take.

'*Su Excellencia, aqui está mi declaracion*,' he began. 'I have no wish to be obstructive. However, I am known to Señor Ramón Enriquez of your Foreign Office Security Department. If you will send for him tomorrow I will tell him everything I know.'

The Police Chief smiled. 'I am glad, señor, to find that you are willing to co-operate. But the Señor Enriquez will pass on to me anything you tell him, so there is no point in waiting until tomorrow. And in this matter time is precious. I pray you, confide in me.'

'I regret, *Excellencia*.' Adam shook his head. 'My mind is made up. I will discuss my situation only with the Señor Enriquez.'

For some minutes longer the Police Chief endeavoured to cajole him into talking. Then, as Adam made no reply and sat there staring at his large feet, he said testily to the detective, 'Oh, take him away, Mejia, and give him the treatment.'

The words were ominous. Into Adam's tired brain there flickered terrifying images of people being plunged into ice-cold baths, beaten with flexible steel rods, and other horrors perpetrated by the Nazis. Endeavouring to fight down his fears, he went with Mejia to a room on another floor. It was sparsely furnished with a table and hard chairs. An adjustable electric light with a cone-shaped shade hung from the centre of the ceiling. The detective told Adam to sit down at one end of the table and adjusted the light so that it shone into his eyes. He then spoke into an old-fashioned house telephone fixed to the wall.

After about five minutes another plain-clothes man, a fair-haired Mexican, appeared. With him was a woman carrying a notebook—obviously a stenographer. Adam was quite fascinated by the narrowness of Mejia's pointed nose as the light shone on it; but next moment the others took places on either side of Adam, and Mejia, sitting down opposite him, said sharply:

'I understand that you have had a long and unusually distressing day. All of us here have been on duty for many hours; so we, too, would like to go to bed. Please therefore be sensible and do not keep us up all night. Your statement, please.'

Adam employed the same tactics as he had in the Police Chief's office. He kept his mouth tightly shut and his eyes lowered to the table. Even so, the strong light from the lamp focussed on him partially penetrated his eyelids, giving them a rosy glow.

How long the session lasted he had no idea. Every few minutes one of the detectives shot a question at him. At times he fell asleep and slumped forward on to the table. Each time he did so the fair-haired young man stood up and shook him into wakefulness. They used no brutality, but the glare of the light was in itself a torture. At last he could stand it no more. Woken for the tenth time, he lurched to his feet, grasped the edge of the table in his great hands, lifted and heaved it right over. Mejia was sent flying backward and temporarily pinned to the floor. The other two went to his rescue, while shouting abuse at Adam over their shoulders. But he did not hear it. Utterly exhausted, he, too, had slumped to the floor and lay there unconscious.

He woke next morning in his cell. His bleak surroundings brought the events of the previous day and night flooding back to him. Turning over on the truckle bed, he groaned aloud. Grimly, he realised that had it not been for Chela he would never have landed himself in this ghastly mess. Almost he was inclined to curse her. But he loved her. She had given him greater happiness than he had ever believed it possible for a woman to give a man. But why, oh why, had the fates imbued her with this damnable fanaticism? She was sweet and gentle, but another side of her was completely ruthless. Under the influence of the sinister Don Alberuque it seemed that she would stick at nothing to further their cause. That she loved him in her fashion he had no doubt, but she had not had the least scruple about using him. And now that the conspiracy had been nipped in the bud by his arrest, what could the future hold for either of them? For him, unless Ramón could get him out, years of imprisonment. For her, since she was so deeply religious, her bitter disappointment at the failure of her plans might well lead her to take the veil and bury herself for life in a convent.

In due course he was brought *tortillas* with a mess of onions, and later more *tortillas* with tomatoes. All day he hoped that he would be sent for to be interviewed by Ramón and, alternatively, dreaded that he would be summoned to undergo another grilling. But no-one came to fetch him and for hour after hour he lay on the bed, a prey to black despair.

That night he slept fitfully, being more conscious of the much colder climate now that he was again at an altitude of seven thousand five hundred feet. In the morning he washed as best he could in the bucket provided, then again lay down with his anxieties revolving in his mind like a squirrel in a cage.

It was about eleven o'clock when the warder who looked like an ex-pugilist came for him. He was taken to another bleak room. Ramón was standing there, and the warder left them alone together.

He greeted Ramón with a pale smile. Ramón did not return it. Instead he regarded Adam with an angry stare and exclaimed, 'So you ratted on me! You bloody fool!'

'No!' Adam protested. 'I didn't. I swear I didn't.'

'Oh yes, you did. It was clear as crystal that you had fallen for Chela. She twisted you round her little finger and persuaded you to play the part of Quetzalcoatl. Well, you've asked for it and you'll get it. Ten years in gaol.'

Adam quailed at the thought of such an awful prospect; but temper came to his aid and he burst out angrily, 'If that happens, it will be you who have let me in for it. It was you who persuaded me to act as your cat's-paw and go spy the land for you during my motor trip. Damn it, owing to you I was nearly murdered by that mob at San Luis. And on my return I reported everything I had found out. You can't deny that.'

'No,' Ramón admitted, his expression still hard. 'I don't. But since that, you've played the turncoat. Chela was with you at Uxmal and you posed for her as Quetzalcoatl. Explain that if you can.'

'I can. I was working on the line I promised you I would: playing along with her to find out for you what I could. But the trouble was that I couldn't get in touch with you to let you know what was being planned.'

'What! Do you mean to tell me that a whole fortnight went by and you were so busy that you couldn't find a moment to ring me up. I don't believe you.'

'It's true, though.' Adam felt that he could not give away the fact that he had spent most of that time honeymooning with Chela, so he went on rather unconvincingly, 'For eight days I was held . . . well . . . incommunicado. Then I was taken down to Uxmal. You must know how difficult it is to get a call through from there to Mexico City. Before I had a chance this thing was sprung upon me. I was faced with the choice of either playing along or throwing in my hand. What would you have done?'

It was now Ramón who seemed a little uncertain. 'I . . . well, I suppose I would have done as you did. But it still doesn't explain why you didn't tip me off.'

'Damn it, man, I've already told you! I was never left alone for a moment. If I had been caught telephoning to you I would have been rumbled. They would have smelled a rat, changed their plans and, perhaps, bumped me off. And this is all the thanks I get for risking my neck on your behalf! For ingratitude you take the cake. I have been counting on you to get me out of here.'

'If I could believe you, of course I would. But I'm not

certain that I do. Give me the names of the ringleaders in this conspiracy and perhaps I might.'

'Don Alberuque is the king-pin. His principal lieutenant is a Father Lopéz.'

Ramón gave a cynical laugh. 'Do you take me for a simpleton? Alberuque is a clever and important man, but he is not a Prince of the Church. This is an attempt by the Church to regain her temporal power in Mexico by using these half-baked Indians. It is the names of the prelates we want—the really big boys who are behind this thing.'

'You are barking up the wrong tree,' Adam replied earnestly. 'I'm convinced that they are not involved. They know nothing about it. With a very few exceptions, this revolt is to be led by Mestizos and Indian clergy who are still half pagan and besotted with superstition.'

'I very much doubt that. It's much more likely that the wool has been pulled over your eyes and that those who stand to gain most if the revolution came off are still keeping under cover.'

Adam shrugged. 'Well, you've got another fortnight or three weeks in which to find out. The party at Uxmal was only what they termed a ceremony of Recognition, held so that local leaders from all over the country could vouch for it that they had seen Quetzalcoatl in the flesh with their own eyes. They are back in their towns and villages by now, spreading the good word. But that is going to take time. The plan was that I should not appear again until everything was ready, and that when I did it should be the signal for the balloon to go up.'

'Then it never will go up,' Ramón gave a sardonic smile, 'because, for a long time to come, you will be sweating it out as a convict in a labour gang. Having been idiot enough to incite these people to revolt, that is the price you will have to pay.'

'Thanks,' Adam retorted bitterly. 'But at least I'll have one consolation. That scheming bastard Alberuque will be wielding a pick beside me.'

'Maybe; but quite possibly not. The government's policy

is the less said about this thing the better. Alberuque has not
been pulled in yet, nor anyone else except yourself. And that
was not intended. The Police Chief down at Mérida was a
bit over-zealous. Information about your party reached him
only at the last moment. He could not raise enough police
on the nod to rope in the whole congregation; so he sent the
few he could lay his hand on, with orders to ignore everything
else and concentrate on bringing in the principal performer.
As you were the star of the show, they naturally went all-out
to get you.'

'I see. Then I, although an innocent party, am booked to
carry the can for all those who are really guilty?'

'That's what it looks like. If you are innocent—and I'm
still inclined to doubt it. There will be no fuss or bother.
You will be tried in camera and quietly put away for a term
of years.'

'You can't mean that!' Adam cried desperately. 'You
can't. I am innocent, I swear I am.'

Ramón shook his curly head. 'You may swear until you
are blue in the face that you are; but you are not. I'll grant
that you may not have intended to provoke a civil war, but
the fact is that you made a speech calling on the people to
overthrow the government. You can't laugh that off and, even
if I would, I couldn't help you. What is coming to you is
the price you must pay for having let Chela make use of you.'

Adam had gone white. In a low voice he said, 'Chela; what
has become of her?'

'Oh, Chela's all right,' Ramón shrugged. 'I had to fly
up to Monterrey on Wednesday, otherwise I would have come
to see you yesterday. But I got back last night and saw
Chela dancing at the Jacaranda. She may be a bit peeved
about having lost your services, but she didn't show it.' After
a moment he pressed a bell and added, 'I don't think there is
any more to be said, so I'll have you taken down to your
cell.'

Utterly stricken, Adam allowed himself to be led away.
As soon as the door of his cell had been locked behind him,
he sat down on his truckle bed and buried his head in his

hands. Too late, he realised what a lunatic he had been not to let Ramón know that he had agreed to act as Quetzal-coatl. If he had really set his wits to work on the problem he could surely have found some excuse to use the telephone which would have fooled Chela. It occurred to him now that he could have said that he had to phone the British Embassy, have got on to Jeremy Hunterscombe and asked him to give Ramón a simple message such as 'Gordon has agreed to play principal lead'. In retrospect, it also seemed probable that his fears of the postal censorship had been greatly exaggerated and that he could easily have got off a letter before setting out for Mérida. But the fact was that he had been too absorbed in his love affair with Chela to give the matter serious thought or realise its importance. Then, when it was too late, he had been pushed into his act without even five minutes' warning.

The thought of a ten-year sentence in a Mexican prison was too awful to contemplate; but Ramón had been right in saying that, even if his intention had been to make a further report on the progress of the conspiracy as soon as he had a chance, the fact remained that he had made a speech to its leaders from all over the country, inciting them to revolt.

He wondered for a moment whether he could plead insanity, but dismissed the idea at once. He could not bring a tittle of evidence to show that he had ever been abnormal, so no doctor would certify him.

Added to his tormented speculations concerning his future was what Ramón had said about Chela. How could she go out and dance at a night club, knowing him to be in prison and about to face a trial the outcome of which was almost certain to be that they would never see one another again?

He recalled their bitter quarrel when, after his rescue by Father Suaréz, he had flatly refused to continue playing the part of Quetzalcoatl. It must be that she had decided to break with him on that account. Yet from the fierce passion of her embraces and unvarying sweetness towards him at Oaxaca, Acapulco and at Uxmal, he could have sworn that she loved him. Perhaps she had, but only in so far as was possible to her on account of her nature. She was twenty-six and had freely admitted that she had been the mistress of other men. It might well be that her hot Indian blood craved constant sexual satisfaction and that she had been sleeping with a succession of men ever since her teens. That possibility was reinforced by the fact that her mother had deliberately left her native village to enter on a life of vice, and in such matters heredity often played a decisive part. If the reason for Chela's conduct was that she was secretly a nymphomaniac, it followed that, having lost one lover, she would soon seek another. Perhaps then, knowing that an arbitrary end had been put to their affair, although she had loved him after her fashion, she had decided that the best way to get him out of her mind was to go dancing with some other man. It was even possible that she had slept with him.

The mental picture of her doing with some new lover the sort of things she had done with him caused Adam suddenly to be stricken with almost insane jealousy. He wrung his hands and groaned aloud. The long hours of the day that followed were the worst he had ever spent.

Night fell at last, but he could not sleep. In vain he endeavoured to quieten his mind with thoughts of other things; but persistently they returned to himself, spending endless months in prison, barely existing on coarse, monotonous food, forced to slave at some uncongenial task and, for his only companions, ignorant, brutalised felons from among the scum of the earth. Alternatively he thought of Chela, moaning with passionate enjoyment beneath some muscular young man.

The hours dragged on until, close on midnight, a key grated in the lock of his cell. Starting up as the door opened, he saw the battered face of the gorilla-like warder. The man told him in a gruff voice that he was wanted upstairs.

With a sigh, he left the bed, tidied himself as best he could and went out into the passage, wondering why he had been summoned. It could hardly be that they wanted to interrogate him again, as Ramón already knew all there was to know about his case.

Then he hit upon it. Ramón had said that there was to be no publicity and he was to be tried in camera. Evidently such secret courts were held at night. There would be no prolonged arguments; at best only a stooge would have been nominated to plead on his behalf. He could ask to be allowed to get in touch with the British Embassy, but he thought it unlikely that his request would be granted. The odds were that, within an hour, he would be back in his cell: tried, convicted and with his life in ruins.

I

15

In the Toils

THE warder took Adam upstairs to the room in which he had first been interrogated. The squat, bald Police Chief was there behind his desk and with him was Ramón, seated in an armchair smoking a cigar. He nodded to Adam, waved a hand towards his companion and said, 'I think you have already met General Gómez, our Chief of Police for the Federal District.' Gómez then greeted Adam with ominous politeness, told him to sit down and went on:

'You must be aware, Señor Gordon, that you are facing a very serious charge. For subversive activities a sentence can be given of up to ten years with, I may add, hard labour. Of your guilt there can be no possible doubt. My colleague in Mérida infiltrated two Mestizos and a mulatto into your organisation. They will testify to the speech you made, inciting to rebellion the considerable number of people who attended the meeting. Our prisons in Mexico are efficiently run, but I cannot too strongly stress that an educated man like yourself, who has been accustomed to every comfort, will find life in one of them almost unbelievably unpleasant.'

When he paused, Adam said bitterly, 'As a writer with some imagination I do not need to be impressed about that. However, before you bring me to trial, I demand that my Embassy should be informed. Without inviting serious trouble, you cannot ignore the right of a British subject to receive advice from a lawyer appointed by his Embassy and to be defended by him.'

The General smiled. 'We do not intend to bring you to

trial, señor—at least, not yet. I was speaking only of possible eventualities.'

Having let that sink in, he went on, 'I have discussed your case very fully with Señor Enriquez. It was only this evening that I learned from him about the tour through several of our towns that you made a few weeks ago, and that during it you voluntarily gathered such information as you could for him about the conspiracy. Of course, I already knew all about the affair at San Luis Caliente; but through some oversight our Foreign Office failed to inform me of how you came to participate in it.'

New hope surged up in Adam. Hardly able to believe that after all there was a chance of his escaping imprisonment, he held his breath while Gómez took his time over lighting a cigar.

When the end was burning evenly, he said:

'The fact that at San Luis you nearly lost your life while working for us, and were compelled to act as a sacrificial priest in order to save it, puts a different complexion on matters; and I now take a much more favourable view of your case.'

'You . . .' Adam choked. 'You mean you're going to let me go?'

'Well; we shall see about that.'

'Su Excellencia, I beg you to! I swear that I was equally innocent in the affair at Uxmal. I had to go through with it if I was to stand any chance at all of securing further information for Señor Enriquez.'

'But you haven't,' Ramón put in. 'Except for that of Don Alberuque, which was known to us already, you have not furnished us with the name of a single person of importance.'

'I couldn't; because there are none,' Adam flung at him. 'No Bishops and very few white priests are involved. I'm certain of that.'

'You cannot be certain. You may be lying or your informant may have been lying to you.'

'It was divulged to me during a highly-emotional scene,

in which there could have been no premeditation to deceive me.'

The Police Chief held up a plump, beringed hand. 'Enough, señores. Let us get back to the present situation. As I see it, to begin with, Señor Gordon, being convinced that as a humanitarian it was his duty to do what he could to save this country from the horrors of a civil war, worked loyally to that end. Later there is reason to believe that he was persuaded to change his views and allow his likeness to the god Quetzalcoatl to be used by the conspirators. But we have no proof that his explanation for having done so is not the truth. Should we not, therefore, give him the benefit of the doubt?'

'Yes,' Ramón nodded. 'I think we should.'

Adam was almost sobbing with relief. 'Oh God be thanked!' he exclaimed. 'And thank you both. As soon as I'm free—tomorrow if there is a seat on a plane—I'll leave Mexico. I meant to stay a good while longer, but I'll willingly cut short my visit so that you can be quite certain that these people have no chance to use me again.'

'Señor Gordon, you go too fast,' Gómez said smoothly. 'As the Señor Enriquez has just remarked, we are by no means satisfied that none of the higher clergy are involved in this. We are going to rely on you to find out for us if that really is so, and any further plans the conspirators may have.'

'No, please!' Adam violently shook his head. 'I've had enough of this. More than enough. Think what I've suffered already as a result of getting mixed up in this business.'

Ramón smiled at him. 'Yes, I'm afraid you've been through some very nasty experiences since you agreed to give me your help; and I'm sorry about that. But I'm afraid, Gordon, that you don't realise your position.'

'Exactly,' added the General, his voice suddenly hardening, 'and I had better make it clear. We can bring and prove a charge of subversive activity against you that will send you to prison for ten years. And that is what we shall do if you refuse us your aid.'

Adam's shoulders sagged and he said unhappily, 'Then I've no alternative.'

'I'm glad, señor, that you realise it. And, after all, if you

In the morning he was brought up to a small courtroom inside the Police Headquarters. Neither the Police Chief nor Ramón was present, but the trial lasted barely ten minutes and followed the lines Adam had been told to expect. Later in the day he was conveyed several miles in a closed van to a prison that lay somewhere on the outskirts of the city. There particulars of him were again taken. To his considerable relief he was then allowed to have the first bath he had had since he had left Uxmal, and afterwards was escorted to a clean cell furnished with an iron bedstead, with sheets as well as a blanket, a table and a chair.

From the warder, who seemed a decent man, he learned that his fellow prisoners were nearly all Mexicans: business men who had committed fraud or sexual offences, debtors and opponents of the government who had aired their views too loudly; also that they were given two hours' exercise a day, one in the morning and one in the afternoon, and that he could draw three books a week from the prison library. Far more surprising, he was informed by the warder that if he was married or had a girl-friend the lady would be allowed to visit him once a week, and that rooms were provided in which for an hour they could enjoy themselves in private.

Giving the Mexican government full marks for its humanity and wise precaution against the spread of homosexuality, Adam resigned himself without anxiety to his ten days in prison.

Next day was Sunday. So much had happened to him recently that he found it almost impossible to believe that only a week had elapsed since he had spent a happy, carefree day with Chela, rambling round the ruins at Chichén Itzá.

He was thinking of her late in the afternoon when the warder came to tell him that he had a visitor. Recalling the lenient regulations regarding the prisoners and women, his heart leapt at the thought that Chela would have learned through the morning papers what had happened to him and had come to see him. For who else could it be?

On reaching a small reception room, he suffered a sharp disappointment. His visitor was not Chela, but Jeremy

Hunterscombe. When they had greeted each other, they were locked in the room, and sat down on two of the hard chairs set round a bare table. The lanky Wing Commander brushed up his flowing moustache and said :

'Well, chum, you've landed yourself in a fine mess. Read all about it in the paper this morning. You'll remember I told you what was cooking and asked you to play along with these revolutionaries, then give me the lowdown on what they were up to?'

'Yes,' Adam admitted, 'and I refused to spy for you on my friends.'

'Fair enough, dear boy. But that's one thing, and it's quite another to have allowed them to use you as their stalking horse. Of course, Chela is quite a wench and at times we all make fools of ourselves over women. But really! To let them dress you up like a peacock, then to spout a lot of Marxist stuff to a mob of yahoos . . .'

'What is done, is done,' said Adam testily. 'Maybe I behaved stupidly but, anyhow, the authorities have let me off lightly.'

'By Jove, they have. You might have been picking the old oakum or sewing mail-bags for a term of years. Someone once told me you had been nicknamed "Lucky" Gordon. Seems jolly apt to me. Still, that's beside the point. In nine days you'll be out of here, but *persona non grata* with the Mexican government. That means you'll have to shake the dust of this country off your brogues—and pronto. At the Embassy it is part of our job to look after British subjects; even when they do behave like nuts. So I've dropped in to offer the old Austin Reed service : get you a reservation on an aircraft, arrange to collect you in a car and see you safely on your way to England, Home and Beauty.'

'It's very good of you,' Adam replied. 'But as it happens, I shan't be leaving Mexico.'

Hunterscombe gave a slightly superior smile. 'Dear boy, I hate to disillusion you, but you certainly will. The Mexican government apart, H.E. has expressed his desire for your absence. Strange as it may sound to your evidently Marxist ears, we don't want British subjects here who are likely to embarrass us by advocating the overthrow of the régime; and your passport will in future be endorsed "not valid" for entry into Mexico. Believe me, chum, the skids are under you and, like it or not, you've got to quit.'

Although at their last meeting Adam had assured Ramón and General Gómez of his co-operation, the willingness he had shown had been mainly inspired by his relief at escaping a long prison sentence. Since then, he had had ample time to contemplate the matter in a more sober light. Reluctant as he was to forgo any prospect of renewing his affaire with Chela, he would have given a great deal to be freed from his dangerous obligation. But he realised that he had no choice, so he said:

'I wish to goodness that when I am released from prison I could go straight on board an aircraft and get out of this bloody country. But His Excellency's desire to be rid of me will cut no ice. The Mexicans wouldn't let me go.'

'Why shouldn't they?'

'Because they've got me on a hook. They're blackmailing me.'

'The devil they are!' Hunterscombe frowned; then, after a moment, said:

'Now look, Gordon. I don't care what you've done and you had better come clean with me. As I said, it is up to us to do what we can for you, and there is no-one else to whom you can turn for help; so tell all.'

Adam gave an unhappy nod. 'Yes, you're right. Well, this is what happened. Although I refused to spy on my friends for you, I was later persuaded by Ramón Enriquez to find out what I could about this revolutionary movement. What followed we need not go into until we come to my arrest down at Uxmal. That would never have taken place if the Police Chief at Mérida had been put in the picture. But he wasn't, and being an eager-beaver type, he had me pulled in. The big boys here have been pretty smart, though. They could treat me either as a criminal or a practical joker, and I was given the choice. Naturally, I preferred ten days to ten years, but the price was that, when I came out, I should work for them again.'

'Well, I'll be damned!' The Wing Commander's lean face broke into a grin. 'So you are now Richard Hannay, Gregory Sallust and Uncle Tom Cobley and all.' His face suddenly became serious. 'But this is a dangerous game you're playing, and your pals in the Mexican Security set-up won't equip you against all emergencies. I mean, real secret agents don't have daggers that spring out of the toes of their shoes, cars that eject flame and tintacks in the path of their pursuers, and all those other silly, amusing gadgets that one reads about in the Bond books. It is only in countries such as this, where it is not illegal to tote a gun, that a chap can even do that without risk of getting himself pinched.'

'I see no reason why anything I do should lead to a gun battle,' Adam replied. 'All I mean to do is turn in anything I pick up; but I'm damned if I'll stick my neck out for Enriquez and Co.'

'That's what you think. But you're in this thing now and, like it or not, you'll have to. That is, unless you want to be framed on some other charge and popped back into prison for keeps. Gun battles apart, if the plotters tumble to it that you are double-crossing them they will have hoodlums around who, at a nod, would stick a knife into you quicker than you could take the first sip of a dry Martini. Look, chum, this is your show and your old Uncle Jeremy has no wish to cramp your style. But you are an amateur: a Babe in the Wood going in against a pack of wolves. I'd bet the Crown Jewels against a handful of peanuts that, before you are much older, you are going to land yourself in real trouble. Your Mexican pals are only putting you in on the off-chance that you'll pull the chestnuts out of the fire for them. They won't lose a wink of sleep if this ends in your kicking the bucket. But you're one of us; so I will. If you do find yourself in a spot, get on to me. I'm used to nasty situations and if anything can be done to pull you out I'll do it.'

'Thanks,' Adam smiled. 'That's very good of you. If I do need help, how do I bring my "Uncle Jeremy" racing to the rescue?'

Hunterscombe fished a small notebook out of his pocket, wrote in it, tore the page out and handed it to Adam. 'There

is the address of my flat and my telephone number. Below it
is the Embassy number. For most of the twenty-four hours
you'll be able to get me at one or the other. If you can't,
leave a message for me; but don't use your own name. Let's
see. Who was that bloodthirsty character in your last book?
I've got it. Ord the Red-Handed. Use Red. That's more common than Ord. Lots of people nicknamed Red. Don't give
any details unless you're quite certain the line isn't likely to
be tapped. Just say where you are and I'll be along as soon
as I can make it.'

As Adam thanked him again, he added, 'Better memorise
the info' on that slip of paper, then destroy it. No need to
swallow it, though, as they do in thrillers. Just give it a good
chew, then spit it out into your slop bucket.'

When the Wing Commander had gone, Adam spent the
best part of an hour repeating to himself over and over again
the address and telephone numbers until he was quite certain
that they would stick in his memory; then he got rid of the
paper.

Since he had so peremptorily turned down Hunterscombe's
request for his help when they had lunched together at the
Ritz, he thought it very decent of him to show such concern
for his safety now that he had admitted to working for
Ramón. All the same, it seemed unlikely that a situation
could arise in which he would need to avail himself of the
Wing Commander's offer. Before he left prison it was certain
that Ramón would furnish him with the means of communi-
cation for anything urgent; so, if he did find himself up against
it, and was able to appeal for help, it would obviously be
more effective to call in the police rather than the solitary
secret agent of a foreign country.

On the Monday, while at exercise, he scraped acquaintance
with two other prisoners and, in whispered conversations,
learned that one was a defaulting lawyer and the other a rich
brothel owner who had refused certain highly-placed persons free access to his houses and, as a result, had been
framed. Of himself he said that he was in on a short sentence
for dangerous driving. By Tuesday, the prison grapevine had
picked up an account in the Sunday papers of the arrest of

an Englishman caught posing for a joke as Quetzalcoatl; which explained an absurd but persistent rumour recently running round the country that the Man-God had returned and appeared to a crowd of Indians at both San Luis Caliente and Uxmal. Adam gathered that his physical characteristics, coupled with the date of his arrival at the prison, had led his fellow prisoners to conclude that he was the practical joker concerned; but their opportunities for questioning him were few, and he refused to satisfy their curiosity.

It was in the early hours of Wednesday morning that he was roused by the sound of an explosion. A few minutes later it was followed by the ringing of an alarm bell, shots and loud shouting. Sitting up in bed, he wondered what on earth could be happening.

The pandemonium continued: single shots, the rat-tat-tat of sub-machine guns, yells and curses. Flying feet pounded down the corridor outside his cell. A shot was fired, there came a scream and the footsteps ceased abruptly. More curses, loud protests, growling voices now outside the cell. A key turned in the lock and the door swung open.

Adam's warder was pushed inside. His face was white, his right arm hung limp at his side, dripping blood. He was followed by a huge Negro and three Indians with long, matted hair. The Negro grinned at Adam and said in a travesty of Spanish:

'You're free now, Lord. Jus' you come wi' us.' Then, turning to one of the Indians, he waved a hand towards the warder and added, 'Jacko, yoo know what t'do wid dis guy. G'ie 'im de works.'

Two of the Indians pushed the wounded man down on to the bed from which Adam had just got up and the one named Jacko grasped him by the throat. Seeing that he was about to strangle him, Adam cried:

'Hi! Stop that!'

The Negro shook his head. 'He gotta die, Lord. Yo'se free now. Yo' come along wid us.'

'But damn' it,' Adam exclaimed furiously, 'he's already wounded. He can't do you any harm. It's senseless murder.'

Turning, he grabbed the collar of Jacko's jacket in an attempt to pull him off.

As he wrenched, Jacko's head was jerked up, but he did not release his grip on the warder's throat. By then the wretched man's eyes were starting from their sockets and he was turning purple in the face.

Unhappily the big Negro stood by watching for a moment, apparently reluctant to intervene. Suddenly making up his mind, he grasped Adam from behind by both arms, and wailed, 'Forgi' me, Lord, fo' touchin' yo. But Ah can't let yo. Ah gotta obey orders. Dey was ter croak de keysman an' git yo outa here.'

A furious struggle ensued. Adam hung on to Jacko's collar until, with a loud, rending sound, the thin cotton fabric tore. By then Adam's pull on Jacko and the latter's on the warder's neck had lifted them both. With a thump they fell back on the bed. His arms being held from behind by the Negro placed Adam at a big disadvantage. The other two Indians lent a hand. Despite his efforts, the three of them succeeded in pulling him away, pushing him through the doorway, then dragging him along the corridor. At its end, realising that by now the warder must be beyond anything except medical help, he gave up trying to break free.

Still held by his captors, he was hustled through the prisoners' dining room. Another warder lay there with his throat cut. In the corridor beyond it a third warder lay sprawled on his face, while a Mestizo who had taken his keys was swiftly unlocking cell doors to release the prisoners. Out in the main hall a battle was raging. A dozen coloureds of all shades were blazing off with pistols and sub-machine-guns at the upper floors. Prison officers on the high galleries round the staircase were exposing themselves only for the minimum of time, but long enough to return the fire of the raiders. On the stone flags lay several dead or wounded. One man had his hands clutched to his stomach and was screaming horribly.

Outside, the courtyard was a shambles. Not only was it littered with dead or dying prison officers and Indians. Adam nearly tripped over a body; then, looking down, saw by a beam of light coming from the hall that the face was that of his new acquaintance, the brothel-keeper. A moment later, to his horror, he saw that a group of coloureds was shooting down the white Mexican prisoners as they poured out from a side door of the prison believing that they had been restored to liberty.

When he reached the prison gate, one half of it was flat, the other hanging crookedly on its hinges after having been blown open. Outside, there were a dozen cars and small vans. Adam's escort ran him over to one of the cars, he was pushed into the back, the two Indians scrambled in after him and the Negro got into the driver's seat. There came a whirring of the self-starter, a screech of gears changed too quickly and they were off.

As far as Adam could see, the suburb in which the prison lay consisted of some rows of small, uniform, modern houses, a short row of one-storey shops and empty back lots. The blowing-in of the prison gates and subsequent shooting had roused the inhabitants. There were lights in most of the windows and people leaning out of them, calling excitedly to one another. A few had come out onto the sidewalks; but no attempt was made to stop the car.

It was driven for some miles out into the country, returned to the city by a circuitous route, ran out again through a good-class district of scattered houses, then through some narrow, twisting lanes, to swerve between gateposts set in a high wall and up a short drive.

Adam had strong suspicions why he had been 'sprung' from prison while the other white prisoners were being shot down, for who but Alberuque would have ordered half a hundred mixed coloureds to attack it for the sole purpose of rescuing him? But he could not be absolutely certain of that, and he felt far from safe in the hands of his murderous captors. As they all got out of the car he had half a mind to attempt to escape. But a swift glance towards the gates showed him that another man, who had evidently been waiting there, was shutting them. That made the odds against him four to one, and the men who had carried him off from the prison were armed. Uneasily, he resigned himself to putting as good a face as possible on the situation.

The car had pulled up in front of the porch of a rambling old house. A light went on, showing up the fanlight over the door. It was opened by a tall man in a monk's habit. His garb at once strengthened Adam's suspicion about the reason for his kidnapping. The lay brother, as he turned out to be, bowed and stood aside for Adam to enter. As he did so, a gabble of words behind caused him to look over his shoulder. Instead of following him in, his escort had gone down on their knees, and the big Negro was mumbling apologies for their having laid hands on his sacred person.

The hall of the house was austerely furnished. On one wall there hung a large wooden crucifix, with a holy-water stoup below it; on the other a few cheap religious prints. The stone staircase that led to the floors above was uncarpeted.

Bowing again, the lay brother waved a hand towards the stairs then led the way up. In the light of the hall, Adam had had his first sight of the man's face. It was that of an ascetic who had consistently mortified his flesh and fasted for long periods. The skin was drawn so tightly over the bones that his head looked almost like a skull, and the dark eyes were sunken in their sockets.

Adam had expected that on the first floor he would be shown into a study in which he would find Don Alberuque awaiting him; but his guide went up a second flight of dimly-lit stairs to the top of the house, signed to him to wait for a moment on the landing, then went into one of the rooms and lit an oil lamp.

Following him in, Adam saw that it was a bedroom and a far from comfortable one. The single bed sagged in the middle and had no valance; there was a prie-dieu against one wall, a single, hard-bottomed chair and an old-fashioned wooden washstand carrying a china jug and basin. The only accommodation for clothes was some hooks behind a faded curtain that screened off one corner of the room.

Many years earlier, the government had deprived the Church of all the great historic monasteries; but recently religious communities had, in limited numbers, been allowed to establish themselves in private houses, and Adam felt little doubt that it was to a small monastery that he had been brought.

Convinced that Alberuque was responsible for this terrible night's work, Adam could hardly contain his impatience to come face to face with him. The fact that he was committed to attempt to worm the Monsignor's future intentions out of him had been completely pushed out of his mind by his sick horror at the massacre he had witnessed. He was inwardly boiling to such an extent that for two pins he would have killed the instigator of that shocking butchery. But, at the least, he meant to shake him like a rat, slap his face until it was purple, then at the first opportunity have him charged with instigating murder. Turning to the lay brother, he asked, 'Where is Monsignor Alberuque?'

The man shook his skull-like head, fished a tablet and stylo out from a pocket in his gown and wrote on it: 'Not here. He will see you tomorrow.'

It was only then that Adam realised that the man was dumb. Thwarted in giving vent to his anger, he shrugged his shoulders and turned away. Unseen by him, the lay brother left the room and locked the door behind him.

At the sound of the key turning, Adam swung round, strode over to the door, grasped the handle and shook it. Certain now that it was locked, he pounded furiously upon it with his fist, shouting to his new gaoler that, unless he returned and unlocked it, he would later wring his neck; but there was no response.

Still seething with rage, he marched over to the window, wrenched aside the flimsy curtain and saw that the window was barred. Suddenly his sense of humour overcame his resentment. He was again a prisoner, but to confine him in such a prison was ridiculous. With his great strength he could have wrenched out the rusty grille of thin iron bars or have smashed down the door.

He was in half a mind to break out there and then, but on second thoughts decided not to. He had no idea where he was and he might be miles from the centre of Mexico City. If he did leave the house he had not a *peso* on him with which to telephone to Ramón. Tomorrow, he decided, would be time enough to have a showdown with Alberuque, then quit.

The ancient bed was not as uncomfortable as it looked. Nevertheless he slept badly, haunted by dreams which were grotesque distortions of the brutal slayings he had witnessed in the prison courtyard.

He woke with a calmer mind and was able to assess better the results of the courses of action open to him. Of one thing he was now fully determined. At whatever risk to himself, he must do his utmost to wreck the conspiracy.

To begin with, Chela's persuasiveness had led him to believe that the revolution would rescue the Indians from the miserable conditions under which they had lived for so long and that it could be accomplished almost bloodlessly. Hunterscombe and then Ramón had convinced him that it must lead to a sanguinary civil war; so he had taken the side which aimed at preserving law and order. Later, again under Chela's influence, he had allowed himself to be used as Quetzalcoatl; but only because he had fallen for the idea that, as the titular head of the revolt, he would be able to prevent his followers from committing excesses, and with the mental reservation that, by letting Ramón know the plans of the conspirators, he would still stop the whole thing if he could.

After his arrest he had again agreed to work for the government, but only because he had been blackmailed. He had resented that intensely, cursing the day that he had first become involved and of a mind to do only as much as would ensure regaining his freedom. But now a new situation had arisen. The attack on the prison the previous night had convinced him beyond all doubt that a revolution would lead to a blood-bath. The fanatical Indians and half-breeds would murder every white man they could lay their hands on. Once they got the bit between their teeth, no leader would be able to control them. So the outbreak *must* be stopped while there was still time.

But how to set about it? If he followed his inclination to beat Alberuque to a pulp, then denounce him to the police, that might put an end to the conspiracy. But if Ramón and General Gómez were right it would not, because they believed him to be only a 'front' for the higher clergy who were at the bottom of the business. Adam doubted that to be true, but admitted to himself that it was up to him to try to find out, and he certainly would stand no chance of doing so if he used violence on the Monsignor.

At about nine o'clock the lay brother brought him a pot of weak chocolate, plain, cold *tortillas* and fruit. Adam tried the chocolate and found it to be a thin, bitter drink, quite unlike the rich, sweet brew that his mother had at times made for her family when he was a boy in Scotland. For the past week he had been unable to take his Enteroviaform pills and had at first feared that tummy trouble, or even dysentery, might result from the prison food. But he had taken the precaution of eating only fruit that could be peeled, and suffered no ill-effects from the cooked messes that had been his staple diet. Now he left the *tortillas* and ate only a big orange and two mandarines.

His gaoler had not brought him any hot water; so, on getting up, he made do with the cold in the china jug and washed as well as he could with a small square of yellow kitchen soap. Then, having dressed, he sat down to await events.

As his watch, together with all his other belongings, had been taken from him when he had first been arrested, he had no means of telling the time. Actually an hour and a half elapsed, although it seemed much longer, before the lay brother returned and signed to him to follow him downstairs.

On his way down he passed four monks. Their heads were downcast and they deliberately avoided looking at him. Earlier, a chapel bell had reinforced his belief that the place was a monastery. But in the hall two very unmonastic characters were lounging. They were Indians and both of them were wearing soiled leather belts from which hung pistol holsters. On seeing Adam they went down on their knees, but, even so, he had little doubt that they had orders to stop him if he attempted to walk out, and would have obeyed them.

The lay brother opened a door at one side of the hall, bowed to Adam and signed to him to enter. The room into which he walked was long and lofty. Two-thirds of the walls were lined with bookshelves. The books on them were old, their calf bindings faded and, in many cases, torn. Behind a desk at the far end of the room sat Monsignor Don Alberuque.

Although for just on a month he had been frequently in Adam's thoughts, this was only the second time they had met; so he took stock of his enemy with special interest. Alberuque was wearing clerical clothes—a black, satin vest and a white lawn cravat—which, with the darkish, high-nosed face framed in the sleekly falling silver hair, gave him an air of distinction. Under the bushy black eyebrows his eyes seemed curiously dead and fishlike. His lips parted, showing slightly uneven teeth, in a smile of welcome; but the smile did not reach his eyes. The effect was almost as though he had been a Zombie.

Again Adam had the queer sensation that his hackles were rising in the presence of a spirit which reeked of evil. How Chela could remain insensitive to it, and regard Alberuque as almost a saint, Adam could not conceive. Fighting down his intense dislike, he managed to greet the priest with a civil 'Buenos dias'.

Rising from his chair, Alberuque returned the greeting and, as he continued to speak, it was borne in on Adam that his voice must account for much of the influence he wielded over people. Its tones were extraordinarily harmonious and, coupled with his charm of manner, gave him an almost hypnotic attraction. It must be, Adam thought, that my dislike of him is a personal thing, not felt by others. Meanwhile the Monsignor was saying:

'Señor Gordon, please accept my apologies for receiving you in such an austere abode. I do not live here but my home is not unlike it. Few foreigners, other than scholars, realise that Spain escaped large numbers of her people being suborned by the Protestant heresy because our Church had already been cleansed by Queen Isabella's great adviser, Cardinal Ximénez de Cisneros. He put a stop to the sale of indulgences and other unethical practices, purged the priesthood of its drones and lechers and gave preferment only to those who led useful, saintly lives. In Mexico the clergy have followed that fine tradition, so you must excuse the poor accommodation and indifferent food with which you have been provided.'

Impatiently, Adam heard him out, but he could not resist

remarking acidly, 'That may apply to the lower orders here; but you showed no reluctance to lap up the caviare and champagne when we were together at Cuernavaca.'

'When in Rome, my son. When in Rome . . . you must know the rest of that quotation. It would ill become me to embarrass my flock by refusing the good things offered at their tables. But that is of no moment. I am most happy to welcome you to this poor house where, at least, you can remain safely concealed; and I rejoice that my endeavours resulted in my restoring you to freedom.'

Adam had meant to keep his temper, but at that it flared and he burst out, 'Happy! Your endeavours! My freedom! Do you realise that a score, perhaps two score, men were killed or grievously injured to achieve it?'

'Indeed I do,' Alberuque replied quietly. 'But the revolution must go on. And you have become an essential element in its fulfilment. That you should continue to play your part as Quetzalcoatl is imperative. To ensure your being able to do so, the loss of a few lives, however regrettable, is unimportant.'

'But damn it, man,' Adam shouted, 'how can you calmly sit there and say that? If you thought it an ace-high priority to get me out, it is just possible to understand your having squared it with your conscience to be the cause of the death of a few unfortunate warders. But that gang of mixed coloured hoodlums you let loose on the place murdered every white man they could lay their hands on: prisoners as well as prison officers.'

'You must make allowances.' The Monsignor spread out his hands and hunched his shoulders. 'For centuries, in spite of the Church doing her best to protect them, the coloured people of Mexico have endured great suffering at the hands of the *gachupines* and their descendants. Given an opportunity, it is only to be expected that they would take their revenge.'

His eyes gone hard, Adam demanded, 'Am I to understand that what happened last night at the prison is the pattern for the revolution you are planning? That there is to be a wholesale massacre of the white population?'

Alberuque shook his head and the silver locks falling about

his ears danced a little. 'I trust not. Once we have triumphed, we shall do our utmost to prevent excesses.'

Adam said scathingly, 'What chance will you have against tens of thousands of Indians and half-breeds gone berserk? Go on with this and I'll tell you how it will end. They will string *you* up to a lamp-post. And serve you damn' well right.'

'Your sentiments are singularly unfriendly,' Alberuque observed coldly. 'But no matter. You will give us your co-operation. I am in a position to ensure that you will.'

'No doubt you think so,' Adam retorted. 'But if I were you I wouldn't count on that.'

With a slightly amused smile, Alberuque said, 'I am well aware that I could not, had I not had you removed from prison.'

'That will make no difference.'

'It will make a great deal of difference. With an astuteness that one can but admire, the government wrote you off as a practical joker of no account and sentenced you to only fourteen days' imprisonment. In a week's time you would have come out. What would you have done then?'

Suddenly Adam realised that his violent temper and dislike of Alberuque had led him into adopting an attitude the very opposite to that he should have taken. Berating himself as the worst possible secret agent, he made an effort to retrieve the situation by replying:

'I would have gone to the Señorita Chela and offered to resume my role as Quetzalcoatl.'

Alberuque's thin lips drew back in a snarl. 'Oh no, you would not! You lie! You would have done nothing of the sort. You would have left Mexico on the first aircraft in which you could get a passage.'

'What leads you to think that?'

'I am certain of it. On your last night in Uxmal, after Father Suaréz had rescued you from the police, you had a bitter quarrel with the Señorita Chela. You told her that you were through with this whole business. That nothing would induce you to appear again as Quetzalcoatl. That is why I had you taken from prison. I can now ensure that you will remain with us and, when the time comes, again appear before my people as the Man-God.'

These angry exchanges and Alberuque's disclosure of his distrust finally cut the ground from under Adam's original intention of appearing to give his co-operation willingly. His resentment at this threat of coercion led him to set his jaw stubbornly and declare, 'You can't force me to.'

'Indeed, Señor Gordon, I can.' The Monsignor's voice had become honeyed again. 'You seem to have forgotten what took place last night. With the assistance of some fifty raiders, you broke out of prison. Owing to this plot, of which it will be assumed that you had knowledge, a number of people lost their lives. For that the government will hold you, in part, responsible. But there is much more to it than that. During the riot an unfortunate warder took refuge in your cell and, to save himself, locked himself in with you. What happened then? In order to gain your freedom you needed his keys. To get them, you strangled him.'

'You swine!' Adam roared. 'That is a filthy lie! I did my utmost to prevent his being murdered by your thug Jacko.'

Again Alberuque's uneven teeth showed in a smile. 'I am aware of that. But who will believe you? My big Negro and his companions are prepared to swear that, when they succeeded with another key, in getting into your cell, they saw you choking the warder to death.'

He paused for a moment, then went on with silky satisfaction, 'Refuse to obey my orders, Señor Gordon, and I will turn you over to the police. My people will give evidence against you. And I will tell you what will happen then. As there is no capital punishment in Mexico, you will be sentenced to life imprisonment. But do not imagine that, as in England, by good conduct you will be freed in time to enjoy a happy middle and old age. Here we are not so soft with murderers who have killed without provocation. Such dangerous and useless mouths are not allowed to remain a charge upon the taxpayers. After a week or two a small paragraph will appear in the papers, simply stating that "Señor Gordon was shot while attempting to escape".'

Again the smooth voice stopped, then went on softly, 'But

I am confident that you are much too sensible to bring upon
yourself such a premature and unpleasant end. Instead, you
will appear again to a chosen audience as the Man-God,
Quetzalcoatl. After you have done that, I shall have no more
use for you.'

Adam realised then that he had been caught in the toils of
this arch-conspirator. Next moment as, disconcerted, he
stared at Alberuque, his heart was gripped with awful fear.
The reason for his instinctive loathing for the man had suddenly been revealed to him. Those cold, dead, fishlike eyes
were the eyes of the High Priest, Itzechuatl, from whom Mirolitlit had saved him. And in those eyes there again lay the
threat of death.

16

The Terrible Betrayal

ADAM'S mind was in a whirl. He was so positive now that Alberuque had been Itzechuatl that he could not think how he had failed to recognise him before. The man's features were different, just as Chela's were from those of Mirolitlit. It was the personality that inexplicably but unmistakably came through. No wonder that at their first meeting he had felt repulsion for the smooth-tongued Monsignor. And now, added to that, there was fear—fear that Itzechuatl had known him from the outset and, once he had used him, intended to exact vengeance for having been cheated of his Man-God victim a thousand years ago.

With an effort, Adam endeavoured to assess his chances in this new and terrifying situation. The reason why Jacko had strangled the warder was now plain. The fiendish Alberuque had ordered the murder so that he could frame the rescued prisoner with it. Who could now possibly fail to believe that all the time he, Adam, had been hand in glove with the conspirators, had never had any intention of letting Ramón know about the gathering at Uxmal and, by secret means while in prison, had connived at the plan to rescue him whatever the cost in lives? It would be assumed by everyone that a lust for power had gone to his head and that, regardless of the strife and misery a civil war would cause, he hoped to rule Mexico as the returned Quetzalcoatl.

Now, if he again fell into the hands of the police, his number would be up with a vengeance. As the man responsible for the murders in the prison, his name would be execrated by all decent people throughtout Mexico. A life sentence would be bad enough; but he had a horrid feeling that Alberuque had not been lying about the fate he might expect, and that for such a crime the government would see to it that he was shot 'while attempting to escape'. The only alternatives left to him were to do as Alberuque wished or, if he could escape, endeavour to disguise himself and get out of the country clandestinely. Fighting down his fear and anger, he managed after a moment to mutter:

'I take it, then, that you intend to hold me a prisoner here?'

The Monsignor shrugged. 'I do not need to. Should you be so ill-advised as to leave this place, I shall take steps to let the authorities know that you are at large, and within a few hours you will be arrested. It will be only a few days now before my plans for your final appearance are completed. During that time you may enjoy the freedom of this house and its garden.'

Adam thought quickly. Chela had got him into this and, if she still loved him, she might help to get him out of it. Owing to her devotion to Alberuque, that seemed unlikely; but it was at least a possibility—in fact his only hope. So he said:

'The time of waiting is certain to prove a great strain. To ease it, would you allow the Señorita Chela to visit me?'

'I see no reason to refuse. But you must content yourself with walking with her in the garden. This house is conducted as a monastery, so it would not be fitting that she should enter it. Later I will telephone her and find out if she is free to come here either tomorrow afternoon or the next.'

'Thank you.' As Adam spoke, it occurred to him that it would be sound tactics to pretend resignation, so he added:

'In the meantime, can I have something to read?'

With a wave of his smooth hand, Alberuque indicated the many shelves of books. 'Choose what you like. I now have some work to do; but it will not take me more than half an hour. At the end of that time, this room will be at your disposal.'

Seeing that there was no more to be said, Adam nodded curtly, turned about and went back upstairs to his room. There, preferring the bed to the hard-seated chair, he lay down and again gloomily contemplated the results of having come to Mexico in search of background colour for a novel. He had hit both the high-spots and the low-spots. The hours he had spent alone with Chela had been sheer heaven, those while in custody at the Mérida airport unadulterated hell. In addition there were others that also seemed to have been out of this world. There were times when he could not really believe that he had sacrificed a pig at San Luis Caliente, or stood garbed in barbaric splendour on the top of the Pyramid of the Magician at Uxmal. Those episodes far more nearly resembled his dreams of past lives. In fact the whole conception of a plot to use him as Quetzalcoatl and launch a revolution that would set modern Mexico back a thousand years seemed utterly fantastic.

Yet here he was, unquestionably awake and, for all practical purposes, a prisoner in this gloomy monastic house. The association with religion brought his thoughts back to Alberuque. Ordained though he must have been, he was no priest of Christ. Mentally he was still Itzechuatl, a servant of the Devil, as represented by the blood-lusting gods who had for so long terrorised the unfortunate people of Mexico.

That made the movement he was leading much more understandable. The superstition-ridden Indians still believed in those old gods, and sacrificed chickens and pigs to them. Many of their half-breed country priests were secretly of the same persuasion and gave only lip service to the Christian God. It had needed only a dominating personality, such as Alberuque's, to imbue them with the conviction that, if they acted with resolution, they could by sheer weight of numbers seize the country and afterwards be able to bring about a return of the old days—the days of human sacrifice.

If that came about, Alberuque would achieve his ambition. Once more he would be a High Priest, able to glut his sadistic craving to hear the screams of his victims as he tore out their hearts and plunged his hands in their warm blood.

What then? Would the United Nations take solemn notice and, after months of debate, call for sanctions, or the United States employ armed intervention? Either was possible, but unlikely. Both had sponsored this new-found doctrine that all peoples were entitled to their independence which, literally interpreted, meant that they were free to persecute and kill their minorities in any way they chose. The pressure they had exerted to force the European Powers to give up their colonies prematurely had led in them to an end of justice, toleration, the liberty of the individual, security of property and life itself. Indonesia, Cambodia, India, Pakistan, Cyprus and the Congo all told the same awful tale of massacres and murder. Would Americans then kill their own 'sacred cow' and intervene in Mexico? Even if at long last they did, it would not be before many thousands of people had lost their lives in a ghastly civil war.

Judging that the half-hour was up, Adam went downstairs again. The library was empty and he browsed there, seeking some work that would distract his mind from his worries. Nearly all the books were in Spanish and on religious subjects; but at length he came upon a row of tall atlases, some of which dated back to the seventeenth century, and he flicked over their pages until he was brought his meagre lunch.

Afterwards he went out into the garden. It was ill-cared-for, the paths overgrown with weeds, but it was a good acre in extent and surrounded by high walls. At the far end there stood a big barn and, finding the door unlocked, he went inside. To his surprise, it housed a helicopter capable of carrying four people. The machine formed a strange contrast to the other contents of the barn: an ancient wagon, two dusty carriages dating from Victorian times, old agricultural implements and, in a half-loft above, some bales of hay.

For a moment he was seized with the wild idea that he might use the helicopter to escape—to fly right out of Mexico down to Guatemala. But he had never flown an aircraft of any kind, so recognised his thought to be a pipe-dream. Besides, on second thoughts even if he could have flown it and it was capable of covering such a distance, he would not have made the attempt. For better or worse, he considered himself committed now to remain there and do his damnedest to wreck Alberuque's schemes.

But how? All the afternoon he paced up and down the garden exploring possibilities. One thing was clear: he dared not communicate with Ramón or the police. If he had been able to go to them with the names of several Bishops and evidence that they were involved in the conspiracy, or an account of Alberuque's plans and the date he intended to set the revolution in motion, he would have gambled on their believing him and, at all events until matters developed, affording him protective custody.

To go to them empty-handed was a very different matter. They had clearly believed him guilty in the Uxmal affair and had given him the benefit of the doubt only because there was a chance that they might gain some useful information by doing so. Now, after the massacre at the prison, obviously staged to get him out, he must be Number One on their wanted list. They would never believe him to be innocent. They would assume that he had come to them only because he had belatedly decided that Alberuque's *coup* would fail; so was now endeavouring to put himself in the clear while there was still time. Even if they kept him on ice for the time being, once Alberuque's account of how he had strangled the warder reached them, his goose would be cooked.

He could think of only one possible life-line: 'Uncle' Jeremy Hunterscombe. Whatever he was supposed to have done, Hunterscombe would not turn him over to the police. He might provide help or, at all events, sound advice on how to get the better of Alberuque. And later, when Adam had to face a police enquiry, the Wing Commander would be able to vouch for it that he had done his utmost to sabotage the conspiracy.

During the course of the day, Adam had seen, in addition to the skull-faced lay brother who appeared to be in charge of him, several monks, as well as four Indian hoodlums who lurked about the place, presumably as guardians; so, after spending a long, dreary evening, he still had to struggle to keep awake for several hours until he could be reasonably certain that the inmates of the house were asleep.

Although he still had no accurate means of telling the time, he judged it to be about one o'clock in the morning when he got out of bed, dressed himself and prepared to leave the building. To have gone downstairs would have been to risk discovery, and the last thing he wanted was for Alberuque to learn that he had attempted to escape or communicate with friends outside. But the door of his room had not been locked, and in the ceiling of the landing on to which it led he had noticed a trapdoor that was obviously a way up to the roof.

Owing to his unusual height, by standing on tiptoe he was able to reach it and, after several failures, succeeded in throwing the trap back. A good spring then enabled him to grasp a rim of the aperture and a moment later he had wriggled himself out into the cool night air.

The ten minutes that followed were fraught with difficulties and dangers, but his strength and reach enabled him to overcome them. Lowering himself from one precarious hold to another, he succeeded in reaching the ground safely. Still undetected, he tiptoed down the drive and out into the high-walled, cobbled street.

So far, so good; but he now had to get to Hunterscombe's apartment, which presented quite a problem, for he had no money and not the faintest idea where he was. As the street was on a slope, he set off downhill and after only five minutes' walk had a lucky break. It ended in an irregular, open space, on one side of which stood a big building blazing with lights, and in front of it were parked thirty or forty cars. After a moment he recognised it as the once-great monastery and now de-luxe restaurant of San Angel.

That gave him his bearings but cause for dismay, as he recalled that this ancient suburb lay about seven miles from the centre of Mexico City. For several minutes he stood in the shadow of some tall trees, listening to the strains of dance music coming from the restaurant, while he wondered what to do. From time to time cars would be leaving, so he could beg a lift; but it was certain that his description would have been circulated by the police. His height, coupled with his red-gold hair and beard, were a sure give-away; so he decided that he dared not risk it and must walk.

After two false casts, he found the six-lane motorway and put his best foot forward. Presently he came to a lighted clock tower and saw that it was only twenty-five minutes to one; so he had overestimated the time he had lain waiting and must have left the house shortly after midnight. But that was now all to the good. Below the tower there was a public telephone box. If only he had had a few coins on him he could have telephoned Hunterscombe to drive out and meet him; but he had not, so, regretfully, had to continue on his way. His long stride ate up the miles and an hour and a half after leaving San Angel he was well into the city.

There he had to make enquiries several times for directions to the street in which Hunterscombe lived. Although it was by then close on two o'clock there were still plenty of people about, for it is rightly said that Mexico City never sleeps. Each time he asked his way he feared to be identified; but he asked only of down-and-outs, thinking that they would be least likely to have read the newspapers, and, to his great relief, none of them showed any special interest in him. After another half an hour of striding along pot-holed pavements, he reached his destination: a block of apartments to the south of Chapultepec Park.

Thankfully, he saw that there was no porter about, ignored the lift and ran up the stone stairs, pausing on each landing until he found Hunterscombe's number, then pressed the front-door bell, praying that he would be at home. Twice more he rang, and was beginning to fear that he had accomplished his seven-mile tramp for nothing, when the door was opened by the Wing Commander—his thin hair rumpled, slightly bleary-eyed and clad in a flamboyant silk dressing gown.

'So it's you,' he muttered with a frown. 'Did the night porter bring you up?'

Adam shook his head. 'No, he wasn't in the hall.'

'Thank God for that! You're a hot potato if ever there was one. But come on in.'

A few minutes later Adam was sitting in a comfortable armchair, a welcome brandy and soda in his hand, giving an account of all that had happened to him. When he had finished his recital, Hunterscombe said:

'Well, chum, you're in the soup and no mistake. I believe you, but the police won't; and everyone is hopping mad about your prison break. I wouldn't be in your shoes for a packet.'

'You're telling me!' Adam retorted bitterly. 'That swine Alberuque has got me by the short hairs and don't I know it. I've not a shadow of doubt that he was speaking the truth when he said that his people will do exactly what he tells them, whatever the cost to themselves. The Negro and those others will swear to it that I strangled the warder and I can't possibly prove that I didn't. But you volunteered to help me if I got in a mess; so the only thing I could do was a moonlight flit and come to you.'

The Wing Commander remained thoughtful for a moment, then he brushed up his large moustache and said, 'If you were a member of the firm we'd have that beard of yours off, dye your hair black, give you a crew-cut and get you out of the country on a faked passport. But you're not; and it's more than my job is worth to issue a faked passport to anyone who is not on the strength. Still, there's no ban on my fixing you up with a disguise if you are game to make a bid to get out of Mexico under your own steam.'

'Thanks for the offer, but I'm not a taker.' Adam took a pull at his brandy and soda. 'When I first heard about this business I was reluctant to get mixed up in it and later I resented being blackmailed by the police into agreeing to give them my help. But now things are different. The massacre at the prison opened my eyes to the sort of thing that will happen all over the country if Alberuque is allowed to let loose his Indians and half-breeds. I left his place tonight only to come to see you. I mean to go back there and do my damnedest to chuck a spanner in his works.'

'Good for you, chum!' Hunterscombe's eyes suddenly brightened and he sat up. 'That is quite another cup of tea and your Uncle Jeremy is right behind you. What line do you intend to take?'

'All I can do is try to find out when and where the big meeting at which I'm billed to appear is to take place; then let you know. If I can do that, it will both enable the police to scotch it and prove to them that I am innocent.'

'That's the drill, if only you can pull it off. How about communications?'

'I got away tonight without much trouble. Providing I don't arouse their suspicions, I see no reason why I shouldn't get out of the house again as soon as I have anything to report. I'm averse to seven-mile walks though; so if you'll give me some money, next time I could telephone from somewhere near the place.'

'That's not good medicine, old boy. You may get caught on your way in tonight, or for some other reason they may decide to lock you up and put a guard on you. D'you happen to know Morse?'

'Yes. I was a W/T operator for a time when I was doing my service in the Royal Navy.'

'Hence the beaver, eh?' Hunterscombe grinned. 'You decided to keep it, just as I have my R.A.F. moustache. Anyhow, your being able to use a transmitter is going to save us a lot of headaches.'

Standing up, he walked over to a chest and took from one of the drawers a long, flat silver cigarette case. Opening it he showed that one side held a row of some fourteen cigarettes; the other side was covered by a metal flap. 'This,' he said, 'is a gadget for just such occasions. Under the flap there is a radio that has a pretty useful range. I'll give you my call sign and will listen in every day for half an hour from 0800 hours, 1700 hours and 2300 hours, then all you'll have to do is to tap me out the gen.'

'Fine.' Adam took the case and examined it carefully. Then he said, 'I'd be grateful if you could lend me a gun.'

'Do you think that's wise? If somebody tumbled to it that you were carrying one, they'd wonder where you got it.'

'I'll take good care no-one sees it and I may need a weapon badly. You see, I've a nasty feeling that if things do blow up Alberuque would not hesitate to do me in. But if I've a gun on me, with a little luck I'd be able to shoot him first.'

'O.K., chum.' The Wing Commander went to the chest again. From another drawer he took a small automatic and an armpit holster. Having loaded the weapon, he fitted the holster on to Adam and said, 'We'll have one for the road, then I'll get into some togs and run you back; but we'll have to keep our eyes skinned for the night porter as we go downstairs. That head of hair of yours is about as conspicuous as a parson wearing a pair of tights with his dog-collar.'

When they had finished their drinks, Hunterscombe left the room to dress. He returned with a wad of notes and some small change. As he gave them to Adam he said, 'With the compliments of H.M.G. against emergencies. I suppose that as well as being a matelot you don't happen to be a flying type?'

Adam shook his head. 'No; and I'm really only a land-lubber.'

'Pity. I was thinking about that helicopter. I wouldn't be surprised if old Alberuque doesn't intend to have you flown to the place where he means to hold his jamboree. If you were a pilot you might have beaten him to it, and left him in the lurch. Still, maybe you could sabotage it so that it couldn't take off.'

'That's certainly an idea. I'll bear it in mind.'

With Hunterscombe leading the way they tiptoed down-stairs. The porter was still absent; so they got clear of the building without being seen, and while Adam waited in the shadows his companion collected his car from the garage. It was a long, low Alfa Romeo of ancient vintage but alarming power and they covered the seven miles in a little over ten minutes. Shortly after four o'clock Adam's 'Uncle' Jeremy dropped him in San Angel, wished him 'happy landings' and roared away into the night.

When Adam reached the house it was still in darkness and he thought it unlikely that even its religious inmates would get up to make their early-morning devotions in the chapel for another hour or more. All the same, he approached with the utmost caution. Clambering down had been a risky business and he was not at all looking forward to his climb back on to the roof; but, having gumshoed round the building, he found a first-floor verandah at the back which he had not seen be-fore, and above it there was an open window.

Judging the window to be on the staircase, he clambered up to it and, holding his breath, peered in. It was so dark inside that at first he could not make out whether he was staring on to a landing or into a bedroom; so for several long,

K

anxious moments he hung there, listening intently for snores or heavy breathing. No sound reached him and by then, his eyes having become accustomed to the darkness, he felt fairly certain that, if he was looking into a room, it had no furniture in it.

The window was not open wide enough for him to get in, so he pushed it up a few inches. As he did so the old frame gave a loud creak that, in the silence of the night, sounded as if it would rouse the dead. Again he froze and hung there, expecting every moment to hear the running footsteps of someone coming to investigate. But the stillness remained unbroken. Reassured, after a long wait he wriggled over the sill and tiptoed forward. Then, by the dim light, he saw that he had been right. He had come in on the landing. Ten minutes later he was in bed and fast asleep.

On the following afternoon, feeling considerably easier in his mind than he had been during his first day as Alberuque's guest, Adam was sitting in the library reading an early edition of Bernal Díaz's famous *True History of the Conquest of New Spain* when the dumb lay brother came in and handed him a small sheet of paper on which was written: 'The Señorita Enriquez will arrive at the garden gate to visit you at four o'clock.'

Adam's first reaction was delight, but it was swiftly followed by uneasiness. It was over ten days since he had seen Chela and they had parted on far from happy terms. The night after his rescue from the police by Father Suaréz, he had declared to her that nothing would induce him to lend himself further to Don Alberuque's plans and that had resulted in their having a furious row. The following morning she had come to him submissively and begged him to talk things over, but they had never done so, because she had gone off to Mérida to buy a hacksaw with which to cut off his handcuffs and before she returned he had again been arrested.

The question was, what front should he present to her now? That she had agreed to come to see him at all implied that she still cared for him and he knew that he was still in love with her. But Alberuque would have informed her of the present situation—that, under duress, he had again consented to play.

To tell her that he did not mean to, let alone that if he got half a chance he intended to bust the whole movement wide open, was out of the question; yet the idea of pretending that he was now reconciled to appear again as Quetzalcoatl, and so win her confidence by deception, was most repugnant to him.

After some thought, he decided that he must compromise with his conscience. She could hardly expect him to approve the massacre at the prison or to be happy at having been coerced by Alberuque into doing as the Monsignor wished. But he could pretend resignation to *force majeure*, and it was clearly his duty to get what he could out of her.

Well before four o'clock he was out, pacing up and down the broad open space of the garden that lay in front of the big barn, keeping an anxious eye on the gate. True to Mexican form, it was not until nearly half past that one of the Indians who had been posted on the gate let Chela in.

Halting abruptly in his pacing, Adam turned and strode towards her. She was dressed in a coat and skirt of scarlet Thai silk and had an absurd hat perched on her black hair. She looked more lovely than ever. Displaying her even, white teeth in a ravishing smile, she ignored the guard and cried:

'Oh, darling! How lovely to see you.'

At the very sight of her, Adam's heart had begun to beat faster. His eyes drank in her superb figure and the grace with which she moved. All the emotions she had previously aroused in him again came to the surface. Seizing both her outstretched hands in his, he said:

'I can hardly believe that I'm not dreaming. There have been times when I feared I'd never see you again.'

'I know.' She shook her head. 'I've been worried out of my wits about you. I can't tell you how delighted I was when Don Alberuque telephoned me to say that you were free and are at one with us again. Naturally, you were upset about things going wrong at Uxmal, but I felt certain that when you had had a chance to think matters over you wouldn't let me down.'

So, Adam thought, Alberuque has not put her fully in the picture. She believes that I have come round and am now willing to play their game out for them. Aloud, he said, 'Don Alberuque has been most kind, particularly in agreeing that you should be allowed to come to see me in this monastic haunt.'

She made a wry face. 'It's a world apart from our villa at Acapulco, isn't it? And I'm forbidden the house. Still, surely there must be some place where we could . . . well, talk in private?'

He glanced over his shoulder. 'There's the barn. In it there is a helicopter; but unless the mechanic is working on the engine, no-one is likely to be there.'

'Let's explore it, then.' She took his hand and they walked over to the barn. As he had expected, it was deserted. Without his aid she ran up the ladder to the open loft where the bales of hay were stacked. He followed, wrenched the bands from one of the bales and spread out the hay to make a couch for them. Picking her up in his arms, he gave her a long kiss on the mouth, then lowered her to the hay. She pulled him down beside her, twined her fingers in his hair, and whispered:

'Darling, I've wanted you so terribly.'

'And I you. It seems an age since we last made love.'

He had one arm round her and was leaning over looking down into her dark, limpid eyes. She closed one of them in a wicked wink. 'I prefer a bed, but there could be worse places than this.'

'Some people refer to it as a "roll in the hay",' he laughed. 'Come on, let's.'

Her slim fingers were already at her waist, undoing her skirt. Wriggling out of it, she spread it beneath her. Eagerly he bared her breasts and kissed one of them. For a few minutes they dallied, exciting each other to a fervour, then she threw back her head and pulled him more closely to her.

Suddenly she gave a little cry. 'No! Stop! You're hurting me.'

Raising himself, he looked down at her in surprise. 'But . . . but it never has before.'

'No, darling. Not there. It's something hard under your left arm. It was digging into my breast.'

In his excitement he had forgotten the small automatic

strapped under his left armpit. Quickly he unbuttoned the strap of the holster and pulled it out.

As she saw the weapon her eyes widened and she said, 'So you are carrying a gun. Where did you get it?'

'I . . .' He hesitated a moment, then inspiration came to him and he lied. 'During that ghastly battle at the prison. There was a dead detective lying in the corridor with his coat open. When I spotted it I thought it might be useful in getting away, so I took it from him.'

She nodded. 'I see. Yes. What a terrible business that was. Just as at Uxmal, everything went wrong. Don Alberuque told me. His men were only supposed to hold up the Governor of the prison at pistol-point and force him to release you. But someone lost his head. I was horrified, because it is such a blot on our movement.'

Adam did not doubt for one moment that she was telling what she believed to be the truth. To learn that Alberuque had not made her a party to the deliberate massacre and the murder of the warder as a means of blackmailing him, was a great relief. Kissing her again, he said:

'My sweet, the whole affair was utterly horrible. But there is nothing we can do about it now.'

Adam had laid aside his gun. The discovery of it had temporarily poured cold water on their passion, but they were still eager for each other. Thrusting from their minds the thought of that night of blood, they renewed their caresses and five minutes later were locked in the divine embrace.

When it was over they lay silent for a while, Chela's dark head on Adam's broad chest. Yet he was far from experiencing the utter contentment which had submerged him in a swoon of happiness on the other occasions after he had possessed her. One tormenting thought nagged at him persistently. Slave as he was to the allure of her cameo-like features, her voice, her laughter and her glorious, dark-golden body, he could no longer believe that, for all her apparent purity, she was not the servant of evil. Even if it meant an end to everything between them, he felt that he must challenge her and force her to admit it, as the first step to saving her from the satanic influence under which she had fallen.

At length, raising himself on one elbow, he looked down into her lovely, sun-tanned face and said, 'Chela, my love. You know who Alberuque really is, don't you?'

Her big eyes widened and she murmured, 'Who he really is? Whatever do you mean?'

'Why, that he is Itzechuatl in a new incarnation.'

'Itzechuatl! I don't understand. I've never heard of him.' She yawned and looked away, turning her head sideways.

At her denial, Adam's temper frayed. Taking her by the shoulders, he shook her. 'Don't lie to me! You can't have forgotten that day when, as Mirolitlit, you enabled me to escape from him. He was the evil High Priest who was set on tearing out my heart.'

His rough handling of her had roused her from her somnolent indifference. Now, staring up at him with mouth agape, she gasped, 'Yes, I remember now. That was the High Priest's name. But, darling, I'm sure you must be mistaken. Anyhow, I wouldn't have recognised him as I did you. I saw the High Priest only that one time on the terrace of the Palace, and then his face was smothered in paint.'

'It's not his physical appearance but his personality that comes through. Surely you must have sensed it?'

'No. I swear I haven't. And I know Don Alberuque so well. You must be wrong. I'm certain you are.'

'I'm certain I'm not,' Adam retorted stubbornly. 'And he is still living in the past. That is the key to this movement in which you have involved yourself. There is nothing Christian about it. His status as a Monsignor is a cloak which enables him to influence others and foster his evil designs. His real intention is to re-establish the old religion and rule Mexico again as High Priest.'

Pushing Adam from her, Chela sat up. 'You are wrong, darling! Absolutely wrong! He is a saint and has only the betterment of our poor down-trodden Indians at heart.'

Sadly Adam realised that it was useless to argue further with her. But the faith she displayed in Alberuque's innocence held such conviction that he could not doubt her honesty; so at least he was able to console himself with the thought that she had not consciously become the tool of evil.

With a sigh he said, 'Beloved, since neither of us believes the other, we had better drop the subject. But time will show. And of one thing I am positive. Alberuque is still my enemy. He has not forgotten that, in our previous lives, I cheated him of a Man-God as a sacrificial victim, and if he can he means to get me now. But forewarned is forearmed. I mean to watch him like a lynx. If he or his people lift a finger against me, I'll kill him without the slightest scruple.'

'Adam!' Chela gave a gasp of horror. 'What are you saying? How could you even think of such a thing?' Her glance fell on the pistol lying in the hay beside him. 'You . . . you can't really mean that you'd shoot him?'

He shrugged. 'God knows I'm not a violent type. I'd hate having to kill anybody. I would, though, if it were to save my own life.'

'But think! Just think! In all innocence he might say or do something that you took to be a threat, then . . . then, suspicious and trigger-happy as you are, you might shoot him before realising your mistake. And he is a priest. Even if you are right about his being a reincarnation of Itzechuatl, in this life he is the Lord's Anointed. To kill him would be the most terrible crime. Whatever happens, I implore you to put any such idea out of your mind.'

Taking her hand, he patted it and gave her a pale smile. 'Don't worry, my sweet. I promise you I won't act rashly, and we'll pray that it never comes to a showdown between him and me.'

For a long time she was silent, then she said, 'Feeling about him as you do, I am surprised that you have again agreed to co-operate with him.'

Instantly Adam was on his guard. He loathed having to deceive her, but had no option. After a moment he said, 'That is different. As you know, at first I was reluctant to play; but you persuaded me that, if the revolution succeeded, as the Man-God I could control our people, and prevent excesses like that which took place at the prison. I still feel that it is my duty to take a chance on being able to do that.'

'But what about your enmity to Don Alberuque?'

'You may prove right, after all; that in this life he is a

reformed character. If so, I'll co-operate. If not, I'll hope to overcome him. But this waiting about is getting on my nerves. All I want now is to get on with the job. Do you know when the big day is to be?'

She shook her head. 'No; but it won't be long now. Within two or three days at most.' As Chela spoke, she looked at her wrist watch, then exclaimed, 'How the time has flown! It's nearly six. I must be going.'

He took her in his arms again. After prolonged kissing they stood up. She put on her skirt and he brushed the pieces of hay from it. As they left the barn, she promised to come again the following afternoon. Then he accompanied her to the garden gate and, once more enthralled by the grace of her tall figure, watched her walk through the gate to her car.

When she had gone he returned to the barn, took the radio cigarette case from his pocket and, judging it by then to be 1800 hours, tapped out Hunterscombe's call sign every few minutes. For a while there was no response, then he got through and sent a brief message that the party was scheduled to take place not more than three days hence. The Wing Commander sent back, 'Good for you. Keep in touch and don't act without me.'

That evening Adam spent a long time thinking over his conversation with Chela about Alberuque, and wondering if she could possibly be right in her belief that he was now an honest fanatic whose only ambition was to better the lot of the Indians and half-breeds; but he could not accept it. His every instinct cried aloud that the intriguing priest had long since sold his soul to Satan and was an active embodiment of malefic forces.

The following afternoon found him eagerly awaiting Chela's promised visit. As soon as she arrived, they went to the barn. Not long after they had settled themselves, they enjoyed another 'roll in the hay' then, still embraced, talked for over an hour. But both of them avoided bringing up the name of Don Alberuque and they had no serious conversation about the 'movement'.

Shortly before leaving him, Chela said that she would not be able to come the next day because she had to attend a committee meeting at the Ministry of Education. When she had gone, he pondered on that; for it struck him as strange that, with the great crisis in their lives now imminent— after which it was possible they might never meet again— she should not have made some excuse to get out of her committee meeting so that she could spend another hour or two with him. Uneasily, he wondered if the committee was a myth and that in fact she had some special preparations to make before the ceremony which was to trigger off the revolution.

If his guess was right, it meant that the balloon was due to go up the following night. Soon after six o'clock he radioed Hunterscombe and told him of his suspicions. The Wing Commander tapped back, 'Will be listening in from 1500 hours till 2400 hours tomorrow.'

The next morning passed uneventfully. In the afternoon Adam went to the barn and had a look at the helicopter, with the idea of seeing if he could sabotage it. But he knew nothing about engines so, short of actually smashing it with a hammer, there was no way in which he could put it out of action. Smashing it would certainly be attributed to him, and would thereby warn Alberuque of his secret intention to rebel at the last moment. So he decided to leave it and, instead, went up the ladder and lay down in the hay where he and Chela had taken their joy of each other.

He thought of her with longing, then dropped off into a doze. Some while later he was roused by voices below, near the helicopter. Peering cautiously over, he saw that two mechanics were working on the machine. Now much relieved that he had not monkeyed with it, he listened intently to their conversation.

One of them had a grouse and, between technical exchanges with his companion about the engine, was grumbling that he would not be able to keep a date with a girl who he had good hopes would let him have his way with her that night. Presently the man said:

'If only the old bastard would have stayed put till midnight, I could have made it; but take-off at ten o'clock means I'll have to stand little Inez up, and the odds are she'll be so furious that she'll not give me another chance.'

So this was 'it', and take-off was timed for ten o'clock. Impatiently Adam waited until the two mechanics had finished work on the helicopter and left the bar. Then he got through to Hunterscombe.

'Good show,' the Wing Commander tapped back. 'Any idea where the 'copter will be heading for?'

Adam replied, 'No, and unlikely I can find out.'

The response was: 'Can't be far. Keep your pecker up. I'll be seeing you.'

As soon as he had eaten his meagre supper that evening, Adam went up to bed. As tonight was the night, he knew that he might need every ounce of strength that he could muster; so even an hour or two lying dozing would be all to the good.

For a long time, or so it seemed to him, he lay there in the dark, thinking of Chela: wondering whether somehow they would both come through this awful business and, if they did, he could persuade her to forgo a Mexican millionaire as a husband and marry him.

Then, as he had felt almost certain would be the case, the dumb lay brother came in carrying a lamp and made signs to him that he should dress and come downstairs.

He took his time about dressing and had so arranged his clothes that, by keeping his back to the skull-headed mute, he could strap on his shoulder holster without it being seen. He had no fear that Alberuque would attempt to kill him until after he had played his part in the ceremony as Quetzalcoatl, unless he refused to do so at the last minute. But he felt certain that there would be a showdown later, and the feel of the pistol under his armpit was a great comfort. Priest or no priest, Adam meant to get in first and send him to hell where he belonged.

Downstairs in the library he found Alberuque waiting for him, sitting, as before, smugly behind the big desk. But what Adam had not expected was to find two Indian hoodlums in the room posted on either side of the door.

As he came into the room Alberuque greeted him politely:

'Señor Gordon, or should I anticipate by a few hours and address you as Most Exalted One, Essence on Earth of the

Supreme Powers, Lord Quetzalcoatl. Tonight is the night of your Elevation. Shortly we shall proceed to the place of the ceremony, where you will be hailed as the representative of the true gods and the restorer of the ancient religion. But first there are two small matters which must be attended to. I have here a paper that I wish you to read.'

As he spoke, the Monsignor pulled open a drawer of the desk and put his hand into it. But when he withdrew his hand, instead of a paper, it held an automatic.

Pointing it at Adam's heart, he smiled and said smoothly, 'I have been informed that you are carrying a pistol in an armpit holster. Be good enough to raise your hands above your head while my men relieve you of it.'

Slowly Adam raised his big hands. He was too stunned, too shattered, even to speak. A single thought seared through his mind with the pain of a hot iron. Only Chela knew that he was carrying a gun; she had betrayed him.

17

While Time Runs Out

THE two hoodlums closed in on Adam, unstrapped the pistol holster and took his weapon from him. They then patted him all over for any hard objects. The only things he had on him were the money Hunterscombe had given him and the radio-cigarette case. As he would not have been allowed to retain money in prison, lest anyone should hear the coins clanking in his trouser pocket, he had put them with the notes in his shoe, under the sole of his left foot. One of the Indians opened the case then, seeing that it contained nothing but cigarettes, snapped it shut and gave it back.

In other circumstances Adam would have thanked God for that. As things were, he was still too overcome by Chela's treachery to care much what happened now. Listlessly, he waited for Alberuque to ask him how he had got hold of the weapon. Since he did not, Adam concluded that Chela must have passed on the explanation he had given her—that he had taken it from a dead detective during his escape from prison.

The search having been concluded, Alberuque ordered the two hoodlums to leave the room, laid his pistol down on the desk and took a sheet of paper from the drawer. His fish-like, black eyes focused on Adam's, he said :

'Your speech to the faithful tonight, Gordon, will be very brief; so you will easily be able to memorise it. Here it is.' From the paper he read :

'My people : true sons of Mexico and rightful owners of its wealth. I, Quetzalcoatl, am come again to release you from your bondage, and restore the worship of the ancient gods who once made you great. From on high I shall watch over you, leaving all power here in the hands of my faithful High Priest, Itzechuatl, whom I charge you to obey.'

Adam gave a bitter laugh. 'So you mean to come out in your true colours, and all this talk of regaining power for the Catholic Church was camouflage.'

Alberuque spread out his long hands. 'One must be practical, my dear Gordon. During the centuries that this country was known as New Spain the influence of the Church was paramount here and she had a fine record as the protector of the people. But since Mexico gained Independence, not only did the Church lose her power, but she suffered from a hidden schism. The lower clergy, who are mainly of Indian or mixed blood, have continued to serve their communities to the best of their ability; the higher clergy bent their necks and became the servile puppets of their atheist masters. A revolt under the banner of the Church could lead only to Mexico's becoming subject to Rome and the Bishops. They are incapable of standing up to the pressure that the oppressors of the people would exert upon them. Within a few years at most, we would be back where we are now. Therefore, the only hope of restoring Mexico permanently to the Mexicans is to do as many other countries have done in recent times. Ceylon, for example; where, having thrown out the foreign blood-suckers, they made Sinhalese the official language and Buddhism the State religion. Here Nahuatl will become the official language and the restored worship of the Ancient Gods the State religion.'

'And you,' added Adam, 'become Dictator.'

'Who could be better fitted for that onerous position?' Alberuque's uneven teeth showed in a smile. 'As you well know I have ruled here before. Incidentally, I was surprised that you did not recognise me at our first meeting. But you did after I had had you rescued from prison, didn't you?'

'Yes, for the black-hearted spawn of Satan that you are.'

'Hard words break no bones, my friend.'

'No, but bullets do,' Adam rapped back. 'And fire-power will prove the decisive factor in this Civil War you mean to start. Your untrained, ill-armed mobs won't stand an earthly chance against the government forces. With tanks, artillery, strafing aircraft, flame-throwers and nerve gas, they'll break up your formations in no time. Those wretched Indians you are misleading will disperse like mist before the sun and make off for their homes with their tails between their legs.'

'You underestimate our Indians, Señor Gordon. There are no more courageous people in the world. During the past hundred and fifty years they have proved it a score of times. When they believe in a cause they become fanatics and prefer death to surrender. Led by Morelos, Santa Anna, Benito Juárez, Pancho Villa, Zapata and in the Cristero rebellion, they died fighting for their beliefs by the tens of thousands.'

'Then this time it will be by the hundred thousand.'

'Even such losses are relatively unimportant. In the French Revolution a million people died and France then had a population of only twenty million. In Mexico today the population is nearly double that. Besides, our plans are well laid: the Militia will fight on our side and a great part of the Army will come over to us. At Uxmal, during the ceremony of "Recognition", I showed you to our leaders from all over Mexico. Tonight, at the ceremony of "Elevation", only those from Mexico City Federal District will be present. At the conclusion of the ceremony they will return to their posts. Then by radio and telephone the codeword will be sent out to all the others who now wait impatiently for it. With simultaneous risings in every city, town and village in the country, the government cannot possibly hope to hold more than a score or so of places where there are large garrisons. Isolated, and with their supplies cut off, they will be compelled to surrender. It will all be over within three weeks.'

The confidence and resolution that Alberuque displayed convinced Adam that the movement was far more formidable than he had previously supposed. But he had one last shot in his locker, and used it.

'All right then. Let's say you do get control of the country. According to your programme, it is to be Mexico for the Mexicans, with all foreigners thrown out. Do you realise what a "foreigner" is in a coloured man's country? He is *any* white man. And *you* are white. Before you are a year older, the odds are they'll run a *coup d'état* of their own and hang you from a lamp-post.'

For a second, Alberuque's eyes dropped. Holding out the sheet of paper, he snapped, 'We waste time. Come now, learn your brief speech so that you may make it with clarity and dignity.'

'What if I refuse? You can't make me.'

'In that you are mistaken. You will do as you are told or live to rue the consequences.'

'Then I will wait until you tell me what those consequences will be,' retorted Adam stubbornly.

Alberuque shrugged and put the paper in his pocket. 'As you will. We shall have ample time for you to learn it at the place to which we are going. And now I have a pleasant surprise for you. By tradition only males are allowed to be present at our great ceremonies, but tonight I am making one exception. The Señorita Chela has rendered such outstanding services to our cause that I am rewarding her by taking her with us.'

As he spoke, he pressed a bell on his desk. A minute later Chela entered the room.

Had Adam passed her in the street he would not have known her. Her own hair was concealed under a beret and from its rim there hung a fringe of greasy, brown, false hair, quite short across her forehead, about four inches long behind and with two matted tufts of about the same length at the sides, which hid her pretty ears. She had on dark glasses and was wearing a rubber raincoat without a belt, so her figure was also hidden. The costume was completed by a pair of scruffy old calf-high boots and she had smeared her lips with something that gave them a faintly purplish look. As she was tall for a woman, even without her high heels, she was well up to the average height of a native; so, with her bronzed complexion and the false brown hair, she would have been taken anywhere for a Mestizo youth.

Adam gave her a withering look and said, 'I hear you are being paid off with a ticket for the party instead of thirty pieces of silver.'

Her pale mouth twitched as though he had slapped her. In a low voice she replied, 'I'm sorry. But . . . but I did it for your own sake. Knowing you had that gun I couldn't possibly risk your using it.'

'Thanks for your concern for my immortal soul, but I'm quite capable of taking care of it myself.' His glance swept her from head to toe. 'Congratulations on the outfit. The Educational Committee you attended this afternoon evidently takes a special interest in amateur theatricals.'

'Don't be so bitter, Adam,' she said sharply. 'How could I tell you that I meant to spend the afternoon perfecting my disguise without giving it away that the ceremony was to be tonight? You have only yourself to blame for being so suspicious and antagonistic towards Monsignor Alberuque.'

'So you thought I might do a bolt, and risk being caught by the police, although that would have meant a life sentence?'

'You can be so stubborn at times, I thought it possible.'

'And that we could not possibly afford to risk,' Alberuque put in. 'My threats, of course, were only a bluff to keep you here. If you had taken to your heels it would have done us no good to have laid an information about you. But we should have temporarily lost you; and, my dear Gordon, you are irreplaceable. No one else could take the role of Quetzalcoatl convincingly.'

'Yes, I see that now,' Adam muttered angrily. 'But even without any false evidence from your people about the murder of the warder, the police would have believed that I connived in the prison break and put me inside for a good long stretch.'

'Exactly.' Chela took him up quickly. 'And everything else apart, I just couldn't let you risk that. Please believe me, Adam, I only acted in what I believed to be your own best interests. I swear I did.'

Angry as he was at having been tricked and deprived of his pistol, Adam was fair-minded enough to appreciate her point of view. Admittedly she had saved Alberuque, but in the present case that did not conflict with the anxiety she must have felt that he should neither commit the sacrilege of shooting the—to her—sacred priest, nor take the bit between his teeth and land himself with a long prison sentence. A little grudgingly he said:

'Oh well, it's evident that you think I should be grateful

to you for saving me from myself. Perhaps I should be. Anyhow, what's done is done, and we'll get nowhere by arguing further about it.'

'That's better,' Alberuque purred, 'much better. Between young people who love one another there always occur misunderstandings. But they should not be allowed to fester.' Standing up, he picked up his pistol and added, 'Come! We still have many preparations to make; so we should be on our way.'

As he spoke, he stepped past the others to open the door. For a second it crossed Adam's mind to seize him while his back was turned and get his pistol from him. Next moment it was too late. Although unconscious of Adam's intention, Chela had stepped between them. Out in the hall the two hoodlums were still on guard. With Alberuque leading and the hoodlums bringing up the rear, they left the house.

The helicopter had been brought out of the hangar and now stood on the rough grass of the open space in the middle of the garden. It was a four-seater. The pilot was already at the controls and, as Adam was told to get into the seat next to him, he noticed that he was not one of the mechanics he had seen in the barn, but a lean man with a scarred face. The two mechanics were only standing by in case they were needed. Chela sat immediately behind Adam and Alberuque behind the pilot. The engine was started up, there came a whirr of blades and, gently, the machine rose from the ground.

Adam's brain was racing. Very soon now must come the showdown. For him to participate actively in the ceremony was obviously essential to its complete success, and he had no intention of doing so. But when he refused to learn his speech—what then? He thought it as good as certain that, furious at being thwarted, Alberuque would no longer hesitate to kill him. In fact, he would probably seize on that to justify the deed in the eyes of his followers. Alone and unarmed, Adam knew that he would stand no chance at all. His only hope of being rescued lay in bringing Hunterscombe and the police upon the scene. But to do that he would need at least five minutes entirely on his own, so that he could use his radio.

As the helicopter lifted, they could see the myriad lights of Mexico City to the north. For a time Adam thought of what must be going on down there. In the crisp evening air following the hot day, millions of people would be looking forward to the pleasures that the night always brought. The chefs at the Hilton, the Rivoli, the El Presidente and a score of other de-luxe restaurants would be preparing rich dishes for the wealthy; the Sandborn coffee-shops would be packed with typists, shop girls and their boy-friends laughing over good if less expensive fare; in hundreds of bistros the barmen would be pouring *tequila*, gin and beer for groups debating every topic under the sun; queues would be filing into the cinemas and countless families starting out for their evening stroll under the palms in the Alameda and other parks.

Unless he could prevent it in some way, overnight this scene of gaiety and quiet pleasure would be replaced by brooding terror. The streets, except for dead bodies here and there and armed men hunting down their enemies, would be empty. No-one's life would be safe. There would be pillage, rape and arson. Ghastly scenes of massacre and innocent people caught in suspicious circumstances being summarily shot. That had happened many times before in Mexico City and would happen again. Even if Alberuque proved right in his assertion that the revolution would be over swiftly—which Adam did not believe—it still meant that many people would lose their lives and a multitude of others suffer grief, loss and misery before order could be restored.

Yet what could he do to save the situation? Only dig in his toes and refuse to make the speech upon which Alberuque was counting so much to inflame his followers with uncontrolled fanaticism; and pray that a chance would come for him to get in touch with Hunterscombe in time for him to save the city from a holocaust.

The helicopter veered east of the city, passing over only the outer suburbs and the marshes of Madero, which were the last remnants of the great lake that had once surrounded it. The moon had just risen and lit the unearthly landscape: the flattish valley sloping away to the east and on either side of it the great ranges of volcanic peaks, their slopes as barren as the mountains of the moon themselves.

When they had travelled some twenty-five miles the helicopter began to descend and Adam then had no difficulty in guessing their destination. Ahead of them, throwing strong shadows in the moonlight, lay the mighty Pyramids of the Sun and the Moon at Teotihuacán. As Adam leaned forward to see them better, he let his right hand hang down between his seat and that of the pilot. Another hand, which he knew must be Chela's, clasped it from behind and pressed it.

He was still furious with her for having robbed him of his chance, in the last event, to shoot Alberuque; but he had not the heart to push her hand away. They had known such wonderful times together, and that she loved him he could not doubt. It was only her obsession with the thought of securing a better life for the millions of wretchedly poor Indians that lay between them and caused her to give unquestioning devotion to Alberuque. Returning the pressure of her fingers, he held them as the helicopter slowly sank on to the reception area of the ruins, enclosed by the museum, the restaurant and the rows of shops selling souvenirs.

As the machine grounded, a group of men ran forward; some of them secured it while others, evidently Alberuque's principal lieutenants, greeted him obsequiously. Several of them were wearing the uniform of officers of the Militia and all of them had white armbands upon which were black crosses surmounted by the snake symbol of Quetzalcoatl.

Alberuque at once started firing questions at them, and their replies showed Adam that the revolution had been far better organised than he had supposed would be the case. Soon after the guides and day staff had gone home for the night, the whole complex of buildings had been taken over without incident. Such personnel as remained were under lock and key. The telephone exchange was now manned by professional operators and any calls would be dealt with so as not to arouse suspicion. The windows of the buildings had all been screened so that no unusual amount of light for that time of night would show, and patrols were out on the main road ready to direct the arriving delegates to the car parks.

Having satisfied himself that all his orders had been carried out, Alberuque led the way over to the restaurant. As they entered it, he said over his shoulder, 'We have a long night before us, so we shall sup here before we change into garments suited to the occasion.'

'Fine,' Adam remarked, having decided to give the impression that he was now more or less reconciled to playing his part. 'But first I must ask you to excuse me. I suppose it's nerves, but I've got a pain in my tummy.'

One of the Militia officers was detailed to take him to the lavatory. Immediately he had bolted the door behind him, he took out his radio-cigarette case. To his fury and distress, for several minutes atmospherics interfered with reception. Impatiently the officer knocked on the door and called to him to hurry up. Sweating now with apprehension that he was going to have to abandon this last chance of getting through to Hunterscombe, he ignored the summons and kept on sending. Then, to his immense relief, the Wing Commander acknowledged his call. Swiftly he sent:

'Have been flown out to Teotihuacán. Party being held here probably midnight. Unless measures taken immediately revolt likely to be nation-wide and very difficult to suppress. Am in fear of life. Hurry.'

Hunterscombe sent back: 'Good show. Stall for as long as you can. Will be with you soonest possible.'

On being taken to the restaurant, Adam found that a buffet supper was being eaten, composed mainly of tinned foods which had evidently been a part of its stock. His mind had been so occupied with his anxieties when Alberuque had said they were to sup that he had not felt like eating anything; but his large frame required considerable sustenance and, for the past few days, the meals given him at the monastery had been so meagre that the mere sight of food gave him a sudden appetite. Helping himself lavishly to ham and half of one of the miserable little Mexican chickens, he set to.

While he ate, he took stock of the types round him. There were about fifty men in the room, but Alberuque was not present. Only a handful of them had light enough complexions to be called whites, and these he assumed to be the more able priests who were hand in glove with Alberuque. The rest varied from light coffee to near-black and a number of them were, he thought, probably priests also. Nearly all of them were on the short side and he was a head taller than any of them; so he had no difficulty in locating Chela, who was in a far corner talking to one of the Militia officers. From a clock on the wall of the restaurant, he judged it to have been a quarter to eleven when he had radioed Hunterscombe, and it would take the best part of an hour for police and troops to get out there; so, while eating, he had been cudgelling his wits for a way to delay the proceedings. Seeing Chela again gave him an idea. Putting down his plate, he moved towards her.

From the time they had landed it had struck him as strange that Alberuque should not have surrounded him with more mystery—brought him there perhaps in a cloak and hood and kept him in a room apart—instead of allowing him to mingle freely with these other men, like an ordinary mortal. He could only suppose it to be because these people were the inner ring of the conspirators, so aware that he was only a stooge who, after he had played his part, was to be dispensed with, and Alberuque become their sole master. Nevertheless, the many covert glances cast at him held a suggestion of awe and, as he moved from the buffet, everyone in his path made way for him deferentially. So did the officer who had been talking to Chela. He gave her the sort of nod he might have given to any Mestizo youth, bowed to Adam and walked away.

'Who do these people take you for?' Adam asked in a low voice.

'The Monsignor's secretary,' she replied.

He gave her a speculative look. 'What will happen if I address the company and tell them you are a woman?'

'I . . . I don't know.' Her eyes widened with apprehension as she spoke. 'It's certain there would be trouble. All the people here are educated men, but that does not prevent many of them from being superstitious. A lot of them would think that a woman being present could bring bad luck, so would strongly resent it.'

'I thought as much, and Alberuque would find himself

with a packet of trouble on his hands for having brought you here.'

She gave a little gasp. 'No! Adam, please! I beg you not to. That would not prevent the ceremony from taking place. But think of me. The only way he could put himself right would be to sacrifice me to them—say that I had only recently joined his staff and had imposed on him—that he did not know I was a woman—then think what would happen. They would take me for a spy and might kill me.'

Adam saw that he was stymied and gave an angry shrug. 'All right. You win again. No doubt you are mighty pleased with yourself about this night's work.'

'No,' she said tearfully, 'I'm not. I would have been if only you had carried out the promise you gave me in the first place, and played your part willingly. I hate your being compelled to it; but the future happiness of millions of poor people hangs on their believing that the revolution is divinely inspired. Thank goodness it will soon all be over now. We'll go back to Acapulco again then; or . . . or if you want me to, I'll marry you and we'll make a home together.'

At that moment Adam felt a light touch on his arm. Turning, he saw that it was Father Lopéz, whom he had not seen before that evening. The priest bowed and said:

'Be pleased to come with me. The Monsignor wishes to have a word with you.'

Adam looked again at Chela, and sadly shook his head. 'I'm afraid things won't pan out like that. You still don't seem to realise that if this revolt once gets going it will lead to terrible times for everyone.' He was about to add, 'And I'll be lucky if I'm not dead by morning.' Instead, he said, 'We can only wait now and see what happens.' Then he turned away and followed Father Lopéz from the room.

Alberuque had installed himself in the restaurant manager's office. An empty plate and a half-empty bottle of wine on the desk showed that he had supped there alone; beside them lay his automatic. When Lopéz had shown Adam into the room he withdrew, closing the door behind him.

Taking from his pocket the piece of paper on which was typed the speech, Alberuque held it out to Adam and said,

'Now, Gordon, there must be no more shilly-shallying. Please learn these few sentences off by heart, then repeat them to me.'

'I have already refused,' Adam replied quietly.

'Very well. If you continue to do so, I must make the consequences clear to you. You will be aware that the old gods were always propitiated by human sacrifices. It was a barbarous custom which I do not intend to reintroduce and I can make our more primitive people accept that by telling them that it would lead to intervention by the United States and a resumption of their oppression by a new influx of white foreigners. But tonight a demonstration must be made.'

Adam paled under his tan as he thought, 'I know what is coming now. He means to bribe me into making the speech with the promise of my life; afterwards, though, the treacherous devil will kill me just the same.' Alberuque went smoothly on:

'For this purpose a Chac-Mool is now being laboriously carried up to the top of the Pyramid of the Sun and, to be sacrificed upon it, I have had a dummy made. It is a very clever dummy, with a tape-recorder inside it that, when started, will scream. It also contains a bladder full of blood and a sheep's heart that I can hold aloft. Of course, only my immediate followers are aware of this; but it is necessary to give the rank and file the sort of spectacle they expect. However, there is nothing to prevent my ignoring the dummy and using a human being instead.'

Passing his tongue over his dry lips, Adam said, 'And you propose to use me. That's it, isn't it?'

'Oh no, my dear Gordon, you are quite wrong there,' Alberuque purred. 'Had it not occurred to you that, however great a woman's services had been to our cause, I am not the sort of sentimental fool who would ignore tradition by allowing her to accompany me here, unless I had a special use for her?'

'You fiend!' Adam roared, and raised his big hands to grab the Monsignor by the throat. But he was standing on the far side of the desk and Alberuque was too quick for him. Snatching up his pistol, he snarled:

'No heroics now; unless you want your stomach full of lead. A very painful death, I'm told.'

Breathing heavily, Adam let his muscles relax and his hands fall to his sides as Alberuque went on, 'Your guess is right, my friend. Should you continue to refuse to learn your speech, I shall have to make it for you. In that case it is the beautiful body of the Señorita Chela, which I am sure you have frequently enjoyed, that will repose in the lap of Chac-Mool when I wield the sacrificial knife.'

18

In Desperate Straits

ADAM stared into the dead, black, pitiless eyes on the far side of the desk. His knowledge of Alberuque, as the High Priest Itzechuatl in the past, told him that this was not bluff. The tale about the dummy might be true, but Adam doubted that. It was probably no more than a concession to the canons of the present day thought up by the modern Alberuque to gloss over lightly the fact that he was still at heart Itzechuatl, the blood-lusting savage who was determined to take again this opportunity to enjoy tearing out the heart of a living human being. Dummy or no dummy, for the past four days Adam had not been able to rid himself of the awful conviction that, somehow or other, at the end of the ceremony, Alberuque would so contrive matters that he, Quetzalcoatl, should supply the heart to be offered to the gods.

After a silence that could be felt had lasted for some thirty seconds, Alberuque went on, 'Please do not suppose that my companions would seek to prevent me from sacrificing the Señorita Chela on the lap of Chac-Mool. As a woman her presence at such a ceremony is a gross sacrilege. High Priests, as you may know, have the power to "smell out", as it is termed, evil-doers and the guilty. I have only suddenly to declare myself to be perturbed, fix upon the Señorita as the cause of my fears that some influence is obstructing the objective of the ceremony, then accuse her of being a spy who has recently entered my service under false pretences. Others will seize her, strip her of her clothes and reveal her sex. I will not have to say another word. Everyone will be howling for her death, and I shall simply accept their verdict.'

This was so exactly what Chela had feared when Adam had threatened to expose her imposture that he could not doubt that was the course matters would take. To allow her to be slaughtered in front of his eyes was unthinkable. Glancing at a small clock on a bureau, he saw that it was now ten past eleven. Hunterscombe and the police might get there by a quarter to twelve. But not before. All he could do was to pray that God would speed them on their way, and continue to play for time. Taking the piece of paper, he said:

'All right, I'll learn it.'

Five minutes ticked by, then Alberuque said, 'You have had long enough. Recite it to me.'

Adam laid down the paper and did so, but deliberately muffed the words.

'Enough of this mulishness,' Alberuque snarled, his dark face now set in anger. 'You are an educated man, Gordon. An author, used to words and phrases. These are easy ones to memorise and I have no more time to waste. Either you will now recite them properly or we will proceed to the pyramid. The sight of the Señorita Chela about to be thrown into the lap of Chac-Mool may loosen your stubborn tongue.'

Seeing that he had no option, Adam spoke his piece. Still holding his pistol, Alberuque went to the door, opened it and said to Father Lopéz, who was waiting outside, 'He has come to heel. Call an escort, then take him over to the museum.'

Two minutes later, Adam was marched between two guards, with Father Lopéz following, across a corner of the open space. The museum was divided into a number of bays by walls, upon which there were photographs of excavated ruins and big glass showcases containing pottery, weapons and other items from the long-dead civilisations of Mexico. In several of the bays, attendants were robing Alberuque's principal lieutenants.

Occupied as Adam's mind was with the danger in which he stood, the significance of the fact that several of the leading conspirators were changing into the barbaric vestments of a pagan priesthood did not escape him. Even the parody of Christianity combined with worship of the old gods, with which so many of the Indian and Mestizo priests had satisfied their parishioners for four centuries, was evidently now to be abandoned. Tonight there would be no mockery of the Mass to precede the ceremony of his 'Elevation', and he had counted on that to gain him a good twenty minutes. It brought home to him more sharply than ever how time was running out, and he began to fear that Hunterscombe might not now come on the scene before the dreaded pagan ceremony was well under way.

In a bay reserved for him, Adam found four men waiting. Laid out nearby was the gorgeous costume of featherwork and embroidery that he had worn at Uxmal. During his wild career down the Pyramid of the Magician and subsequent arrest by the police he had lost his great feathered head-dress, his shield and the wand crowned with his jewelled symbol of power. But he saw that replacements, probably stolen from one of the museums, had been procured for him.

To delay matters a little, he again demanded to be taken to the lavatory. Father Lopéz showed annoyance, but could hardly refuse his request; so he was led away to one just inside the entrance to the museum. Getting out the cigarette case, he repeatedly gave Hunterscombe's call sign. As he had hoped, there was no reply. That cheered him a little, as it showed that the Wing Commander was not still in his apartment telephoning various authorities; the police could now definitely be assumed to be on their way.

Knowing that Alberuque would be extremely loath to proceed with the ceremony without him, Adam sat down and lit a cigarette. After a few minutes Lopéz rattled the door and called on him to come out. He ignored the shouts and went on smoking. But he was not allowed to do so for long. The door was kicked in and Alberuque stood outside. He was now dressed in the flamboyant robes of a High Priest, his face was painted with stripes and circles and he presented the same terrifying appearance as he had when in his incarnation as Itzechuatl. Glaring at Adam, he snarled :

'We leave in five minutes. If you are not ready to accompany us, stay here and I will send you a pair of human ears that you may recognise.'

At this threat, Adam quailed and surrendered. Hurrying

now, he returned with Lopéz to the bay where his vestments were laid out. As he passed the other bays, he saw that they were all empty. The men who had been changing in them had disappeared.

Suddenly seized with panic at the thought that Alberuque might carry out his threat to leave without him, and Chela pay the penalty, he refused to take off his suit and insisted that the men who were attending him should arrange the princely robes over it. Neither would he allow them to remove his shoes so that they could put on his feet the gilt leather sandals. In less than three minutes he was again feeling the weight of the solid gold breastplate, leg gyves and arm bucklers as he strode towards the entrance to the museum.

Alberuque was waiting there. Beside him stood another, slenderer, figure, also berobed in splendour and with fans of gorgeous Quetzal plumes appearing to sprout from every limb. Only the blue eyes in the lavishly painted face enabled Adam to recognise Chela.

As they walked out on to the open space, Adam thought of trying to warn her that the evil priest to whom she had given such devotion would kill her without the slightest scruple. But he decided that there was no point in doing so at the moment since, as long as he obeyed Alberuque's orders, she would be in no danger.

Adam had expected to have to walk the quarter-mile to the base of the pyramid, then make the long, tiring climb to the summit; or, as had been the case in the vision he had had of himself some weeks earlier, be carried up it in a sedan-chair. He had counted on that to take not less than a quarter of an hour, and there would at least have been a chance that Hunterscombe, with the forces of law and order, would have arrived by then. But Alberuque had thought of a much more impressive way for the Man-God to make his appearance. Instead of turning right, in the direction of the pyramid, he walked straight ahead towards the helicopter.

As Adam realised that they were to fly up, his heart gave a sickening lurch. He had assumed that the ceremony would not start until midnight. Now it was evident that by midnight it might be over. In four minutes or less they would be on the top of the pyramid and the last chance of Hunterscombe's arriving in time be gone.

This was the second time that Adam's hopes of a delay had been unexpectedly disappointed. Now he could no longer hope to be rescued. When help did come, he would be marooned on the summit of the pyramid, at the mercy of men who would certainly murder him in their fury at seeing their followers down below being dispersed by police and troops.

Chela was leading the way, Adam walked just behind her, and Alberuque, his automatic again in his hand, brought up the rear. Realising that death stared him in the face, Adam was sorely tempted to break away and run for it. But the double threat of Alberuque's pistol, and what would happen to Chela if he did, kept him walking towards the helicopter. When they reached it, Adam saw that the pilot was now robed as a priest and his scarred face painted. They took their places as before: Adam beside him and Chela and Alberuque in the two rear seats. There was a whirr of blades and the 'copter lifted.

As it rose in the air, the bright moonlight revealed the scene below. In three open spaces scores of cars and small vans were parked. The men who had arrived in them were assembled on the pyramid and round its base. Its three terraces were packed with people and those who had arrived too late to get a place on them were grouped on the mounds and uneven ground where, weeks before, Adam had had his fall and knocked himself out. It was possible to arrive only at an approximate estimate of their numbers, but he guessed that the assembly could not be fewer than one thousand.

The helicopter went up high, made a wide circle so that the car parks and crowds temporarily passed from view, then it returned, hovered and landed with a slight jolt that made it lurch sideways on the great square of tumbled stone blocks which had once formed the temple, and now rose in a tangled mass a few feet above the level of the flat summit of the pyramid.

When they alighted, Adam saw that only six of Alberuque's lieutenants, including the pilot, had been granted the honour of donning priestly robes to assist him in the ceremony. With

him that made seven, and it passed through Adam's mind that
seven was the magic number common to all ancient reli-
gions. Five of them had climbed the pyramid in advance and
were standing on the broad, flat terrace that had once had the
temple as its background. They now formed a line there and as
Alberuque, followed by Adam and Chela, picked his way
across the big, uneven stones towards them, they genuflected.

Alberuque halted for a moment to adjust his robe. The
pilot quickly passed him and joined the group. It then divided,
three on each side, and Adam saw that, while standing in a
row, the bodies of the five had concealed the stone image of
Chac-Mool. It reposed there, silent but infinitely menacing,
the head turned sideways, the knees and shoulders raised,
waiting as of old to receive a sacrificial victim in its lap.

But there was no cleverly constructed dummy to be seen.
The absence of one confirmed Adam's grim supposition that
it had been only a figment of Alberuque's imagination, invented to disguise temporarily his intention to sacrifice a
human victim.

Walking past the sinister stone image, Adam advanced to
the edge of the broad terrace and for some moments gazed
down at the silent, expectant crowd gathered below. He recalled his dream, in which he had stood there before to be
received and acclaimed as a Man-God. In the moonlight the
clothes of the people down there could not be distinguished,
so they might just as well have been wearing the cloaks with
gaudy patterns that their ancestors had worn a thousand years
earlier. The blur of upturned faces was the same.

He decided that he must be dreaming again. It was absurd,
fantastic, unbelievable, that there could really be a plot in this
day and age to destroy modern Mexico, with its booming in-
dustries, skyscrapers, achievements in science and art, magnificent motorways and broad-minded government which was
slowly, but surely, turning it into a Welfare State; to turn the
clock back hundreds of years, leaving the country at the mercy
of hordes of primitive Indians led by a handful of fanatics.
The whole conception of such a revolution was hopeless:
utterly impractical. It could be no more than an idea con-
jured up in a nightmare. He must soon wake up in his bed at

the El Presidente, or perhaps in London.

Like receiving a bucket of cold water in the face, he was brought back to earth by one of the priests handing him a microphone, a spotlight that completely blinded him being switched on from somewhere, and Alberuque's voice coming from within a few feet of his ear with the harshly whispered ultimatum, 'Now say your piece, and clearly; otherwise I'll smell out your woman, have her stripped naked and give her to Chac-Mool.'

Although it was cold up there, beads of perspiration started out on Adam's forehead. He had played for time, had done his utmost to enable Hunterscombe to arrive before the assembly below dispersed, carrying his message, and the codeword was sent out that would inflame the whole country. How could he possibly send them away inspired to commit themselves to a ruthless civil war in which thousands of their kind and thousands of other entirely innocent people must be killed.

But if he refused, what of Chela? Strong as he was he could not hope to overcome the seven priests, and Alberuque was armed. The thought of her being murdered before his eyes was positively horrifying. He must continue to play for time. Even while he was speaking Hunterscombe might arrive.

Fearing that half-measures would probably drive Alberuque into such a fury that to revenge himself he would carry out his threat and sacrifice Chela, Adam resisted the temptation to mumble and declaimed his speech in a loud voice. It was received by the crowds below with an awed murmur of appreciation.

The wave of sound had hardly subsided when Alberuque took the hand microphone from him and shouted into it:

'Sons of Mexico! Rightful owners of its soil and silver. You have heard the Man-God delegate temporal authority over you to me. There is one way only in which we can hope to triumph. It is by swift and ruthless action. The masters must be destroyed root and branch before they have time to organise against us. When you go forth from here, kill! kill! kill! Death to the descendants of the *gachupines*.'

As he paused, there came a thunderous burst of applause. The cheering lasted a good minute and it was only as it began to fade that Adam caught Chela's voice coming through it from behind him. She was shouting:

'No! What are you saying? No! No! No!'

Drowning her cries, Alberuque resumed his speech. 'I call upon you now to witness the ancient ceremony of Elevation. The Man-God has made his will known. As in the past he again ascends to rejoin his Divine Brothers. The shedding of his blood will rejuvenate our nation.'

It had come—the dread decree that Adam had been fearing ever since he had recognised Alberuque to be Itzechuatl. Yet still he could hardly believe it possible that in this modern age such a thing could really happen. Even now, at the eleventh hour, he thought again that he must be suffering from a ghastly dream and, as is the way with nightmares, would wake at the critical moment to find himself in bed, sweating but safe.

Fear for Chela had kept him obedient up to the moment of Alberuque's final sentence. The actual announcement that he was to be the victim of the ritual murder put her out of danger. Suddenly he woke to the reality of his own peril. Alberuque was standing on his right and within a yard of him. Had his hands been free, he could easily have seized him and thrown him down the pyramid. But they were not. In his right hand he held the long staff of authority tipped with his cypher in jewels; in his left the big shield from which dangled his plumed head-dress.

Letting fall his impedimenta, he thrust out his right hand to grab Alberuque. But the evil priest had anticipated that he would make a fight for his life, and had taken precautionary measures. Unseen by Adam five of the other priests had closed in behind him. The second he moved, they flung themselves upon him, grabbing him round the neck and waist and by both arms.

His only assets in a fight against such odds were his towering height and the powerful muscles in his big limbs; but although small men, the priests were muscular and, except for one, they were in the prime of life.

Exerting all his strength, he wrestled with them, striving to throw them off. As he did so, he caught a glimpse of Chela.

The seventh priest was holding her back from coming to his assistance. Through the almost deafening shouts of excitement that rose from the crowd, he could hear her screaming at Alberuque:

'You cannot do this! You cannot! Oh, what have I done that this should happen? Holy Virgin, have pity. Save him! Save him!'

Adam got an arm free and brought his clenched fist down on the head of one of the priests. The man fell like a pole-axed ox. But another of them seized his arm again. With both arms held, his body was vulnerable. One of the priests, lowering his head, ran in and butted him in the stomach. The blow winded him. The breath driven from his body, he doubled up. His limbs went slack. Seizing their advantage, the priests dragged him towards the Chac-Mool.

Again he caught a glimpse of Chela. The priest was holding her with her arms behind her back. She was struggling violently with him and still screaming, 'Oh Lord, have mercy! Holy Mary intercede for me! Save him! Save him and I'll become your handmaiden. I have sinned; I know it! But I repent! I repent!'

It was then that Adam subconsciously became aware that new sounds were vibrating in the air. From overhead there came the roar of aircraft while the shouting of the crowd no longer held a note of fanatical elation; it had changed to pandemonium. Out of the night sky above the massed people, row after row of flares descended, dropped from fighter aircraft. Help had come, but too late; for aircraft could not rescue him.

Yet the thought that succour was so near lent him new strength, and he had got back his wind. Desperately he turned and twisted like Laocoon among the serpents. Snarling with fury, the four priests strove to force him down on to the Chac-Mool. For a moment he let himself go limp, gave a terrific heave and broke free. But, as he jumped clear, the older priest tripped him. He went down heavily, hitting his head on the raised knees of the hideous idol. The blow did not knock him out, but he was momentarily blinded. Stars and whirling circles flashed before his eyes. Involuntarily his muscles slack-

L

ened, and he was rendered temporarily helpless.

Panting from their exertions, the priests got him down. One of them tore off his gold breastplate, another ripped away his shirt; the two others were using their full weight to pin down his arms. As his vision cleared, he saw Alberuque standing over him. The High Priest's painted face was demoniac. Grasped firmly in his hand he held the obsidian sacrificial knife. He raised it to strike.

Adam knew then that his hour had come. As the government forces had arrived before the completion of the ceremony, the codeword that was to rouse the mobs all over the country would not yet have been sent out from the museum telephone exchange. He had saved Mexico from a terrible Civil War. But he must pay for it with his life. Fate had decreed that Itzechuatl should, after all, wreak his hate and vengeance on the victim who had escaped him a thousand years before.

At that very moment there came a piercing yell. A second later, two shots rang out. With a wail of agony, Alberuque dropped the knife and clutched his side. For a moment he swayed, then heeled over and fell. Another shot followed. The priest who had torn off Adam's breastplate gave a sudden grunt and went over backwards. The other three hastily let go of Adam and took cover as well as they could behind the Chac-Mool.

Gasping for breath, Adam heaved himself to his feet and looked towards the place where Chela had been standing. The spotlight was still on. In its glare he saw that the priest who had held her was dabbing at his face, from which blood was dripping. She now lay sprawled at his feet.

Instantly Adam grasped what must have happened. She had somehow managed to get her head round and fix her teeth in the man's chin. Then, as he released her, she had drawn the little automatic she often carried strapped to her thigh and shot Alberuque. The infuriated priest who had been holding her must then have knocked her down.

Adam took a stride in her direction. Having no longer anything to fear from Chela, the priests behind him sprang to their feet and came at him again. The man with the bitten chin ran to their assistance. Once more Adam found himself fighting for his life against four of them.

Like a pack of wolves attacking a big reindeer, they fastened on to his limbs and strove to pull him down. Staggering from side to side, the group reached the very edge of the terrace. One more step in that direction and all five of them, with arms and legs whirling, would have pitched down the steep steps.

Adam was facing that way. Over the heads of his shorter assailants he had a swift view of what was taking place below. The road to the pyramid was made as bright as day by the glare of the headlights on a long line of vehicles. The leading ones had already drawn up and police or troops were tumbling out of them. The mob had dispersed and was running in all directions. But there were scores of people still on the pyramid terraces, and some of those on the nearest were making for the top.

Again he was near despair. Even if he could succeed in fighting off the priests who clung to him, help would soon reach them. Assailed by greater numbers, he must succumb. He was fearful, too, that now they would all go over the edge. Splaying his feet, he made a violent effort to heave himself backward. It took the others by surprise. All but one of them lost their hold on him. Jerking up his elbow, he struck the man under the chin with it. His teeth snapped together, his head fell back and he dropped to the ground.

Chela had been left unguarded. For a few moments she had been knocked out. Now she had come round and again came into action. Raising her pistol, she shot in the back the priest whose chin she had bitten. With a hideous scream, he sank to the ground.

There remained two unwounded priests, and the one Adam had hit on the head, who had now staggered to his feet. All three of them had to be dealt with if he was to stand any chance at all of escaping with Chela down the rear side of the pyramid before the mass of shouting Indians coming up its front was upon them.

The nearest priest was the one who had piloted the helicopter. Rushing at him, Adam seized him round the body.

The other two ran at him. With sudden dismay he saw that they had drawn their knives. It was clear that, realising they could no longer hope to overcome him and get him down on the Chac-Mool, they meant, if they could, to kill him where he stood.

Desperately he looked round for a weapon. His glance fell on the long staff of authority. It would not be as effective as a spear, but the jewelled serpent-head at the top could inflict an ugly wound on a man's face. Snatching it up, he fended off the attack. Backing away, he jabbed with it first at one priest then at the other, while hoping that Chela would use the rest of the bullets in her pistol to shoot them before one of them could stab him. Ten seconds later he realised that hope to be vain. To escape their first rush he had leapt aside and turned; so now he had his back to her. She would not dare shoot at them for fear of hitting him.

The two priests had their backs to the edge of the terrace. Adam was sparring with them at a distance of only four feet, so he could see beyond them down the steep slope. Howling like dervishes, the thirty or forty Indians and Mestizos who were pounding up the steps from the lower terrace were now within twenty feet. A few flourished knives and sabres, but most of them were armed with pistols.

He dared not turn his head and so take his eyes off his two assailants, but with all the strength left in his lungs he shouted to Chela, 'Run! Run for your life!'

As he urged her to flee, he knew that within the next two minutes he must be overwhelmed and hacked to pieces by the ferocious mob that was surging up towards him.

19

A Truly Bitter Pill

TIME is entirely relative to circumstances. At school, the last lesson of an afternoon can seem endless and the hands of the clock barely crawl. Yet a long evening spent together by two lovers seems to be over when it has only just begun.

To Adam, fighting for his life, the next minute seemed an eternity. Automatically he parried the knife thrusts of the two priests and struck out at their faces with his staff. But through his mind flashed a multitude of jumbled thoughts. Hope that Chela would get away; grim satisfaction that, at last, Alberuque had paid for his evil intentions with his life; a sudden speculation about what Aunt Flora would do with all the money he had left her as his only relative; a gripping fear of the pain he must suffer from knife thrusts in his flesh and bones smashed by bullets before he finally expired; a longing to be through with this terrible end decreed to his life as Adam Gordon, and again free of his mortal body.

Suddenly, above the din that was coming up from below, there came from close at hand the staccato rattle of a Sten-gun. Fearing that he was about to be shot down from behind, Adam gave a swift glance over his shoulder. To his amazement, he saw Jeremy Hunterscombe standing only a dozen yards away from him on the edge of the terrace.

It then flashed upon him that Jeremy, having alerted the police, had driven out to Teotihuacán in his racing car and must have come up the rear side of the pyramid.

Hunterscombe had his weapon pointed slightly downward and was swivelling it from side to side. Screams and curses made the night hideous as the bullets ripped into the mob that was streaming up from the nearest terrace.

Although it seemed to Adam that he had been fighting for his life for half an hour, actually less than six minutes had elapsed since Alberuque had pronounced his death sentence. Now, the sight of Hunterscombe gave him, for the first time, real hope that he would survive. But that one glance over his shoulder nearly proved his undoing.

Both his attackers rushed in. He jabbed wildly at the face of one of them. The jewelled serpent caught the man in the left eye. Letting out a long-drawn howl, he slumped back on to the Chac-Mool, but the staff snapped off short. At the same moment, the other priest ran in, stabbing upwards with his knife at Adam's heart. With not the fraction of a second to spare, he swerved aside. The blade ripped through his robe and the man's evil, painted face came to within an inch of his. Seizing the man's wrist, Adam gave it a savage twist. The knife fell with a clatter on the stone flags. Still holding the priest by the wrist, Adam swung him round and away. Bringing up his right foot, he kicked him hard in the crotch and let him drop.

Trembling from the violence of his exertions and nearly exhausted by the terrible fight he had been through, Adam turned on his heel to see Chela and Hunterscombe standing side by side.

'Come on, chum!' the Wing Commander shouted. 'Into their old kite before these devils get us all.' Then he and Chela began to run towards the helicopter.

There came the crack of a pistol. Chela staggered, seemed to trip, then, with outflung arms, pitched forward on her face.

Adam had believed Alberuque to be dead. But he was not. When, clutching at his wounded side, he had fallen, he had hit his head on one of the big, uneven chunks of stone and knocked himself out. A minute earlier he had come round, managed to get out his pistol and seized the chance to use it. Adam was only a couple of yards away from and behind him. In one bound he reached him, lifted his foot and kicked him hard in the face. The toe of his shoe caught Alberuque on the side of the jaw. With a groan he rolled over and lay still.

Whimpering with pain, Chela had scrambled up, but stood

precariously balanced on her left foot. Alberuque's bullet had gone through the calf of her right leg. Hunterscombe was beside her. Putting one arm round her shoulders and the other under her knees, he lifted her and staggered with her to the helicopter.

Adam was about to follow. Checking his stride he turned back. Snatching up Alberuque's pistol, he seized him by the scruff of the neck. Berserk with fury, he shouted at the unconscious man, 'You bloody swine! So there's still life in you. But I'll see to it that you're not rescued by your murderous friends. You're coming with us.' Exerting all his remaining strength, he dragged the unconscious Monsignor across the uneven area of tangled stone.

When he reached the helicopter, Hunterscombe had already got Chela into the front seat beside that of the pilot's in which he was sitting; and evidently being familiar with such machines he had got the engine started. Adam heaved Alberuque up on the floor beside them, then scrambled into one of the back seats.

They were none too soon. Hunterscombe's volleys had taken by surprise the men who were swarming up the pyramid, accounted for a number of them and temporarily checked the rest. But, as he turned away, they had come on again. Many of them had pistols. As the helicopter took off, they let fly a hail of bullets at it. Lurching forward, the Wing Commander cried:

'Oh God! I'm hit!' The helicopter lurched dangerously, then gained height and flew on down the valley.

Adam leaned forward and asked anxiously, 'Badly?'

'Not . . . too good,' Hunterscombe grunted. 'Got me through the back. But this kite's easy to fly. No need to fuss.'

Only partially reassured, Adam tried to relax. He felt incredibly tired and was aching all over. Although his height had enabled him for most of the time to keep his face clear of blows, when he had been down one of the priests had given him a kick above the left ear that still made his head sing. Another had struck him in the mouth, so that his lips were bleeding. His legs and body were one mass of bruises from their kicks and his scalp was smarting where one of them had seized and tugged at his hair.

Looking back on the fight, he felt that he could count himself lucky that the thugs had not used their knives from the beginning and, in fact, that he was alive at all. He owed that to Chela, who was moaning in the seat in front of him. He could only hope that both her wound and Hunterscombe's were not serious, and that he would be able to get them to hospital quickly.

With that in mind, after a few minutes he became worried. From the height at which they were flying, the glow coming up from Mexico City was plainly visible; but they were heading away from it, in a north-easterly direction. Abruptly he said to Hunterscombe:

'What the devil are you up to? We're far enough now from the pyramid not to be shot at. For goodness' sake, turn her round and head back to the airport.'

The Wing Commander gave a far from gay laugh. 'D'you think I'm steering away from the city on purpose? Think again, chum. Those bastards shot away . . . away most of the controls.'

'Good God!' Adam exclaimed in horror. 'D'you mean you can't turn her?'

'S'right.'

'Then get her down, man! We're still over the valley. You can land her in any field.'

'Wish I could. But she's stuck on course. Not a hope till we've . . . till we run out of petrol.'

Grimly Adam took in this frightening news. Faced with a fresh danger, his tiredness suddenly dropped from him. He was tempted to ask Hunterscombe further questions, but refrained because obviously to talk at all was an effort for him, and upon his remaining strength their lives now depended. He alone was capable of landing the helicopter when the petrol did give out; and if he collapsed before then, a crash that might kill them all was a certainty.

The glow from Mexico City faded behind them. Chela continued now and then to give a low moan. She had not spoken since Hunterscombe had lifted her into the machine,

so Adam hoped that she was only semi-conscious and unaware of their perilous situation. Leaning forward, he found
her hand and held it. Alberuque was sprawled on the floor
between them, still apparently out from the kick on the side
of the jaw that Adam had given him.

They had been in the air for some twenty minutes when
Adam suddenly became aware that the angle of their course
was bringing them closer to the chain of mountains on the
north side of the valley, and that if they continued on it they
must either go over or crash into them. With rising apprehension he stared ahead at their rugged silhouette, made visible against the night sky by the moonlight. After another few
minutes he discerned a plume of smoke rising from an active
volcano. They were almost on a level with the crest and flying
straight towards it.

Hunterscombe had seen it, too. Suddenly he said, 'This is
curtains, unless we can fly over it.'

'How can we?' Adam asked desperately, 'if you can't
make her fly higher.'

'Simple,' came back the laconic reply. 'Push that bloody
sky-pilot out and she'll lift herself.'

At his suggestion Chela suddenly roused. 'No!' she exclaimed. 'No! You can't! You can't! Whatever he has done,
he is an anointed priest. I shot him to save Adam, but only to
wound him. To cause his death deliberately would be the
most terrible sacrilege.'

'Couldn't care less,' muttered the Wing Commander. 'Un-
load him, Gordon. It's . . . our only chance.'

They were rapidly approaching the crater. The decision
had to be taken swiftly or it would be too late. Adam looked
down at Alberuque. His eyes were open and held abject terror. Evidently he had been shamming unconsciousness for
some time and had heard what it was proposed to do with
him.

'Get going, damn you,' Hunterscombe's voice came with
renewed strength. 'Throw the bastard out or we'll all have
had it.'

At that moment the helicopter was within fifty feet of the
near lip of the volcano. Adam cried, 'O.K.,' and gripped

Alberuque by the throat just as he was about to scream for mercy.

Chela turned in her seat and pleaded desperately, 'Don't, Adam, don't! The Lord Jesus has saved us once and He will again. Any risk is better than that we should have this awful sin on our consciences.'

'Go on, man,' shouted the Wing Commander. 'Out with him or we'll not clear the crest and all be killed on it.'

To spare Chela's feelings, Adam told a swift lie. 'We'll be committing no sin. He is already dead.' Continuing to choke Alberuque into silence with one hand, he put the other under his knees and lifted him. But before he could heave him out, the crest seemed to rush up at them.

'Quick!' gasped Hunterscombe. 'For God's sake . . .'

There came a scraping noise as the undercarriage of the machine grazed the lip of the crater, but she just cleared it. Next moment Adam got Alberuque's wildly kicking legs out in the rushing air, gave a final push and let him drop, to roll down the inner slope of the crater into the red-hot, bubbling lava.

The helicopter lifted at once. Another few seconds and it entered the plume of smoke. The hot air lifted it still higher. The smoke blinded them, they were half choked by it and by the awful stench of sulphur. The machine rocked crazily, filling them with terror that it would fall apart under the stress and that they, too, would end up screaming their lives out in the boiling mud beneath them.

Suddenly they shot out of the smoke and passed well above the far lip of the crater. Gasping for breath and with their eyes streaming, they felt immense relief. But only for a matter of moments. The engine began to splutter; then it died. From Mexico City it had flown some sixty miles, and the petrol tank was now empty.

Rapidly, it sank. There was nothing that Hunterscombe could do to check it. In an agony of apprehension they stared down at the barren, rocky slope below them, then braced themselves for the crash. It came with a grinding of splintered metal. They were all flung forward, then jerked upright; for luck had saved them from the worst. Owing to the formation of the ground, the light machine bounced and came to rest thirty feet further down on an uneven shelf of rock.

For more than a minute they sat there, stunned; hardly able to believe that they were still alive and had escaped serious injury. The lights had gone out, but pale moonlight seeping in made the head and shoulders of each of them stand out to the others in silhouette.

Adam was the first to recover. As he rose to clamber down, he slipped in Alberuque's blood. The interior of the machine was smothered with it and with that from the wounds of Chela and Hunterscombe. The smell of it was strong in their nostrils, mingled with that of the sulphur given off from the volcano.

Adam lifted Chela out, then helped the Wing Commander down. Supported by a hand on the fuselage, she stood beside the machine on her good foot. He tottered a few steps, then sank to the ground. Bending over him, Adam asked anxiously, 'Just how bad is it, old chap?'

Hunterscombe gave a travesty of a laugh. 'Pretty nasty. That bullet may have had my number on it.'

'Don't say that. You're as tough as they make them. You'll be all right if only I can get you to a doctor.'

'That's what I meant . . . If you could, I expect he'd patch me up. But you can't . . . You've Chela to look after and . . . I'd never get down this mountain without help.'

'I'll manage.' Chela spoke bravely. 'That is, if you can find me something to use as a crutch.'

Adam climbed back into the machine. There was nothing suitable there but, rummaging in the pockets, he found a first-aid kit, a big torch and a flask of brandy. Hunterscombe's wound was obviously the worse, so he went to him first and took a bandage from the pack. But their rescuer shook his head :

'No good, chum . . . look at my back.'

The light of the torch showed below the right shoulder a large, dark patch where blood had soaked through his jacket. Staring at it, Adam realised that, even if he could get the coat off, to deal efficiently with such a wound would prove beyond him; so he turned to Chela.

Her wound was worse than he had expected. He could not tell if the bone was splintered, but the bullet had torn the ligaments in her calf. She had lost a lot of blood and was still bleeding. When he applied the iodine, she fainted. Propping her up with her back against a boulder, he bandaged the wound and fixed a tourniquet beneath her knee.

Going back to Hunterscombe, he said, 'We can't stay here. These sulphur fumes are poisonous. If we keep on breathing them, we'll be dead before morning.'

The Wing Commander spoke tersely. 'Don't argue. Get the girl down.'

'We can't possibly leave you here.'

To that the wounded man made no reply. Laboriously he fished out of his pocket a lighter and a pack of cigarettes, then lit one.

Chela had passed out only for a moment. She was now sitting with her head bowed on her knees. It was a terrible decision for Adam to have to make, but he knew that Hunterscombe was right. Love apart, his first duty was to the woman of the party; even if leaving the man up there meant that he would die from the poison in the air.

Kneeling beside Chela, he whispered, 'I've got to get you down the mountain, and Jeremy is not up to making it on his own. He insists that we should leave him.'

She sat up and, in view of her state, spoke with surprising firmness. 'We can't. He saved us. It would be an awful thing to do.' Then the fumes caught her in the throat and she was shaken by a bout of coughing.

'We must,' Adam insisted. 'These fumes are deadly.'

Putting a hand on his shoulder, she levered herself up and said, 'You can go if you like, but I'm not going without Jeremy.' Then she looked across at Hunterscombe and added, 'You heard what I said. For all our sakes, you must make the effort.'

He, too, was coughing now and had thrown aside his cigarette. With a touch of his old humour he muttered, 'Little idiot. But . . . anything to oblige a lady.' Then he struggled to his feet.

'One moment,' said Adam. Taking the second bandage

from the pack, he draped it round Chela's neck and tied it under her right foot, so that it should not drag on the ground and cause her injured leg to give her greater pain. From the first-aid pack he gave her half a tablet of morphia and a whole one to Hunterscombe. Knowing that he could not afford to carry any unnecessary weight, he took off and regretfully abandoned his gold armbands and leg gyves. As he did so, he thanked his stars that in those last hurried moments at the museum he had refused to let the attendants put on the soft, gilded sandals, and was still wearing his own stout shoes. But it was cold up there on the mountain-top, so he decided to keep the featherwork kilt and cloak that he had made them put on over his suit.

Two minutes later they had formed up. Adam had Hunterscombe on his right and Chela on his left, with an arm round the waist of each, while they both had an arm round his neck. Chela held the torch in her free hand, and they set off on their attempt to get down to safety.

The going was rough, but it might have been much worse, for the slope was steep only in places they were able to avoid by the light of the torch; but that meant their changing direction every dozen yards or so, and several times they had to make their way round patches of jagged rock that Chela and Hunterscome could not have got over. In silence, except for their heavy breathing and an occasional gasp, they gradually made their way downwards.

After a quarter of an hour they had to take a rest and sat for several minutes on a broad stone shelf, panting and wheezing. But the air was better there as the sulphur fumes were less pungent. While they recruited their strength, Adam's thoughts were gloomy. He reckoned that, so far, they could not have covered more than two hundred yards and there might well be a mile to go before they could hope to come upon some habitation. The priests had given him such a battering that his body ached all over and, even had he been in the pink of condition, he doubted whether he could have got his two companions down to the valley.

Soon after they set out again he was cheered a little by coming upon a broad, smooth slope formed by an old river of lava. In the next quarter of an hour, gasping and sweating, they covered nearly double the distance they had before. But by the end of that time their state was desperate. Hunterscombe's head was hanging forward on his chest and Chela's jerking backwards and forwards with every hop she took. Owing to the gradient, Adam had all the time to lean back; otherwise he could not have held back the others, and all three of them would have broken into a stumbling run, then tripped and fallen on their faces. The strain of taking such a dead weight was appalling, his knees were beginning to give under him. Strong as he was, he knew that he could not support them for much longer.

The flow of hard lava ended in a small plateau, on one side of which there rose a ten-foot-high cliff with a cave in it. As Adam looked about for a place for them to rest again, Chela dropped the torch and slumped forward. She was all-in and had fainted.

Fortunately, the bulb of the torch had not broken. Lowering her to the ground, he picked it up, then said with a sigh to Hunterscombe, 'It's no good. We'll never make it.'

'Crazy to try,' the Wing Commander wheezed. 'Get me to that cave. I . . . I'll stand a better chance lying still there than . . . And . . . and without me you can carry her.'

Adam had already realised that, the morphia he had given Chela having had time to take effect, it was not so much pain as loss of blood during their twenty-five minutes' flight from the pyramid that had caused her to collapse. He knew, too, that when she did come round, her good leg could not possibly stand up to hopping more than another few hundred yards; so his only chance of getting her down was to carry her.

To leave Hunterscombe seemed an awful thing to do; but at least they were now clear of the poisonous sulphur fumes and he was no doubt right in believing that if he lay still for the remainder of the night he would lose less blood than if he continued to stagger down the mountain. Clearly the sensible course was for Adam to try to get Chela down then, if he succeeded, he could return next morning with a doctor and stretcher party to collect Hunterscombe.

Without further argument he helped the Wing Commander

across the open ground to the cave and shone the torch round
it. The beam revealed a primitive fireplace in which there
were dead ashes, the rind of a paw-paw and the stubs of
several cigarettes; so evidently the place was used in bad
weather by some goatherd to take his midday meals and
siesta.

Sinking to the ground, Hunterscombe muttered, 'Worse
places . . . to spend a night in. Give me the morphia.'

Retaining the odd half-tablet for Chela, Adam handed him
the little phial. As he did so, he thought of giving him the
flask of brandy as well, but decided against it because he recalled being told by someone that the effect of taking brandy
on top of morphia could prove fatal. Instead, he took off
his feather kilt and cloak, then folded the kilt into a pillow
for Hunterscombe and covered him with the cloak.

There seemed nothing else he could do and he was anxious
to carry Chela away from the plateau while she was still unconscious, lest she should again refuse to leave their rescuer.
After a moment, he said :

'I hate to leave you like this, and nothing would induce me
to if it weren't for Chela. But, having lost so much blood,
she may die from the cold up here if I don't get her down. In
the morning, as soon as it's light enough to find this place
again, I'll be up here with a doctor and a rescue team.'

'No!' Hunterscombe held up his hand as Adam was about
to turn away. 'A stretcher party, but no doctor.'

'What the devil do you mean?'

'Have to go to the nearest town for a doctor. You'd be
recognised.'

'Well, what if I am?'

For a good minute Hunterscombe remained silent, recruit-
ing his strength, then he said in a hoarse voice, 'Until you're
certain I'm going to live you . . . you mustn't show your face
to anyone who might fetch a policeman.'

Adam stared down at him in amazement. 'Why on earth
shouldn't I?' he asked. 'Alberuque is dead. There will be no
rebellion now. On my information Mexico has been saved
from a bloody civil war. Far from my having anything to fear,
they should treat me . . .'

'You have,' the Wing Commander cut in harshly. 'I've let you down, chum. Took the credit to myself for giving the Mexicans the gen. Not . . . not for myself, really. But for the old firm . . . British Secret Service. Meant to see you right later. And . . . and will, of course, if they can get me to a hospital alive. But I'm in a pretty bad way so . . . so don't gamble on that. If I do kick the bucket . . . make for the coast. Get out of the country. Otherwise . . . otherwise you'll be for the high jump.'

20

'There's Many a Slip . . .'

SLOWLY the full implication of Hunterscombe's confession sank into Adam's tired brain. In the past hour of fear, distress and exhausting effort, he had had little time to think about what the future might hold for him; but while they had been in the helicopter it had crossed his mind that, if only they could land safely, he would once again be able to count himself 'Lucky' Gordon.

Not only had he twice escaped with his life—once when he had believed that no more than a moment lay between him and death under the sacrificial knife, and again when Hunterscombe had saved him from the mob of Indians swarming up the pyramid—but he had earned the gratitude of the Mexican government and people for saving them from a bloody revolution and, above all, Chela had offered to marry him.

Now, in a few rasping sentences, Hunterscombe had rendered all those glowing prospects horribly uncertain. Unless Hunterscombe did live, Adam foresaw the awful situation in which he would find himself. Ramón Enriquez and the Chief of Police had never been fully convinced that by his speech at Uxmal he had not deliberately incited the assembly to rebellion. They had given him the benefit of the doubt only because they thought they could make use of him. There had then been the horrible affair at the prison in which, on his account, a score or more of people had been murdered. Lastly, only a few hours ago, he had again appeared as Quetzalcoatl and had given his blessing to a great crowd which was about to take up arms against the government. After that, how could anyone possibly believe him to be innocent?

Already the police all over the country must have been alerted to keep a look-out for him. If he were captured, a life sentence was a certainty—or, most probably, worse. Grimly he recalled Alberuque's telling him that prisoners who had committed particularly heinous crimes were, unofficially, executed and it was then given out that they had been shot while trying to escape. Unless Hunterscombe did survive to clear him, he thought his chances of saving himself looked about as good as of his becoming Prime Minister of Britain.

To abuse the man who had let him down so badly was futile; so, with a heavy sigh, he said, 'What a bloody fool I was ever to let myself get involved in this and, from what you say, it seems I'm still in it up to the neck. But while there's life there's hope, and I'm sure there's plenty of life in you yet. For both our sakes I'll be praying that you don't take a turn for the worse before I can get up here tomorrow. Anyhow, if you hadn't pulled Chela and me out we'd both be dead; so I've at least that to thank you for.'

'Decent of you to . . . to take it like that,' Huntersombe murmured. 'Don't worry too much. I'll stick it out. Only warned you just in case . . . Good luck, chum.'

Turning away, Adam walked over to Chela. She was still unconscious. He felt her pulse and found it was very slow, which was far from reassuring. Grasping one of her wrists, he heaved her up in a fireman's lift so that her head and arms dangled over his left shoulder and her long legs over his right. In his free hand he held the torch and scanned the ground ahead for the path by which the goatherd reached the cave. After a few minutes he found it. Planting each foot firmly, he followed its downward course.

When he had covered only a hundred yards it forked, and he took the path that appeared to lead more nearly to the valley. Ten minutes later Chela came to and began to moan; so he put her down and tried to comfort her. When she asked where Hunterscombe was, he told her and said that now their friend was clear of the sulphur fumes he stood a much better chance of living through the night than if he had continued to aggravate his wound by lurching along with them. On that

assurance she made no further protest at their having abandoned him.

Adam gave her the other half-tablet of morphia then, after
resting for ten minutes, picked her up and resumed his trudge
down the winding path. For half an hour he staggered on,
resting from time to time, generally at places where the path
forked, as it did at quite frequent intervals, so that it seemed
as though the whole mountainside was a maze of goat tracks.
Three times he took long pulls from the flask of brandy, now
more than ever selfishly glad that he had not risked Hunterscombe's killing himself with it. Only those gulps of the sustaining spirit restored his energy enough for him to go on.

As they descended, he realised dully the change in the terrain. Soon after leaving the plateau with the cliff and cave,
they were passing tufts of coarse grass and, here and there,
bushes. Then they entered an area of man-made terraces
where low, stone walls supported narrow strips of cultivation. But the way down the mountain seemed endless. Slender
as Chela was, she was tall for a woman and her weight on
Adam's shoulders caused him to bend almost double. In spite
of the cold, he was sweating profusely and his legs ached
intolerably.

When he set her down for the eighth time, he knew that he
could carry her no further. To attempt it meant that, at the
next rough patch, he would stumble and fall. Then they would
roll down the steep path together and, perhaps, be unable
to save themselves at the next bend from going over the edge
of a ravine.

For a while he sat hunched beside her, savouring the bitter-
ness of defeat. Then he roused again, struck by a new thought.
If he left her there and went on alone, he might yet find a farm
at which he could get help. He told her of his idea, and she
replied in a hoarse whisper.

'Darling, I'll hate your leaving me, but no ordinary man
would have got me so far; so I'd probably have died up there.
Now we are in cultivated land a farm can't be far off, if only
you can find it. Try to, while I wait here for you, but . . . but
will you ever be able to find me again?'

He handed her the torch. 'I will if you can prevent yourself from passing out, or falling asleep. Flash this every four or five minutes, then I'll be able to locate you.' Even talking now was an effort; so he kissed her on the cheek, got to his feet and forced his aching legs to carry him down the track.

The moon was now low in the sky, but its light saved him from blundering on uselessly until he dropped from sheer exhaustion. All sense of time had left him; but he could not have covered much more than three-quarters of a mile when he happened to glance to his right and saw a cluster of low roofs, which he would have passed had not the moonlight revealed them to him.

Halting, he stared at them uncertainly for a moment, suddenly becoming conscious of a new danger. Soon after he had arrived in Mexico City he had been told that recently an aircraft bound for Acapulco had had to make a forced landing on the mountains. Primitive Indians from a nearby village had robbed the passengers and crew of all their possessions, then stripped and murdered them. Here, in this remote valley, the Indians might prove equally hostile and pitiless.

But there could be no going back now, with Chela up there alone on the mountainside. Whatever the risk, he must take any chance that offered to secure help to get her down. Bemused as his mind was with fatigue, he then remembered that he still had Alberuque's pistol in his pocket. Taking it out with shaking hands, he withdrew the magazine and found that only one bullet had been fired from it. Ruefully, he realised that in his present state he would be incapable of taking proper aim with any weapon. But, if the Indians did prove hostile, the sight of it might at least overawe them.

He took another pull from the flask of brandy, straightened himself up and, with dragging feet, walked towards the silent group of buildings. As he approached, a dog began to bark, then a cock crowed raucously. Ignoring them, he went up to the door of the largest of the squat dwellings and, with the butt of his automatic, hammered hard upon it.

As soon as he heard sounds of movement inside, he put the pistol back in his pocket, so that he would not be taken for a bandit. A light then showed through some cracks in the door, there came the noise of a wooden bar being pulled back on the far side and the door swung open. Just inside it an Indian was standing, sideways on, holding up a lantern on a level with his head. Twelve feet away stood two others, covering Adam: the one with an old Service rifle, the other with an antiquated shotgun.

At the sight of him, their mouths fell open and their eyes opened wide with amazement. Lowering their weapons, they hastily crossed themselves, fell on their knees and bowed their heads.

For a few seconds he was equally nonplussed; then the explanation came to him. The lantern, shining full upon him, revealed his height and golden hair and beard. Added to which, although he had left his featherwork robes with Hunterscombe, he had since become so dazed with fatigue and anxiety that he had not thought of taking off the ear-rings that had been clipped to the lobes of his ears, the bracelets on his wrists or the splendid serpent insignia that hung by a thin chain on his chest; and all of them were flashing with jewels. They took him for Quetzalcoatl.

Rallying his strength, he spoke to them in Spanish, telling them that they had nothing to fear and that he needed their help. All three shook their heads, obviously not understanding. He then tried with the few words of Nahuatl that he could muster, but that, too, proved useless. Anxious to show his pacific intent, he put a hand under the arm of the man who held the lantern and raised him to his feet, then walked forward and did the same to the others. All three of them were trembling, but his smile reassured them. The eldest muttered some words in his dialect, bowed himself double, then left the room.

While he was absent, Adam took in the fact that he had been lucky to come upon a farm of some substance, instead of a native hovel in which a family and their livestock were all crowded together. The living room was quite large. It contained a cooking range, a dresser displaying two rows of cheap plates, a home-made table, several stools and even an elbow chair. But evidently the men slept there, as there were three tumbled, straw-stuffed palliasses spread out on the floor.

Thankfully, he took the weight off his legs and sank down in the only chair.

When the elderly man returned, he brought with him two women. One was an old crone with a face like a wrinkled apple, the other a plump, passably good-looking girl of about twenty-five. The old woman was swathed in black garments; the young one had on a gay, coloured dressing gown and her black hair was done up in curlers. Both crossed themselves, and the mother, as Adam assumed her to be, regarded him with fear-distended eyes, whereas those of the girl showed intense curiosity. Hopefully, Adam addressed her in Spanish.

She replied at once. 'You do our humble house a great honour, Lord. My father, mother and brothers do not speak the tongue of the *Gachupines* but my father wishes me to say that we are your servants and everything here is yours.'

Having thanked her, Adam went on, 'You will realise, señorita, that as a Man-God, when I take human form I have all the weaknesses and needs of any ordinary man. Tonight I have travelled far and am very spent. I started out with a companion—a lady. She is injured and still some way up the mountain. My most urgent need is help to bring her here.'

Rapidly the girl translated. The father issued orders and the two younger man quickly left the house. The girl told Adam that they had gone to knock up a stretcher, then explained that the name of the family was Zupango and hers Juanita.

Displaying respect, but no fear of him, she continued to chatter away. The nearest village, about three miles distant down in the valley, was Xalcatlan and the nearest large town, nine miles off, was Apizaco. Her father and brothers culti-vated the terraces on the slope of the volcano and, as these faced south, good crops of maize were grown on the lower ones and of grapes on those higher up. They also had a few cattle, pigs and poultry, and enough fruit trees scattered about the place to supply their own needs. Her first job had been as a waitress in Apizaco; she had then spent four years in Mexico City as a chambermaid in a good hotel. She was at home only because she had returned to marry her fiancé. The district was famous for its wood-carving. He was a skilful craftsman and, now that so many American tourists bought such work, he made good money at his trade.

Her father and mother meanwhile produced *tequila*, some slices of cold meat, onions, the inevitable *tortillas* and a bowl of fresh fruit, and nervously offered them to Adam. He was no longer feeling the cold but, loath to hurt their feelings by refusing, he drank the fiery spirit and ate a banana. As he finished, the brothers returned, carrying two stout poles to which they had attached several empty sacks. Their father picked up the lantern and, bowing to Adam, signed to him to lead the way.

Now that Chela's rescue seemed to be so close at hand, his heart was gripped with a new fear. Would they succeed in finding her? In the past half-hour he had been incredibly lucky. Instead of having to force himself to walk for another hour or, perhaps, collapse from exhaustion, he had come upon a habitation within a comparatively short time of leaving her; instead of it being a peasant's shack, it had been a well-equipped farmstead; instead of being received with hostility, he had been treated as a god; instead of a single native, three strong men had been available to carry her down to safety; and instead of his being unable to communicate with them, Juanita had chanced to be at home, so was able to translate his need and its urgency.

But would his luck hold? In the past half-hour Chela might have fainted again or, as a result of the morphia he had given her, fallen asleep. If so, there would be no flash of the torch to guide them to her, then in the darkness it would be next to impossible to find her. Again, there were so many tracks on the mountainside, and in the pale light of the setting moon there was no way of telling one from another. If he took a wrong one, it might lead them round a shoulder of the mountain; then Chela might flash the torch for the next hour, but they would not see it.

His fatigue temporarily forgotten in his acute anxiety, he set off at a good pace. Yet very soon he realised that had it not been for his brief rest he would not have had the strength left to make the climb at all. As it was, he had not been in the house for much longer than ten minutes; so before they had

gone far he had to shorten his stride. Coming down he had
counted it fortunate that the long rivers of lava from past
eruptions had, to some extent, smoothed out the sides of the
volcano and made the slopes by no means precipitous; but
now, going up, it seemed to him that they were almost as
steep as the roof of a house.

With labouring breath he rhythmically pushed one foot
in front of the other, but a new wave of weariness caused him
to start stumbling again every time his eyes left the track to
search the heights above for the flash of the torch. At last one
of the brothers saw it. Adam's heart missed a beat, then he
sent up a prayer of thankfulness. He had not led them in the
wrong direction and Chela had not dozed off. Soon now she
would be warm and safe.

But, for him, 'soon' was not applicable. He had yet to drag
himself up another hundred and fifty yards. When they
reached Chela he could do no more than croak out a greeting as he sank down beside her. Then came the descent. It
had to be made slowly, lest either of the brothers, who were
acting as stretcher-bearers, tripped and fell with her. Yet,
even at this modest pace, to Adam the way down seemed
interminable. Towards the end he could not even keep his
eyes open and the older Zupango had to support him.

Afterwards he could not remember reaching the farmhouse. His gruelling fight with the six priests, the nerve-racking flight in the helicopter, the awful strain of supporting
both Hunterscombe and Chela down to clean air, having carried the dead weight of Chela for so far, and his final effort
of going down the last slope, then up and down again, had
drained the last ounce of strength from his body. When he
did enter the farmhouse he slumped to the floor, having passed
out cold.

When he woke, memory seeped back to him—the terrible
ordeal of the previous night, then Hunterscombe's last words,
conveying that every policeman in Mexico was by now on the
look-out for him as the most wanted criminal in the country.

With a groan he raised his head and looked about him. He
was lying on a palliasse in a narrow room. A few feet away

Chela was lying on another. Between them Juanita was sitting on a stool, knitting.

Seeing that he had woken, she stood up, smiled down at him and said:

'You have slept well, Lord. Eight hours, and it is close on midday.'

Raising himself on an elbow, he looked across at Chela and asked, 'How is the Señorita?'

'As well as can be expected. When they brought her in she was in a high fever. My mother gave her a herbal drink which is better than the doctors in the cities can prescribe. When she became drowsy we looked at her wound, cleaned and dressed it with a healing ointment. The bone of her leg is not broken, but the tendons are torn. She may become a little lame, but she is very beautiful and a slight limp will not lessen her attraction.'

Greatly relieved that Chela was being so well cared for, Adam's mind turned to his other anxieties. He now cursed himself for having slept so long. His freedom and possibly his life hung on his getting Hunterscombe to hospital and it was now nearly twelve hours since he had been wounded. Lying untended in the cave, his condition would deteriorate with every hour and he might not last out the day. He alone could testify that it was Adam who had enabled him to warn the authorities and, that apart, no effort must be spared to reach in time this friend who had had the courage to arrive alone among the fanatical priests on the top of the pyramid.

Pulling himself together, Adam told Juanita about Hunterscombe and said that as soon as possible a rescue party must go up to get him. She said that her father and brothers had, as usual, been working up on the terraces all the morning, but would shortly be back for the midday meal, and would then be entirely at his disposal.

After his collapse they had taken off only his jacket and shoes before laying him on the palliasse and putting a single blanket over him. As he threw the blanket off and sat up to put them on, he was smitten with a dozen aches and pains from the kicks and blows he had received the previous night. Striving to ignore them and the stiffness of his limbs, he went over to look at Chela. She was very pale from having lost so much blood, but sleeping peacefully under the drug that the old woman had given her. When he felt her pulse it was slow but regular so, satisfied that her state was somewhat better than he could have hoped for, he asked Juanita where he could wash.

First she gave him two pots of salve, one to rub into his cuts and the other for his bruises, then she led him outside to a shed in which there was a big trough, several buckets of clean water, a bar of soap and some rough towels. After stripping, he put into one of his pockets the jewels he was wearing, then washed off the grime he had accumulated during his terrible night's journey. His eight hours' sleep had done much to restore him and the shock of the cold water proved a further stimulant. The herbal ointments, when applied to his abrasions, quickly dulled the pain. By the time he was dressed again he was feeling in better shape, although by no means his normal self.

On re-entering the living room, he found that the men had returned from their morning's work and that the midday meal was ready. They were waiting only for him to partake of it first. The urgency of going up for Hunterscombe being uppermost in his mind, he was greatly tempted to insist that they should start at once; but it was thirteen hours since he had had even a snack and he knew that he ought to recruit his strength before setting out to climb the mountain. Moreover, he saw that in his honour his hosts had provided a banquet: chickens, a leg of pork, mutton chops, three kinds of stuffed *tortillas*, several strange puddings, and flagons of wine. Obviously, during the morning the old mother had performed prodigies of cooking, and he had not the heart to refuse her tribute.

Taking the elbow chair, he insisted that the family should join him at table. All of them except Juanita, who was evidently restraining herself, to give a lady-like impression, ate voraciously. Adam, in spite of his normally big appetite, found it difficult to do full justice to the feast. His thoughts remained focused on Hunterscombe and in what sort of state they would find him.

As far as he had been able to judge, the bullet had pierced

the Wing Commander's right lung; so it was a nasty wound but not one from which a man was likely to die, given proper medical attention. The cave where he lay had been dry and the chill in it was not too great to have offset the warmth of the feather cloak in which Adam had wrapped him. While piloting the helicopter and staggering down from the area made poisonous by sulphur fumes, he must have lost a certain amount of blood; but once he had settled in the cave there was a good chance that the blood had coagulated where his shirt stuck to the wound. The biggest feature for hope lay in his not being the type of man to turn his face to the wall, and he had said himself that, somehow, he would stick it out till help came; so it seemed all the odds were in favour of his still being alive when they reached him.

Nevertheless, Adam's anxiety about him was acute and he did his best to hurry the others into finishing their big meal. It had, also, occurred to him that, although there was every reason to hope that he would find Hunterscombe again much as he had left him, when they did move him his wound would begin to bleed again, and a further loss of blood before they could get him to hospital might prove fatal; so, as soon as Juanita ceased eating, Adam asked her if she could let him have a pen and paper.

From a drawer in the dresser she produced a Biro pen and a pad. On a sheet of it, he wrote:

'I, Wing Commander Jeremy Hunterscombe, of the British Embassy, Mexico City, hereby testify that Mr. Adam Gordon has, at my request, been investigating a conspiracy against the Mexican government; and that it was solely due to information received by me from him that I was enabled to warn the authorities about the subversive meeting held last night at Teotihuacán. Between us we captured Monsignor Alberuque, the leader of the conspiracy, who later died of wounds received during the fighting on the top of the Pyramid of the Sun.'

He added the date and put the Biro in his pocket. As soon as they reached Hunterscombe he would get him to sign the statement and, if the Indians proved unable to write, they could put their marks under the signature, as witnesses. Then,

if the Wing Commander did succumb on the rough, twelve-
mile journey into Apizaco, Adam felt confident that when he
produced the document he would have nothing to fear.

By the time he had completed this precautionary measure,
the others were ready to start. While the brothers collected the
home-made stretcher, Adam went in to look at Chela. Finding her condition unchanged, he quickly joined the three Indians and they set off up the mountain.

Seeing it in daylight, Adam realised how lucky they had
been not to have landed on the top of one of the much loftier
peaks that still had snow on them, and that the Zupango
farm was a good halfway up it, instead of near the bottom.
Had either not been so, they would all by now have been
dead.

Looking back over the roofs of the farm, the view was
magnificent and far below could be seen a little cluster of
houses that one of the brothers pointed out as Xalcatlan. Far
away on the other side of the long valley there rose the other
chain of mountains, their peaks, some of which were snow-
capped, outlined against the pale-blue sky. Two of the highest
were veiled in cloud and in the bright sunlight the vivid colouring of the countryside made a perfect picture-postcard landscape. Where they were, halfway up the volcano, the air was
crisp and windless, so there could not have been better conditions for climbing. But soon they were in difficulties.

Adam had already learned through Juanita that none of
the men knew of a cave high up on the volcano that was sometimes used as a shelter by a goatherd; so it fell to Adam to
guide the party as best he could and the paths branched so frequently that he had not the least idea by which one he had come
down. By half past two they reached the sulphur-affected
level, and he knew that he had left Hunterscombe well below
that; so they turned back and traversed the mountain lower
down, ascending again from time to time by other routes.

As they trudged up and down the winding tracks they
yodelled now and then, but only the echoes came back. When
coming down Adam had naturally always taken the easiest
way, with the least steep slope, which had frequently led to
his having to proceed for some way almost at right angles to a

line of straight descent. In consequence, he was not even certain on which side of the mountain he had left Hunterscombe, and that made the area to be searched very large. Moreover, the surface was far from being as comparatively smooth as in the darkness he had supposed it to be. The relatively easy ways of descending were along the rivers of lava which had flowed down the volcano sides; but between them were high cliffs, elbows that stuck out forming overhangs and great humps of piled-up boulders. The little plateau where Hunterscombe had been left might lie hidden behind any of these and probably could be seen only from above. On the other hand, alongside the lava flows, there were many small plateaus with low cliffs and caves in them; so they might have passed the place more than once without Adam recognising it.

For the first hour of their search Adam had not been particularly worried but, as time went on, he became more and more so. Although he regarded it as unlikely, he had visualised the possibility of finding Hunterscombe dead; but he had put that thought from him and it had never even occurred to him that they might not be able to find him at all.

At five o'clock they were still high up on the mountain. It was still light there, but the late February dusk still comes early. It had fallen in the valley and was creeping upwards. By then it was getting on for four hours since they had left the farm and, although the hardy little Indians did not show fatigue, after the gruelling Adam had been through the previous night he was feeling terribly tired.

For a further twenty minutes he cast desperately about, shouting Hunterscombe's name until he was hoarse. Then, as the shadows gathered about the little party, he had to confess himself defeated. As they had failed to find the Wing Commander during the hours of daylight, it was certain that they would not be able to do so in darkness. By pointing downwards towards the farm, he indicated to the Indians that he was calling off the search.

To renew it the following morning would be pointless. By then it would be over thirty hours since Hunterscombe had received his wound. He could not possibly last so long without even a drink of water. The thought that he must have been tortured by thirst all day was a terrible one. Perhaps that explained their not having found him. Desperate for a drink, he might have left the cave, attempted to make his way down the mountain and gone headlong over a precipice. It was not Adam's fault that he had slept on until midday; but he had meant to be up there first thing in the morning and now he felt that, indirectly, his friend's death lay at his door.

His having slept for so long was not Hunterscombe's tragedy alone; it was also his. All too well he realised that, with the failure of the search, his one hope of proving his innocence was gone. Now, only his wits and endurance could save him from years of imprisonment, or perhaps death.

21

A Bid for Freedom

ON HIS way down the mountain Adam had had ample time
to consider the bleak prospect that now confronted him. When
warning him of the situation in which he might possibly find
himself, Hunterscombe's advice had been to make for the
coast. To do so and hope to get aboard a ship certainly
seemed the best bet; in fact there appeared to be no promising
alternative. But Adam had no illusions about his poor chances
of keeping clear of the police. His height and red-gold hair
alone were a complete give-away. Something must be done
about them, and he would need a number of things for his
journey.

To secure them presented a major problem, as he dared
not show himself in the village. On further thought, too, he
felt that he would be unwise to remain in the farmhouse, even
for another night. During the morning, the wrecked helicopter might well have been spotted from a searching aircraft. If so, the authorities would assume that he and Alberuque were somewhere not far off and already, perhaps, police
and troops were being mustered to scour the whole district.

Obviously, if he set out as he was, he would stand no chance
at all, so he decided to enlist the help of Juanita.

When he reached the farmhouse, he found her sitting with
Chela, who had come out of her drug-induced sleep that afternoon. But to his considerable annoyance he learned that the
old woman, after feeding her with some broth, had given her
another potion from which it was unlikely that she would
wake until early the following morning. As he must be on his
way long before then, that meant he must go without being

able to tell her why it was imperative that he should leave her, what he planned to attempt and say good-bye to her. But the chance had gone and there was nothing he could do about it.

While he had been feeling Chela's pulse, Juanita had left the room and now returned with a noggin of *tequila* which, bobbing respectfully, she offered him. Tired after his hours of climbing, he drank it down gratefully, then said to her:

'Juanita, you are a sensible girl and I can talk frankly to you. I expect you have heard rumours about my return to earth to lead a movement which would overthrow the present government and restore the land to the descendants of its original inhabitants?'

She nodded, and he went on, 'The *coup* was planned to take place last night. It failed. As a result the government people are now hunting for me everywhere to capture and, perhaps, kill me.'

Giving him a puzzled look, she said, 'But, Lord, if you really are a god, surely . . . ?'

He cut her short. 'No. Matters are not ordered like that. I am not a god but a Man-God. It is decreed that I should spend certain periods on earth and I am not permitted to shorten such visits by a single second. During that time, as I told you last night, I am subject to all the weaknesses and needs of an ordinary man.'

'I understand,' she said gently. 'You are like our Lord Jesus, and while on earth must suffer without complaint.'

At the comparison he had unconsciously led her to suggest, he felt profoundly ashamed; but, knowing that his life might depend on securing her help, he forced himself to respond. 'Yes; that's it. But . . . well, I have work to do here, and I'm not willing to allow myself to be put to death yet. I've got to get away.'

Her face glowed and in a low voice she said, 'I should be proud, Lord, to have helped you.'

Again he felt shamed at taking advantage of her belief in him, but he said, 'You can, Juanita. At present my appearance would give me away to the first policeman I ran into. To stand any chance at all, I've got to have my hair cut and my beard shaved off. Have you a pair of scissors, and is there a shaving kit in the house?'

'I have scissors with which I could cut your hair. The men of my family shave on Sundays and on the days of the great feasts of the Church. I will borrow their razor for you.'

He smiled at her. 'Bless you, my dear. Then I'll need some sort of haversack and a good supply of food to carry in it, because for several days I don't want to enter any village in case someone identifies me. I mean to make my way through the fields and forests. For that my present clothes are far from suitable. Do you think you could get me some spare clothes which your menfolk have worn, and maybe a hat? Of course, I would pay for them.'

Juanita returned his smile. 'All these things I will get for you, Lord. But how soon do you need to have them?'

He heaved a sigh. 'After last night and the hours I spent on the mountain this afternoon, I'm very tired. I must have a few hours' rest, but I ought to leave here by about two o'clock in the morning. There is one other thing, though. Your parents and brothers have not your education. It might prove difficult to explain my situation to them; so it would be better if they knew nothing about it. Do you think you could get the things I need without their knowledge, stay awake to give them to me and cut my hair in the middle of the night, then afterwards keep the secret of what you have done for me?'

Suddenly she knelt down, seized his hand, kissed it and, her eyes shining, exclaimed, 'Dear Lord, even torture would not drag a word from me. All my life I shall remember this day with joy, and be so very proud of having had the privilege of serving you.'

Again Adam felt a qualm at being treated as though he really were a divinity. For such a situation to occur in the age of space travel seemed hardly believable. Yet the lives and mentality of the Zupangos differed little from those of a farming family living in Palestine in the first century A.D. Just as the Jews had been brought up to expect a Messiah, so the Mexican Indians had long believed that Quetzalcoatl would return to them. And Adam could not doubt that young

M

women similar to Juanita had shown equal joy and devotion when serving Jesus of Nazareth.

Their conversation had taken only a few minutes and, as Adam had passed through the living room, he had seen that the evening meal was ready; so he and Juanita went through to join the others. Normally, he felt sure, the Zupangos would have eaten earlier and their supper consisted of a few *tortillas* and a beaker apiece of acid, home-made wine; but the dishes provided were again a feast.

Not knowing when he would again have sustaining food, he tucked in heartily; with the result that the heavy meal, taken while he was still tired after his climb, gave him an overwhelming desire to go to sleep. But he resisted it, for he had another matter to see to before he could allow himself to rest.

After his failure to find Hunterscombe, he had to consider what to do about Chela. While he was fully confident that the Zupangos would give her every possible care, and thought it probable that the old crone's treatment of her wound would prove as efficacious as any she might receive from a proper doctor, he was most averse to leaving her with them for longer than was absolutely necessary. The fact that the bone of her leg was not broken at least meant that there was no urgency about getting it properly reset; but the Zupango household was far from sanitary and the palliasse on which she was lying would prove anything but comfortable when she was no longer under drugs; so he must get her taken to hospital as soon as possible.

The snag was that, in order to do so, explanations would have to be given; and as soon as it became known, if it was not already, that the helicopter had come down on the nearby volcano, the whole area would be alive with police. After much thought, Adam had decided that Chela's wound would not be adversely affected if he gave himself twenty-four hours' start, and he could be reasonably certain of gaining that time if he sent a telegram that would not reach Mexico City until late the following afternoon.

Producing the Biro he had borrowed from Juanita, he asked her to let him have the writing pad again. Then, while the family regarded him with interest and awe, he wrote out a telegram, and a letter to Chela.

He addressed the telegram to Bernadino Enriquez, stating, with Juanita's help, where the farm was situated and adding only that Chela was there, wounded but not dangerously, and being well cared for.

To Chela he explained why he was compelled to leave her and said that, if he did succeed in getting away, immediately he was safe he would let her know. He mentioned the great debt they owed the Zupangos, then ended by saying how greatly he loved her and that, although they might never meet again, he would treasure the memory of her all his life.

By the time he had done, the men of the family were, as well as they could, politely suppressing their yawns. Knowing that in the ordinary way they would have turned in soon after sundown, he asked Juanita to thank them for all they had done and tell them to go to bed, while she and he repaired to the other room.

With smiles and deep bows they wished him good-night in dumb show then, the mother included, they proceeded to spread their palliasses on the floor in front of the cooking range.

When he and Juanita had settled themselves in the bedroom, he gave her the draft of the telegram and asked if she could send it the following afternoon from the village.

She shook her dark head. 'No, Lord. It is a little place and has no post office. But I could take a mule and ride in to Apizaco with it.'

'Good enough,' he smiled. 'It is important, and I am sure you will not fail me in getting it off. But I don't want you to hand it in before four o'clock.' Giving her the letter for Chela, he went on, 'I want you to give this to the Señorita as soon as she is sufficiently recovered to read it. She is a great lady and her father is immensely rich. You may be sure that he will reward you and your family handsomely for all your kindness to us.'

At that Juanita bridled. 'We need no reward, Lord. To have had you in our home is a great honour.'

He smiled again. 'I am sure that your father would have

felt insulted if I had offered him money in return for his hospitality. But you have promised to provide me with some clothes, the razor and other things. For those I insist on paying. There is also the telegram.'

A week or so earlier, Hunterscombe had given him approximately fifty pounds of Secret Service money to use, if need be, for bribes or in an emergency. The handful of coins concealed in his shoes had been to enable him to telephone from a public call box; by far the greater part of the money was in notes, which he had since hidden in the lining of his jacket, just below his right armpit. Fishing them out, he gave Juanita three hundred-*peso* notes.

As she took them, she said, 'That will be more than enough, Lord. I will collect the things as soon as the others are sound asleep.'

'There is one other matter,' he told her. 'The day after tomorrow, the police will come here. They may take you all in to Apizaco to question you about the Señorita and myself. She, of course, will still be in bed here, but I shall be gone and they will press you to tell them all that you have learned about me. I am counting on you to say nothing about your cutting my hair before I leave or the clothes you are going to get for me. Say only that I arrived here in the middle of last night, went up the mountain today to search for my friend, and left during darkness tonight, while you were all asleep. Is that clear?'

'Yes, Lord,' she assured him, wide-eyed. 'Not a word more shall they get from me.'

He patted her on the cheek. 'Well said, Juanita. But you will all be subjected to a lot of unpleasantness and for that I am determined to compensate you.' As he spoke, he took the pair of magnificent ear-rings from his pocket, held them up to her so that their pear-shaped drop pearls glistened in the light of the lamp, and went on:

'These are for you; but you must not attempt to sell them, otherwise you might get into serious trouble. Before the Señorita leaves here you are to give them to her. They are worth several thousand *pesos*. She will either buy them from you, or sell them for you and send you the money. She has

many jewels; so no-one will question her ownership of them
and what they fetch will make a handsome dowry for you,
with which you can buy a pleasant house where I hope you
will live happily with your man for many years.'

Hesitantly she accepted the jewels, then dropped him an
awkward curtsy and murmured, 'Lord, your generosity
overwhelms me. I have done nothing . . . nothing to deserve
this wonderful gift.'

'You have done more than enough,' he assured her. 'As
for your parents and brothers, the Señorita's father will see
to it that for all their lives they will never know want. And now
I must sleep. Can you keep awake for six hours or so?'

She glanced at a cheap wrist watch she was wearing. 'It is
now a quarter to eight. At what time, Lord, do you wish to
be awakened?'

'Let's say two o'clock. But should you feel yourself dropping off before that, you must rouse me.'

'Have no fear, Lord. I shall be doing my knitting and will
wake you on the minute.'

Gratefully he stretched himself out on the palliasse. She
moved the lamp so that his face was in shadow. Within minutes he was fast asleep.

Faithful to her promise, at two o'clock she shook him by
the shoulder until he opened his eyes. For a moment he did
not know where he was, then memories of the previous day
came back to him. Sitting up, he knuckled the sleep from his
eyes, and asked Juanita:

'Did you manage to get all the things?'

She smiled. 'Yes, Lord. I took them out after my family
had gone to sleep, and they are now in the wine-press shed.'
Producing a pair of scissors, she added, 'If you will turn
round, I will cut off your hair.'

A quarter of an hour later she had given him a crew-cut
and trimmed his beard as closely as possible. She then brought
him a saucepan of warm water that she had left on the range
and gave him the family razor to shave off the rest of his
beard.

Standing up, he stepped across to Chela. For several
moments he looked down on her lovely face, now a little

drawn. Silently he cursed the conspiracy that had been the cause of all his troubles and now forced them to separate. They had known such wonderful happiness together; but now it seemed certain that they must part for ever. Taking from his pocket the finest of the jewelled bracelets that had been put on him as Quetzalcoatl, he slipped it on over her wrist and kissed her lovingly on the forehead.

Turning to Juanita, he asked, 'Do you think we can get out of the house without rousing your family?'

She shrugged. 'They all sleep like logs, Lord. But what matter if one of them does wake? They would never think of stopping you.' Having turned down the wick of the lantern until it gave out only a faint glow, she opened the door and he followed her into the living room.

The other Zupangos were sound asleep, two of them snoring loudly. Adam and Juanita tiptoed past them and eased back the wooden bar of the outer door. Once it creaked loudly; the old woman gave a grunt and turned over, but went off again. Two minutes later they were out in the cold, crisp air.

Juanita led him to the wine-press shed, turned up the lantern and got out from behind a cask the things she had procured for him. The clothes consisted of a pair of blue dungarees that were just broad enough to take his shoulders but much too short for him, a checked cotton shirt and a loose-fitting leather jacket with tarnished brass buttons. Quickly he changed into them then, pointing to his own clothes on the floor, he said:

'I want you to burn these. And tonight. It is important that the police should not find them.'

She nodded. 'It shall be done, Lord. Here are the other things.'

He saw then that she had got for him the type of pack used for countless generations by the Indians, which is worn on the back and supported by a strap across the forehead. He feared that at first he would find it awkward; but it had the advantage that, when wearing it, he would have to lean his head forward, which would make him appear less tall, and it was in keeping with his new role.

When he had tucked his torch, her scissors and the shaving kit into a corner of the pack, she helped him adjust the single strap, then handed him a battered hat. It was no high-crowned, broad-brimmed sombrero, such as one frequently sees in pictures of Mexicans, but a more ordinary affair, now in much more general use: a narrow-brimmed, oval-crowned straw. Putting it on his close-cropped head, he took both her hands, kissed her on the cheek and said:

'Juanita, you have proved a true friend. I thank you from my heart for all you have done for me.'

Her dark eyes shining like stars, she sank to her knees, still looking up at him. As he turned away, she murmured, 'May heaven defend you, Lord. I pray that you may come to me again in my dreams.'

With a last smile to her, he went out into the night.

At a rough estimate he believed the coast to be a hundred and twenty miles away; but that was as the crow flies. Owing to the mountainous nature of the country, the roads made many detours; so he expected to have to cover at least half as much ground again and perhaps twice that distance.

The track from the farm wound down the lower slope of the volcano. At about four in the morning he entered the village of Xalcatlan. The moon was still well up and by its light he could see that the place was the usual huddle of, mostly, one-storey houses with patched roofs and plaster peeling from the walls, grouped round a small, dusty square. The village was utterly silent, the windows of the houses shuttered, the stalls in the square now empty of fruit and vegetables. There was only one road leading out of the village, and he knew that it must lead to the local town of Apizaco.

Juanita had said that it was about nine miles from the farm; so, even walking at a good pace, he could not expect to reach it before half past five. By that time people would be stirring, so it would be dangerous to enter it. In any case, he had decided to make his way round it for, although he had rid himself of his wavy hair and beard, his unusual size might still draw attention to him. Once the hue and cry was up the odds were that, had he passed a policeman, the man would remember having seen him and his only certainty of remaining uncaptured lay in keeping out of sight of everyone for several days to come.

When the first few straggling houses of Apizaco came in view, he left the road and took a turning that led east. The moon had set, but the grey light preceding the early spring dawn was now sufficient for him to see his way without using his torch. To his annoyance, the road curved south towards the town, so he had to leave it for a track. The track led only to a farm. As he approached, the sound of an empty pail set down with a clatter on the stone-paved yard warned him that the inmates were already up and tending their cattle. Taking to a field, he skirted round the farm and soon found himself in open country.

By then a rosy glow crowning the distant range of mountains to the east told him that dawn was near and gave him his direction. He walked on towards it for another hour, keeping, as far as he could, to paths between patches of cultivation. During this time there were always one or more dwellings in sight, but no wooded areas, and the peasants were already coming out to work in their fields. As he looked about for a suitable place to go to earth during the day, he became increasingly anxious at not being able to find one.

At length the fields gave way to an area of coarse grass and, ahead of him, he saw a mound about fifty feet in height. As he came nearer, he recognised it as one of the smaller pyramids, still covered with the earth of centuries, that are scattered about the country. When he reached it, he found that near the base at one side there were some broken stone steps leading down to a low arch. Getting out his torch, he went down the steps and flashed it round. The arch gave on to a passage blocked about ten feet from the entrance by earth and fallen debris. It was quite roomy enough to serve as a hideout, but was by no means a pleasant one, as the floor showed that it had been used many times by the field workers to defecate. None of these unpleasant souvenirs left by human visitors appeared to be recent, which led Adam to hope that he would remain undisturbed there; and, although the place stank of urine, he decided that 'beggars cannot be choosers'.

Taking off his pack, he sat down with his back against

the wall and looked through the items that Juanita had secured for him. There was a good blanket, a large piece of lean bacon, a knife to cut it with, some two dozen *tortillas*, a slab of guava jelly, a great hunk of coarse cocoa-chocolate, two packs of cigarettes and a box of matches. From what must have been the very limited supplies available at the farm he thought she could not have done better. The bacon, being smoked, would not go bad, the guava jelly would make the cold *tortillas* much more palatable, and few things were more sustaining than chocolate. Again he blessed his luck that he should have come upon such a well-disposed and intelligent girl.

As he had fed so well the previous day, and knowing it to be important to conserve his stores, he decided that he would not eat until evening; but he had a cigarette while he calculated roughly the time it should take him to reach the coast. With his long legs he could easily cover four miles an hour, so if he walked for eight hours a day he should do it in less than a week. But it might not prove so straightforward as that. There would be times when he had to leave the road, and he meant to move only at night. If there was no moon, having to cross open country in the dark would greatly reduce his speed. Again, if clouds prevented him from using the stars as a guide, he might go for several hours in a wrong direction before he discovered his mistake. Anyhow, he would be certain to lose his way now and then and have difficulty in finding it again, for he had no map and the strange names of towns on signposts would convey nothing to him.

Although it was less than five hours since he had slept, his past two days had been extraordinarily onerous ones and he soon began to feel drowsy. Stretching himself out, he used his pack for a pillow and soon dropped off. Well before midday he awoke and had to face the long afternoon with nothing to occupy him. The minutes seemed to crawl by, but at last the sun set and he was able to leave his smelly refuge.

After trudging along paths and across fields for over two hours, he came upon a road and, taking his direction from where he knew the mountains lay, turned left along it. But now he had to use greater caution, as he was anxious not to get caught in the headlights of a car. Fortunately, there was little traffic; but each time a vehicle approached he had to get off the road quickly, crouch down with his back to it in order to remain unnoticed and keep still until the car or lorry had passed.

From time to time he took a brief rest and, at about midnight, a long one during which he made a meal off a strip of bacon and a *tortilla*, washed down with a draught of water from his flask, for which he again blessed Juanita, as she had had the forethought to fill it for him.

An hour later he came to a township, skirted round it and lost the road again. Another hour went by without his succeeding in finding it. Judging by the moon, he knew that there was still a long time to go until dawn; but he felt too tired to go any further, so dossed down under a hedge. At first light he woke and covered another two miles, by which time the peasants were coming out into the fields and, as he was most averse to risking an encounter, he began to look about for a hideout. Soon afterwards he came upon a burned-out shack. Settling himself in a corner, he ate some of the chocolate and tried to sleep, but found that he could not get off.

The day seemed never-ending, but at last sundown came and he was able to go on his way. Again, after walking for some eight hours, he had to give up and spent the rest of the night sleeping among some bushes.

And so, with little variation, matters continued. Each night, when fatigue forced him to stop and sleep, he grudged losing the hours of darkness during which he might have covered another eight or ten miles. But the days were the worst.

Again and again he went over in his thoughts scenes through which he had lived since his arrival in Mexico: Chela—tall, broad-shouldered, superbly gowned and incredibly lovely— as she had made her entrance in her father's penthouse on that first evening they had spent in each other's company; Alberuque—hawk-faced, cynically smiling at the moment he had admitted that he was a reincarnation of Itzechuatl; the top of the pyramid at San Luis Caliente with the slaughtered pig and the smell of its hot blood; Chela, naked, laughing, utterly adorable, as he had known her in her villa at Acapulco;

Jacko strangling the wounded warder; Alberuque, his dull black eyes radiating evil when he had threatened to sacrifice Chela; the crowd, the smell and the mosquitoes at Mérida airport; Jeremy Hunterscombe lying *hors de combat* in the cave; Ramón playing the gracious host at the Bankers' Club; the Zupango family falling on their knees, believing him to be Quetzalcoatl; Alberuque's face showing stark terror as he was thrown from the helicopter to die in the boiling lava of the volcano; Father Lopéz discoursing genially on the life of Cortés beside the swimming pool of the Hacienda Hotel at Uxmal; Chela, wan and still under the herbal drug, as he had last seen her at the farmhouse.

These and many other memories kept passing through his mind like the pictures made by a Victorian revolving silhouette wheel. Utterly weary of them, he tried to pass the time by thinking out plots for stories, reciting all the poems he could remember, repeating the multiplication tables, endeavouring to do intricate sums in his head, playing noughts and crosses against himself and inventing other games.

Several times he succeeded in sending his spirit back to the past and lived again for a while either as Ord the Red-Handed or Quetzalcoatl, whom he now knew to be one and the same. On one such occasion he found himself as the Man-God, alone, tired and hungry, making his way by night through a forest. He was lost, yet dared not go into a village to ask his way in case the inhabitants proved to be enemies. Eight days earlier he had succeeded in escaping from Itzechuatl and was now about two hundred miles from Tenochtitlán; but he still had a long way to go before he could hope to rejoin his own people. He was not only still in danger from the warriors whom he knew must have been sent in pursuit of him, but sad at heart because he had fallen in love at first sight with the beautiful Mirolitlit and knew it to be most unlikely that he would ever see her again.

When Adam came out of his dream he thought how strange it was that he should have made his present journey, or a very similar one, in that long-past life and in almost identical circumstances; for in this present incarnation he was again tired, hungry, lost, pursued by enemies with little hope of

ever again seeing the great love whom he had had to leave
behind. Nevertheless, this vision gave him new courage to
endure. As Ord the Viking become Quetzalcoatl, he had
succeeded in reaching Yucatán; so he should be ashamed of
himself now if, as Adam Gordon, he failed to reach Vera
Cruz, which was nowhere near so great a distance.

None of his other returns to the past was of any special
interest and, although they gave him something to think
about, they were useless for killing time. The many hours, or
even days, they seemed to cover were an illusion; when he
came out of his visions the sun had not perceptibly moved
in the heavens, so, in fact, he had not left his body for more
than a few minutes.

Travelling mainly over rough ground eight hours out of
twenty-four was as much as he could manage and the dis-
comfort of his resting places made it impossible to sleep for
more than six hours; the remaining ten had to be got through
somehow. His every thought grew stale and, day after day,
waiting for darkness to fall again so that he could go on his
way almost drove him mad with impatience and frustration.

At no time could he with certainty have put a pin-point
on a map within twenty miles of where he was. No road led
directly towards the east for more than a few miles, then it
curved either to north or south. After a time the cultivated
lands gave way to jungle. Often he found difficulty in finding
a stream of fresh water from which he could refill his flask
and sluice his face. To eke out his rations, he stole fruit from
trees growing on the outskirts of villages and twice ran down
chickens which he afterwards encased in mud and baked over
a wood fire. Once he trod on a snake and narrowly escaped
being bitten, another time when the moon was hidden by
clouds he fell headlong into a pond and he was bitten by
mosquitoes until he thought he would go mad.

But one thing buoyed him up. Day after day during his
wearying journey he managed to avoid coming face to face
with any human being. In the early morning of the twelfth
day he emerged from a patch of mimosa bushes to see the
sun rising over the sea.

Hardly able to believe that he had at last reached the

Atlantic, he retreated into the bushes and considered his next move. The past fortnight had greatly changed his appearance. Three times during his journey he had shaved and trimmed his hair as short as he could with the scissors; but he had allowed his moustache to grow and, by feeling the bristles, he knew that it must now be an obvious feature. Even though he had remained in hiding for the greater part of each day, the torrid sun baking the lower lands had considerably increased his tan; his face was puffy from mosquito bites and his fingernails were black with grime. As he now looked, and in his cheap Indian clothes, he thought it very unlikely that anyone he had met while in Mexico, except perhaps Chela, would recognise him; so he need no longer fear to enter a town.

The great port of Vera Cruz was the obvious place to try to get aboard a ship, but the problem was how to set about it. Without a passport, he could not sail as a passenger, even had he had the money to buy a ticket. Out of the money with which Hunterscombe had provided him he had given Juanita three hundred *pesos*. That left him with six hundred and fifty and some small change—about nineteen pounds. Far too little to offer a sea captain as a bribe for getting him out of the country illegally.

Taking out the remaining jewels that he had worn as Quetzalcoatl, he looked them over. In addition to the beautiful jewelled serpent, there were five thick gold bracelets studded with fair-sized but ill-cut gems. As he examined them they brought back to his mind the treasure he had found in Scotland when a boy. So many things had happened to him since that that seemed a whole lifetime ago, although, actually, it was only a little over fourteen years. Crude as they were, these stones were much larger and, if recut, would be worth a lot of money. But no buyer would be such a fool as to remove the stones from their settings. As genuine antiques, the bracelets must be worth a small fortune and the serpent symbol be almost priceless. To dispose of them, though, was another matter. No jeweller would consider such a purchase unless he had first checked up on where they had come from, so to sell them in Mexico was impossible. With a sigh, Adam put the jewels back in his pocket.

That evening he set off north along the coast, hoping that Vera Cruz lay in that direction. Here on the sea, villages were much more frequent. At the first he came to, lights in all the houses told him that the inhabitants were taking their leisure after the long, hot day. Having for close on a fortnight gone to great trouble to avoid contact with anyone, he felt considerable reluctance to enter the village. But the plunge had to be taken some time, so he nerved himself to walk on to the little *piazza*.

In it there was a small eating house. No-one had taken any notice of him, so the temptation to enjoy a hot meal proved irresistible. The fare offered was simple, but included freshly caught fish; and he ate voraciously, enjoying the meal more than he would have a carefully-chosen dinner at the Ritz.

As he paid his bill he got into conversation with the waitress and told her that he had hiked from Puebla with the idea of getting a job as a seaman, but had lost his way the preceding night, so had only a vague idea were he was. He learned from her that Vera Cruz was about fifteen miles further north.

Proceeding on his way, he passed through three more villages and covered two-thirds of the distance to the great port, then dossed down for the remainder of the night in a hut on the beach. Next morning, another two miles brought him within sight of the steeples of Vera Cruz, but immediately in his path there lay a smaller town. On entering it, he found it to be called Boca del Rio. It had quite a good harbour and, lying off it were three ships, one of which was flying the Stars and Stripes.

As he stood on the quayside looking out at them, it occurred to him that there would be many fewer officials in a small port like this than at Vera Cruz; so he would stand less risk of detection if he made his attempt here to get aboard a ship and stow away.

To do so would require careful planning and might take several days; so, although he was loath to register at an hotel, he decided that it would be better to do that than to spend the nights on the streets and risk being picked up by the police.

Choosing a small inn that looked fairly clean, he gave his name as Sancho Bracero and enquired for a room. When he was asked for his papers, he said that the previous night he had got drunk in Vera Cruz, gone to a brothel and been robbed of his wallet; then he produced some money as evidence that he could still pay his reckoning. The fat landlord shrugged, deducted the price of a room for the night, said Adam had better see the police about getting new papers, then took him upstairs.

Adam would have given a great deal for a bath, but had to make do with sluicing himself down with water from a tap in a stone-floored washroom at the end of the passage. He then went out again to reconnoitre the harbour and find out where each of the three ships was bound for.

From a wharf-hand with whom he got into conversation he learned that one ship was only a coastal trader, another was taking aboard a mixed cargo for Havana, and that the United States tramp had come across from Campeche with a cargo of sisal; she was now calling at Boca to load fruit on her open decks before proceeding to New York.

The American was obviously the best choice if he could get aboard her, as in New York he would at once be able to get money from his American literary agents and, on their vouching for his identity, he would have no difficulty in securing a new passport from the British Consul General. But, as she was not alongside the dock, there could be no easy business of slipping over her side in the middle of the night; so to stow away in her presented a major problem. It seemed that his only chance was to persuade one of the crew to help him.

After a hearty midday meal and a siesta, he returned to the dock, sat on a bollard and kept watch on the ship. In due course, as he expected, several of the crew put off in a boat to come ashore for an evening's amusement. On landing they formed two groups of nine seamen or stokers and three officers, then separated, the officers evidently heading for a somewhat better place than the ratings would patronise. Adam had intended to scrape acquaintance with the members of the crew, but he chanced to overhear a fair-haired, freckle-faced young officer with the rings of a Second Engineer speak to his two companions in a broad Scottish accent. Following a hunch, he tailed the three men to a café that looked about the best the small port had to offer.

Giving them a few minutes to settle down, he went in, took up a position near them at the bar, ordered himself a Scotch and soda and plonked down a hundred-*peso* note to pay for it. As he did so they gave him a curious glance, for his appearance was that of a down-and-out Mexican who would not ordinarily have ordered such a drink or have been able to afford it. Then they went on talking and took no further notice of him.

Having waited until the glasses of two of them were empty, he looked along at the Engineer and, reverting to the accent he had had before going to Marlborough, said, 'M' name's Adam McTavish, an' seeing we baith hail fra north o' the border, I'd like tae stand ye an' ye're friends a drink.'

They looked at him in some surprise, then readily accepted. Other rounds followed and they were soon all talking in a most friendly fashion. The young Engineer, whose name was Bruce Sinclair, came from Glasgow; the others—the ship's First Officer and 'Sparks'—were Americans. Adam gave them a partially true and partially false account of himself. Having spoken of his time in the Royal Navy, he post-dated his trip as a supercargo who had been left high and dry at Recife, then spun a yarn that he had worked his way north through Venezuela, Panama and Guatemala to Mexico where, for the past few months, he had acted as a foreman in a silver mine.

Later they all had a meal together, during which Adam drew lavishly on his novelist's imagination to recount amusing fictitious happenings in which he had played a part while on his way up from Brazil. After they had eaten, he found an opportunity to leave them for a few minutes, get an order slip from one of the waiters and write on it:

'I have a good proposition to put up to you if you can meet me here alone for a meal at two o'clock tomorrow.'

By that time they were all half seas over, so he had no difficulty in slipping the note into Sinclair's hand unobserved by the others. The young man read it under cover of the marble-topped table to which they had adjourned, and nodded. Round about midnight Adam, by then well loaded himself, saw his new friends off from the dock with mutual expressions of undying friendship.

Next day he went to the café well before two o'clock and wondered anxiously whether Sinclair would turn up or if, having been decidedly tight the previous night, he would have forgotten their appointment. But on the hour, with his nautical cap at a jaunty angle over his freckled face, the young Engineer joined him.

Until they had enjoyed a good meal, Adam refused to satisfy his companion's curiosity. Then he said, 'See you, Bruce, I'm in trouble. While I was working in that mine I came on a cache of old Indian jewellery, really valuable stuff. I didn't see why I should turn it in to the management, so I decided to make off with it. Unfortunately, I was rumbled and there was one hell of a row. They ran me for stealing antiques rightly belonging to the Mexican government, and I was given six months. Five weeks later I had a lucky break and managed to escape from prison. Being a cautious chap, I had hidden a few of the things I had come upon; so they didn't get them all back, and I collected the rest. But they had taken away my passport; so, although I've got several thousand pounds' worth of loot in my pockets, I can't get out of this damned country. Now, if I make it well worth your while, are you game to help me?'

Sinclair considered for a moment. 'I'd like to, but it would be taking a big risk. What is there in it for me?'

Fishing out of his trouser pocket the least valuable of the bracelets, Adam showed it under the table and said, 'This. I've friends in New York to whom I'll take you and I'll guarantee that they'll give you at least a thousand quid for it.'

As the young man looked at the jewel, he drew a deep breath. Considering their responsibilities, the officers in small ships are about the worst-paid class in the world, and there was a bonnie lass in Glasgow that Bruce Sinclair was saving up to marry.

'All right,' he said, 'but how is it to be done?'

'That's for you to say,' Adam replied. 'But there can be nothing against your asking me on board some time when things are quiet, and it won't be noticed if I don't go ashore again. You'll have to think of a place where I can hide for twenty-four hours. I'll come out then, and I'm quite capable of working my passage.'

'What about when we dock in New York?'

'Leave that to me. I'll find a way of getting ashore. Maybe in one of those crates of fruit you are loading. Or, if you lay off, I'm a good swimmer and could swim ashore.'

Again Sinclair remained thoughtful for a minute, then said, 'Coming aboard at night would look a bit fishy. To-morrow at about three in the afternoon would be best. Everyone will be having a shut-eye then, even the deck watchman who is supposed to keep a look-out while we are in port. We don't want any of the crew to see you come aboard, though; so you'd better get a boatman to take you out to the ship and I'll be waiting for you.'

So the matter was arranged, and an hour later Adam saw Sinclair off from the dock.

The following afternoon, hopeful but nervous about the outcome, he hired a small motor-boat which chugged with him out to the *President Cleveland*, as the American ship was named. When he reached her, he told the boatman that he might have to remain on board for some hours, and that when he had done his business one of the ship's boats would bring him ashore; then he paid him off.

Sinclair, looking far from happy, received Adam as he came over the side. But after they had had a few drinks in the deserted Mess under the stern deck, he cheered up considerably and said, 'There is a spare cabin not far from mine which should be occupied by a Fourth Officer. But in this tub we don't run to one, and I don't think anyone has even looked into it for weeks; so you should be quite all right there.'

A quarter of an hour later Adam was installed, lying in the narrow bunk and, delight of delights, after being without books for so long, starting to read one of half a dozen which he had bought that morning. With him he had also brought food enough to see him through the next forty-eight hours; and the *President Cleveland*, having completed her loading, was due to sail on the tide early the following morning.

After reading until sunset he had a meal, then undressed, got under the blankets and went to sleep. A few hours later he was rudely awakened by the door of the cabin being unceremoniously pulled open. Starting up, he blinked a few times, then saw that a big, heavy-jowled man who, from the rings on his sleeves, he knew must be the Captain of the vessel, and a much gold-braided Mexican Customs officer, were framed in the doorway. Behind them were grouped several other men.

'What's this?' the Customs officer snapped at the Captain. 'You told me this cabin was empty.'

'So it should be,' retorted the American in atrocious Spanish. Scowling at Adam, he demanded, 'Who are you? What the hell are you doing here?'

Adam's mind jumped to it that he had been caught in a search that Sinclair could not have foreseen. Instantly he decided that he must protect the young Scot who had befriended him, so he refused to explain how he came to be there. His stubborn refusal to answer all the subsequent questions fired at him resulted in the gold-braided Customs officer drawing a revolver, covering him with it and ordering in a junior to search his belongings.

Within two minutes the Customs man came upon the jewelled serpent-head and the bracelets. With a cry of triumph, he held them aloft.

'Now what have you to say?' sneered the senior Customs officer at the unhappy Captain. 'We were tipped off that your ship was smuggling out valuable antiques which should belong to the Mexican government. Evidently the people for whom you are acting do not trust you, so sent this man to carry the most valuable pieces himself, and keep a watch on you. I have no doubt now that we will find many lesser Mexican *objets d'art* hidden among your cargo.'

Adam was then locked in the cabin and left to brood on his extraordinary bad luck in having tried to get away in a ship which was under suspicion as an antique-runner. Hours later two policemen came to the cabin, handcuffed him and took him up on deck.

There, under the arc-lights, he saw that many of the fruit

crates had been broken open and set out on the deck were a score of pieces of fine pottery, several small jade images of gods, obsidian axe-heads, knives and other items which had evidently been destined for antique dealers in New York; and the Customs men were still searching.

He was taken ashore and, half an hour later, put in the local lock-up. Next morning he was questioned but refused to give an account of himself. That afternoon he was transferred to the police headquarters in Vera Cruz. Again he was questioned and again he refused to talk.

They photographed him, took his fingerprints and sent them to the capital with a full description of the jewels that had been found in his possession, to find out if he could be identified as an habitual criminal.

Two days later he was brought from his cell to face the ex-pugilist who had been his warder in Mexico City after he had been brought there from Mérida. In vain he denied that he had ever before set eyes on this human gorilla. His denial was ignored. That night he was sent back under guard to Mexico City, to stand his trial as the man who had incited rebellion in the role of Quetzalcoatl.

22

Out on a Limb

FOR the second time Adam made the flight to Mexico City handcuffed and under guard. Soon after he arrived at Police Headquarters, he was brought before the bald General Gómez, from whom he had last parted after a convivial supper. He was then formally charged with: conspiring against the government; subversive activities; inciting the civil population to rebellion; breaking out of prison; inciting the Armed Forces to mutiny and creating a public disturbance. It seemed a formidable list, but he had little doubt that, to their own satisfaction, they would be able to prove the lot.

On this occasion he was not subjected to prolonged and searching questioning, which, he rightly guessed, was due to the authorities already having all the evidence they needed to convict him. He was simply asked if he wished to make a statement.

All he could do was to tell a near-enough version of the truth, although he did not expect to be believed, and, during his long recital, the Police Chief showed by his bored manner that he considered listening to it a waste of time. However, he agreed to Adam's request that the British Embassy should be informed of his situation.

The following morning the Embassy solicitor, a Mr. Wilkinson, who was a partner in a Mexican firm, came to see him, and they went over in detail a copy of Adam's statement.

Wilkinson obviously took a dim view of his prospects. Now that Hunterscombe could not vouch for Adam's innocence, the only ways in which his guilt could even be brought in doubt was (1) by testimony from Chela, (2) by evidence that he had been held in the monastery against his will, and (3) that he had, belatedly, fought the priests on the top of the pyramid; but Chela's testimony would be regarded as biased in his favour, it was very unlikely that anyone at the monastery would be inclined to speak in his defence and it would be urged that he had turned against the priests only when he had found that, by taking the role of Quetzalcoatl, he had fallen into a trap which was about to cost him his life.

The lawyer could give him no information about Chela, but he was able to tell him about the results of the abortive ceremony at the pyramid.

The government was maintaining its policy of belittling the movement, in order to discourage possible risings in the provinces. It had been given out that a group of fanatics who dabbled in occultism had held a type of Sabbath, their object being to reintroduce the worship of the old gods. The leaders had dressed themselves up as priests and endeavoured to impose on the credulous by again producing the English eccentric who had played the part of Quetzalcoatl at Uxmal and later escaped from prison. The movement had been condemned as anti-social and liable to lead to breaches of the peace. On these grounds it had been made a penal offence to belong to it.

'You will no doubt be surprised to hear,' Wilkinson added, 'that, according to the official statement, the crowd was simply dispersed and no arrests were made. That, of course, is quite untrue. All those rounded up were screened; the small fry were allowed to go, but the leaders, among whom were a number of Militia officers, were detained and they have since simply disappeared. No doubt by this time several of them have been induced to talk and the Security Service is hard at it rounding up people in the provinces who were involved. The only warrants issued, as far as I know, were for Monsignor Alberuque and yourself. He is believed to have escaped and still be in hiding. According to your statement, you and Hunterscombe took him prisoner and later, while struggling with you, he fell out of the helicopter. But I don't think they will believe that for a moment. Their theory is that you and he took Hunterscombe prisoner and made off in the helicopter. So they will assume that you are trying to cover up for him and that he is still at large.'

That afternoon Adam had another visitor—Bernadino Enriquez. White-haired, fresh-faced, his eyes as bright and his manner as forceful as ever, the millionaire smiled genially as he shook Adam's hand and said:

'My dear Gordon, I'm most terribly distressed to find you in this situation. I made the police show me the statement you made and, of course, I've had the whole story from Chela; so I know it to be true.'

'How is she?' Adam asked.

'She is still a little lame, but the injury to her leg was nothing that the surgeons could not put right. Naturally, she has been terribly worried about you and when she heard yesterday that you had been captured she had a collapse.'

'I'm sorry about that, but glad her leg is going on well. I've kept her out of this as far as I could; but, as we were at the Zupangos farm together, I had to explain how she got there.'

'Yes, you behaved very chivalrously, and it is entirely her fault that you are here. If it hadn't been for her you would never have played any part in this wretched business. In a sense I feel responsible myself, so I mean to do everything I can to help you.'

At this ray of hope, for the first time in days Adam brightened and he said quickly, 'That's good of you, sir.' But after a moment he added, 'I'm afraid, though, that the cards are stacked against me.'

'You are right about that,' Bernadino agreed. 'If you were charged with an ordinary crime, even murder, I could buy you off. But, although the government is playing this business down as far as the public are concerned, they are very well aware of how dangerous it could be. In consequence, they mean to make sure that any conspirator they may fail to pull in shall never again have the chance of using you to represent Quetzalcoatl. I don't think there's a chance of getting you off altogether, but there is a faint one that we might be able to shoot down all the charges except "creating a public disturbance". Then you would be given only a nominal sentence with a very much heavier suspended one, should you ever return to Mexico after you had served the short term and been deported. Anyway, I can provide you with the best legal help in Mexico City, which will ensure that you get a fair trial and that no point in your favour remains unstressed.'

Adam smiled wryly. 'Well, that's something. The British Embassy are doing their best for me, too. Unfortunately, Chela is the only person who could testify to the truth about what really happened. But I doubt if they'd believe her; so it's better that she should protect her reputation by keeping out of it. Besides . . .'

'She won't. She is fully determined to give evidence on your behalf, and a woman of twenty-six is entitled to do as she likes. Her friends won't think the worse of her for having been your mistress. You were going to add that she might land herself in prison, but you needn't fear that. In Mexico women are looked on as temperamental creatures, and not always accountable for their actions. At least, not if they have rich fathers who can pull a string or two. I suppose you know that she is not really my daughter?'

'Yes, she told me that; and about her awful childhood.'

Bernadino nodded. 'That's the root of this whole damnable business—her Indian blood. She has never forgotten what she suffered as a child. We all know that the natives lead a pretty miserable existence. But so they do in Peru, Chile, India, China, Arabia and a score of other countries. Their condition here is being improved gradually as more money becomes available. That's all that can be done for them, and her idea of making them overnight lords of all they survey was sheer lunacy.'

'It was Alberuque who put that bee in her bonnet.'

'Yes. He was crazy, too, of course. It couldn't possibly have worked, but he was a meglomaniac, simply out for himself with a mad dream of power. Chela told me that you chucked him out of the helicopter, and a damn' good job too.'

'I haven't admitted that,' Adam said hastily. 'Otherwise

they would probably have added "murder" to all the other charges.'

'No; even if they believed you, it's best that we should keep that under our hats. But Chela takes it badly, because he was an anointed priest. As soon as she was well enough to be moved from a nursing home, she went into retreat at the Convent of Santa Monica, and it's my belief that she spends most of her time now on her knees, praying that you will be forgiven.'

'I don't see why. As far as she knows, he was dead when I chucked him out.'

'No,' Bernadino disagreed. 'She heard him scream as he went down. Still, don't let that worry you. It's your defence we have to concentrate on, and I have given orders that your meals are to be sent in from a restaurant. The warder will bring you the menu. Order what you like and keep as cheerful as you can.'

When the millionaire had left him, Adam felt distinctly more cheerful. It was good to know that he had such a powerful friend, and a really good dinner that night with a bottle of French wine to wash it down enabled him to sleep well for the first time since his arrest.

Next day, Bernadino's lawyer came to see him. Señor Urquiza was a tall, thin man with a bulbous nose and slightly shifty black eyes. They spent two hours together going over the whole story. Summing up, Urquiza said :

'As I see it, the defence rests upon being able to prove that you were supplying Hunterscombe with information. You did this through a radio transmitter. What happened to it?'

'The police took it from me in Vera Cruz,' Adam replied.

'Then it will have been sent on here with the jewels and any other things that they confiscated on your arrest. It is certain that the set will have a number. I'll find out what the number is and check with the British Embassy. If that particular radio-cigarette case was issued to Hunterscombe, it could be argued that he must have given it to you so that you could communicate with him. There is, of course, a rebuttal to that; but, with luck, the prosecution might fail to realise and use it.'

More hopeful now, Adam continued to fortify himself with the good meals sent in during the three following days; then he was brought up for trial. In the well of the Court he saw Bernadino, who gave him an encouraging smile; Wilkinson and Urquiza bowed gravely to him.

After the charges had been read out, a score of witnesses were produced by the prosecution: most of them prisoners who had been brought to the Court to testify. Among the witnesses were: the priest for whom he had sacrificed the pig at San Luis Caliente; the police officer who had arrested him after the débâcle at Uxmal; a warder who had been present during the massacre at the prison; the dumb lay brother from the monastery, who wrote out evidence to the effect that Adam had been an honoured guest there and on the best of terms with Monsignor Alberuque, the mechanics of the helicopter which had taken them to Teotihuacán, who vouched for it that Adam had gone willingly; several people who had seen him in the restaurant there, apparently a happy participant in the proceedings; and others who had heard his speech from the top of the pyramid. Lastly, Juanita and her family were put in the box and, reluctantly, testified to Adam's having passed himself off to them as the Man-God, Quetzalcoatl.

For the defence, Ramón came forward and told how Adam had voluntarily agreed to assist the government by investigating the situation in towns near Mexico City, while making a tour of them. He added that he was convinced of Adam's innocence. Chela was then called. She was dressed in black and wearing a veil. Accompanying her was an older woman, also swathed in black. In a low but firm voice, Chela told the whole story of how she had suborned Adam to give his assistance in the plot.

A representative of the British Embassy then took the stand. He gave evidence that Adam was a well-known author of respectable character, who had at no time involved himself in politics of any kind. Questioned by Señor Urquiza about the radio-cigarette case, he testified that an office in Whitehall had confirmed that its number was that of one which had been issued to Hunterscombe; so Adam could have obtained it only from him.

The prosecution ignored Ramón, but recalled Chela. Under cross-examination, her replies were frank. She admitted that since Adam's arrival in Mexico she had been frequently in his company; that they had stayed at the same hotels at both Oaxaca and Uxmal. Questioned about her villa at Acapulco and Adam's having stayed with her there, she became defiant and hysterical, acknowledged that she had been his mistress, swore that she had suborned him into playing the part of Quetzalcoatl, and took all the blame on herself for his present situation. It was a courageous effort, but had the unfortunate effect of conveying the impression that nothing she had said could be relied on, as she was simply making a desperate effort to save him.

Finally, the prosecution tackled the matter of the radio-cigarette case. As Urquiza had feared might prove the case, the flaw in his argument was exposed. Admittedly, Adam had secured it from Hunterscombe; but the belief of the prosecution was that the Wing Commander had flown the helicopter off, only because he had a pistol at his back. Therefore, when they landed Adam had no doubt searched him and taken the radio-cigarette case from him.

Adam knew then that his last hope was gone. Stoically, he listened to his sentence: as a dangerous disturber of the peace, through whose activities a number of people had lost their lives: hard labour for life.

Rousing himself, he made the request that before being taken away he might have a few minutes' conversation in private with the Señorita Enriquez.

His request was granted. Five minutes later they stood facing each other in a bare room. But they were not alone. A warder stood by the door and the elderly, black-robed woman who had accompanied Chela into Court was sitting in a corner, telling her beads.

When Chela lifted her veil, her eyes looked enormous and tears were running from them. 'What can I say?' she murmured. 'Oh, Adam, what can I say? I have ruined your life.'

He attempted a smile. 'You couldn't help it, darling. It's

just Fate. You hoped to bring happiness to many people. That you have failed, and that to lose one another has been the price of your failure is the will of the gods. Perhaps in our next lives they will be kinder to us.'

'Oh, I hope so.' She took his hands and pressed them. 'But, even if you had been freed, there could have been nothing more for us in this life.'

He frowned. 'I don't understand. You offered to marry me.'

'I know. But that was before . . . before the culmination of that awful night.'

'Do you mean that you wouldn't have married me because I . . . of what happened to Alberuque?'

'No; evil as he was, it is still a terrible sin to kill a priest. But I might have done so myself when I shot at him—after I had suddenly realised that you were right about his being a reincarnation of Itzechuatl. It's not that. When he declared his intention to sacrifice you on the Chac-Mool, I prayed to the Holy Virgin. I offered to become her handmaiden if only she would intercede with our Lord Jesus to save you. She did, and you were saved. I cannot go back on my pledge.'

For a moment he stared at her lovely face, then he exclaimed, 'Chela! Beloved! You can't mean that you're going to bury yourself alive and become a nun?'

She gestured to the black-robed figure with downcast face in the corner. 'Sister Maria there is waiting to take me back to the Convent, and I shall never leave it. Owing to my past, I may not be acceptable as a bride of Christ, but I could become a lay Sister and continue with my teaching. Even were you free, that would still be my destiny for this life.'

Two minutes later they parted and Adam was taken down to his cell.

. . . . .

That night Adam knew the depths of black despair. His career ruined, his freedom gone, condemned for years to hard labour with only brutal felons for his companions; not a ray of hope to brighten his foreseeable future.

The following midday he was still at Police Headquarters, awaiting transfer to a prison to begin his sentence, when Wilkinson was shown into his cell.

The Embassy lawyer was smiling and clapped him on the shoulder. 'Take it easy, old chap, but I've got a surprise for you. Hunterscombe isn't dead. A goatherd found him in that cave, brought up some other men and got him down. He couldn't be moved from their place for a week, but since then he's been in hospital. He kept mum because he thought you'd got away. But last night he heard over the radio about your trial. This morning he got through to us on the telephone. He'll swear an affidavit that will put you in the clear. The formalities may take a day or two, but you've got nothing more to worry about.'

Two days later Bernadino, Ramón, Wilkinson and Urquiza saw Adam off from the airport on his way back to England. He had lost his great love of this life, but he had regained his freedom. And he had plenty of material for a book on Mexico. Yes, plenty of material for a book.

Dennis Wheatley's work has also been published in:

BELGIUM
BRAZIL
CZECHOSLOVAKIA
DENMARK
FINLAND
FRANCE
GERMANY
HOLLAND
HUNGARY
ITALY
MEXICO
NORWAY
POLAND
PORTUGAL
RUMANIA
SPAIN
SWEDEN
SWITZERLAND
THE UNITED STATES

Also in:
ARABIC
ARMENIAN
FLEMISH
GREEK
MALTESE
RUSSIAN
SERBIAN
TURKISH
HINDI